Seven Will Out

A Renaissance Revel
by JoAnn Spears

Copyright © 2015 JoAnn Spears
All rights reserved.

ISBN: 1514775891
ISBN 13: 9781514775899
Library of Congress Control Number: 2015910900
CreateSpace Independent Publishing Platform
North Charleston, South Carolina

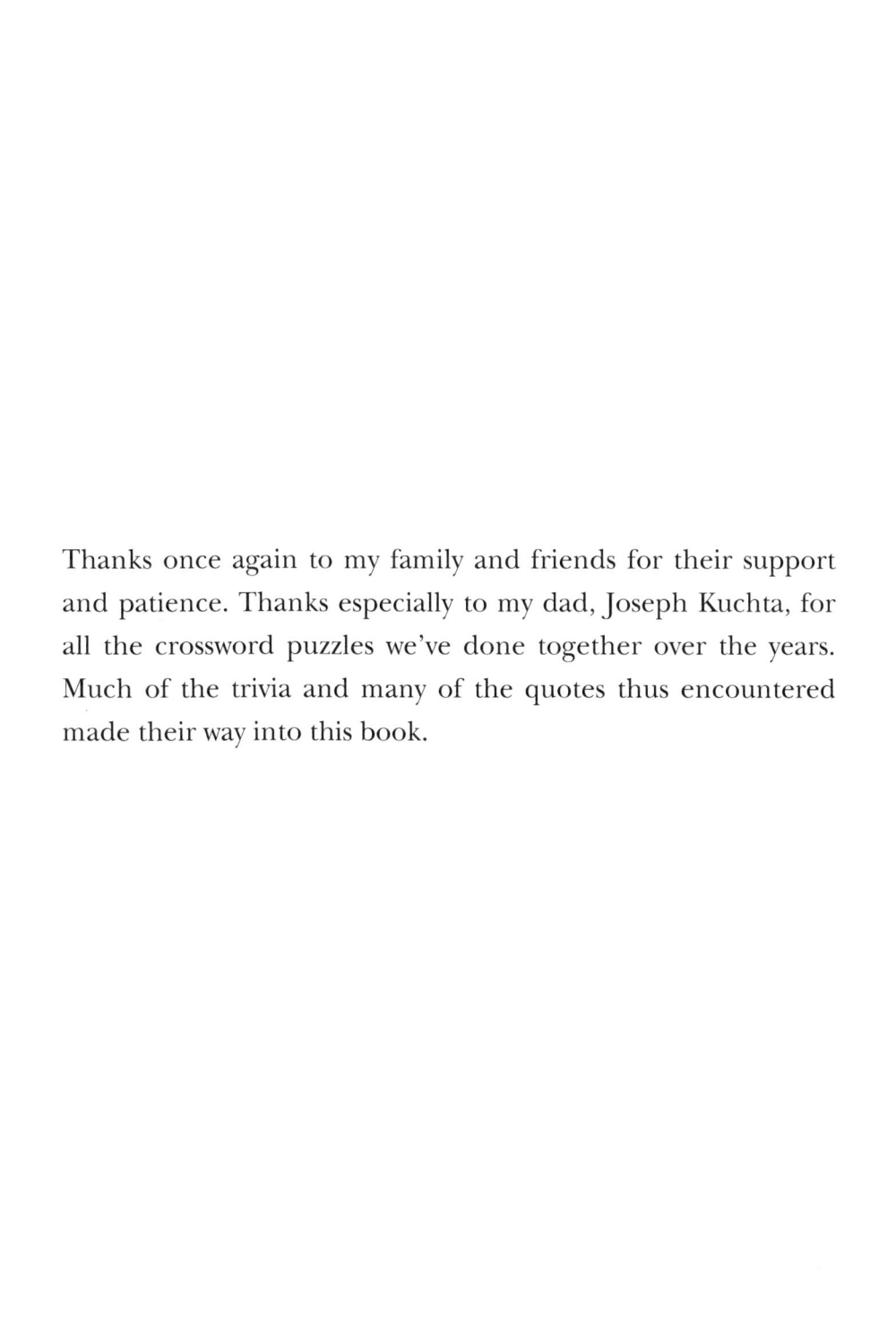

Thanks once again to my family and friends for their support and patience. Thanks especially to my dad, Joseph Kuchta, for all the crossword puzzles we've done together over the years. Much of the trivia and many of the quotes thus encountered made their way into this book.

Author's Notes

For checking the accuracy of the various Shakespeare quotations in the book, and for miscellaneous fact-checking, *Open Source Shakespeare* (http://www.opensourceshakespeare.org/) and the Folger Library website (http://www.folger.edu/shakespeares-works) were most helpful. Quotes from the Bible were sourced with the help of *Bible Gateway* (https://www.biblegateway.com/).

Relationships among the various characters presented here are complex. In the interest of simplifying them for the reader, the word "cousin" is used throughout the book to denote cousinly relations both direct and at varying degrees of distance.

Table of Contents

Act One

Chapter One: 1
    Betwixt Mixed Bags

Chapter Two: 3
    Meeting and Greeting

Chapter Three: 7
    True Love's Course and the Source of Divorce

Chapter Four: 9
    Puck'll Chuckle

Chapter Five: 11
    The Rest of the Guest List

Chapter Six: 13
    Burr Puts a Burr under Dolly's Saddle, by Golly

Chapter Seven: 17
    Aviation and the Odd Relation

Chapter Eight: 21
    A Ragtag Chin Wag

Chapter Nine: 23
    Mary and Lizzie Go All Bizzie

Chapter Ten: 27
    The Lives of Six Wives

Chapter Eleven: 29
   To Go, Or Not To Go, Commando

Chapter Twelve: 33
   Dear Me, Syncope!

Act Two

Chapter Thirteen: 37
   Déjà Vu Plus Two

Chapter Fourteen: 39
   Menagerie and Query

Chapter Fifteen: 41
   The Mission Condition

Chapter Sixteen: 45
   Canny about Grannie

Chapter Seventeen: 51
   Hello, Marlowe!

Chapter Eighteen: 53
   Tête-à-Tête on a Reprobate

Chapter Nineteen: 57
   The Statutory Story

Chapter Twenty: 61
   Spring Fling

Chapter Twenty-One: 67
   Rendezvous and Parlez-Vous

Chapter Twenty-Two: 73
    The Permanent Termagant

Chapter Twenty-Three: 77
    Of Stoolies with Brass Goolies

Chapter Twenty-Four: 81
    Disaster on the Morning After

Chapter Twenty-Five: 87
    Used Sorely by Morley

Chapter Twenty-Six: 91
    Hero of the Zero-Sum Game

Chapter Twenty-Seven: 95
    Mythology's Follies

Chapter Twenty-Eight: 101
    The Breakdown of a Shakedown

Chapter Twenty-Nine: 103
    Bess Is Tightest with the Best and Brightest

Chapter Thirty: 107
    Hot to Plot

Chapter Thirty-One: 111
    Bring on the Bling

Chapter Thirty-Two: 113
    Regalia Inter Alia

Chapter Thirty-Three: 121
    Sidekick and Psychic

Chapter Thirty-Four: 125
    Must We Force It into a Corset?

Chapter Thirty-Five: 129
    How to Deck Dolly's Neck?

Chapter Thirty-Six: 137
    Ring-a-Ding-Ding

Chapter Thirty-Seven: 143
    The Distinguished and the Extinguished

Chapter Thirty-Eight: 145
    Hearts Afire and Dolly for Hire, More or Less

Chapter Thirty-Nine: 149
    The Names of Three Dames

Chapter Forty: 153
    A Little Mystery in the History

Chapter Forty-One: 157
    More than One None-Too-Cheery Theory

Chapter Forty-Two: 159
    The Rustic and the Prick

Chapter Forty-Three: 163
    Keep Calm, Rest Still, and Call Cecil

Chapter Forty-Four: 167
    The Pair Who Missed the Fair,
    or Of Potions and Emotions

Chapter Forty-Five: 171
   Of Empty Houses That Haunt Absent Spouses

Chapter Forty-Six: 175
   Assumption and Gumption,
   or A Dame in the Patriot Game

Chapter Forty-Seven: 179
   Of Climacterics and Tricks

Chapter Forty-Eight: 185
   A Team on the Same Beam

Chapter Forty-Nine: 189
   Quaff, Drop, and Roll Is the Goal

Chapter Fifty: 193
   Caught Red-Handed and Wedding-Banded

Chapter Fifty-One: 197
   The Chi-Chi English Lady and Catherine de' Medici

Chapter Fifty-Two: 201
   Circumspection and Escaping Detection

Chapter Fifty-Three: 205
   By Dint of Madame Serpent

Chapter Fifty-Four: 211
   Solution Convolution

Chapter Fifty-Five: 219
   A Gal in a Gallery

Chapter Fifty-Six: 223
    Genial Genealogy

Chapter Fifty-Seven: 227
    One Tear More or Less and the *Devonshire MS*

Chapter Fifty-Eight: 233
    On Sorrowing and Borrowing

Chapter Fifty-Nine: 237
    Star-Crossed and Pillow Tossed

Chapter Sixty: 241
    Termagants and a Song and Dance

Chapter Sixty-One: 245
    The Party Line on a Maligned Spine

Chapter Sixty-Two: 249
    The Royal Matron and the Literary Patron

Chapter Sixty-Three: 253
    The Accessory That Tells a Story

Chapter Sixty-Four: 257
    Being Practical and Waxing Theatrical

Chapter Sixty-Five: 261
    The History of the Sisters Grey,
    or the Thwarted Departed

Chapter Sixty-Six: 263
    On Disparaged Marriages

Chapter Sixty-Seven: 267
    Mary Grey's Matrimonial Testimonial

Chapter Sixty-Eight: 269
  A Little Ire and Irons in the Fire

Chapter Sixty-Nine: 273
  Mary Grey Tells It to Liz Like It Is

Chapter Seventy: 277
  Iniquities and Ditties

Chapter Seventy-One: 283
  Time for Catherine to Chime In

Chapter Seventy-Two: 285
  Character Building and Gilding the Lily

Chapter Seventy-Three: 289
  Confinement, Wine, and On Down the Line

Chapter Seventy-Four: 295
  Holy Folio!

Chapter Seventy-Five: 301
  Doggy Style for a Little While

Chapter Seventy-Six: 305
  Hypocritically, Literally?

Chapter Seventy-Seven: 309
  Remorse, of Course

Chapter Seventy-Eight: 313
  Hindsight Is All Right

Chapter Seventy-Nine: 319
  Execution, Exile, and Exculpation

Chapter Eighty: 323
   How They Were Hand-to-Handed,
   and Whence They Landed

Chapter Eighty-One: 329
   Paeans to Three Queens

Chapter Eighty-Two: 333
   Family Dysfunction Junction

Chapter Eighty-Three: 337
   The Spin on Ann Boleyn

Chapter Eighty-Four: 341
   A Quote or Two to Float Your Boat for You

Chapter Eighty-Five: 345
   Of Druthers and Mothers

Chapter Eighty-Six: 351
   The Concussed and the Nonplussed

Chapter Eighty-Seven: 357
   Literary Notions and Going through the Motions

Chapter Eighty-Eight: 361
   The Riled and the Exiled

Chapter Eighty-Nine: 367
   Tiswas at Amboise

Chapter Ninety: 371
   The Gift That Fixed a Rift

Chapter Ninety-One: 375
    See 'Em Later, Alligator

Chapter Ninety-Two: 379
    Propinquity with Antiquity

Chapter Ninety-Three: 381
    The Lots of Some Scots

Chapter Ninety-Four: 385
    Stitch and Bitch

Chapter Ninety-Five: 389
    In the Stir with the Green-Eyed Monster

Chapter Ninety-Six: 393
    Gore in Store and Walking the Floor

Chapter Ninety-Seven: 397
    About a Lout

Chapter Ninety-Eight: 401
    Moor and More

Chapter Ninety-Nine: 403
    Imogen and Imagining

Chapter One Hundred: 407
    A Gem of a Stratagem

Chapter One Hundred-One: 411
    Amnesty, Your Majesty

Chapter One Hundred-Two: 415
    Ruff and Bluff

Chapter One Hundred-Three: 417
    Bucolic Frolics

Chapter One Hundred-Four: 427
    Winter's Chill Fits the Bill,
    or Nothing Finer than Paulina

Chapter One Hundred-Five: 433
    No Greater Collaborator

Chapter One Hundred-Six: 439
    The Rom-Com Bomb, or a Winning Way with Twinning

Chapter One Hundred-Seven: 447
    Validating Vacillating

Chapter One Hundred-Eight: 451
    Fare-Thee-Wells and Dare-Thee-Tells

Chapter One Hundred-Nine: 455
    A Toast That Is the Most

Chapter One Hundred-Ten: 459
    What's Supposed to Be Sub-Rosa

Chapter One Hundred-Eleven: 463
    Enigmas, Anyone?

Chapter One Hundred-Twelve: 469
    Routing and Outing

Chapter One Hundred-Thirteen: 475
    Spouse in the House

Chapter One Hundred-Fourteen:... 479
    Secreted and Defeated

Chapter One Hundred-Fifteen: 483
    A Man of Parts, a Change of Heart, and a Departure

Act Three

Chapter One Hundred-Sixteen: 491
    Arise and Surprise

Chapter One Hundred-Seventeen:.. 495
    The Shindig and the Big News

Chapter One Hundred-Eighteen:.. 501
    Bliss and Synthesis

Act One

Chapter One
Betwixt Mixed Bags

In general, I agree that "no legacy is so rich as honesty," but I wasn't exactly feeling it that morning. I had let out a feeble "Fine, thank you," when my solicitous husband inquired how I was feeling, even though I'd skipped my usual hearty breakfast because of a slightly upset tummy. I knew he'd fuss over me like a mother hen if I told him of my indisposition, and I'd not built any fuss time into the day's crowded agenda.

As my husband was observant as well as solicitous, he redirected the fussing to a mini-intervention on my abuse of mood-altering substances.

"Really, darling—*three* of these? All at once?"

I carefully extricated three Lipton tea bags from the tangled web that dangled into my teacup. "Yes, *three!*" I replied more grumpily than I'm proud to admit. "I can't be expected to stay awake through a Monday morning staff meeting on any less caffeine than that."

"Well, then?" asked Wally, directing his gaze toward the two bags of chamomile tea that remained steeping in the same cup.

"You know what Monday morning meetings do to me on a good day! And with everything else that's going on today, this should be just enough sedation to keep me from snapping before the meeting is over."

"Really, Dolly—I've never known you to have nerves like this. I'm concerned enough to think that you should see a doctor."

Wally squeezed me in a hug and then squeezed out all the tea bags and handed me my teacup. The cup was actually a gift from him to celebrate my getting my current job. It had holograph pictures of Henry VIII's six wives on it. The wives' images came and went, ghostlike, as the tea in the cup went from hot to cold.

My disproportionate fondness for that teacup has always perplexed Wally. He knows, of course, about my Henry VIII obsession; that's why he purchased the cup. What he has no way of knowing is the story of my otherworldly encounter with the shades of the Big Man's six wives or the impact that their advice to me has had on both our lives. The portraits on the cup remind me of my faraway Tudor girlfriends and of my various family members and friends who are, in a way, their counterparts here in the real world. At times I long to tell Wally about my memorable night with Henry VIII's women, and that I live in something of a parallel Tudor universe. I am unable to, though; the Tudors—or, to be perfectly accurate, Ann Boleyn's daughter, Elizabeth I—made it clear to me when I met her that telling tales out of Tudor School is against rule number one.

"'There are more things in heaven and earth than are dreamt of in your philosophy,' Wally," I reminded him, hoping to end the reverse-curtain lecture with some feminine mystery. It worked.

"I'll be dreaming about *this* in my philosophy all day long," Wally said, tapping me fondly on the behind. "Although I'm sure it's not exactly what the Bard meant when he said that. And anyway, if you aren't in better spirits by tomorrow, I may just have to spank it again."

It seemed to me that it would be a win no matter which way my spirits went. As it turned out, however, there were more things in heaven and earth than were dreamed of in *my* philosophy as well.

Chapter Two
Meeting and Greeting

My commute to work involved some very pretty English countryside, and the morning was so fine that I opened the car windows; the drive revived my spirits nicely. My appetite had returned by the time I sat down at my desk and raised my office teacup in a toast to no one in particular.

"'Now for the tea of our host, now for the rollicking bun, now for the muffin and toast, now for the gay Sally Lunn!'"

I hoped that a little Gilbert and Sullivan for my breakfast order would make a change from the Shakespeare-awareness that had recently overtaken our little college. A major Shakespeare festival was in the works. It had subsumed pretty much everything about academic life lately, at least in the humanities; everyone was all about the comedy and the drama. In keeping with the drama portion of the theme, a tempest in a teapot was brewing among our support staff that morning. Staff meeting refreshments set up, the ubiquitous tea and buns, promised to be disputatious.

To begin with, our two administrative assistants, Katie and Merrie, were both in a hormonal haze. This was not unusual, because of the rather dreamy, romantic nature they shared. In their little world, love conquered all; the work ethic certainly did not stand a chance. We did not ask too closely about Katie's man, who was by all accounts a questionable choice. Her bestie, Merrie, was there for her, though, to support her through her various romantic trials.

Merrie, a petite little thing at well under five feet, was a gal who liked them tall. Her true love, all seven feet of him, was chief of college security. Merrie's swain made it a point to visit our department daily on his rounds. The distant sound of his heavy shoes clumping along the corridor that morning was like starter's orders to Merrie.

"I am *so* excited about him! I think he might just be the one, you know! Golly," she said, "I'll bet he's got his escutcheon with him today!"

"I think you mean truncheon, dear," Katie said patiently. Correcting Merrie's grammatical lapses was not in Katie's job description, but it may as well have been.

After a truncheon sighting, Merrie was pretty much useless the rest of the day. The relationship made us all feel well looked after in terms of security, if not well served on the administrative end.

"I shouldn't be expected to handle the bun detail while I'm battling morning sickness!" Katie said, looking like she was about to lose the battle.

"I can't do it, either," said Merrie. "It's almost time for my scheduled tea break, and *he* will be here any second now. I will *not* see my man with his truncheon stood up!" I had a feeling that eventually she would, one way or another, but I declined to comment. The crisis seemed insoluble until the dean's assistant, Amy, handily resolved it.

"I will take care of the tea, and the buns are a done deal. I baked some myself last night!"

"Leave it to you, Amy!" I said. The old-fashioned term doughty-handed always came to mind when I witnessed an example of Amy's solid, no-drama efficiency. That and her porcelain-skinned milkmaid looks spoke of her rustic roots.

Some of our staff considered Amy a country bumpkin and wondered how she had secured a position in credential-aware academia with only a lot of horse sense to recommend her.

Sex and a soccer star named Lester were at the bottom of it.

Chapter Three
True Love's Course and the Source of Divorce

Lester had wed the pulchritudinous Amy when he was the star of the soccer team here at our college, and she was a waitress at a local village eatery. Amy was able to keep up with him socially—though barely—as he worked his way up to soccer coach for his home team. Lester's career really took off from there; he rose to prominence in the international soccer community in what seemed like no time flat. It wasn't long before he outgrew the sweet, simple Amy, who was not inclined to change her down-home ways. Eventually, the two divorced, with Lester using his connections at the college to swing a good job for Amy, thus reducing his alimony payment. Lester moved on to bigger and better things, at least in the bustline department, with his second marriage.

In the Jeeves stories, Bertie Wooster's deserving Aunt Dahlia warns him against girls with oddly spelled names such as Gwladys. She might have sung a similar siren song about Lester's second wife. Like the moon pulling at the ocean tide, Gladous had a downright magnetic effect on testosterone seas.

Gladous probably deserved to have been warned as much as warned against—at least according to my would-have-been step-daughter, Lizzie.

"Lester raked Gladous over the divorce court coals even worse than he raked Amy over them!" Lizzie told me once. "I'd like to see him try to get the better of *me* that way!"

It occurred to me that a woman sometimes "scorns what best contents her," but I wasn't about to point that out to Lizzie, who dallied with Lester herself whenever she visited England but preferred to keep the exact nature of the relationship a mystery.

Letty, Lester's third and current wife, had recently become our department head. In a stunning example of life imitating marriage, Letty took on this position after none other than the aforementioned Gladous vacated it.

Letty's special area of academic expertise was fashion history; stage and screen producers of costume dramas clamored for her consulting services. Photos of celebrities dressed in period best to which she had given her blessing filled her office. The woman was certainly in her element with the upcoming Shakespeare festival; as she was often heard to say, "The play's the thing!"

The *plays* are the *things* would have been more accurate, if less literarily fortuitous. Our little university had fallen on tough times, and that Shakespeare festival that I mentioned was intended to bring attention, cache, and funds our way. Personally, I thought it a long shot. Nevertheless, our department's role in the festival would form the bulk of the agenda at our morning staff meeting.

Chapter Four
Puck'll Chuckle

Our department had never been involved in theatrical doings as grand as those now being planned, but we had helped out over the years in the various productions that the college had put on. My Wally was known to lend a hand to the cause on such occasions, and he knew some of my work associates passingly well.

"I don't mind getting 'bear' for a good cause," Wally had said puckishly, rustling up a tame bear for a production of *The Winter's Tale.* That act of ursine kindness had made him the go-to man for theatrical livestock. He'd had to put his foot down once or twice, though. "I cannot and will not participate in animal body part procurement on a nonessential level," he had insisted when approached to supply lizard leg, dog tongue, frog toe, and so on for the weird sisters' cauldron in *Macbeth.* I knew that one of the plays we would be discussing today was *A Midsummer Night's Dream.* Hard to know what Wally would have to say if getting Nick Bottom suited up meant that he would have to contribute a piece of ass to the production; I chuckled at the thought. As our all-girl department gathered at the meeting table, I chuckled as well at Wally's nickname for the assembled contingent: "mixed bags."

"We'll be talking about work soon enough, Dolly; the meeting will be starting in a few minutes. You still have time to take a look at this catalog, though. Lots of new items, and several lovely pieces marked down. Some of them just struck me as so 'you' that I circled them for you in red ink. Tell me what you think after the meeting!"

"I shouldn't have to, Blanche," I said, laughing. "You could just read it in my palm!"

Hard-pressed to make ends meet on an academic salary, Blanche had taken to reading the odd palm and to selling jewelry as a franchisee. Her sideline had become quite successful, as evidenced by the preponderance of baubles, bangles, and beads in our department.

"Necklaces are the way to go, Dolly," advised Gladous, peeping into the catalog companionably and offering some expert advice. "The right lavalier does wonders for the cleavage, you know."

"Enough about cleavage, Gladous; I am calling this meeting to order. Time to get down to business!" Letty said, gathering her papers about her. Once things were underway, Letty announced that she would be introducing two guest attendees at the meeting. I already knew both of them.

Chapter Five
The Rest of the Guest List

Marge, running a little late and entering the room as Letty made her opening remarks, seated herself to my left upon her arrival. "Heard from Uncle Harry lately?" she whispered convivially. Marge was a niece, several times removed, of my former fiancé, Harry, as well as an active member of our college's board of trustees. I inquired politely about Marge's two unprepossessing sons, and Marge then settled in with one of Blanche's jewelry catalogs hidden behind her meeting agenda. A large, ornate brooch seemed to have caught her eye.

Our other guest attendee sat next to Marge. A woman of substantial girth, she went by the unlikely nickname of Demi, an abbreviation of her full and unpronounceable Italian moniker.

"How is Wally's sheep-rescue project going?" she leaned toward me and whispered as Letty made her way down the meeting agenda.

"The flock is prospering finely," I whispered back, "thanks in no small part to you."

Demi was a woman of substance in more ways than one. She was present at our meeting today as a board member and as a primary funding source for our college. The woman's pockets ran deep, and she could be generous when she wanted to be. Wally had charmed financial support from Demi for his animal charities more than once. He referred to her as *paisana* whenever they spoke and as *buy-sana* once he was safely back at home with me, her check in his hand.

The meeting made its way to what was more or less the seventh-inning stretch, and I fell to thinking of all that was on my home plate. I had a bevy of company coming to stay at the house, and in fact, I needed to pick them up at the airport as soon as the meeting was over.

As the proceedings concluded, Gladous was kind enough to kick me under the table and bring my reverie to an end. I sprang into action, grabbing my car keys and making a dash for the door.

"'They stumble that run fast,'" Letty reminded me. "What's your hurry?"

"'Time and the hour runs through the roughest day,'" I pointed out. "I have a plane to meet!"

Chapter Six
Burr Puts a Burr under Dolly's Saddle, by Golly

There were two preoccupied spouses in our marriage, I thought as I drove to the airport after leaving work. My husband had seemed a bit restless of late, like something was bubbling up in him, and he could barely contain it. I wondered what it could mean.

His work life was the first and most obvious thing to come to mind. Wally had come to the Cotswolds to bring his world-class veterinary research skills to an ovine variant of mad cow disease that was threatening the very fiber of the wool business across the globe. He had, as he said, pretty much unraveled that tangled problem, and sheep, as Bach said, might safely graze again. Now he had only a bit of cleanup work left to do.

I wondered if Wally had received some secret call to his next world-improving feat of veterinary, medical, sanitary, or engineering brilliance. It wouldn't be the first he'd had since we'd married and moved to the Cotswolds; he was quite in international demand. He had said no to all the professional calls I knew of on the pretext of being caught up with his sheep. But I knew he also did it to allow me the opportunity to develop and birth my magnum Tudor opus in the conducive quiet of the country.

My groundbreaking historical treatise, *Henry VIII, Man of Constant Sorrow*, had made quite a splash in Renaissance academic circles. It had been conceived, so to speak, the night I was privileged to meet the six wives of Henry VIII on an astral plain and to learn the secret that each wife had harbored, heretofore safe from history. Developing the pursuant thesis on those secrets in a scholarly fashion, when the primary sources were, shall we say, undocumented, had taken some doing—and some time. While accomplishing the task, I had grown personally and professionally, and now I yearned to expand my horizons even further. Academic advancement was the obvious possibility, and well within my comfort zone. But somehow, I wasn't so sure about it.

I wasn't the only one concerned about my professional development; Burr—my first mentor in Renaissance history and a dear friend—had mentioned it as well. We'd spoken about it on the phone several times, in fact, as recently as the week before.

"After all, Dolly," he'd said, "you've had the last word when it comes to Henry VIII's wives."

Not having been there himself when I was among that legendary bevy, he could not have known that having the last word with those gals was pretty much impossible.

"I take your point, Burr, but where do I go from here? That is the question."

"I thought 'to be or not to be' was the question," Burr had said smugly, his own academic specialty being all things Shakespearian. "You can always come over to the dark side with me, Dolly. Some of the latter-generation Tudors coexisted with Shakespeare, as you well know."

"I am all about my Tudors, Burr, and nothing is going to change that. I feel in my bones, though, that changes are afoot in my life; that the direction I am supposed to go will be made clear to me—and soon."

"You can get out of that dusty little college you are working at, for a start," Burr said, never one to pull any punches. "It may have been all right while you had to work on your six wives treatise, but now that that task is over, I think it is time for you to move on to bigger and better things."

"Well, I have had some interesting offers, but I just can't seem to settle down to a decision. I am giving the commencement address at my college in a couple of days, and some of the parties who are interested in me will be present. Maybe that will shake something loose, somehow."

"You've got to shake loose that death grip you've got on that little 'six-wives-of-Henry VIII' world you live in, Dolly. Let it go a little bit. You'll never know what wonderful things could be in store for you, if you don't!"

"I'll ponder that advice a bit, Burr; really, I will!"

"Well, good luck, Dolly. And the same to Wally as well; tell him I asked after him and his husbandry."

"Animal or conjugal, Burr?"

"I suppose he'd think I was some kind of pervert either way!" Burr said, sounding flustered. His inner nerd tended to come out at the oddest times; it made the scholarly genius quite human and lovable. "Best just give Wally my kindest regards, Dolly."

"I will, Burr," I assured him.

"And the same to young Lizzie, if you're going to see her while she's in England," he added. Burr was inordinately fond of that almost-stepdaughter of mine, and not in a creepy way, either. Lizzie had been his student back in the day—in fact, a star pupil. She was likewise very fond of Burr and had recently used him as a cultural context consultant for her business, about which more later.

After I hung up the phone with Burr, I told Wally what we'd talked about.

"I have to agree with Burr that perhaps you have come to some sort of crossroad; that the game is soon going to change for you. It might be time for you to let something go to pick up on something new. Wasn't it Shakespeare who said, 'When you come to a fork in the road, take it'?"

"No, dear," I said fondly, charmed as I always was when Wally made one of his rare mistakes. "Yogi Berra, I think."

"I should have known better," Wally conceded. "After all, they tell me that I am smarter than the average Berra."

Chapter Seven
Aviation and the Odd Relation

I hold to the philosophy that it is better to be three hours too soon than a minute too late, but between staff meeting and traffic, this would be one time I did not make the grade. I hoped, as I came to the end of my drive to the airport, that my kith and kin would not have been long on the ground when I arrived to meet them.

My cousins Jean, Kath, and Bella wouldn't have dreamed of missing the commencement speech I would be giving the next day. They were flying in for it together, accompanied by darling Auntie Reine Marie. Miss Bess, an old family friend, had also strong-armed her way into the band of travelers. Based on a lifetime of experience, I knew what to expect when they all deplaned.

Miss Bess was the first off the plane, with relieved-looking flight attendants clearing the way for her.

"I'm what is known as a *badass*," Bess said to the flight attendants in passing.

"*Hardass* is more like it," one of the flight attendants whispered to the other.

"I didn't think much of the attendants on this flight," Bess confided in me as we hugged in greeting. "Short on brains, I can tell you! A couple of…of…"

"'Knotty-pated fools'?" I ventured.

"I was going to say idiots, but have it your own way, Dolly."

My cousin Jean, singularly unencumbered by excess baggage, greeted me next. "I love my new travel bag," she said, showing me a most efficient-looking multicompartmented marvel. "I was able to get nine days' worth of outfits in here!"

"How did you manage that?" I asked.

"Careful folding," she replied, her inner overachiever peeping through. "I've been complimented on my packing by airport security, you know."

Cousin Kath, on the other hand, was sure to be bursting at the seams in every sense. Her predilection for stretch pants was a fond family joke; she had them in every conceivable style and pattern, and she was oblivious to ever outgrowing a single pair.

"What kind of leggings did Kath press into service for this trip?" I asked Jean, as we waited for the rest of the family to deplane.

"You mean what kind of leggings did she *stretch* into service, don't you?"

"Come on, Jean, the suspense is killing me! Polka dots? Leopard spots? Forget-me-nots?"

My question was answered as Kath stepped off the plane sporting red leggings with a little black Yorkshire terrier silhouette print. Her little pet dog amplified the canine and the "bursting" themes, breaking free from his traveling restraints and leaking pee once at ground level.

Kath greeted me fondly. "I've got two checked bags to pick up, Dolly. You know I can't cross the Atlantic without bringing you fashion from home!"

"What is it this time, Kath?" I asked, trying not to show my trepidation. I generally hold that wearing a particular type of garb the first time it was in style necessitates avoiding the mutton-dressed-as-lamb trap by eschewing it the second time it comes around. Kath had no such compunction, though, so I would not have been surprised at anything that made its way into the "fashion from home."

"It's leggings!" she said jubilantly. "Leggings in all the latest colors and textures, Dolly, with plenty of tops to wear over them. I know you will be pleased with the assortment. I even managed to find a pair of leggings with pictures of Henry VIII's wives on them!" Kath said. Her pup circled about in shared delight—or perhaps dread—of those Henry VIII leggings.

There was no convincing Kath that fashion of all kinds was available to me, should I want it, by means other than her kindly auspices. I waved at her as her little caravan of chaos headed off toward the baggage carousel, and cousin Bella, who had just stepped off the plane, watched them walk away.

"I don't know if it's a blessing or a curse that cats don't travel well," Bella said, giving me a big hug. I was inclined to think *blessing*, as I emerged from the hug with my share of the cat hair that festooned pretty much everything my cousin wore.

"Your cats are with you in spirit, anyway," I said, offering the little lint brush that experience had taught me to bring to any reunion involving Bella.

"No thanks," she said, brushing her clothes off perfunctorily. Bella's fashion preference tended toward what Barbara Pym would have called a fusty Bohemianism; cat hair counted as an accessory in her little world.

Auntie Reine Marie deplaned last, bringing up the tone as well as the rear. She was tall, lissome for a woman of her years, and flat-out stunning, rocking maturity, as they say, like a boss.

"Everyone else is off the plane, *n'est-ce pas?*" she asked before stepping into the airport proper. A combination of native graciousness and knowledge of how to make an entrance informed her question.

"All clear," I assured her. "Everyone else has already disembarked, hugged, kissed, stretched, scratched, and orienteered toward the nearest ladies' room."

Auntie Reine Marie descended like Venus stepping off the half shell, with a scarf trailing behind her á la Isadora Duncan. If anyone can descend from a plane that is actually on the ground, it is Auntie Reine Marie.

It probably will come as no surprise to you to learn that my family is what you would call well known at the airport.

Chapter Eight
A Ragtag Chin Wag

Once we were all safely crammed into my vehicle—actually, Wally's Land Rover—and driving out of the airport, my visitors and I turned our attention to thoughts of our absent family and friends.

"I hope we get to see Mary and Lizzie!" Jean said. She was referring to my two would-have-been stepdaughters. "They are such international travelers these days that it is hard to keep track of where they are."

"You just might see them, Jean. They are this side of the pond for the next few days."

"Yes, they are here to get that award we've been hearing so much about. It is all over the news; you just can't escape it," said Miss Bess.

"It is as though Lizzie and Mary are being crowned queens of enterprise!" said Auntie Reine Marie, glowing with pride at the younger generation.

"Well, those girls come by their business acumen honestly," said Miss Bess, doing the in-character thing by bringing the cold, hard facts of reproduction into the conversation. "They get it from their father, surely."

"Mary and Lizzie no doubt got their executive abilities from Harry. And of course, Mary is so like her mother. She and Kay are both so intelligent, so capable, and *so* consistent," commented Auntie Reine Marie.

"And Lizzie, of course, is so like that Anna Belinda," Miss Bess added. "Mother and daughter both so intelligent, so capable, and so, so…"

"I think 'mercurial' is what you are looking for," I offered.

"What did Harry have to say about his two daughters getting this award?"

"Nothing whatsoever, Bess, for the first full minute or two after the news broke," I said, recalling what I'd heard about it through the grapevine.

"That doesn't sound like Harry," Jean said.

"Apparently he was so dumbfounded that his bickering daughters could accomplish *anything* together that the news rendered him speechless for a bit. He soon recovered, though."

"What did he say about his progeny *then*, Dolly?" asked Miss Bess.

"I don't remember the exact words," I admitted. "Something to the effect that 'the age of miracles is not past.'"

I didn't know it then, but I'd soon be coming to that same conclusion myself.

Chapter Nine
Mary and Lizzie Go All Bizzie

Mary and Lizzie's business model was, to say the least, a remarkable partnership. It ran on a winning combination of Mary's solid grounding in traditional humanities and Lizzie's hipper interest in science, technology, and style. It was nothing less than a schematic for subliminally encoding classical messages into modern-day social and entertainment media. The twist was that new art, products, services, and so on were to be promoted by leveraging well-worn, even archaic, axioms that had withstood the test of time.

Lizzie's was the face associated with the advertisements that were inescapable pretty much anywhere you went to access news or information. She was probably not someone you would think of, at first blush, as being well equipped to do it. Slender to skinniness, fair and freckled in a tanning-bed world, and flat chested to boot, she was even further removed from traditional cover girlhood by geek-level intelligence. Clearly, though, she was better equipped than Mary to do the front work. Mary, though a lovely and intelligent girl, was the serious type; too little the geek and too much the old-school librarian to suit trendy tastes.

"I make a whisper a sell," Lizzie would say softly, staring frankly and ingenuously from TV, computer screen, tablet, or smartphone as she delivered the company tagline. And most were inclined to believe her, if the success of the girls' operation was any indication. There was something appealing about the fresh and intelligent young face juxtaposed against the outfits and accessories she chose for her appearances. Lizzie being Lizzie, she could never do anything like everyone else did, and in this case, it paid off.

"Sex sells," she had informed me once, thinking that I did not already know it. "But not," she added, apparently thinking that I suffered a mercantile deficit as well, "if you give it away." Not only was Lizzie not giving it away, but she was also keeping it under some very impressive wraps.

"I wonder," Jean pondered aloud, "if Lizzie will accept her award in one of those famous outfits of hers."

"Famous is an understatement! The world waits with bated breath for each of her new ads, and so do I," admitted Bella. "I'm not sure what I look forward to finding out most: what kind of fashion statement she is going to make with her over-the-top outfits or which body part she will choose to expose."

"My personal favorite of her ads thus far is the one in which she's wrapped from head to toe in furs," I said. In this particular ad, a truly lovely, long, slender, and elegantly jeweled hand was the only part of Lizzie's body, other than her face, that was exposed.

"Wally isn't crazy about that particular ad though," I went on. "His veterinary view makes the whole fur thing a bit much for him, even though the furs were faux."

"Which ad does Wally prefer?" Bella asked.

"The one where she's swathed in velvety red roses, seated with arms wrapped around knees, with the roses falling away to expose her left kneecap. He calls it the petals-and-patella ad," I said, showing off his scientific prowess just a little bit.

"I like that one too! But not as much as the cat lady one," Bella said.

"I'm not surprised," said Miss Bess, flicking a cat hair off Bella's shoulder.

Auntie Reine Marie—so stylish and well equipped to make suggestions along these lines—had given Lizzie the idea for this very popular ad. She was proud of it and rushed in to correct Bella's fast-and-loose interpretation.

"Cat *woman*, Bella, not cat lady. Cat ladies do not wear elegant leather cat suits with navel cut outs."

"Nor would they think to make the cat suit white instead of black," Jean added. "What a well-received break with fashion tradition that was!"

"The world is certainly Lizzie's stage these days," Miss Bess admitted.

We were nearing home. My own little world, I was sure, would be a plenty big enough stage for me that evening.

Chapter Ten
The Lives of Six Wives

The Rainbow Chateau is the name Wally and I chose for our little Cotswolds cottage. Surprisingly, the prismatic aspect of the home was not pointed out to us when we set about purchasing it. We were pleasantly surprised the first time we walked out our back door after a rain shower and found our Shakespeare garden nestled under an absolutely perfect arc of a rainbow. Most rainy days gift us with a rainbow as perfect as that first one. In fact, Wally and I actually look forward to precipitation nowadays.

As my relatives and I crested home, the skies were sunny. We moved into gossip cleanup mode about the last six of our acquaintances who were currently gossip worthy: the six exes of my former fiancé, Harry.

"Kay is so happy living on the West Coast," my cousin Jean said of Harry's first ex. "She's turned out to be such an effective political activist and asset to her community—and of course, there's her work on the international scene as well." I was glad to hear that the kindly Kay was living a full and productive life.

"Anna Belinda has been migrating between the States and the UK; she's working on a music video with Lady Gaga!" said Bella. "She's going to do the 'ebony' bit in a remake of the McCartney/Jackson pop hit 'Ebony and Ivory.' With those raven tresses of hers, she'll be perfect for it."

Taking Harry's wives in numerical order, I inquired what was going on with Jane, his third ex.

"Jane is traveling abroad, and Cleva has joined her for the trip," said Miss Bess, accounting for ex number four as well. "Jane had taken a great notion to take a grand tour of Europe and broaden her cultural horizons. Cleva is acting as her traveling companion for the Amsterdam leg of the trip."

"I can see the ill-advisedness of letting someone as dippy as Jane go around unaccompanied in a party city like Amsterdam," I said. "And Cleva would likely enjoy a stint of chaperonage, seeing as no one chaperones the chaperone."

"Kitty and Kate are traveling too. They are touring the Orient together!" said Bella, bringing in Harry's fifth and sixth wives, respectively.

"Kitty got out of the Betty Ford clinic a couple of weeks ago," Jean said. "She says she is done forever with sex, drugs, and rock and roll."

"I feel pretty sanguine about the drugs and rock and roll part. Not so much about the sex part, knowing Kitty the way I do. Still, she has my best wishes for her getting clean and sober."

"Well, you know, Dolly, Kate is not much of one for the swinging high life. So, she kindly volunteered to accompany Kitty on a meditation tour of India to get her away from all the old people, places, and things," Jean went on.

"Well, Kate is unequalled when it comes to being serious and sober, and if anyone can pull off a geographical cure for Kitty, I guess it is Kate," I said as we pulled into the drive.

Wally was waiting for us at the door, arms full of flowers—a bouquet for each of us. "I will get the luggage, ladies. I've gotten the guest rooms all ready for you, and dinner is waiting on the stove."

If I'd had any envy at hearing about Harry's exes having adventures all around the globe, it melted then and there.

Chapter Eleven
To Go, Or Not To Go, Commando

I entertained my company in the good old-fashioned way, around the kitchen table. We joked, speculated, and gossiped the way close friends and family will. When dinner was over, my guests headed out to see a movie to allow me to work in peace and quiet. I had to put a few finishing touches on the commencement address I was finalizing for the next day.

My *Henry VIII, Man of Constant Sorrow* had been well received, if controversial, in Europe as well as in the United States and the United Kingdom. I'd had the honor and pleasure of speaking about it to academic audiences all over the world in the months after its completion. International interest in my treatise, and in me, had been flattering indeed. It had also given me a certain cache at the institution where I worked—hence my being asked to give the aforementioned commencement address. Several professional contacts who could easily turn into prospects for the career change that I'd discussed with Burr would be in the audience for the address; they had come, in fact, from several countries. Because my future felt so very much in the balance, I especially wanted my speech to be impressive.

Of course, I also wanted to look drop-dead amazing while I delivered the address. There is only so much you can do about that, though, when it comes to a doctoral robe. Still, I wanted to be sure that my garment was in tip-top shape for the upcoming event, even if hiding my own shape was all that it would do. Truth be known, I also had an ulterior motive for wanting that doctoral robe to look good.

Taking a break from my speech, I unfolded and examined the robe.

"Sexy?" I asked, holding the garment in front of me.

"Depends what you will be wearing under it," said Wally with a grin I can only describe as hopeful.

Wally has this fixed fantasy about attending a commencement ceremony at which I am wearing nothing but the doctoral robe, a secret known to no one in the commencement audience but him. I am not averse to fulfilling the fantasy but have held off on doing so. I have always advocated that every wife should have at least one coital contingency plan for keeping the interest going, and this was mine. Given both Wally's and my restlessness lately, I wondered if perhaps it was time for me to play the robe-and-mortarboard card. While I considered it, I assumed a poker face—no pun intended—and answered Wally's question.

"You never know," I said, batting my eyelashes and untangling the tassel on my mortarboard with what I hoped was a provocative gesture.

"'Lend me your gentle hand, and take my heart,'" said Wally, tenderly untangling my fingers from the tassel and raising them to his lips.

"All that puttering you've been doing in the Shakespeare garden is showing on your hands," he said with concern, rubbing a finger over some chapped skin. "They must be frightfully sore."

I looked at my fingers and had to admit that I could probably grate cheese on them. Wally laughed.

"Some lanolin on them ought to set things right," he said, kissing each of my five fingers. "I'll get Janie to compound some for you."

One of the nice things about being married to a man who works in the sheep industry is that you are never at a loss for moisturizing agents. The research assistant Wally mentioned had quite a sideline in variously scented lanolin-based emollients.

Wally had Janie on the cell phone in a moment and handed the phone over to me.

"I'd suggest lavender scent for your lotion, Dolly. I endorse it for its soothing effects. Your Mary swears by it," Janie added. Said Mary, my would-have-been stepdaughter, was Janie's best customer.

"Anything to make my hands, and the course of true love, smoother," I joked, finalizing the order and handing the phone back to Wally.

"Now I shall allow you to finish your sartorial and speechifying arrangements in peace," Wally said, heading for the kitchen to clean up the dinner dishes. "'Is this a dagger which I see before me, The handle toward my hand?'" asked Wally dramatically, gesturing toward the carving knife that Cousin Kath had left dangerously close to the table's edge. "'Come, let me clutch thee!'"

As Wally bustled about contentedly in the kitchen, I turned my attention to finishing my commencement speech. I hadn't gotten very far when the phone rang.

"For you, Dolly," Wally said, handing me the phone. "It's those publishing women again!"

My publishing team, as they liked to call themselves, were fairly regular conference callers, but their timing on this particular night left something to be desired. I took the phone and explained the situation about the upcoming commencement address.

"Well, Dolly," said Helen, the lively redhead who was in charge of the team of three, "we will contact you in a few days, then, when all the excitement has died down. Mark your calendar for this time next Wednesday. We don't want too much time to go by, you know."

"Yes," commented Emily, the foreign markets gal on the team. "The sooner your story about Henry VIII's six wives makes it out of the academic world and into the international media, the better!"

I was still on the fence about going mainstream with my academic research; the idea was intriguing, but it took me well out of my comfort zone.

It was as if Annie, the editorial brains of the publishing team, could read my thoughts over the ether. "Time to bust out of the old, tried and true academic world, Dolly; it's so confining. Let it go, and cast your lot with us. You'll have the world's premier publishing team behind you; nothing second best about our operation!"

I thanked the team for their enthusiasm, got off the phone, and applied myself again to my speech, with pleasantly surprising and rapid success. Checking on a few last-minute event details rounded out my night.

"All things are ready, if our mind be so," I thought, as somehow, after I perfected my speech and committed it to memory, everything else came together by the end of the night. With guests settled in at our cottage, the international professorial contingent phoned in and contentedly ensconced in their hotels, and doctoral robe and mortarboard at the ready, I turned in for some of "tired nature's sweet restorer."

Chapter Twelve
Dear Me, Syncope!

Things went smoothly the next morning at the cottage. My husband and guests breakfasted, but I abstained because of a bit of performance-anxiety dyspepsia. While the others ate, I dressed for commencement. I decided this *was* the occasion on which I would choose to indulge that fantasy of Wally's and assumed doctoral robe and shoes and nothing else. Mortarboard in hand, I climbed into the car with Wally and shivered a bit. "Chilly," I commented.

"Really?" said Wally, with a gleam in his eye.

"Yes, really!" I returned, with a gleam in mine. And with that, we and our guests caravanned off to commencement.

When we arrived at the college, Wally shepherded my family and friends to their places in the audience and then went over to say a few words to those international colleagues of mine who had come to hear my speech. I eventually saw Wally settle into a seat toward the front of the audience as I began to climb the steps to the stage from where I would give my speech.

About halfway up the steps, I started to feel woozy and faint. My knees wobbled and my vision bobbled. I felt myself starting to fall. As the foundations of the earth slipped from under my feet, I recalled my complete lack of foundation—or any other-nondoctoral garments. I fleetingly prayed that my doctoral robe would stay down around my ankles somewhere as I fell down the steps, but I knew there was little hope of that. Then, next thing I knew, Wally was bolting out of his chair, leaping over several members of the audience. In a trice, he was at my side, grabbing my mortarboard as it fell from my head. I felt a wisp of draft at my thighs as I continued to fall, but only the slightest wisp; Wally handily clapped the mortarboard over my exposed nether regions with one arm as he held out the other to break my fall.

And then everything went black.

Act Two

Chapter Thirteen
Déjà Vu Plus Two

When I awoke, I realized I was in a great big bed with some fairly rough-textured bed linen under and above me. Old-fashioned bed-curtains hung around the bed; I reached over and opened them a bit to see outside of it. As far as I could tell by the ambient candlelight, the walls of this round room were made of stone. They were also innocent of windows as we know them, being punctuated only by arrow slits at evenly spaced intervals. It was nighttime in this place, or at least I assumed so, as only inky darkness was visible though the arrow slits. The air in the room was chilly and dampish.

There was hope of warmth soon to come in a fire that had been newly started in the fireplace and the tapestries that hung on the walls. The textiles were impressive, depicting Bohemian revels á la Botticelli's *Primavera,* only with the participants sporting Tudor-era beards and coiffures and the odd Elizabethan ruff or glove.

The tapestries were new to the room, I knew. Otherwise, the room was in fact entirely familiar to me. It might seem odd to you, my having a feeling of déjà vu about so singular a room. But, you see, I had been in it before—on that memorable night when I somehow transcended time and space and met the six wives of Henry VIII, not to mention the distaff side of the extended Tudor family.

On that earlier instance, my ensemble dishabille had consisted of an old-fashioned white nightdress, all billowing linen. I hoped my present garment was not the same one; I hate being seen in the same outfit twice, particularly on special occasions. I decided to toss off the bedclothes for a nightdress check. It wasn't as easy as I expected. Eventually, though, thanks to all that Jazzercise triceps work I'd been doing, I was able to move the weighty satins and brocades that were piled high on top of me. After some further tugging and tussling, I was also able to more fully open the heavy satin draperies around the bed and take advantage of what little light there was in the room.

My Herculean efforts revealed to me that I was, indeed, wearing the nightdress I remembered so well. I discovered something else too; I was not alone. I was sharing my quarters with not one, but two other occupants.

Chapter Fourteen
Menagerie and Query

My two welcoming companions were not, as on my last visit, those two medieval beauties, Margaret Beaufort and Elizabeth of York, grandmother and mother of Henry VIII.

On my last stay here, I had learned that this was a strictly ladies-only domicile. That is why I rapidly concluded that my companions, who were a couple of dogs, were likely also a couple of bitches. This is not as rancorous a statement as you may think.

You see, my stirring about had agitated two toy-size dogs that had been lying at the foot of the bed, setting them to romping and frolicking around. I settled them down a bit and then zeroed in for a closer look at my strange bedfellows.

One of them I had met before. I had not gotten its name, but I knew it to be the terrier that had belonged to Mary, Queen of Scots, at the time of her death. Said pup had attended Mary's execution, hidden under her skirts; it barked piteously as it emerged, bloodstained, unable to decide whether to stay with the decapitated queen's body or with her head. Eventually it mourned itself to death.

My understanding had been that, after my last visit here, the Tudor denizens of this celestial way station would have vacated the premises for good. But if this dog—and another to boot—were present here, then likely the queen of Scots was again, or perhaps still, in residence. And heaven knew who else.

I looked a little closer at the other dog to try to figure out what, or at least, whose, it was. It appeared to be a sweet little bichon frise, and it looked back at me with head atilt and tail wagging.

"*Por quoi!*" a female voice called from without the room, and the little bichon perked up its ears.

"*Por quoi* to you too!" I sang out, playing for time as I tried to recall some of my high school French. As I did, I realized that I had just unintentionally given someone "what for." I hoped this wouldn't mean that my stay here this time was going to start off with me giving a bad impression. Wanting to take no chances, I got out of bed and began to smooth, as best I could, the wrinkles from my nightdress. As I did so, the person outside my room, getting closer by the sound of her voice, riposted my comment.

"Your French accent is execrable, Dolly!"

I wondered fleetingly if Marie Antoinette was in residence, but this was not the case. The lady who eventually rounded the doorway and entered my room was someone I had met before. She sported the Renaissance equivalent of a hippie-chick outfit that had seen better days. A parrot was circling above her in a holding pattern, and she was trailed by several feline friends whose orange calico markings resembled her own ginger coloring. I knew whose tragic and fascinating presence I was in.

Chapter Fifteen
The Mission Condition

"Arabella!" I called out happily as she entered the room and began to nuzzle my two canine companions. I was happy for two reasons. First, I had taken a shine to Arabella Stuart when we met on my last visit here. Second, I was pleased that, at least for my first interview of the night, there would be none of the guess-who that had featured in my initial visit. Back then, unidentified Tudor ladies had come out of the woodwork at practically every turn, and it was disconcerting until I got used to it. Starting this visit off with a familiar face gave things a different feeling altogether.

"Welcome back, Dolly!" Arabella greeted me with an embrace and a kiss on the cheek.

"Well, thank you very much, Arabella!"

"I'll bet you thought you'd never visit this place again," she conjectured.

"You've got that right," I responded. "Looks like the place hasn't changed all that much from last time."

"The conditions of exile in place the last time you were here no longer hold, Dolly. That applied to Henry VIII's six wives only, for reasons that you are of course already aware of. This time, it is a little different. All in residence at present are not exiled; they are here voluntarily."

"Who, Arabella, besides yourself, is in residence this time? And why?"

"The linchpins of the current house party could be said to be your old friends, Mary and Elizabeth, Henry VIII's daughters, and their cousin, Mary, Queen of Scots. Accompanying them are various cousinly and other relations, and a few of what I guess you might call hangers-on."

"The latter-day Tudors," I recapped. "None of the Tudor old guard are here today?"

"None of Henry VIII's wives are currently in residence. Ann Boleyn and Katharine of Aragon have recently taken possession of the last empty guest chamber for a brief visit, but it is strictly an ad hoc event."

I'd not heard combustion, racket, or explosions of any kind since my arrival, and this now surprised me.

"Your guest quarters must be quite commodious to hold those two peaceably in the same room," I commented.

"Ann Boleyn and Katharine of Aragon have gotten quite companionable since your last meeting with them, Dolly," Arabella informed me.

I was pleased to think that I'd had something to do with that. It was hard to imagine them as besties, but perhaps they had come into their proper relationship as frenemies. I'd managed to get each to pay the other a compliment the last time I was here; apparently, the relationship had flourished even more finely from there.

"What is the ad hoc purpose of their visit here?" I inquired. "Anything," I asked, hoping I was not being too egocentric, "to do with me?"

"Well, yes and no," Arabella replied. "It primarily relates to their daughters."

"So something is afoot with Bloody Mary I, Elizabeth I, and company," I pondered aloud.

"Yes, Dolly; something is indeed afoot—something that required your presence here for another visit, obviously."

"Well, I hope they won't be dragging their feet about whatever is afoot. I have commencement activities to see to back home and a house full of guests!"

"You were in a hurry to leave the last time you were here, and you are in a hurry to leave this time. Rest assured we will get you back to your world in good time."

"So give me the rundown, Arabella, on why I'm needed here again."

"Based on their mothers' advice, Henry's VIII's *daughters* have decided to entrust you with a vital mission. As the spacious accommodations we are now in were vacant, they petitioned the Almighty for their use to meet with you and set things up. He graciously permitted Mary, Elizabeth, and their compatriots to set up shop here for purposes of the mission."

Chapter Sixteen
Canny about Grannie

It had taken *much* longer than this to cut to the chase during my last visit; quite frankly, I was stunned to so quickly learn what was at the bottom of my return here. I displayed my amazement by not saying a word for what must have been a full minute, and unfortunately, my uncharacteristic silence put Arabella on her guard.

"I've shocked you," Arabella said, showing a talent for understatement that I had not previously noted. She looked concerned.

"Don't fret yourself," I said, recollecting that in life, Arabella's sanity had been at best a touch-and-go proposition. I certainly did not want to cause her any undue stress. And, less becomingly, I also wanted to keep her sweet so that I could pump her for additional information. "I just haven't been myself lately, Arabella; please, do not take my silence personally."

"Not been feeling well, Dolly?"

"A bit off my food lately; I've had a lot on my plate, you know."

"Overindulged in rich foods, have you?" Arabella inquired.

"No, I was speaking metaphorically," I said. "I think my nerves have unsettled my mind, not to mention my digestion. Company in the house. Chaos in the workplace. Career crossroads. Distracted husband. Big speech to deliver. In short, too much to think about!"

"Well, Dolly, you'd best get a grip on yourself. You'll have plenty more to think about soon enough. Won't she, my darlings?" Arabella queried, as she took a seat on a nearby chair and beckoned for the pets that had followed her into the room to assume a place on her lap. They cavorted about her elaborate Renaissance garb, taking what could only be called liberties with her finery.

"Do tell!" I invited, trying not to let a wheedling tone creep too obviously into my voice. My attempt at subterfuge was not successful.

"I've revealed too much already," Arabella decided aloud, voicing a sentiment with which I was unable to agree. "Elizabeth might get cross with me. But of course, when it comes to the queen, one is used to having her cross with one. My grandmother might get cross with me as well, and as usual. The thought of it all is enough to make *me* queasy too."

"Which of your grandmothers are you worried about?" I asked with curiosity tinged with pity.

Fate did not gift Arabella with the traditional encouraging, milk-and-cookies grandmothers; unsweetened granola and admonishments would more likely have been on the menu. On her father's side, the woman in question would have been Margaret Douglas, niece of Henry VIII and relentlessly ambitious mother of two handsome but ultimately disappointing sons. One of those sons sired Arabella; the other paved the way for the downfall of Mary, Queen of Scots.

When it came to the maternal side of her family, fate had been even less gentle with Arabella. The grandmother in question there was none other than Bess of Hardwick.

"My maternal grandmother is the one to whom I was referring," Arabella clarified, "although both of my grandmothers are currently in residence. My grandmother of Hardwick is *always* cross with me about something."

"Well, Arabella, if it eases your mind any, I will not let Bess know—should I happen to meet her—what you've divulged. And even if I were to tell her, she'd surely have no reason to be cross with *you*. If I've got a job to do for the next Tudor generation, the sooner I can get down to brass tacks, the better."

A little surprised at how quickly I had gotten used to the idea of being on a Tudor mission, I continued on. "You've done nothing but start the ball rolling, so to speak, Arabella. Anything else you have to tell me will only serve to *keep* the ball rolling," I said hopefully.

"Not the happiest of similes, Dolly, in a place as cursed by rampant decapitation as this one is. We'd hoped your last stay here would have cured you of such foolishness."

"I thought I'd about run out of execution *faux pas* the last time I was here," I admitted. "Guess I had one more left. But please, don't let my ramblings derail your train of thought."

"There's nothing else I can give you in the way of information about your mission," Arabella confessed. "I told you how it is the last time you were here. I am a little bit mad and not, as far as my relatives are concerned, to be trusted with much information on matters of importance."

I looked at the pretty but plump Arabella, stuffed into an opulent, velvet gown of clashing hues perhaps a bit too bright for good taste. The Elizabethan ruff that encircled her neck quivered ever so slightly even while Arabella herself was as close as she could get to repose, attesting to overstrung nerves. Bits of the lace on both ruff and gown were torn and damaged, attesting to her overindulgence of the felines that she was so fond of.

It saddened me this time, as it had on my last visit, to think about Arabella's story. As a small child, she was the pampered mascot of Mary, Queen of Scots. When she was an adolescent and young adult, there might have been room at the top for her in the royal succession, but things never worked out that way. Eventually, an emotionally overwrought spinsterhood turned her into the crazy cat lady equivalent of the Tudor and Stuart courts. A disastrous, late marriage unraveled her completely, and she eventually died in prison, starved and emaciated, quite possibly suffering an eating disorder on top of everything else. I assumed she appeared to me now as the plump Arabella of her youth because, as I had learned during my last visit, the denizens of this place appeared to me at the ages of their choosing.

I had also learned during that last visit that the Tudor ladies then present had entertained numerous earth-dwelling women here down through the ages. This had enabled them to keep up with worldly social and linguistic developments to a degree, making my communications with them fairly easy, at least on a semantic level. On an emotional level, it was different. I have to admit to getting a bit teary eyed thinking both of Arabella's history and of her present situation with her grannies. My maternal instincts, I was surprised to find, were aroused.

A sigh from Arabella, followed by the scuffling of the dogs as they scampered around in an effort to amuse her, brought me back to reality. Or at least as close to it as I could get in a distaff Tudor court on an unknown astral plane.

"It is not easy to have turned out a disappointment—or worse, a bad luck charm—to everyone one cares about," she began. I sensed a counseling session in my near future.

"Surely you were not that," I said, as comfortably as I could. "Look at Mary, Queen of Scots, for example. You were the apple of her eye when you were a child. You probably brought what little joy she had to her prison years."

"I suppose so, but we all know what end she came to, don't we?"

I winced as I considered the point.

"And my husband, William, imprisoned for marrying me. Even though he managed to escape, he wound up marooned in Ostend and in exile for years. To boot, he was disappointed of the crown I might have brought with me into the marriage."

I recollected that the William Arabella had wed was William Seymour, second Duke of Somerset. The Seymour line had pretty consistently brought ill luck to the Tudor house, at least the males of the family did. Arabella was imprisoned for marrying the much younger William, having spent all of maybe a year as his bride. William's grandfather—Edward Seymour—had been the ruin of Tudor descendant Catherine Grey.

And then of course there was yet another, earlier Seymour: Thomas. He was the brother of Henry VIII's third wife, Jane. In addition to being a royal in-law, he was also an epic horn dog and came damn near to ruining the life and prospects of Henry's daughter Elizabeth when she was still in her teens. History is divided on what actually occurred on old Tom's romps in young Elizabeth's boudoir. Although I'd never delved deeply into the subject with Elizabeth herself, I did have the opportunity of discussing Tom Seymour at some length with her mother, Ann Boleyn, when last we met. Between the two of us, we'd called him just about everything but a bull pizzle. I suppose it would have been kinder for us to pity poor Tom, considering his eventual end on the executioner's block—kinder but not nearly as gratifying.

"And my poor father," Arabella went on, expanding the hard-luck theme. "Dead before I could even talk."

"Must be difficult to lose someone so close without ever really having known him," I sympathized.

"Even worse to lose someone close, *with* really having known him," she replied.

I took a moment to try to determine who Arabella was speaking about, but I drew a blank.

"Thinking about someone in particular?"

"Yes. I was thinking of my poor, lamented Morley."

"First name Christopher?" I inquired hopefully, my scholar's blood well up.

"Yes, first name Christopher," Arabella confirmed.

Chapter Seventeen
Hello, Marlowe!

"So he *was* your tutor!" I exclaimed. "Some scholars in my time have purported that the famous poet and playwright, Christopher Marlowe, aka Morley in Elizabethan-speak, had the honor of providing you with instruction. Mind you, the reasoning behind the theory was speculative at best, given the paucity of Marlowe evidence that has survived the ages. How fascinating to find out that it is true!"

"Nice to be able to make *someone's* day," Arabella replied glumly.

"Surely, you brought joy into Marlowe's—or Morley's—short life when you were his pupil. A bright young Tudor sprite like you must have been a charming pupil to be sure!"

"I was not all that young when he tutored me, Dolly; I was in my teens, you know."

Having so recently considered the depredations of the elder Tom Seymour against the teenage Princess Elizabeth, I had a sinking feeling that I knew where this was going.

Chapter Eighteen
Tête-à-Tête on a Reprobate

When Arabella had said she *knew* her Morley, was she telling me that she had done so in the biblical sense? Inquiring flat out about such relations with, say, Henry VIII's lubricious fifth wife, Catherine Howard, would have been easy. It was not, however, the kind of inquiry one would directly make to someone as sensitive as Arabella.

I decided to try a nice, open-ended question instead.

"What was Morley like?" I asked.

"Beautiful," Arabella said dreamily. "Almost pretty enough to have been a girl."

This so far accorded with the possibility of Morley being the sexually ambivalent Christopher Marlowe.

"I'm rather surprised that your grandmother Bess would have put such a handsome fox into the henhouse, so to speak. I'd have thought she'd be worried about your developing a crush on him," I ventured.

"Grandmother was convinced that Morley was not, as she put it, a 'woman's man.' She granted him the same privilege and trust she granted my female attendants because of her assumption."

Score another point for the Morley/Marlowe theory. If anyone in the Renaissance era would have had gaydar, it surely would have been Bess of Hardwick.

"So you had a crush on Morley as a schoolgirl, and he, unfortunately, came to that sad end in a bar fight that the literati have mourned for centuries. That is sad, Arabella, but surely not a result of any bad karma on your part. After all, look at how the man lived outside of your schoolroom!"

There is, of course, no shortage of theories on the life and death of the enigmatic Christopher Marlowe. Many say he would have emerged as a greater writer than Shakespeare had he lived longer than the twenty-nine checkered years allotted to him. The high-minded might think that his being stabbed in the head during a brawl was a fitting end to a classic bad-boy life. Romantics tend to attribute his end to some sort of sexual melodrama, possibly involving the lowlife of Renaissance London. Conspiracy theories about his death abound too, of course, bringing in everything from theatrical jealousy to the Babington Plot to Elizabethan espionage gone bad.

"It wasn't how the man lived *outside* my schoolroom that led to the man's death, Dolly. It was something that happened while he was employed by my grandmother as my tutor."

Just then, Arabella looked like someone who wanted nothing more than to have a good old heart-to-heart with a gal who wouldn't dismiss her out of hand as mad. Of course it was obvious that she was a few stays short of a corset. But as someone who was quite at home with being on a mission for a bevy of dead Tudors, who was I to hold that against her?

"Do you want to tell me about it?" I asked simply.

"I do, Dolly," she said. "Because of family feeling and fellow feeling, I can't talk about Morley and his end to the women here. It raises all sorts of negative emotions, especially with Ann Boleyn, for one."

"Because it reminds her of what happened with her daughter and Tom Seymour?" I inquired.

"Yes. That and the whole idea of a sharp object being taken to the head. She finds both upsetting."

The little bichon, I'd noticed, had perked up his ears a moment ago when Ann's name was mentioned.

"Arabella! 'Por Qoi'—Purkoy—this little fellow is Ann Boleyn's dog, isn't he?" I asked.

"Yes, indeed, Dolly."

"It's very sweet to think that Ann and her pup were reunited in the afterlife! They say Ann was quite upset when little Purkoy fell out of a castle window to his death," I recollected aloud, getting a bit more misty eyed at that thought than was my wont.

Arabella looked a little fearful at my Ann Boleyn sympathies. "You mustn't ever tell Ann I've chosen to share my story with you," she warned. "Eternity with Ann Boleyn being cross with you is no joke."

"*Silence á la morte!*" I exclaimed dramatically.

"Until death and after death, Dolly; I require a truly eternal promise, regardless of how bad the pronunciation is."

I bowed my head and held my finger to my lips, gesturing my promise. "I promise to keep mum when it comes to your grandmum, Bess, as well."

"That is a kind thought, Dolly. I'd ask that you not discuss the intimate details with her gratuitously. As to the bare bones of the story, though, you need have no worries."

"Pun intended?" I inquired.

"No, but I trust you to pick up on it," said Arabella.

"Why don't I have to worry about those bare bones?" I inquired.

"Because when it comes to those bare bones, Bess of Hardwick," Arabella informed me, "knows all."

All, it turned out, and then some.

Chapter Nineteen
The Statutory Story

For my Morley discussion with Arabella, I had to suspend modern-day mores, more or less, and accept the ways of the Renaissance world for what they were. Fortunately, I had learned something about this the last time I was here. In meeting and greeting Elizabeth I, I had chatted quite normally with a woman who had ordered the execution of her own cousin. Sweet Jane Seymour had become engaged to Henry VIII the day after he had his prior wife executed, and it never even occurred to me to call her out on that. Bess of Hardwick performed duty as a prison wardress in her own home, but I conversed with her with no less trepidation than I would have had with any other matron. And speaking of matrons, I had listened with interest, but not surprise, to Margaret Beaufort, a widow and a mama at age thirteen, spin tales of her son, Henry VII.

So when Arabella told me of her relations at the age of fifteen or sixteen with the grown-up and heathenish Morley, I did my best to suspend contemporary judgments. In Arabella's day, fifteen or sixteen was, handily, marriageable age.

I dragged a chair across the stone floor—not an easy task when the chair is one of those weighty medieval numbers, all wood and finials and minimal upholstery. With my chair placed next to Arabella's, I climbed into it and curled myself, cross-legged, into its generous seat. Purkoy, seeing a vacant lap, hopped into the chair with me, and together we listened intently as Arabella began her story.

"Greek was never my best subject," Arabella began. "My late cousin Mary Tudor, of course, was a solid Greek scholar long before she ascended the throne, as was my cousin Elizabeth. Grandmother did not want me to be found wanting should the day come that *I* would ascend England's throne."

"You're forgetting Jane Grey," I commented. "She was likewise renowned for her scholarship before that nine-day reign of hers."

"*Grandmother* certainly did not forget her," Arabella commented. "I recall her throwing Jane Grey in my face as well. When Morley first met me, he described my Greek as 'middling,' but as far as Grandmother was concerned, it was much worse than that. She said it was…was…" Arabella paused as she tried to summon up the word.

"Execrable," I suggested.

"Well, not nearly as execrable as your French, Dolly. Such a degree of deficiency would have put me beyond even Morley's erudition."

Tempted though I was, I concluded that sticking my tongue out at Arabella for that one would be unwise. I vented my feelings by making a face at Purkoy, who yelped and jumped ship for Arabella's already crowded lap. She genially made room for him.

"So, Arabella, your grandmother, Bess of Hardwick, considered you linguistically challenged. How came she upon a ne'er do well such as Christopher Marlowe—or Morley, as you call him—as a prospective tutor to so close a claimant to the throne as yourself?"

"You could be more considerate of my feelings than you are, Dolly, when you bandy words such as 'ne'er do well' about in reference to those I hold dear."

I humbly apologized. "'Ne'er do well' probably wasn't very accurate, considering his contribution to literature," I admitted. "How does 'scapegrace' suit you?"

"Much better," Arabella said; "much more accurate!"

Marlowe/Morley didn't so much escape grace as he'd run screaming from it as though his backside were on fire. In deference to Arabella's feelings, however, I declined to share the imagery with her. Arabella addressed my earlier question.

"Grandmother, I am sure, turned to any number of her friends at court for suggestions for a tutor for me," Arabella said.

I thought about the prominent Elizabethans Bess of Hardwick would have numbered among her friends. It was heady stuff for a Tudorphile such as me. William Cecil, Baron Burghley; Sir Francis Walsingham; Robert Dudley, Earl of Leicester—could one of them have been responsible, I wondered, for the Morley-Arabella connection?

"I am equally sure," Arabella went on before I could speculate aloud, "that, having canvassed sage advice, Grandmother would have chosen not to take it. It is her way. Anything that even remotely resembles a decision being in someone else's hands is anathema to her."

Having met the redoubtable Bess, I did not doubt that one bit.

"I suspect Grandmother would have then applied to Cambridge directly, requesting recommendations for suitable tutors. Having decided on a candidate, she likely made inquiries at court and received no information to make her go back on her choice."

Considering Marlowe's history and reputation, I concluded that Bess could not have inquired about him too closely and had made an uncharacteristically poorly informed or careless decision. That would be another one I got wrong.

Chapter Twenty
Spring Fling

"So Marlowe/Morley arrived at Hardwick Hall to take up his duties as tutor. What did he find when he arrived there? Tell me what you were like as a girl," I prompted. I was interested to hear how Arabella saw herself in the years before trial, tribulation, and house arrest had taken their toll.

"I can remember well what I was wearing when Morley and I first met," Arabella recollected.

Eyeing Arabella's current couture, I prepared myself for the worst.

"That outfit was quite a favorite of mine, all my favorite colors included in the ensemble. Grandmother thought it in poor taste and insisted that it was too much of a good thing—or rather, too much of too many good things. Grandmother did not believe in mincing words."

Of course, Elizabethan ladies' apparel was nothing if not over the top, and not only in the low-neckline, push-up-corset sense. "Many good things" pretty much summed up the Elizabethan fashion plate: sumptuously textured fabrics, accessories laid on by the pound, ruffs and skirts that were outstanding—literally, finishing up inches, if not feet, from the body. Under the circumstances, it was frightening to imagine what might have been considered too much in those days.

"Having met your grandmother, I'm not surprised about her not pulling any sartorial punches," I confessed to Arabella.

"Even if she was hard on you though, she was surely fond of you. After all, she has gone down in history as calling you her jewel."

"True, but when it came to my fashion and accessory decisions, Grandmother was known to say that her jewel was a few carats short of a diamond."

"With all due respect to Bess of Hardwick's fashion and gemology credentials, I would like to hear about your ensemble firsthand and come to my own conclusions."

"Well," Arabella said, blushing becomingly, "I thought it the most flattering outfit that I could assemble at the time: violet underskirt—green partlet and sleeves—blue kirtle—muslin ruching—and of course, the gilt embroidery and spangles. All my favorite pieces assembled into one outfit! What would *you* think of such an outfit, Dolly? Too much?"

My initial response, surprisingly, was to be charmed by the fact that the Tudor offshoot before me had inherited the family predilection for green sleeves. I then thought of my own favorite adolescent outfit. Those shiny tights and that neon, scoop-necked ballet leotard clinging precipitously to me and my AA-size bra! And what a job it had been, holding up those striped legwarmers when I'd yet to actually develop any calf muscles. Not to mention the six-foot-long vintage *Dr. Who* scarf that I'd found at a flea market and was so very proud of. The memory made me smile fondly, both for Arabella and for myself.

"For a woman of your grandmother's years and dignity, yours was certainly not the outfit of choice," I answered with perfect honesty. "But if anyone could pull off such an outfit, surely it would be a burgeoning young lady, generously endowed with the showman's genes of the Tudors," I concluded, satisfied that I'd not just told too much of a whopper.

"Once we were out of Grandmother's company, Morley complimented me on the outfit quite extravagantly," Arabella confided. "He favored the scent I was wearing as well."

For a moment, I could smell the perfume that I had practically bathed in as a girl. I was glad for Morley that Love's Baby Soft had not been invented yet in the Renaissance era.

"Attar of roses, perhaps?" I inquired, hazarding a guess.

"A compote of flowers," Arabella corrected me. "It was ever so inviting. I had to stay upwind from the apiaries whenever I was wearing it, or the bees would make real pests of themselves."

I considered that perhaps Morley would have been better off with Love's Baby Soft after all.

"And so, with the first blush of youth firmly on your side, you charmed the legendary Christopher Marlowe. Spare me no detail in your narrative, Arabella. History knows so tantalizingly little of the man. What a golden opportunity this is!"

"Morley had quite a way with words, to begin with."

"No kidding!" I said, trying to keep the sarcasm from coming through in my voice. Surely she could find something to tell me about Marlowe that I didn't already know.

"Morley knew I'd just returned from a visit to court. He said he would not call me 'Venus,' because those who gave that appellation to any but the queen, and were found out, would have hell to pay. But he did start off our acquaintance by saying quite prettily what a lovely acolyte of the goddess of beauty I must have made."

I knew that extravagant mythological references were pretty commonplace in the Elizabethan era; I was sure most would have taken Marlowe's glib line of patter for what it was worth. For someone as high-up in the low-self-esteem club as Arabella was, though, it was clearly dynamite. And Marlowe, the rapscallion, would have known it.

"What had your grandmother to say about Morley's flattery?" I inquired.

"She had no way to know of it," Arabella said. "*I* was not about to tell her. I lived to hear Morley's sweet words. Had grandmother heard them, she'd surely have taken Morley to task and ruined it all."

I had no doubt that Arabella was correct on that point.

"So Morley spoke sweetly to you and had access to the privacy in which to do it, protected by your grandmother's estimation of his not being, as you said, a woman's man. She must have had no compunction about your being left alone in the schoolroom with Morley."

"It was not just in the schoolroom that Morley spoke to me of love, Dolly. It was springtime when we first met. The grounds of Hardwick Hall were at our disposal. Grassy knolls far from the house, fern beds sheltered by the bracken in the woods, cool rocks overlooking a stream—all were at our disposal."

"How charming! Mother Nature kept you safe from prying eyes of the servants and family. Not to mention the bees from the apiary, if the wind was right. And of course the queen bee herself, good old Bess."

"Nature afforded us gifts as well, Dolly. Poor Morley could not afford to buy me presents, with grandmother paying him so little. The woods and fields offered him ample resources to make me the most charming, simple *cadeaux*. There were necklaces of ivy, daisy chains, nosegays, fans of plumy fern fronds, and flowers and vines to stud my veils and my hair."

"'There will I make thee beds of roses; And a thousand fragrant posies; A cap of flowers, and a kirtle; Embroider'd all with leaves of myrtle,'" I quoted. The words brought some dignity, I felt, to a young lady who otherwise came off looking like the Renaissance era's cheapest date.

Arabella was impressed with my ability to quote Marlowe's *The Passionate Shepherd to His Love* extemporaneously. Given the short notice I'd had to recollect it, I was too.

"Yes, it was just as Morley described it in that pastoral of his. At least, it was through the summertime, with the outdoors available to us. The game changed when winter came on," Arabella said wearily.

"Did winter's chill cool your passionate shepherd off, my lamb?" I asked, feeling, I had to admit, a bit like a riled up mama bear at the thought of Arabella's Morley breaking her heart that way.

"No," Arabella said, "quite the opposite."

Chapter Twenty-One
Rendezvous and Parlez-Vous

"As the weather started to cool down, things were at a fever pitch between Morley and me," Arabella continued. "I found it increasingly difficult to harden myself against his importuning; I was actually relieved when an unseasonably early winter drove me to the relative safety of the interior of Hardwick Hall. Unfortunately, it didn't stay safe for long."

"Your grandmother got wise to the whole thing once it was in the house, right there under her nose! Bess of Hardwick—the queen bee—got her stinger going and broke up your little idyll before things went too far, saving you from a fate worse than death in the nick of time. That is what happened," I hazarded hopefully. "*N'est-ce pas?*"

Arabella winced. "Sorry to put it so baldly," I apologized. "I did not mean to hurt your feelings."

"It's not my feelings you hurt, Dolly, but my ears—your appalling French again!"

"*Je suis désolé,*" I responded. This time Arabella just rolled her eyes.

"Morley and I were not the only lovers in the house that winter," Arabella informed me. I found no surprises there; I knew all about these stately homes. I hadn't missed a single episode of *Downton Abbey*.

"Who were these paramours behind closed doors?" I asked.

"The waiting woman who was assigned to sleep in my room with me had also taken a lover at around that time. She was so stealthy about it that to this day, I am not sure who he was. What I do know is that she would wait until she thought I was asleep and then sneak out of the room and be gone till almost light. She didn't know that I was up half the night every night myself, pining for Morley. It didn't take Morley and me long to find a way to take advantage of the opportunity this afforded."

Arabella's mien changed right about then; she went from dispiritedness to animation in an instant when it came to talk of plotting. I remembered the half-baked escape plot that was cooked up for her and her husband later in her life, complete with male garb for Arabella and a missed midnight sailing across the channel. Clearly, the girl had a taste, if not a talent, for subterfuge. I awaited developments with trepidation.

"When I found myself alone in my chamber," Arabella continued, rubbing her hands together conspiratorially, "I would light a candle stub and place it on the floor near the door. Morley was able to sneak from his quarters out to a spot from whence he could see the light shining through the bottom of the door. He would come to join me as soon as he saw the signal."

"A plot that is beautiful in its simplicity," I commented. "It must have worked out well for you."

"It did, for our first few meetings. What a dance I led Morley! I'd let him get closer and closer to the castle keep without actually letting him storm the citadel. I quite enjoyed the sexual tension."

"Ann Boleyn would have been proud of the way you played that situation," I commented.

"Perhaps so. In any event, the dance between Morley and me did not last nearly as long as Ann and Henry VIII's. After a few weeks, there came a night when Morley came to my door after considerable delay. He was quite shaken, and his nightclothes were in a terrible state. You see, he'd been accosted as he broached the hallway."

"By Bess of Hardwick?" I asked, shuddering.

"No," she replied. "By my uncle Gilbert."

"Really!" I exclaimed. "Why on earth did Gilbert, having caught Morley on his way to your chamber, let him continue on after roughing him up a bit?"

"Because Gilbert had the same thought about Morley that my grandmother had; you know—that he was not a woman's man."

"Gilbert roughed him up on general homophobic principles?" I inquired.

"No, quite the opposite; Gilbert was not a woman's man, either."

I recalled what I knew about Gilbert Talbot, son-in-law of Bess of Hardwick. He went down in history as a fractious fellow, falling out with just about everyone he encountered in the Tudor world. His sexual preferences are not on record to my knowledge, but I had no reason to doubt Arabella's estimate.

"So Gilbert made a grab for Morley in that dark hallway—what did Morley tell you happened next?"

"Morley said that Gilbert tried to entice him back to Gilbert's quarters, but Morley played dumb. Gilbert was not amused."

"Not as much one for the sexual tension as you," I commented.

"No, indeed! Gilbert got tired of the games pretty quickly and attempted to drag Morley back to his room. Morley eventually managed to break free of him."

"And he sped to your room? That was brave, but foolish, certainly."

"Morley was nothing if not a fast thinker. He did not want to give in to Gilbert. But he did not want our own forays to come to an end before things came to their natural climax."

"So?" I asked.

"So," Arabella continued, "Morley stopped Gilbert dead in his tracks by saying he heard someone coming. He played for time. He took off running, calling softly back to Gilbert, 'Not the morrow, my lord, but the day after.' When the coast was clear, he came to me."

It was getting more like *Downton Abbey* every minute.

"I must say that Morley looked quite fetching in his night attire. Something about the disarray of his garments—what he had risked for the sake of our romance—just added to my excitement!" Arabella confessed.

"'What a pretty thing man is when he goes in his doublet and hose and leaves off his wit!'" I mused aloud.

"Yes, indeed!" Arabella agreed. "We came very near to consummating things that night; I allowed Morley liberties that shock me, when I think of them today, but that were still short of the ultimate prize. I decided to save that for the next night, which we both feared would be our last together, what with Gilbert on the prowl."

"The next day must have been a long one for you both," I commented. "Nothing makes the nanoseconds crawl by like sexual tension."

"Morley said that last foray of his across Hardwick Hall was likely to be the longest trip of his life. He likened it to crossing the Hellespont. He made it to my chamber, though. And was he surprised at what he found when he got there!"

I hoped against hope that it wasn't Bess of Hardwick.

It wasn't.

"He thought I'd be waiting for him, eager to get things under way, but I played my game to the last! I made a tent of my bed linens and hid from him in it. It made him quite mad with excitement. And that made *me* quite mad with excitement. We almost came to blows, things became so heated."

"You two were ahead of your time, playing cowboys and Indians so long before the American continent was even settled," I commented.

"Cowboys?" Arabella asked, looking at little Purkoy as quizzically as he was looking at her. "Morley was not above calling me his little lambkin. Neither he nor I was particularly interested in the bovine element though," said Arabella quite seriously.

I could have made a comment about them taking the bull by the horns for that last encounter, but I thought it would only serve to muddy the waters. I listened as Arabella seemed about to wrap up her tale.

"Of course, the blows eventually gave way to caresses, and all was heaven on earth, at least for the space of a night," Arabella said dreamily. As sordid as I suppose the whole thing was, I was glad that Arabella had at least experienced a little glimpse of unadulterated bliss in an otherwise thwarted life. The morning after had to come though; it always does.

"Morley departed my room before I awakened the next morning," Arabella said. "I never saw or spoke with him again after that night; at least, not directly."

"He wrote to you, perhaps?" I inquired.

Before Arabella could answer, footsteps were audible from just beyond the doorway, and a strident voice beat Arabella to the punch.

"He wrote all right, but not *just* to Arabella!"

"*Sacre Bleu!*" Arabella and I called out in unison, with less than perfect French on both our parts. Arabella was clearly shaken by the voice in question—or more to the point, by the lady to whom the voice belonged. Purkoy dove under the bed and the dog belonging to Mary, Queen of Scots, ran into a wall, stunning itself temporarily. The cats arched their backs, and Arabella's parrot took off for parts unknown as said lady rounded the corner.

Chapter Twenty-Two
The Permanent Termagant

Bess of Hardwick crossed the threshold with the determined step one would expect of the foremost force of nature in the Elizabethan universe. She was dressed in an outfit similar to one that she wears in one of her extant portraits. It featured an unusual ruff made of white fur, which was the only warm and fuzzy thing about her.

"Bess!" I said, genuinely pleased to see this friend from old times, if the relationship we established on my last visit here could be characterized as such. "You look wonderful—it's as if you've not aged a single day."

"One doesn't in the afterlife," Bess reminded me. "As for you, Dolly, you look well, if a trifle plumper than you were last visit."

Bess cordially grasped me by the hand. Her words may have been brutally honest, but her tone with me was genial, proving that she likewise thought of me as an old friend.

"I suspected that Arabella would attempt to tell you her pathetic tale, Dolly, and I see I wasn't wrong," Bess began, taking Arabella's chin in her hand and turning the girl's face toward her own. Bess struck me as one who would be a proponent of the "one upside the head" school of discipline, so I stepped closer to the two of them just in case it should come to blows and I might need to separate them.

Up close and personal, I was shocked at how little these two famous relatives resembled each other. I carefully studied them, feature by feature, in the brief silence that followed but found nothing denoting kinship. It was as if Bess of Hardwick could read my thoughts.

"She takes nothing after my people, Dolly! This one is all Stuart, I can tell you; Stuart by looks and Stuart by nature—foolish to the bone!"

The protective bent I had developed toward Arabella was inexplicable but nonetheless impossible to suppress. I leaped—metaphorically speaking—to Arabella's defense.

"What you just said wasn't very nice!" was the best I could do at short notice. Arabella smiled at me conspiratorially though, at least appreciating the effort.

"It would have been nicer had you let me finish my thought, Dolly," Bess said briskly. "I was about to say, foolish to the bone and charming enough to get away with it, at least for a while."

"I don't know about 'nice,'" I said grudgingly. "Passive-aggressive is more like it."

"But accurate, you must admit. I do believe in being accurate." Bess was relentless. "You know the history, Dolly; surely, you must acknowledge that what I say is so."

I thought of Arabella's uncle, Henry Stuart, Lord Darnley. He had charmed himself into the pants, or rather the farthingale, of Mary, Queen of Scots, in short order. In shorter order still, he had managed to alienate pretty much everyone in Scotland, including his wife; when blowing him up in his quarters with gunpowder failed to arrest his downward trajectory, some good old-fashioned strangulation answered just as well. I took Bess's point.

"And of course," Bess persisted, "one could say the same of Morley as well."

Arabella bridled. Bess called her on it.

"The child is past reasoning when it comes to her Morley!" Bess informed me.

"Reason has little to do with first loves, whatever the circumstances," I offered in Arabella's defense.

"You dignify Morley and Arabella's skirmishes beyond what they were," Bess said, heartlessly, I thought. Arabella winced, took a deep breath, and gave forth, taking herself from victim mode to a surprising degree of dignity in a moment. "I cannot change my perspective on my and Morley's story, Grandmother, to please you or anyone else. I know my limits."

"Foolish, charming, and stubborn!" rejoined Bess of Hardwick.

"And," Arabella continued, with a gracious bow toward Bess, "I know my grandmother's limits as well."

Bess turned a shade of purple likely similar to Arabella's erstwhile underskirt at the implication that she had limitations. It was not a pretty sight, but Arabella did not let it daunt her.

"My grandmother is no more able to change *her* perspective on my and Morley's tale than I am able to change mine," Arabella went on. "And when her face goes that shade of purple, there is no holding her back from sharing what is on her mind."

I expected Arabella should know.

"Even," Arabella continued, "when she knows how distressing her discourse will be to someone she loves dearly enough to call her 'Jewel.'"

I got to my feet and pulled myself up to my full height, with as much dignity as I could muster, wearing nothing but a nightdress. I walked over to Arabella, planted myself next to her, and gave her a side hug. I did not find this easy, given that the recipient was wearing an Elizabethan ruff as big as a ballet tutu and a farthingale to boot. Nevertheless, I kept my arm about her shoulder.

"'A friend should bear her friend's infirmities,'" I said to Arabella. "I am here for you, *on* your side, and *at* your side, *mon amie*. Everything is easier when you've got a friend to buck you up. Bring it on, Bess!" I said with a tone of challenge in my voice. My tone apparently inspired confidence; Purkoy came out from under the bed, and Mary, Queen of Scots's dog, having recovered its senses, joined Purkoy in capering about at Arabella's feet.

Arabella returned my side hug with feeling. "I can't tell you what this means to me, Dolly, having someone take up for me like this," Arabella said, tearing up a bit as she spoke.

"Enabling is more like it," Bess cracked.

It occurred to me that Bess might just be right about that, but I'd have died before I'd have admitted it. I was in too deep to turn back now. "You heard me, Bess," I said, calmly. "Knowing your reputation for efficiency as I do, I am sure you'd be the last one to want to waste time. We," I said, as Arabella and I joined our free hands for good measure, "are ready like Freddie!"

Chapter Twenty-Three
Of Stoolies with Brass Goolies

Bess lugged a chair next to mine and Arabella's and settled herself into it. Arabella and I resumed our seats, and I folded my hands in my lap. Arabella could not keep her hands still and pulled little Purkoy onto her lap to pet. Bess cracked her knuckles twice.

"I am flattered that not just Arabella but you as well are prepared to confide your stories in me," I said. I thought it would be best to oil Bess up a bit, but I strove to keep my tone from being too unctuous.

I strove unsuccessfully.

"None of your soft soap now, Dolly," Bess chided. "It is not for your benefit that I tell the tale. It is for Arabella's. Hearing it baldly told and seeing a third-party reaction from someone she trusts may do her some good. It may make her see this whole thing for what it really was. That would certainly make Arabella's and my propinquity here a more peaceful affair."

I was familiar with the intervention principle but had to wonder about its usefulness in breaking Arabella's particular species of denial. "You're hoping to give her a reality check," I reflected. "Have you attempted to do so before, Bess?"

"Yes, I have!" Bess snapped.

I was not surprised at this answer, given the four hundred years' worth of opportunities to do so that Bess had had. My heart bled for Arabella.

"How well has that worked out for you, Bess?" I asked.

"It has not worked out for me! Arabella is as recalcitrant as ever. But all my previous third parties were people with a stake in the game. You are a true and unbiased third party, someone removed from the whole sordid affair. And your status with Henry VIII's six wives makes you a person whose opinion must have weight and importance," Bess concluded.

I bowed my head in acknowledgment of Bess's compliment. As I did so, it occurred to me that if I continued to point out the ineffectuality of Bess's ways, I might be outsmarting myself out of the once-in-a-lifetime opportunity to get some heretofore unknown Elizabethan history. As the pieces of unsuspected Tudor information that I had picked up on my last visit here had given me a taste for such things, I actually shut up at that point and let Bess do the talking.

"Where has she gotten to in her tale?" Bess asked me.

"Arabella has caught me up to speed to the point of her and Morley's last meeting," I said.

"An excellent place for me to start *my* tale," said Bess, cracking her knuckles again. I hoped she wasn't going to make it a habit.

"I call your attention to the morning after that meeting, Dolly," Bess began. "It started, for me, with my son-in-law, Gilbert, banging upon my chamber door before the sun was fairly up."

"Was he looking to start an argument of some kind with you, Bess? It seems likely, given his reputation. It can't have been very pleasant to cope with him first thing in the morning. Especially," I said feelingly, rising and gesturing illustratively about the skirts of my nightdress, "if you were *en dishabille*."

"I was not *en déshabillé*, Dolly," said Bess. "Please note the pronunciation, and please note that my habit, unlike that of *some* people I know, is to dress to greet the day immediately upon arising!"

Bess had put me in my place, sartorially chastened, by reminding me of my last visit here, when I did not find my way out of my nightdress and into formal Renaissance garb for quite a while after my arrival.

"Gilbert quite rightly came to apprise me of what had been going on at Hardwick Hall over the past two nights," Bess went on. "He told me that two nights prior, he had intercepted Morley skulking in the hallway near the family chambers and sent him packing."

"What explanation had he for waiting a day, rather than coming to you with news of the skulking the same day that it happened? The two of you had a potential heiress to the throne to protect, after all."

"Gilbert said it was because he had business outside Hardwick House to conduct early that morning and that he didn't dare commit anything about it to paper or depute telling me about it to anyone else. He said he'd scared Morley to death and felt confident that all, including my Jewel here, were safe. Mind you, knowing my son-in-law, I suspected a vulgar intrigue of some kind on Gilbert's part. I did not take that up with him, though. It was not worth putting him on his guard about his sexual proclivities when I needed the information that he had."

I was right. Bess did have the gaydar.

"Gilbert then told me that while he himself was up and about in the wee hours that very morning, he had heard a stirring *again* in the hallway. He went to investigate. He said he caught sight of Morley, in his nightclothes, exiting Arabella's chamber. At that point, Gilbert dressed himself and came straight around to me to tell me about it."

"And while he did so, Arabella was asleep, all blissful unawareness," I conjectured.

"That didn't last long," Arabella quipped.

"I should say not!" Bess confirmed. "I dismissed Gilbert with commands to not mention any of this to anyone, ever. I told him I would take it all into my own capable hands, and that would be the end to it. I forbade him to tell even his wife—my own daughter—about it."

Mrs. Gilbert Talbot, Bess's daughter, Mary, was probably quite a lot like Bess; in fact, history has been pretty specific about who wore the codpiece in the Gilbert and Mary Talbot relationship. Sir Francis Bacon himself famously said that Mary was a greater man than her husband was. I actually felt a little sorry for Gilbert—but only for a moment.

Chapter Twenty-Four
Disaster on the Morning After

"After I dismissed Gilbert, I took a minute or two to compose my thoughts," Bess said.

"I guess you needed that little interlude after hearing about your Jewel being mounted in a way that you'd never intended for her to be."

Arabella giggled, and Bess gave both her and me the fisheye. You have seen nothing in the way of fisheyes until you've seen one from Bess of Hardwick.

"Once I had collected myself," Bess continued, "I went straight to Arabella's chamber. The sun was not yet up. As I rounded the bend near Arabella's room, I caught sight of her chamber-woman skulking about the hallway, preparing to enter Arabella's room. I sent her away and entered the room myself, stood beside the bed, and waited for Arabella to awaken. I positioned myself so that the first thing my Jewel would see upon awakening would be her grandmother's face."

I wasn't sure if what Bess was going for here was the element of surprise, the guilt trip, or the flat-out horror-movie shock value; whatever her intent, I was willing to bet that the latter was what she got.

"When I woke that morning," Arabella recollected, "I felt around among the bedclothes for Morley before I opened my eyes. When I ascertained he was not there, I finally stretched out, threw off the covers, and prepared to greet the dawn. The sight of grandmother's face looking down at me was…was…"

Arabella struggled for words, and one could hardly blame her.

"*Diabolique?*" I suggested.

Arabella winced. "I was about to say, not what I expected."

"I should say not!" Bess said. "You can imagine my thoughts, Dolly, when I looked down into the eyes of my disgraced granddaughter."

"'Have I caught thee, my heavenly Jewel?' comes to mind," I said.

"I'd caught her, all right! The child dove, stark naked as she was, back under the rumpled bedclothes. The picture told the whole sordid story without Arabella's having to say a single word."

"Surely not the setting for her Jewel that a grandmother would like to see," I commented sympathetically.

"I should say not! And Arabella was quite cheeky about it, to boot!"

Considering that Arabella was naked at that juncture, I just had to ask: "Pun intended, Bess?"

I took the sharp smack Bess administered to my right ear as a no.

"Arabella had the audacity to attempt to defend her position and to bring her mother's history into the case as well. She said that if true love at first sight was good enough for her mother, it was good enough for her."

Arabella set her chin determinedly, rose from her chair, and stood with arms akimbo, defiantly attempting to stare Bess down. Only a madwoman would attempt to do that, I thought. I gave Arabella full marks for courage, if not sense.

"Well, Arabella had a point about her mother," I pointed out to Bess, earning myself a smack on my other ear.

The historian in me would not be quelled by mere physical abuse. I had to have my head but didn't put it into those words in consideration of the decapitation sensitivity of the environment.

"Come on now, Bess. You and Margaret Douglas are said to have been the ones to facilitate the off-the-cuff love match between your daughter and Margaret's son, who went on to become Arabella's parents."

"Margaret Douglas and I faced a dilemma when those two fell in love and wouldn't be talked out of it. We had to make the best of a bad job, Dolly!"

"I would appreciate you not referring to my parents' love story as a 'bad job,' Grandmother!" cried Arabella.

"Well, whatever you want to call it, it did not last long," I pointed out. "Charles Stuart, Arabella's father, was dead before Arabella was out of nappies. His wife passed on to leave her daughter, your Jewel, to your care just a few years later, Bess."

"Yes, and care for her is exactly what I did, Dolly, to the best of my ability. She had her place in the succession, and I kept her safe for it. I saw her through the childish ailments that claimed so many little ones in those times. I educated her as thoroughly as Henry VIII had educated the royal daughters!"

"*More thoroughly*, surely, considering what the tutor you hired for her accomplished," I said, the words out of my mouth before I could stop myself.

Having run out of ears to box, Bess contented herself with smacking me hard on the bottom.

"Ouch!" I cried. "That hurt! Excessive force, surely, Bess!"

"Sorry, Dolly," Bess said. "I'm used to having to smack hard enough to make the impact felt through a bumroll and a farthingale. I'd forgotten that you aren't wearing either."

I doubted the last part of that but decided to forgo the argument. I was anxious to hear the rest of Bess and Arabella's story.

"I hope you were gentler with Arabella, when you chastised her, than you were with me just now, Bess."

"Too gentle? Too rough? I chastised her roundly but fairly, I thought, Dolly. Given the way things turned out with Arabella, it is hard to know where I went wrong and where I went right," Bess admitted in a rare moment of humble introspection. Clearly, the dilemmas of parenting teenagers had not changed much over the centuries.

"What happened after the chastisement?" I asked Bess.

"A thorough cleaning of house as to the support staff happened. So did closer personal supervision of Arabella by myself, my daughter, Mary, and my son-in-law, Gilbert," Bess answered.

"Don't forget the extra cushions on my chairs until my backside ceased to sting," Arabella said, looking at Bess and rubbing her rear end in reminiscence.

"Yes, but what about Morley?" I asked. "You said he was in touch but that he didn't write *just* to Arabella, Bess. Who else was he in communication with? You? Gilbert? And why? Based on what history tells us about Morley, he can't have been up to anything good," I speculated.

"Say that again, Dolly!" Bess requested.

"I said, 'Morley can't have been up to anything good,' Bess. Based on what history has told us."

"Direct your comments to Arabella, if you please, Dolly."

"I think she's already heard them, Bess," I said as I looked at the crushed Arabella. Some damage control was in order.

"It's always the smartest, classiest, goodest girls that fall for the baddest boys," I said. "Don't take it to heart too much, Arabella."

"Your English isn't much better than your French, Dolly," Bess pointed out.

Arabella was more interested in my theory than in my delivery. "How do you know this, Dolly?" she asked, looking as though maybe she could just see daylight.

I decided that if Bess of Hardwick could be humble on Arabella's behalf, so could I.

"My experience with some of the men who came into my life in the interval between my early days with Wally and our meeting again," I said. "Sneezy, Bashful, and Grumpy, as I like to think of them, come to mind."

"Have you any more scholarly wisdom than that to offer, Dolly?" Bess asked pointedly.

"Well, history is full of examples of the bad-boy phenomenon," I said. "Modern history offers us the Clinton and Kennedy presidential unions, not to mention first daughter Alice Roosevelt. Going a little further back and into Hapsburg country, there is Empress Maria Theresa and Francis I. In your own country's history, Catherine of Braganza and Charles II come to mind."

"Thank you for the perspective, Dolly," Arabella said, smiling through misty eyes. "I am not familiar with all the figures you speak of, but clearly, they are women of standing and importance. That's made me feel better somehow."

"*Ces't magnifique!*" I exclaimed.

"I can't thank you for your French, Dolly," Arabella said, "but I will bid you a fond *adieu. Dieu vous bénisse!*"

"Why are you leaving, Arabella?" I asked. "I thought you were pleased about what I said."

"I am pleased, Dolly, and comforted; I can let go of a lot of the negative emotions I have been harboring all this time. But I must absent myself, as Grandmother prepares to bring her tale home. Even with this wonderful new perspective you've given me, I just can't bear to listen to what Grandmother has to say."

With that, Arabella rounded up her canine and feline companions. Her parrot swooped about the room. En route to Arabella's shoulder, the bird dropped his regards, unbeknown to Bess, on the back of Bess's gown.

"*Adieu* to you too, Grandmother," Arabella said as she exited, smothering a laugh as she noticed the embellishment on her grandmother's garments.

"'A doo,' indeed," I said, saluting Arabella as she passed.

"Dolly, your French gets worse and worse!" exclaimed Bess.

"On the contrary," said Arabella, waving me good-bye, "I think Dolly's French is quite *apropos.*"

Bess and I were silent as Arabella moved out of view. Once she was well away from us, I turned toward Bess.

"Now that Arabella is gone, and I don't have her feelings to consider, I want you and me to get down and dirty about the rest of this story, Bess."

"Are you asking me, of all people, for the unsavory details of Arabella's peccadillos? I knew you were silly, but I didn't think you a *prurient* person, Dolly," Bess said, emphasizing the word "prurient" just as my dear Miss Bess would have back on earth.

"Sorry—I'll rephrase that, Bess. I want the two of us to get down to cases about the aftermath of Morley."

Chapter Twenty-Five
Used Sorely by Morley

"You told me earlier, Bess, that Morley did not communicate with, or at least write to, Arabella *alone* after the escapade we just discussed. I am thinking he must have communicated with *you*, as well, then. I've read that after his tutoring tour with your Jewel was over, he tried to extort a forty-pound pension from your family in recompense for tutoring Arabella and for being away from the life of the university. Is that true?"

"You could say that," Bess replied.

"So Morley—Christopher Marlowe—didn't know that you were aware of what had occurred between him and Arabella? Surely he wouldn't have approached you for a pension if *he* knew that *you* knew!"

"Morley didn't directly approach *me* for the money at the outset of it all. He was reprehensible enough to write to *Arabella* to ask for the money first! Arabella, being *non compos mentis* and having no resources she could access independently, had the audacity to apply to *me* for the funds. She felt that a pension was the least he deserved! I think it was at that point that I really started to realize just how removed from reality my Jewel was."

"So what did Morley do when he was disappointed of his pension?" I inquired.

"He wasn't disappointed of his pension. I corresponded with him and agreed to pay it to him."

Knowing Bess as I did, this surprised me.

"Bess—why?"

"Naiveté can be charming in a girl like my Jewel, but really, Dolly, coming from you—be your age, girl! Why was Morley paid his pension? Surely, with what you knew about Morley's reputation before and what you know about him now, you can figure it out!"

The lightbulb went off. Or perhaps, given the medieval setting I was in, I should say that the candlewick took flame. "Extortion?" I inquired.

"Extortion. Blackmail. Hush money. Call it what you will, Dolly. I willingly paid the money to defuse Morley, so to speak."

"Wait a minute, Bess. Morley was a man of humble rank—a nobody, compared to Arabella. If word got out that he had—well—interfered with a young lady of the blood royal, he'd put himself right in the way of treason charges, not to mention execution!"

"Thank you for pointing out the bloody obvious, Dolly."

"Just can't help it, Bess. My professional Tudor knowledge, you know."

Bess nodded in acknowledgment.

"So," I continued, "Morley was in no position to make his doings with Arabella generally known without serious personal repercussions. A woman as savvy as you should have known that, Bess!"

"Of course I knew it, Dolly! But you see, Morley wasn't threatening to directly expose the Arabella incident to the authorities. At least, he wasn't at that juncture."

"Then why in the world did you choose to lie down, so to speak, with a dirty, blackmailing dog like Morley, Bess?"

Bess made a moue of repugnance at the mental picture I had drawn. "I told you why I did it, Dolly. I did it to defuse Morley!

The man was sitting on a time bomb of his own creation and would not have hesitated to set it ticking if he did not get his way. Forty pounds was a lot of money to Morley but little enough to me, when it came to buying some much-needed time."

Bess of Hardwick has come down through the ages as one of the great business and political powerhouses of Elizabethan times. She was independent enough to build great estates off her own bat, and trustworthy and competent enough to be entrusted with the era's most famous political prisoner, Mary, Queen of Scots. Why in the world would someone as "together" as Bess was feel the need to buy time, and to buy it from the likes of Christopher Marlowe?

Chapter Twenty-Six
Hero of the Zero-Sum Game

I pondered the life of Christopher "Kit" Marlowe awhile. He was surely flaming and volatile enough for incendiary purposes; Bess's defusing simile was apt, to say the least. His origins were humble. From such unpropitious beginnings, he was bright enough to shoot himself skyward and eventually land in university at Cambridge. He produced a little bit of poetry and some weighty and impressive plays, including *The Jew of Malta, Dr. Faustus,* and *Tamburlaine the Great.* Some say that had it not been for Marlowe's early death, he, rather than Shakespeare, would have burned bright as the greatest of English writers. There is, in fact, a conspiracy school of thought that posits Marlowe as the author of all or some of the Shakespeare canon.

Extant evidence points to Morley being, as well, a player in the Great Game: espionage. He may have answered to Elizabeth I's spymaster, Walsingham, or to Elizabeth I herself and was likely involved in the infamous Babington plot of Mary, Queen of Scots. It all exploded for Marlowe during a barroom brawl over a reckoning, or bar bill, when he was stabbed in the head—over the right eye to be precise—and died at the age of twenty-nine, in 1593.

I looked at the formidable, middle-aged woman before me; she was an unexpected protagonist against the flaming youth just described, to say the least.

"So, Bess, if Morley was effectively hamstrung by the specter of treason charges and execution when it came to officially blowing the whistle on the Arabella affair—what game was he threatening to set afoot?"

"You know, of course, Dolly, of Morley's literary endeavors."

"I do! Some of the juiciest drama of the Elizabethan era. Murder. Revenge. Evil. Lots of evil."

"I am not referring to Morley's plays, Dolly. Plays! Fodder for the masses and for people seeking a cheap thrill."

It seemed to me that Bess was being a little hard on the entertainment industry of her day, which had, after all, produced the likes of *Hamlet* and *Macbeth*. I shuddered to consider what the woman would make of reality TV. Truth be told though, she wasn't making any judgments that the more straitlaced of Elizabethans wouldn't have shared.

"Well, Bess, if you are not referring to Christopher Marlowe's plays, then what are you referring to?"

"His *serious* output, Dolly. His poetry."

"Of course!" I said, and I quoted:

Come live with me and be my Love,
And we will all the pleasures prove
That hills and valleys, dale and field,
And all the craggy mountains yield.
And we will sit upon the Rocks,
Seeing the Shepherds feed their flocks,
By shallow Rivers to whose falls
Melodious birds sing Madrigals.
And I will make thee beds of Roses
And a thousand fragrant posies…

"*The Passionate Shepherd to His Love* is a delightful pastoral, *I* think, Bess. And Marlowe wrote it in his youth, *before* he met Arabella. Man and boy, Marlowe probably had dozens of scrambles in the brambles, not to mention beds of roses, before Arabella. Did the subject matter just hit too close to home for your liking, Bess? Were you paying him to suppress the poem to spare your heightened sensibilities?"

"Beds of roses, indeed!" Bess sputtered. "A shepherd who cannot afford proper bedding for his ladylove is a shepherd beneath my notice."

I smiled in reminiscence of the rose petals with which Wally had adorned our marital bed on our honeymoon and on more than one occasion afterward. "I'm afraid I don't share your estimation of *The Passionate Shepherd*, Bess."

"I don't know if that makes you a cheap date, a poor judge of poetry, or both," opined Bess. "It doesn't matter much either way though, as *The Passionate Shepherd* is *not* the poem in question."

"Well, Marlowe's translations from the Greek can't have been offensive to you, Bess. That just leaves his single, unfinished, epic—*Hero and Leander*."

Bess looked at me pointedly and said nothing. The unaccustomed silence gave me a moment to recollect my thoughts and what I could of the content of the lengthy and lusty little ditty in question. As the words and phrases came back to me, the information I had so recently received from Arabella took on a whole new significance.

Chapter Twenty-Seven
Mythology's Follies

> The outside of her garments were of lawn,
> The lining purple silk, with gilt stars drawn;
> Her wide sleeves green, and bordered with a grove,
> Where Venus in her naked glory strove
> To please the careless and disdainful eyes
> Of proud Adonis, that before her lies.
> Her kirtle blue…

The outfit that Arabella remembered so fondly—the one that her Morley first saw her in—corresponded very closely, I realized, with the garments worn by Hero, the heroine of Christopher Marlowe's epic *Hero and Leander*.

"'Fair was Hero, Venus's nun,'" I recited aloud as I further recollected snippets of the poem. "Hadn't Arabella said something about Morley likening her to one of Venus's acolytes when first they met?"

"She said something about it to you, perhaps, Dolly," Bess said. "She'd have known better than to share such drivel with me."

I was not at all surprised to hear that the vinegary Bess was not one for honeyed words. The word "honey," however, brought back another bit of *Hero and Leander*.

> Her veil was artificial flowers and leaves
> Whose workmanship both man and beast deceives.

Many would praise the sweet smell as she passed,
When 'twas the odour which her breath forth cast;
And there for honey bees have sought in vain,
And, beat from thence, have lighted there again.

Here were Arabella's bee-pleasing compote of flowers—and apparently the girl herself—immortalized in enduringly epic and erotic love poetry, unless I was very much mistaken; an apian paean, one might say.

The story of Hero and Leander dates back to Greek mythology and a telling by no less than Ovid himself. Christopher Marlowe's variation on the theme is what is known as an *epyllion* because, in the 1590s, 818 lines of iambic pentameter qualified as a little epic. Marlowe was said to have put the finishing touches on it while at a loose end sitting out the plague in London.

The story involves two lovers: our leading man, the über-sexy Leander, and a gal named Hero, a priestess of Venus. They lived on opposite sides of the Hellespont; a Renaissance Running Bear and Little White Dove who came to the same kind of sad end in the drink. Hero and Leander, however, had the advantage of having consummated their relationship prior to death, thanks to Leander's swimming skills and Hero's handy way with a lantern in a tower window.

Marlowe's version of *Hero and Leander* took the lovers to consummation only. A contemporary of Marlowe's, George Chapman, took the story home to its sad ending when he published it, after Marlowe had died, in 1598.

I needed to explore this newfound theory about *Hero and Leander* being about the relationship between Arabella and

Christopher Marlowe—my historian's curiosity would settle for nothing less. Bess would have to be carefully sounded though; my usual insouciance and forthrightness would not do for this undertaking. An attempt at subtlety would be necessary, and Lord knew that would not be easy for me. I started out by focusing on Marlowe's part in the poem rather than on Arabella's.

"Marlowe spends a good few lines going on about how good-looking his young hero, Leander, is," I mentioned. "Apparently he was pretty full of himself when it came to looks and personal charms."

I felt this to be beautifully understated, considering the description of Leander in the poem. "Leander, thou art made for amorous play." "Dangling tresses" on par with the golden fleece. "Smooth breast." "White belly." A "heavenly path" running down his back. And of course the rather disconcerting neck, like "delicious meat." Apparently, vampire erotica goes back much further than most people realize.

"If one likes men who look like girls, I suppose Morley would have been just one's cup of tea, Dolly. Clearly, that is why a girl as young and virginal as my Jewel was so taken with the man. He certainly didn't strike me as someone a *grown* woman would have any interest in."

"Marlowe would be the grown *man's* cup of tea though, if the orientation were right. I am thinking of your son-in-law, Gilbert, Bess." Bess had made mention of it herself not so long ago, so I felt on safe ground bringing it up.

As it turned out, I was correct, and then some. A little Gilbert-bashing was just what the doctor ordered, as far as Bess was concerned.

"Gilbert! He and my daughter, Mary, managed to make a going concern of their marriage, but only because my girl, Mary, at least, was able to wear the doublet and hose in that family."

I thought it best not to comment too much about which garments Gilbert or Mary Talbot assumed for marital purposes. I was comfortable, though, in making an assumption about Gilbert's part in *Hero and Leander*.

"Marlowe immortalized Gilbert in *Hero and Leander* too, didn't he, Bess? Surely the Gilbert who tried to tumble Marlowe in the hallway in the wee hours was the prototype for Neptune, who did the same with Leander when he was crossing the Hellespont to get to Hero." I quoted:

> And, looking back, saw Neptune follow him…
> He clapped his plump cheeks, with his tresses played
> And, smiling wantonly, his love betrayed.
> He watched his arms and, as they opened wide
> At every stroke, betwixt them would he slide
> And steal a kiss, and then run out and dance,
> And, as he turned, cast many a lustful glance,
> And threw him gaudy toys to please his eye,
> And dive into the water, and there pry
> Upon his breast, his thighs, and every limb,
> And up again, and close beside him swim,
> And talk of love.

"It was the closest Gilbert ever got to being considered godlike, that much is for certain," Bess replied. "What with his being so cantankerous, I'd think Mars or Ares would have been more appropriate choices for comparison than Neptune—although of course, not in keeping with the mythology."

I knew that staying in Bess's good graces would mean forgoing any discussion with her of the parts of the poem that involved Arabella and Marlowe's more intimate moments. That was a shame; Marlowe's description of their youthful cowboys-and-Indians game sounded much more sophisticated and erotic than Arabella's ingenuous description.

> And, as her silver body downward went,
> With both her hands she made the bed a tent,
> And in her own mind thought herself secure,
> O'ercast with dim and darksome coverture.
> And now she lets him whisper in her ear,
> Flatter, entreat, promise, protest and swear;
> Yet ever, as he greedily assayed
> To touch those dainties, she the harpy played,
> And every limb did, as a soldier stout,
> Defend the fort, and keep the foeman out…

At least, "Till gentle parley did the truce obtain," anyway, and love, or lust, conquered all.

Chapter Twenty-Eight
The Breakdown of a Shakedown

It occurred to me that an ego as healthy as Bess's might want the attention focused on *it* every once in a while, so I directed my mind away from the golden lines of Marlowe's epic and toward Bess.

"So, Bess, when Marlowe contacted Arabella, seeking to extort funds, what exactly transpired afterward?"

"I arranged for him to come and see *me* personally, after I'd refused Arabella's request for the pension money he was seeking. He arrived with a draft of *Hero and Leander* already in hand. You are familiar with the content of it, Dolly. If he published it and surreptitiously set rumor loose in London about what the poem was *really* about—"

"Zowie! Talk about a 'subtle, perjur'd, false, disloyal man; a man willing to set word of mouth out to do its worst.' Morley was downright Machiavellian, wasn't he?"

"Yes, indeed!" Bess confirmed. "He could handily use the publication of *Hero and Leander,* and the rumor mill, to circuitously embarrass Arabella, to embarrass Gilbert, and, by extension, to embarrass *me*. At the same time, with the poem clearly based on a well-known myth, he could claim all innocence if burdened with the charge that he had written it about his own experiences with our family."

"And once he'd secretly started that rumor train in motion, it would be the carriers of the scuttlebutt, if anyone, who would be liable for libel. Marlowe himself, with such a well-established and familiar mythological story as the basis of his poem, had a solid alibi if brought up on any kind of charges."

"He had me and my family over a barrel. Should he have published it and gotten some of his unsavory associates to put the word out on the street that the poem was about Arabella, what could we have done? *Fighting* the rumor would be *acknowledging* it! Keeping silent on it would be the lesser of two evils, but there we'd be, humiliated whether it was true or not."

"The man had 'no more mercy in him than there is milk in a male tiger'—but you've got to hand it to him for pure one hundred percent slickness," I said.

"Yes," Bess agreed. "But fortunately, the ally I chose to assist me with the Morley problem was even slicker than that."

Chapter Twenty-Nine
Bess Is Tightest with the Best and Brightest

Bess of Hardwick associated with many of England's political powerhouses over the course of her career. My professorial mouth watered as I considered the brains she'd have had available to pick for her endeavor.

"Well," Bess began, "Marlowe thought he had triumphed over our family, having had his way with Arabella and then weaseling money out of us to boot. I refused to give him the forty pounds in cash. I gave him a ring instead, a ruby ring worth forty pounds and then some, and was handed the manuscript of *Hero and Leander*. In Marlowe's presence, I read it carefully once and then consigned it to the fire that was burning in the chamber at the time."

I winced as I thought about what Marlowe the writer must have gone through, seeing his manuscript go up in flames. The professor in me winced even more at the thought of such wanton destruction of primary source documents.

"Of course, I knew that while Marlowe was silenced for the time being, our transaction was not a final solution," Bess said.

"Well, of course, you were pretty strong on slick yourself, Bess. You must have suspected that other copies of the manuscript existed. And obviously, you were correct about that."

"No," Bess corrected me. "I was *certain* that other copies of the manuscript existed. Even if they did not, the man himself, with his gift for words and what he knew, could create yet another work to accomplish his purpose."

I supposed this was so.

"I needed final resolution to the Morley problem, and I needed it fast. Arabella's reputation and future as an heiress to the throne hung in the balance. I did not hesitate to call in the big guns, but I had to be careful regarding which of them I would entrust my tale to. Discretion was imperative; it was crucial; it was—"

"'The better part of valor!'" I interjected.

"That as well," Bess acknowledged dryly. "At first I considered getting Dudley into the picture. He was an old friend and had proposed his own little boy for Arabella before the lad unfortunately died. I eventually decided against Dudley, though."

"Why, Bess?" I asked. Robert Dudley, Earl of Leicester, was the favorite—if not the true love—of Queen Elizabeth I and was well placed, surely, to help out an old friend like Bess.

"Dudley may have had friendliness and resources aplenty to offer, but he was sadly wanting in the discretion department," Bess said. "I mean, look at how badly the whole Amy Robsart affair went—and of course, Douglass Sheffield to follow."

One woman vulnerable and eventually dead under mysterious circumstances, and one pregnant and desperate and pointing the finger when he wormed out of the relationship. One could hardly give him full marks for discretion or valor, at least based on the relationship history.

"I did briefly consider calling Dudley's stepson, Lord Essex, to my aid. Newly appointed privy counselor, young, full of ideas, and with a soft spot for Arabella to boot."

Arabella had been aware of that soft spot, if the Essex mentions in the rambling letters she wrote later in life—probably in the manic phase of some sort of bipolar crisis—were any indication. Those letters are the basis of the modern-day theories regarding Arabella's troubled mental health.

"In the end, though, I decided against Essex too," Bess continued. "For much the same reason I decided against his stepfather."

"Marital indiscretions?" I inquired. "He certainly cheesed Elizabeth I off when he married Frances Walsingham, the daughter of her spymaster."

"Indiscretion in general," Bess said, encapsulating into three words the life and career of Robert Devereux, Lord Essex. Maniac episodes may have featured in his ultimately unhappy trajectory as well; perhaps his fondness for Arabella had something to do with like calling to like. In any event, as he wound up on a gibbet of his own devising at the end, Bess's call there was probably a good one.

"Sir Walter Raleigh might have done," Bess added.

"Since he 'might have done,' I'm guessing he didn't make it off the short list, Bess. Why not? The man must have been sympathetic to Arabella; he was executed for his treasonous efforts to place Arabella on the throne of England, with Spanish backing, in the Stuart era." Thus died the original Renaissance man and my favorite among them: explorer, romantic, scholar, scientist, poet, warrior, and politico.

"Why not? Timing is why not! Raleigh had been foolish enough to dally with Elizabeth Throckmorton, whom he eventually married. He wound up jailed for it, of course—as she was one of the queen's ladies," Bess reminded me. "I didn't want to get too close to the man at that particular moment in time."

Raleigh was on the outs and in the clink during the reign of Elizabeth I, and later James I, as often as not, even if they did let him out every so often to go exploring. I could see where it would be tricky trying to catch the man in the good graces of the current monarch.

Bess sighed.

"Walsingham! Now, there was a man for valor and discretion!"

"Was he your choice for the Marlowe project then, Bess? The man was steeped in politics, statecraft, and espionage. He used all the means at his disposal to achieve his ends, including torture. I imagine the two of you would have worked quite well together."

"Yes, I suppose we would have, but Walsingham was not available."

"Indisposed by the kidney stones he so famously suffered from?"

"No, Dolly; he was dead. The man had died a short time earlier, around 1590."

"Yes, of course," I said. "It was silly of me not to recall. So who *did* you finally select for your mission, Bess?"

"Knowing what you know, Dolly, you can surely guess his name."

The idea of guessing games brought back memories of my last visit here and some of the fast thinking I'd had to do. Not wanting to diminish the reputation for smarts that I had established at that time, I put on my thinking cap and thought hard.

I knew the name, all right. And it was one to conjure with.

It was, in fact, Cecil: "a man full of wise saws and modern instances, surely, and so to play his part."

Chapter Thirty
Hot to Plot

At the time in English history of which we were speaking, the Cecil in question would have been the first Baron Burghley, William Cecil—arguably the original beta male. The man was a political and administrative genius but was content to live a life of useful and productive civil service in the shadow, if not under the thumb, of the flamboyant Elizabeth I. It could not have been easy for a man as steady and unwavering as Cecil was to run the English government under his unmercifully mercurial monarch. Shakespeare's protagonist in *Hamlet* may have had the male prize for not being able to make up his mind, but Elizabeth I was far and away the front-runner for distaff honors.

For the most part, Elizabeth appreciated Cecil's efforts, making him her secretary of state and lord high treasurer, ennobling him and nicknaming him her "spirit." She visited his estate at Theobalds periodically when she was on progress; when Cecil was on his deathbed, she visited him and took the unprecedented measure of feeding him with her own hands. The two went back a long way; after all, Cecil was part of the old flock of Hatfield, the talented intellectuals who served Elizabeth so faithfully when she was still a young and vulnerable princess.

"So, you confided all to Cecil, Bess?"

"All that I have told you about Arabella and Morley, yes."

"I'll bet Cecil was surprised about all that!"

"He was! He was even more surprised when I tasked him with a suspicion that my son-in-law, Gilbert, had voiced to me as the whole sorry Morley blackmail episode unfolded."

"What suspicion was that?" I asked.

"Gilbert had told me he suspected that Morley was a plant; that he'd been suggested for my employ by the head men at Cambridge at the behest of Cecil's administration. It made sense; Arabella's proximity to the throne made her a political time bomb, and it would have been like Cecil to want to keep tabs on what went on around her."

"What roused Gilbert's suspicions?" I inquired.

"Gilbert started discreetly asking around about Morley once our troubles with him started. Word on the street was that Morley had done a spot of spying for Cecil on more than one occasion. I used this information to tax Cecil with therefore being *himself* responsible for the whole unfortunate Arabella situation by setting Morley loose in my home."

"Were you *certain* Morley was a plant, or were you just trying to deflect attention from what might be considered a lapse in your own responsible governance of the royal personage of Arabella, Bess?"

Bess was honest enough to admit to both. After she had boxed my ears again, that is.

"Cecil, it turned out, had had his tribulations with Morley as well. You see, Morley had been involved in espionage at the highest levels."

"The Babington Plot?" I asked, recollecting that his name had been bandied about in association with it.

"To name just one," Bess said. "Cecil said the others were so sensitive that he couldn't even hint to me what they were.

He went on to say that he had been concerned for some time about Morley's mental stability and his worthiness for the high-level kinds of assignments he was being given. He said he knew that the man had been foolish enough to engage in some counterfeiting and tried to have him arrested for that, but the powers that be went against him and demanded that Morley be spared. That Morley would be idiot enough to interfere with an heir to the throne had never occurred to him and was the last straw for Cecil. He said he would be more than happy to provide me with the way out of the situation that I was looking for."

"So Morley's death in that bar fight was orchestrated by Cecil, on his own behalf and yours, Bess?"

"Exactly. I asked Cecil to spare me the gory details of exactly how he would arrange it. I asked him one favor, though."

"And that was?" I asked. Bess looked so like a termagant as she recalled it that "his head on a silver platter" would not have surprised me as an answer.

"I wanted Morley to know, when it happened, that it was his reckoning for interfering with my Jewel, Arabella."

"So that famous 'reckoning' over which Marlowe was killed was not the bar tab that history tells us it was?"

"The bar tab, as you call it, was mere invention. The document presented to Morley just before that fatal tavern scuffle was a note from me. I remember well what I wrote: 'To one Morley, in reckoning for a Jewel,' signed, E. Talbot."

"You give the term 'dead reckoning' a whole new meaning, Bess! And you worded your note very cleverly too. Had anyone discovered it at the scene or after, it could be fobbed off as having something to do with an exchange of fashion accessories.

And there had to have been dozens of E. Talbots floating around Britain at the time."

"Cecil thought me clever as well," Bess confided.

"I think what you did was *brilliant!*" I said. Renaissance literature and the better angels of my nature took a backseat for just a moment in deference to my feminist leanings and my fondness for Arabella and Bess.

Bess pulled herself to her full height and raised her right hand, exposing a beautiful, jeweled ring; in fact, a ruby ring. She raised it to her lips, puffed on the gem, and rubbed it to a shine on the fur of her ruff.

"Dolly," she said, holding out her finger and admiring the ring, "you flatter me."

"'The lady doth protest too much, methinks,'" I replied.

Chapter Thirty-One
Bring on the Bling

I noticed at the conclusion of Bess's tale that the cheerful, low fire that had been burning earlier in the grate was reduced now to mere embers.

"Time does fly," I said, "when history is turned on its head for one's benefit. I've enjoyed our visit, Bess, but I think it is time to move things along."

"I suppose you are right, Dolly."

"And you know, Bess, it is getting rather chilly in here."

"I hadn't noticed," Bess answered. I wasn't surprised. She was likely the low-thermostat, wear layers, conserve-energy type.

"Maybe I could get out of this nightdress and into some warmer work clothes?" I asked.

"Delighted to oblige, Dolly."

"Will Beaton, Seton, Livy, and Flamina be dressing me this time, as they did the last?" I asked hopefully. With Flamina being a Renaissance Vera Wang, I could be sure of being dressed to impress if she were at the fashion helm. And I needed a copilot, if not several, when it came to managing the considerable mechanics of full period dress.

"Not this time, Dolly. The four Maries of Mary, Queen of Scots, are not in residence at present. But have no fear. You will be well served and well dressed. And unless I am much mistaken," she called out as she disappeared out of sight around the doorway, "accessorized like you have never been accessorized before!"

Chapter Thirty-Two
Regalia Inter Alia

From the outside hallway, I heard two female voices talking indistinctly. I could not make out the words, but the general tone was one of excitement and laughter, and they were clearly nearing me.

The first lady to round the bend and come into view had garments of all hues and textures piled high in her arms. The weight of the textiles must have been considerable; it was hard to see how she managed to carry them all without falling over. It was likely hard for her to see as well; the garments in her arms were piled up over her head.

While the garments obscured her face, they could do nothing to hide her proportions; her hips stuck out quite a ways on either side of the garment pile. Not in this case the bumrolled or farthingaled backside; this lady's contours could only have come from a generous Mother Nature. I remembered reading somewhere that "robes and furred gowns hide all," but with this lady, they wouldn't have stood a prayer.

I got up to help the woman with her burden. As I lifted a foot or two of garment from her arms, I found myself looking into the face of an old friend.

"Kat!"

The lady before me was none other than Kat Ashley, the lady who acted in loco parentis for Ann Boleyn in raising Queen Elizabeth I. Some of her decision making in Elizabeth's adolescence was more loco than parentis, but of course, nobody's perfect.

As Kat and I divested ourselves of the textiles and shared a hearty embrace, another lady came through the door bearing as many jewel boxes as her arms could carry. She put them down on the bed next to where we had placed the garments, turned to me, and made a slight bow.

She was like Mutt beside Kat's vertically challenged Jeff; tall, slender, and with posture that could go toe to toe with Bess of Hardwick's ramrod spine any day. The black and tawny ensemble she was wearing set off her ginger coloring to perfection.

"Here are the jewels! I'm off again for some ruffs and whatnot, now. Won't be a moment! So happy to meet you, Dolly, having heard so much about you," the lady said in passing as she issued out of the room.

I wondered who this woman was. She had an accent that differed from those of the other ladies here; it was soft and lilting, with gently rolling *R*s. I concentrated hard as I watched her walk away, trying to deduce who she was.

The attention I paid to the lady seemed to rub Kat the wrong way. "I hope she doesn't neglect to bring the headpieces!" Kat said. "It would be," she added, looking exasperated, "just like her."

As I opened the various jewel chests and peeked into them, I was surprised at Kat's allusion to the lady's inattention to detail. The jewel collection she had assembled indeed seemed complete. Rings, earrings, bangles, bracelets, pendants, brooches, and chains were all well represented. Gems precious and semi-precious, pearls, enamel, and finely carved cameos peeped out at me from their coffers.

"It would be a mistake, Dolly, to start with the jewels and then assemble an outfit around them. Surely you'd want to do it the other way around. Come here and look at what I've brought for you! Skirts! Bodices! Sleeves!"

"No farthingales though, I see," I said, hopefully.

"We will have Jane bring the correct foundations for your outfit once you have chosen it, Dolly."

"Jane! Is that the name of the lady who is out there acquiring ruffs for my delectation?"

"No, Dolly, it is not!" Kat was standing with her hands on her hips, an impressive sight when one had hips like Kat's. I'd seen the like before, whenever my dear cousin Kath was cross with me, but the familiarity did not blunt the impact. That stance and Kat's tapping foot told me that I'd best move from the jewel trove to the garment pile and pay Kat—and my outfit-to-be—some attention.

"You've gained weight, Dolly, since your last sojourn here," she pointed out, evening things up, I supposed, for my inattentiveness to her.

"Only a few pounds, and just lately, Kat; I must be comfort eating more than I realized. Lots of stress at work and at home these days, you know."

"Well, we'll work around it," she assured me. It was something I was sure she had plenty of personal experience with.

"You've certainly outdone yourself in selecting outfit makings for me, Kat. So many colors—a veritable rainbow! I'm practically giddy with the fashion!"

I'm generally not a flamboyant dresser and firmly believe that a little black dress goes a long way. I noticed no black garments, however, among those present. Going all Audrey Hepburn on Kat seemed ill-advised, so I didn't comment on the omission and set about selecting some garments around which to build my outfit.

Some plum-colored velvet sleeves caught my eye; I lifted them to take a closer look.

"Dolly," Kat said softly, fingering some sapphire-blue damask pieces, "take a closer look at *these*. They would be pure magic with your chestnut hair and brown eyes!"

The way the fabric scintillated in Kat's hands was magic indeed. On closer inspection, I could see that it was generously embroidered with metallic thread.

"A beautiful effect," I admitted, "but maybe a little too showy for a humble college professor such as myself. I think it would be best for me to dress simply if I am to be meeting with the great Gloriana of fashion, Elizabeth I. It wouldn't do for her to think that I was trying to show her up, fashion wise."

"Ha! As if you stood the slimmest of chances of doing that!" Kat said, laughing heartily.

"I suppose you are right, Kat; fat chance of me showing up Elizabeth I!"

"Snowball's chance in hell of you achieving that level of elegance and élan, Dolly."

"You may not fancy my chances, Kat, but perhaps you would be kind enough to humor my fancy. That plum color is just too pretty for me to let it go."

"Well, I'd love to see you in the blue, Dolly. My poppet, when people started starching their ruffs blue, issued an edict against the use of blue starch because blue was the color of Scotland. It made people reluctant to wear blue at all. It meant that some lovely garments, such as this one, were consigned to oblivion for a long time. Now that my poppet is in a place where old politics don't matter, I think we can bring the blue out without risking upsetting her."

"Yes, Kat, but the rich plum color of those sleeves—it is speaking to me!"

"Well, then, I suppose you should listen to what it says," said Kat, holding up the sumptuous sleeves. As I fingered the rich fabric, I realized that the sleeves had slits in them.

"We could put a damask chemise beneath the sleeves, Dolly, and pull it through the slits for a puff-and-slash effect. Imagine that, combined with the blue of the kirtle and gown I chose for you!"

I could indeed imagine the combination. "The outfit would be very like the one worn by the sitter in Titian's *La Bella*, Kat!"

"Really?" said Kat.

"You are not impressed, are you?" I asked her.

"*La Bella* is nothing next to the portraiture of my poppet! *The Pelican Portrait*! *The Phoenix Portrait*!"

"I know those two portraits well, Kat, and I must admit they are spectacular. One doesn't know where to look for the jewels, the embroidery, and the embellishments in general. So much texture, color, and symbolism! Such conspicuous consumption, with the Pelican and Armada jewels prominently featured. Hilliard certainly did Queen Elizabeth I—your poppet—proud in those works of art!"

"And Gowers's portraits of her, of course, further amplified her glory."

"Yes, indeed, Kat, with everything Hilliard had and then some! Such creative use of props! Who'd have thought to paint a portrait of the queen of England with a sieve?"

"It was a fitting tribute to the woman known as the virgin queen!" Kat said with spirit.

"Of course, Kat; it was a skillful allusion indeed to Petrarch's story of a vestal virgin who proves her chastity by carrying water in a sieve and not spilling a drop. Some trick!"

"And what Marcus Gheeraerts did for my Elizabeth's image! Outstanding!"

"If you say *outstanding*, you must be talking about the *Ditchley Portrait*, Kat. The uber-farthingale that Elizabeth wore in one that was something, wasn't it? It must have stuck out a yard. And from a waist that was noticeably narrower than the wearer's sleeves."

"And don't forget," Kat added, "the crotch-level rope of pearls, the lacy halo, the glove, and the fan to complete the ensemble. And of course, that world-atlas carpet beneath her feet!"

Kat threw her head back, reaching her arms out sideways and then upward in a great big, heavenward V. "My poppet was magnificent!" she said.

Kat surely had every reason to be proud of the woman she had raised. However, there was something about Kat and her enthusiasm for all that portraiture that was just not sitting right with my professorial side.

"Kat, pardon my mentioning it, but those stunning portraits—all were painted when Elizabeth I was at the height of her fame and success. Those were not portraits of the young virgin queen but of Gloriana, the mature Elizabeth. Surely you must have been—excuse my mentioning it—dead when they were painted."

"Well, yes, Dolly, that is true. But here in this place, we have been permitted by a higher power to surround ourselves with many of the comforts and luxuries we were accustomed to in life. There are the clothing and jewels we've brought for you, the furnishings in this room, the tapestries on the walls, the portraits that my poppet has brought here. They are all shades of the possessions we owned in life, just as we are shades of ourselves as we were in life."

"So those portraits exist here, in shadow form?"

"They do! A whole gallery full of them."

"What a thrill it must have been for you to see them when you arrived here!"

"It was indeed!"

"But you were not impressed with Titian's *La Bella*—how were you familiar with that? Surely that portrait is not here as well? How could it be? Other than very recent overseas tours, it has been in Italy ever since it was painted—except for a brief stint in the Louvre during the Napoleonic Wars. And that was well after your time, Kat."

"As you know, Dolly, we have had guests here many times over the ages. Not all have been as low maintenance as you are. Some of them demanded all sorts of furnishings and supplies during their brief stays here. One such was Josephine—Napoleon's wife and one-time empress of the French."

"She was here to process marital issues, I presume, based on my last stay here."

"Yes. As I recall, it was something to do with size."

"Her husband Napoleon's short-man syndrome, or some disappointment of Josephine's with his other endowments—a teeny-weeny situation, perhaps?" I inquired.

"As I recall, Dolly, both."

"I can't say I'm surprised, given Empress Josephine's, shall we say, zest for life."

"What had to be brought here to satisfy Empress Josephine, even for a brief stay!" Kat said. "Fashion, *objet d'art*, portraiture, jewels, even a rose garden had to be installed! The Titian was here awhile during her visit, and that was when I got to see it. I have to admit that *La Bella* seemed rather plain Jane to me, Dolly, at least compared to my poppet."

"Well, compared to your Elizabeth, Kat, who *wouldn't* seem plain Jane?"

"Who, indeed, Dolly?" said the ginger lady with the pretty accent. She had returned, bearing the promised ruffs. "And though I shouldn't say it," she added, "I am proud and happy that *I* had something to do with that!"

Chapter Thirty-Three
Sidekick and Psychic

With her armload of ruffs safely piled up in a convenient chair, my newest acquaintance made her way toward me and grasped my hand. "Blanche Parry, Dolly. At your service!"

The lady turned over my hand, and looked into my palm with a gimlet eye not unlike that of my eponymous palm-reading friend back in the real world. She traced a line or two in it with her finger. "Change in store for you in the near future, Dolly!"

"Good or bad, Blanche?" I asked. Do not think I was being forward, addressing a new acquaintance thus by her first name. On my last visit, I had been instructed to address everyone here that way. Given the disputes among the various residents with regard to certain titles, they had decided it politic to do away with titles altogether.

"It will be a good change, I think, Dolly," Blanche answered.

"I'm taking that as a thumbs-up for trading this nightdress for my sapphire-and-plum ensemble," I said as Kat held up the garments in question to a discerning Blanche.

"Very well; we shall get you a Spanish farthingale for that ensemble, I think, Dolly."

"Was the farthingale I wore on my last visit here a Spanish model?"

"Yes, Dolly, it was. Would you prefer a French farthingale?"

"What is the difference between them?"

"The French farthingale swells the hips more distinctly and rocks back and forth quite charmingly when one walks about!

And of course, it nips in and elongates the waist so much better than the Spanish."

I had a fleeting vision of Scarlett clinging to the bedpost and Mammy doing everything short of putting her foot up Scarlett's behind and pushing to lace Scarlett down to a nineteen-inch waist. There were bedposts aplenty available in this room, and Kat and Blanche looked like they could muster considerable strength—not to mention four feet—between the two of them.

I took the coward's way out.

"One Spanish farthingale, sale on approval, please, Blanche. I like the idea of a softer, gentler, unstructured look."

"Not too unstructured, Dolly," Blanche warned, glancing covertly at Kat's backside as she went to the doorway and hollered down the hall. "Jane! The Spanish farthingale! And those cordovan slippers, I think. The port wine–colored ones."

"Well, we can't dress you till we get the farthingale or bejewel you till we've dressed you, Dolly," Kat pointed out.

"What does one do to kill time around here?" I inquired.

"I can do a full reading of your palm, Dolly," Blanche offered.

I'd read that Blanche, child of the Renaissance and its fascination with the pseudosciences, had been quite the palmist. Surely, I reasoned, this was an opportunity not to be missed.

Kat did not agree. "Piffle! Tall, dark strangers. Blond, well-muscled strangers. Strangers with promising codpieces. Strangers with deep purses. Dolly is happily married, Blanche. She is not interested in your questionable prognostications."

"I can see all sorts of things in palms, not just potential suitors," Blanche responded. "When I was rocking our mistress, then the Princess Elizabeth, in her cradle, I peeped into her baby palm. I told her mother then and there that she would be England's most glorious queen one day!"

"What had Ann Boleyn to say to that?" I asked.

"As I recall, she said, 'That is the plan.'"

Given what I'd learned from Ann Boleyn on my last visit here, I was not at all surprised by this response. Or, for that matter, by Ann's being brave, or foolish, enough to say it aloud in the face of Henry VIII's obsession with being succeeded by a male heir.

"Anyone who knew our mistress in her childhood could have told what the future held for her without looking into her palm. Her cleverness, her beauty, her courage—they spoke for themselves. No spurious sixth sense needed!" said Kat.

"First off," Blanche replied, "my sixth sense is not spurious. Second off, I predicted the outcome *before* the child was old enough to show her wits, her full beauty, or her courage. You seem to forget, Kat," Blanche said, walking over toward the jewel boxes, "that, unlike you, I was there from the very outset. I rocked our mistress in her cradle."

"I don't forget it, Blanche," Kat replied. "Your constant mentions of the fact make forgetting about it impossible. And my memory, of course, is excellent. I am, after all, a scholar—our mistress's first educator, in fact."

The two glowered at each other from across the chair that held the ruffs. The competition between Elizabeth I's two oldest and closest retainers was promising to erupt into quite a little dustup. Being conflict avoidant, I felt compelled to head this off at the pass.

"So!" I chirped. "My palm has been held by the hand that rocked the cradle whose occupant rocked the world." Blanche glowed. Kat scowled.

"*And,*" I added immediately, "I have discoursed in art history with the lady who laid the foundation for Elizabeth I's contribution to both art *and* history; her first teacher. It's 'lucky joys and golden times' for me!"

As the lady I presumed to be Jane entered the room, I realized that I had rhapsodized too soon about my good fortune. She was bearing, among other things, the Spanish farthingale. My free-form time in my nightdress was over. The poets would have it that "iron bars do not a prison make." I could tell them a thing or two about donning a farthingale with bars of whalebone, as I was doughtily about to do.

Chapter Thirty-Four
Must We Force It into a Corset?

Jane turned out to be Jane Dormer, lady-in-waiting and best friend of Bloody Mary I. She was young and lovely; what a contrast she must have been to the aging and plain woman Mary had become by the time she assumed the throne. Jane had suitors but Mary, valuing her company, would not see her marry. When Mary eventually died, Jane wed the Spanish ambassador, de Feria, and moved with him back to Spain.

With Jane's assistance, getting me into my cambric foundation garment was easy. I was surprised at the softness of the material; it put my Cuddleduds to shame. The corset, farthingale, gown, skirt, and sleeves that were to follow looked a lot more like work.

I was skeptical, when first I eyed the corset and farthingale presented to me, that I would fit into them. A brief flashback to Scarlett, Mammy, and that antebellum bedpost ensued.

"Needs must when fashion drives," I thought to myself and headed over to the bedpost, embracing it firmly in my arms. "Bring on the farthingale and corset, Jane! I am prepared!"

With less agony than I thought possible and a little assist from Kat in the way of muscle-and-tussle, Jane managed to get me into my foundation garments.

"England lost an ace fashionista when it lost you to Spain," I said to Jane, impressed with her skill. As if to confirm my estimation, she turned her attention to my proposed garments with an expert air.

"Your outfit will mirror that of Titian's *La Bella*, Dolly," she said.

"And you are an art history maven, as well," I added.

"I, for one, approve your choice of outfit," Jane said kindly. "It is so nice to see some continental flair for a change! My mistress, while always beautifully turned out, was never, shall we say, venturesome when it came to fashion; always conservative and good-old-English, even with her cosmetics and toiletries. The woman did love her lavender; I always kept a generous supply of it on hand," Jane said.

"So Mary I was ardently Catholic with a capital C, but not catholic with a small C, at least not when it came to dress."

"You could say that, I suppose," Jane replied.

"Grammatically correct, Dolly!" Kat assured me with a scholarly look.

"We are not here for academics; we are here for costuming and ornamentation," said Blanche, the woman who had served as Elizabeth I's keeper of the jewels in life. "Into your skirt now, Dolly! We can't choose your jewels and accessories until you are dressed!"

Getting into the skirt was the work of a moment, thanks to Jane's efficiency and skill.

"The French gown next!" said Kat, crowing with satisfaction as I donned the garment she had recommended.

"I think you were right about the sapphire damask and Dolly's coloring, Kat!" Jane's pronouncement made Kat glow.

"And I never realized," I added as I moved about the room in the gilt-embroidered garment, "what gilt embroidery looks like on, and in a candlelit room. The way the light from the flickering candles plays off the gilt as I move about is just enchanting!"

"If you think that is something, just wait until we get you bejeweled!" said Blanche.

"Not until we've got the sleeves on, thank you," said the practical-minded Jane, as dab a hand at puff-and-slash as she was at farthingales and corsets. She had wispy puffs of cream-colored fabric peeping through the slits of my sleeves in no time flat.

"What do you think, Dolly?" Jane asked, stepping back and admiring her handiwork. She was clearly pleased with the ensemble and the look.

There was no full-length mirror in the room, but I caught a long-distance look at myself in a picture-sized mirror across the room.

"The full effect is a bit puffier than I am used to," I began.

"Well, you have gained a few pounds, Dolly," Kat reminded me again.

"Puffy, I was about to say, but not stuffy; puffy in a full, sensuous, feminine sense. And the richness of the colors adds to the opulence of the effect. Overall," I concluded, "a triumph for style."

"You are ahead of yourself, Dolly, proclaiming the outfit a done deal," said Blanche, aghast.

"Oh my," I said, as Blanche headed over toward the pile of starched lace and linen that had been brought in earlier. "Things are about to get ruff for me, aren't they?"

Chapter Thirty-Five
How to Deck Dolly's Neck?

"Titian's *La Bella* does not wear a ruff; must *I*, Jane?" I queried, turning to the woman I had come to look at as in overall charge of the outfit.

The group glower I received from Jane, Blanche, and Kat put me in mind of a similar experience when I had bucked the fashion advice of the four Maries of Mary, Queen of Scots. Clearly, the least of a dozen evils was the best I could hope for.

Blanche carefully laid each of twelve ruffs onto the bed so that I could inspect them. They were, to say the least, "fearfully and wonderfully made." Lace, linen, tulle, spangles, muslin, and filigree were all represented, and they were crimped, pleated, curled, and starched to a never-you-mind.

"I think those that are closed at the front will not quite go with my outfit," I said hopefully. Carrying my point here would be a strategic victory. It would eliminate six of the ruffs outright, including the widest ruff at easily eighteen inches in diameter, and the highest ruff at four one-inch layers of stacked, figure-eight pleated linen.

"I'm afraid Dolly is right," said Jane, adding Renaissance taste and weight to my argument. "Let's remove those and work with the six remaining, open-fronted ones."

I tried on a three-inch tall number but found it was a little too big for my proportions. "I have such a small neck, you see," I mentioned, still vaguely hoping to opt out of the ruff.

"Where have I heard that before?" Kat asked, scratching her head.

Blanche Parry was able to answer the question. "From Ann Boleyn, shortly before she died. You recall, Kat, the negotiations for the sharp Calais swordsman for her execution instead of the dull-hatchet man."

"Yes, of course!" Kat said. "And the argument worked, didn't it?"

As it had, we all bowed our heads in respectful silence for just a moment, remembering Ann's tragic but classy demise.

"I suppose it was fortuitous, in a way, that Ann Boleyn did not live to see a time when ruffs would be so fashionable," Blanche commented. "With her little neck, she could never have gotten away with wearing one of these stacked ones. And she wouldn't have been caught dead in garments that were not the very last word in fashion."

"She got her wish, then, didn't she?" said Jane Dormer, getting one in for her mistress, Mary I, Ann Boleyn's sworn enemy.

"Too bad scarves were not in fashion for necks when Ann Boleyn trod the boards," I said. "An ace fashionista such as Ann would have had a field day with the multitude of ways there are to tie and drape them."

"We had another guest here who made the same conjecture," Kat recollected. "Mistress Isadora Duncan. She was a great proponent of the scarf, apparently. And what a talented terpsichorean! She entertained us so pleasantly while she was here, dancing about."

"Why was Isadora brought here?" I asked. "To be advised on her rather convoluted love life by Henry VIII's six wives?"

"No, she was brought here for career advisement. Henry VIII's daughters have had many ladies brought here for this purpose.

Elizabeth and Mary witnessed their mothers' experiences over the centuries as they counseled women in precipitous marital situations and decided they wanted to do something similar. Being independently anointed monarchs in their own right, they thought that career counseling would be right up their street! They applied to the Almighty for permission to bring guests here for that purpose, and it was graciously granted."

"What kind of advice did Isadora need from them?"

"Isadora's dancing career had gone to seed, and her life was in shambles. Elizabeth thought that if Isadora wrote an autobiography, she might be able to capitalize on past glory and ensure her future."

The free-spirited Isadora Duncan was a denizen of Gertrude Stein's Paris, an alcoholic, and an improvisational dancer extraordinaire. I'd have given a lot to see the meeting between her and the self-disciplined Elizabeth I.

"Well, Isadora did take Elizabeth's advice about the autobiography," I recollected; the book was written in the late 1920s.

"Yes, but she would not heed my advice about the scarves," said Kat, shaking her head sadly. "I tried to convince her that a ruff-style collar would be much more flattering to her than those scarves that were waving around all over the place, getting tangled into things and in the way all the time. None of that inconvenience with a ruff!"

Inconvenience was putting it mildly. Isadora's demise in a convertible auto accident has been attributed to her signature long scarf getting tangled in the turning tires of the moving car and choking her to death.

"If we might return to the subject of *my* neck for just a moment," I requested, hoping for a shift of mood before things became too somber.

"Well, since one three-inch-tall number is eliminated by virtue of size, I am taking the other two ruffs of that height out of the running as well," Jane said, all efficiency. "No use wasting time trying them on, Dolly."

Because the overall effect of my outfit was one of wavy femininity, I was inclined to go for the softest and most free-form of the remaining ruffs. I reached for that particular pile of snowy lace and inspected it more carefully. It was actually, I discovered, a length of lace an inch or two wide; the kind that busty but demure ladies used to tuck into their low-cut bodices for modesty's sake.

"Not interested in these other two ruffs, Dolly?" Blanche asked. They were not stacked high but of a single layer of fiercely starched linen fabric, edged with equally starched lace and stiffened to stand up a bit behind the head and then slope down toward the front. I had a Catholic school flashback; they looked like Peter Pan collars on crack.

"No, thank you, Blanche; doctor's orders. Advised to stay away from starches, you know."

"Wise advice, considering the weight you've put on around the middle, Dolly," said Kat fondly—or at least what I hoped was fondly. I declined to comment and turned my attention to my chosen lace accessory, rejoicing in being able to forgo the rigid pleats or folds of the traditional ruff for a sweet and wispy neckline instead. Jane secured the lace to my garments for me and directed me to the mirror. I was sold as soon as I caught sight of it.

"*Bellisima!*" I said.

"Headpiece now, Dolly," Jane directed.

In among the garments in the room were some coifs and snoods as well as a single little late-Tudor era doll hat, a compact fascinator complete with a vaguely peacocky-looking little plume.

"I'll take the hat," I said, perching it on my head at a jaunty angle. Jane faced me toward the mirror as she secured it.

"I look just like a 1940s film star in this hat! You know, Bette Davis, Joan Crawford, or Katharine Hepburn."

"Mistress Katharine Hepburn! She was here with us for a visit, wasn't she, Kat?"

"Yes, she was," Kat confirmed.

Recollecting my last stay here, I hazarded a guess. "Was she here for advisement about her affair with Spencer Tracy?"

"No, she was not here for that. She met with our mistresses. They brought her here to give her advice about her performing career. She was on the stage, you know."

"And in motion pictures, as well, a medium you ladies would not be familiar with, perhaps. It was a means of capturing theatrical performances for posterity."

"We've had quite a few guests here who were employed in that business," Kat assured me. "As I recall, Mistress Hepburn told us she had made quite a splash in the motion pictures you mention, even though she'd not been in the field for long at that point."

"Well, she won her first Academy Award for her third film well before she was thirty years old. 'Splash' is probably a good word for it."

"She told our mistresses, though, that she longed to replicate her success on the legitimate stage. To do so, she was considering appearing in a production at very low remuneration. Our mistresses advised against it, but Mistress Hepburn could not be talked out of her plan, or at least so she said."

"Hepburn's stubbornness comes as no surprise to me," I said in her defense. "The woman was a byword for courage, independence, and following one's own star."

"My poppet recognized those traits in Mistress Hepburn, probably because they featured so prominently in her own personality," Kat said.

"Yes, indeed, and that is why Elizabeth tried so hard to convince Mistress Hepburn not to sell herself too cheaply. It was sound advice," Blanche said.

"It was, indeed!" I confirmed. "Shortly after winning that first Oscar, Hepburn attempted to win stage fame by appearing in a production called *The Lake*. It was a disaster."

"I suppose 'splash' is probably a good word for that as well," Jane commented, proving herself as ace a punster as she was a *modiste*.

"Hepburn was able to buy her way out of the production of *The Lake*, but the legend of her poor performance in it has lived on and on. It's been famously described as 'running the gamut of emotions from A to B.'"

"How sad for Mistress Hepburn! We figured it wouldn't turn out well. Such a shame—she was awfully talented, you know. She was kind enough to give us a little cameo of her role in that play. Do you remember, Blanche?"

"I do, indeed! 'The calla lilies are in bloom again.' Isn't that one of the lines that Mistress Hepburn gave us?"

"That would have to be correct," I confirmed on hearing the great actress's tagline.

"Of course, we had no idea what calla lilies were, but did not want to break her stride by asking her."

"They are elegant, spathe-like flowers that would look very well on this hat," I said, touching my *chapeau*. "But for now, the jewel-toned feather that someone so wisely added to it will do quite nicely. I think I can say, with confidence, that 'I have a good face, speak well, and have excellent good clothes'; the latter, thanks to the three of you."

"You do look a treat, Dolly," said Jane.

"But not as much of a treat as she is about to look," said Blanche as the queen's keeper of the jewels prepared to come into her own. "Time," Blanche practically trumpeted, "for some accessories!"

Chapter Thirty-Six
Ring-a-Ding-Ding

I slipped my feet into the claret-colored leather of the tooled cordovan slippers that Jane had provided for me and headed over to the jewel boxes and the beckoning Blanche.

My jewelry collection back in the real world consisted of a tangle of gold chains, lockets, and pearls as well as a few carefully chosen pieces that Wally had purchased for me as gifts on various occasions. His taste, like mine, ran to the simple and classic. Achieving simple here would not be easy, given the treasure trove Blanche had provided.

"I think a Victorian choker look would be lovely with this outfit," I commented, pulling out several brooches that might achieve the desired effect. Blanche anticipated the mental image I had conjured up with surprising acumen.

"This brooch will meet your requirements, I am sure," Blanche said, gesturing toward a plum-colored cameo.

"The Gatacre Jewel!" I said, recognizing a lovely bit of Renaissance cameo work in gold, pearls, and amethyst.

Together, Jane and Blanche anchored the brooch onto a filigreed ribbon and then fastened the ribbon around my neck. The effect was just what I had hoped; I complacently admired my refection in the mirror.

"What next, Dolly?" Jane asked leadingly. "A brooch for your gown? Earrings? Some long chains? A small purse? A fan? A belt?"

"All the above?" Blanche asked hopefully.

"Well, I rather thought I would stop right here. You know what they say—'Less is more.'"

"Grammatically and rhetorically indefensible, Dolly," Kat opined.

"Sartorially inexplicable!" said Jane Dormer, child of the lushly outfitted and jeweled Renaissance.

"Just call me 'a fool in good clothes,' ladies. I don't mean to offend, but I don't want to be the gal who 'wears her cap out of fashion, richly suited, but unsuitable.'"

Blanche was riled up by this and not pulling any punches. "Bollocks, in my opinion! Whoever heard of a single piece of jewelry completing an ensemble? As the mistress of the jewels of Elizabeth I, I simply cannot let you out of here with just one piece of jewelry to your credit, Dolly. My mistress would have my head!"

Kat, Jane, and I winced at the oblique decapitation reference. "See how you've upset Blanche, Dolly?" Kat scolded.

"She must be upset to have made a decapitation *faux pas* like that one. It isn't like her—she is usually so discreet!" Jane added.

"Very well," I said, willing to take one for the embellishment team if necessary. "I think I could live with adding a ring or two to the ensemble."

"I've brought some lovely ones," Blanche said invitingly. As I combed through the jewel boxes for rings, two azure beauties caught my eye. One featured a single sapphire. The other boasted a rich burgundy-colored onyx cameo, set in deep blue enamel.

"Your mistress?" I asked Blanche as I looked closely at the features in the tiny cameo.

"Yes, it is!" said Blanche, turning a similar shade of purple to the cameo.

"You disapprove of this ring, Blanche? Why? I should think your mistress would be pleased and flattered by my choice of this ring."

Kat and Jane looked pointedly at Blanche. "How," Kat demanded, "did the sapphire and sardonyx rings get in among the jewels you prepared for Dolly, Blanche?"

"Elizabeth," Jane added, "would be furious if she knew!"

"Someone," Blanche hissed, "or, more likely, *two* someones, have been up to their old tricks."

"Catherine and Philadelphia, surely."

"The Carey sisters?" I conjectured, naming two of Elizabeth I's cousins on her mother's side, via her aunt Mary Boleyn, the Tudor-era good time that was had by all.

"Yes. These rings are their claim to fame, you know. They trot them out at every possible opportunity."

"Much to Elizabeth's chagrin," Kat added. "And understandably so."

Given what I knew about the history of the Carey sisters, I was inclined to agree with Kat, as I stared at the cameo ring.

"This is—what shall I call it—the Essex Promise Ring, isn't it?" I asked.

My trio of modistes nodded in confirmation that it was.

The Earl of Essex, the last and looniest of Elizabeth I's male favorites, had a knack for getting in trouble with his queen. It may have been overweening ego, poor judgment, a bipolar disorder, or some combination thereof. In any event, pardons from Elizabeth were something he found himself in frequent need of.

The cameo ring I was proposing to wear was given to Essex by Elizabeth as a sort of "get out of jail free" card. It was given with the promise that it could be turned in to Elizabeth in the future in exchange for one unconditional pardon.

Essex eventually went the full lunacy mile and led, or attempted to lead, an armed rebellion against his queen. Locked up in the Tower, he tossed the ring that he hoped would be his redemption out a window and, he thought, on its way to Elizabeth. Enter the Carey sisters, and the young boy who gave the ring to the wrong one of them. Catherine Carey diverted the ring from Elizabeth, who eventually had Essex executed. When Elizabeth learned, after the fact, that Essex had tried to call in her ring promise, she is said to have been devastated. She lived for two years after that execution, by some accounts with the starch pretty much knocked out of her, which, given the size of the starched ruffs she wore, was saying something.

I turned my attention to the sapphire ring in my hand.

"So, this ring is associated with the Carey sisters as well. With Philadelphia Carey, specifically, I am thinking."

My friends nodded once again.

Philadelphia Carey had her moment in the sun when Elizabeth I was on her deathbed with the succession to her throne still very much up in the air. Philadelphia, in cahoots with Elizabeth's chief adviser Robert Cecil, forwarded a sapphire ring of Elizabeth's to James VI of Scotland immediately upon Elizabeth's death. It was an agreed-upon message from Cecil to James to come-a-running to claim the English throne. Philadelphia managed, at the epicenter of a brewing succession crisis, to transfer the ring to her brother Robert. Robert rode with it posthaste to Scotland, and into history, as the muddied man who broke the news to James that he was now king of England as well as Scotland.

"Well, it is going to be fun to wear two such interesting pieces of history, at least for a little while," I said, slipping each ring on to one of my fingers.

"On your own head be it, if Elizabeth notices you are wearing those rings," Blanche warned.

"Execution awareness, please, Blanche!" said Kat, obviously pleased to be able to take Blanche to task.

"I am willing to take the chance of Elizabeth's disapprobation for an accessorizing opportunity like this," I said, my inner historian taking precedence over my common sense as it so often does.

With that, Kat, Blanche, and Jane gathered up the rejected garments, accessories, and jewels that were scattered about the room and prepared to take leave.

"Wait!" I said, suddenly feeling a little bit let down as all the personal and undivided attention I had been receiving was coming to an end.

"Kat, Blanche, Jane—take one last look at me, just to make sure all is as it should be," I said, spinning slowly around on one foot, allowing them to fully inspect, for one last time, my ensemble.

"Is my apparel marvelous to behold?" I asked.

Kat spoke for the trio.

"It is, and it is our pleasure to tell you so, Dolly. Good luck when you meet with my poppet and her sister Mary. With the outfit you have chosen, you are certainly dressed for success!"

"'I know not what the success will be, my lady; but the attempt I vow,'" I said, reminding myself that in spite of a fun round of dress-up play, I had a mission at hand; a mission I knew nothing about as yet.

"It's been a pleasure dressing with you all," I assured my three fashion consultants fondly. "It was wonderful to see you again, Kat. And Blanche and Jane, 'for fashion sake, I thank you too for your society!'"

My three friends bowed and nodded graciously as I took note of the dwindling length of the tapers in the candelabra. "We'd best be moving on with things. Now that I'm dressed and bejeweled, will I be seeing the two queens, Elizabeth and her sister Mary?"

"Not quite yet," said a voice from without as a whiff of smoke drifted into the room.

Chapter Thirty-Seven
The Distinguished and the Extinguished

The whiff of smoke was backed up by not one but three ladies. I wondered who they were.

"Been at the tobacco again, have you, ladies?" asked Kat.

"You might have asked me to join you, if you were," said Blanche. "I like a companionable puff now and then."

"You really shouldn't, ladies!" I said. "Modern science has discovered that it is very bad for your health!"

"You forget where you are, Dolly," Jane kindly said. "We ladies of the court are but shades in this place; not of heaven at the present but well past the worldly plain. We are, not to put too fine a point on it, dead."

"So, even though we weren't smoking just now, we shall smoke if we want too, and as much as we like!" Thus spoke the sexiest of the three newly entered ladies—the sexiest, at least, if you like the squishy Marilyn Monroe type.

"I thought Dolly was supposed to see Elizabeth and Mary next. What is going on?" Kat asked.

"There has been a conflagration," said the new trio's most elegant member.

"Is everyone all right?" I asked.

All five of my companions looked at me pointedly. Had there been a Renaissance equivalent for the word "duh," they'd have said it. The prettiest gal of the newly entered three overlooked my blunder and explained what had occurred.

"An unfortunate accident in the dressing room; an upset candle sconce," she said. "The outfits that Mary and Elizabeth had chosen to wear were badly damaged. You know how quickly a ruff can go up in flames."

Considering the size of the ruffs I was surrounded with and the air pockets within them, I could only imagine.

"And you know how easily whalebone can snap!" the elegant lady added.

"No, I didn't, actually," I confessed.

"When one must step on a whalebone corset, full weight with both feet, to get to a burning ruff to put it out, collateral damage will occur."

"It's been all snap, crackle, and pop in your little world lately, hasn't it?" I asked.

"Elizabeth and Mary have requested that Kat and Jane come to assist them in improvising replacement ensembles," the elegant gal informed me. "Blanche, the jewel boxes will be required for the accessorizing of the contingency royal outfits. Run along and deliver them. We," the elegant lady said, as she and her two companions assumed seats, "shall entertain Dolly until all is ready."

Chapter Thirty-Eight
Hearts Afire and Dolly for Hire, More or Less

My three new friends set up chairs for themselves. The squishy gal and the elegant lady sat on either side of the third woman in the set—a pretty girl in a soulful way, with huge, dark eyes. Simply dressed, she made quite a contrast to her two companions.

I took a chair and pulled it over to where my three new roommates were seated. I placed the chair facing them and sat down. Contrary to my usual practice, I was the "pattern of all patience," and said nothing. Actually, "ignorance waited upon patience," if truth be told. I had no idea who these women were and therefore no idea what to say.

The elegant lady leaned toward me, her hand upright against her lips in a furtive gesture. "We," she said, speaking for the trio, "have a commission for you, Dolly."

"You and everyone else around here," I said. "There is some misinformation, I presume, that you want corrected for posterity? Some reputation rehabilitation you need me to do?"

"Well, yes, Dolly, exactly. Unfortunately, we have no way to pay you for the undertaking, being that you can't take anything back with you when you leave here."

"Well, it's hardly a commission then, is it? More like a favor, wouldn't you say?"

"Well, we feel that we'd be doing you a favor too. You are a scholar who specializes in the history of our era. Surely, discovering heretofore unrevealed information about our lives and times would set your curiosity alight and kindle your professional interest."

"You've quite a thing for flames, haven't you?" I inquired, nonchalantly moving a nearby candelabrum a little farther from the lady's reach.

"We all three knew how to set a heart on fire," the squishy gal told me, "but we were none of us burned by the flames in the way that history has handed the story down. We mastered the flames of love; we were not consumed by them. And we want the world to know all about it!"

"Well, if the world is to be thus illumined, I need to know all about it first. And right now," I confessed, "I do not even know who you incendiary ladies are!"

"I've never been called 'incendiary' before. I think I like it," said the soulful-eyed gal. "Of course, Dolly, my two companions are more used to flattery than I am, having been at court."

"Well, we were at court awhile—till the fat hit the flames anyway," said the elegant lady. "Then I was consigned to the stagnation of the countryside."

"And I," the squishy one said, "was consigned to foreign shores and the French court. Very exciting, of course, but there is no place like home, even when you know you are not welcome back."

I pondered the bits of personal history I had just been given and felt the incandescence of awareness happening in my head. If anyone had asked me how many Renaissance ladies it took to screw in a lightbulb, I would have had to say "three"; the very three before me.

"Friends," I began, hoping I wasn't being too presumptuous. Apparently I wasn't, for they quite beamed when I said it. Knowing I had their approbation, I wanted their respect as well, and I wasn't going to get that by making a scholarly error. I decided to test my facts before I got too fired up.

"Tell me something about the heart, or hearts, that the three of you set alight. I am guessing it is the former; that each of the three of you set the same heart afire. Am I right?"

"Yes!" they said in unison. Apparently, the unison was unintentional because they laughed heartily together after it happened. It made me glad to see the three of them so companionable together. Many in their places, if my surmise was correct, would have had a hard time behaving civilly together.

I stood up, reached for the candelabrum I'd moved a moment ago, and raised it up to look more closely into the three faces before me. In that of the elegant lady, I detected more than a little bit of the Boleyn. In the face, not to mention the form, of the squishy one, I was put in mind of Catherine Howard, Henry VIII's juicy fifth wife.

The resemblances supported my suspicions.

Chapter Thirty-Nine
The Names of Three Dames

Anyone who's studied Tudor history knows how confusing it can get, sorting out the myriad Anns, Janes, Catherines, Marys, Margarets, and Elizabeths one from the other. Here, if my suppositions were correct, I had not a one of the traditional names to deal with it, and it was going to be a pleasure. I dove right in, addressing myself first to the gal with the Boleyn DNA.

"Lettice, isn't it?" I asked, putting my hand on her shoulder in a friendly fashion. "I must say, your outfit is lovely!"

I wasn't just currying favor there; her outfit really was something. Lettice had clearly inherited Ann Boleyn's fashion sense. If such a thing is possible, she brought simplicity and sophistication to the excesses of the late Tudor era, sacrificing nothing of either the simplicity or the excess.

Her outfit was all gold and white; no other color marred the effect. The jewelry she wore was in keeping, all gold and pearls, but plenty of both on wrists and fingers, in hair, and around neck and waist. Everything that was white on her gown was spangled, embroidered, or bordered with gold or gilt. In the candlelight, every breath she took, making her chest rise and fall, made the glittering gold and the shimmering white twinkle, sparkle, and dance.

"Thank you for the compliment, Dolly. If you know that I am Lettice—Lettice Knollys—then perhaps you can guess who my companions are as well."

"Douglas Sheffield, of course," I said, taking the hand of the squishy lady.

"You won't meet many ladies with an odd name like mine, I am sure!" Douglas said.

"Oh, I don't know," I said. "In my era, naming baby girls has become an exercise in one-of-a-kind names and unique spellings. It keeps one on one's toes, getting everyone's daughters' names straight and not offending anyone with an incorrect spelling or pronunciation."

"I wish it had been like that in my lifetime!" Douglas said, and I could tell that she meant it.

"Can't have been easy for a man in your day to be called Douglas among all the Henrys, Edwards, Jameses, Johns, and Roberts. To be a girl called Douglas must have been even more difficult—like the song, "A Boy Named Sue.""

"Tell me about it, Dolly!"

The best thing to do seemed to be to sing it, so I did the song as much justice as I could. When I got to the last line, of course, I sang, "'And if I ever have a son, I think I'm gonna name him…'"

"Douglas!" said the third of the ladies, giving said Douglas a friendly little shoulder massage as we all had a good laugh. "You are quite the songstress, Dolly, at least when it comes to talking blues rather than actually singing them."

"And you are clever, Amy," I said to her, "at least when it comes to jokes you can see coming from a mile away."

I was addressing, I was sure, the subject of one of the Renaissance era's great unsolved mysteries: Amy Robsart.

"You sound surprised that I might be clever, Dolly."

"I am, Amy; you see, history has painted you otherwise," I said, hoping that I wasn't being too brutally honest.

"History," Amy said, "can go and hang!"

"You aren't nearly as execution-sensitive as most are around here, are you, Amy? Interesting, considering the circumstances of your—umm—demise," I said.

"Good lord! History hasn't decided that I was hanged, has it?"

"No," I said to Amy, as gently as I could. "It has not."

Mind you, hanging is about the only means of extinction that has not been posited about Amy Robsart down through the ages.

Chapter Forty
A Little Mystery in the History

I call her Amy Robsart, but of course her married name was Amy Dudley. She was the mysterious first wife of Queen Elizabeth I's true love, Robert Dudley, the Earl of Leicester. Amy has been largely portrayed as a country bumpkin, a mistake of Dudley's youth—a downright inconvenience as his love affair with the queen developed. Amy languished in the country all her life, reportedly with ailments both mental and physical. Theories as to the cause of her untimely death continue to emerge; given the bizarre circumstances of it, this is not surprising. Amy's end could be said to be the original empty house mystery; she was found in said empty house dead, at the bottom of a staircase.

I took a moment to consider Amy's dress and demeanor. For all the soulfulness of those eyes, the overwhelming impression, on closer look, was one of a down-home mix of horse sense, sass, and sweetness. Amy apparently had never strayed far from her farmer's daughter roots among the Norfolk gentry.

Her outfit, while very flattering to her, was simpler and more flowing than those of her companions. It was, in fact, of an earlier Tudor vintage, looking more like Henrician than Elizabethan fashion. She wore a French hood and caul over her dark hair, and her dress featured the exaggerated bell sleeves I'd seen so much of on my last visit here. Her neck was innocent of any type of ruff whatsoever.

"I love the vintage look of your outfit, Amy," I said. "It brings back fond memories of my time here with the earlier Tudor generation. I suppose fashion changes came and went a bit more slowly where you were, in the country, than they did at court." As I spoke, Douglas adjusted her décolletage a bit, and Lettice primped her gilding.

"Life in the country is not all that behindhand, Dolly," Amy said, standing up for the virtues of the simple life. "My outfit was quite stylish during my lifetime. You seem to forget that death took me out of the fashion picture, so to speak, a mere two years into the reign of Elizabeth I."

I admired the aplomb with which the probable victim of one of history's notorious murders could discuss her own death, which occurred well before she was thirty. I got a bit teary-eyed as I thought about it.

"You're awfully emotional, aren't you, Dolly?" Amy asked. "It certainly isn't what we expected of you. Based on your behavior during your last visit here, we were told that you were not the sensitive type at all."

"I don't usually cry so easily, it's true," I said. "It's just that I've been under a lot of pressure lately, and things will erupt, you know."

"You mean Blanche and Kat got carried away and laced your corset too tight?" the curvaceous Douglas asked, no doubt from the perspective of plenty of personal experience with girdle overflow.

"I shouldn't think so!" Lettice said, looking at my midsection and then back to her own waspish Boleyn waistline.

Douglas proceeded to massage my shoulders sympathetically. There was no doubt that she had a soothing, comforting way about her.

"I was referring to pressures back in the real world," I said sheepishly.

I was more than a little bit embarrassed at being unable to cope as well with day-to-day career and family stressors as Amy did with abandonment, adultery, and a violent death. However, Douglas's minimassage did me good, and after a few moments, I was closer to my usual form.

"I must say, Amy, that I admire your—what should I call it—sangfroid?"

"That's exactly what I'd call it," said Lettice.

"Why so impressed, Dolly?" Amy asked with what looked to me like genuine humility. "Facing life, up to and including its end, on life's own terms; surely, there is nothing so exceptional about that."

"I guess you are right, Amy, since you lived life down on the farm and out in the country. Close contact with the visceral life must have been inevitable. Animals husbanded, hunted, and butchered; one's pet rabbit eventually out of the hutch and into the hasenpfeffer; chickens running around with their heads cut off. Maybe that's why it's not so difficult for you to talk so handily about your own murder."

"Dolly," said Amy gently, coming to my chair, "I know how emotional you are right now, and I know that a blow to your scholarly cred is going to sting. But you see, dear," Amy went on, taking my hand, "I wasn't murdered at all."

Chapter Forty-One
More than One None-Too-Cheery Theory

"Your husband didn't put a hit out on you, Amy, to get you out of the way so that he could marry the queen?"

"No."

"The queen didn't put a hit out on you so that she could marry your husband?"

"No."

"Cecil—Lord Burghley—didn't put a contract out on you to frame your husband for your murder, thus making him too hot to handle as a possible king consort for Elizabeth I?"

"No."

There was my pet theory, pounded into the dirt.

"The French royal family did not assassinate you to allow Elizabeth I to discredit herself so fully by marrying your widower that she would lose her crown to Mary, Queen of Scots?"

"No."

I was out of theories and shrugged, holding my hands outward to indicate as much to Amy.

"I was not murdered. I can't put it any more simply than that, Dolly."

My scholarly cred had taken a minor body blow but certainly not a TKO. I was aware of the other, less accepted theories on Amy's death. I tackled the toughest one first, with all the tact I could muster.

"There are those who theorize, Amy, that you ended your own life in despair. Some say that depression over your husband's affair with the queen caused you to throw yourself down that now-famous staircase in your country home."

"Wrong again, Dolly."

"Others say you despaired because of a major clinical depression; severe melancholia, it might have been called in your day."

"Not so, Dolly. I had the odd sad moment, of course—especially when Auntie Flo was due to come around—but nothing out of the ordinary in terms of melancholia."

"Well, personally, Amy, I always thought the final theory that remains about your death was the weakest."

"What is the final theory, Dolly?"

"It is that your death was because of a malignant illness. That perhaps your fatal fall had to do with a cancer that started in your breast and traveled to your bones. That a bone in your spine, weakened from tumors, may have broken, causing you to fall and then tumble down the staircase."

"You are right about that theory being weak, Dolly. It is not just weak; it is incorrect. My death was not accidental."

"Well, if it wasn't assassination, a despairing suicide, or disease or accident that landed you at the foot of that staircase with a broken neck—what was it?"

I settled back into my chair as Amy Robsart proceeded to "murder impossibility, and to make what could not be, slight work."

Chapter Forty-Two
The Rustic and the Prick

"Really, Amy, in deference to Dolly's scholarly feelings, perhaps you should begin your story with the fact that some of Dolly's surmising has an element of truth to it," Lettice said kindly.

"It couldn't hurt to throw Dolly a bone," Douglas agreed.

"What part of my surmising was the most accurate?" I inquired.

"Well, Dolly dear—the part of the story that you found the least likely was really at the beginning of it all. I did suffer breast cancer, and I knew, in the weeks before my death, that my days were numbered. Cancerous lumps were appearing in other parts of my body. I knew that painful and certain death awaited me."

"What an enormous reality to have faced when you were so young! And of course, you had to face it more or less alone, didn't you?"

"Yes. My husband had the queen's eye and, I was certain, her heart. I was the only thing that stood between him and the achievement of his ambition and dearest wish—marriage to the queen—and I knew it."

"It must have been dreadful for you, Amy, being abandoned that way. Stuck in the country, denied the glory and the hurly-burly of the court, because your husband was in hot pursuit of another woman—one who just happened to be the queen."

"Dolly, my dear, sorry to cause you embarrassment, but I'm afraid you've got it wrong again."

"I'm getting used to it," I said humbly. "Don't try to spare my feelings. Just tell on, please, Amy."

"I loved the country life, Dolly; the simple pleasures, the dignity of honest folk living honest lives, the neighborliness, all that was familiar to me. I loved it far too much to wish to give it up for the cutthroat atmosphere of the court. My companions will forgive me—I know they both thrived on the intrigue of it—but such was not for me. I'd have felt like a slave in the arena at the Coliseum if I went to court, wondering who or what was going to come after me next."

"And the loss of your husband's affections, Amy—how did you feel about that?"

"Early in the marriage, Robert and I were fond enough of each other in our own way, it is true. But it never evolved further than that. He was away in London, which he loved, far too much of the time, and I resisted his importuning me to join him back at the beginning. You see, I loved the country life far more than I loved Robert."

"Well, you know what Shakespeare said: 'God made the country, and man made the town.'"

"I think you will find that that was Cowper, Dolly," Lettice pointed out.

"Of course, once things really took off between Robert and the queen," Amy resumed, "his importuning for me to join him at court ceased. Once I was able to let go of the minor blow that it was to my pride, it was a relief, if truth be told. My husband was so happy at court, so very in his element. I was happy in the country, in my own element. My husband was able to pick daisies with the queen, so to speak, but not able to take it much further than that because of his marriage to me."

"You sound quite satisfied with the whole arrangement."

"I was! I had the life I enjoyed and was accustomed to. And I considered that I was doing a duty to queen and country just by my existence. My slender self was a like a bulwark between Elizabeth and my husband. As long as I was alive, and as long as I was Robert's wife, he could not marry her."

"He could have divorced or annulled you, couldn't he?"

"He could have. But with the experience Elizabeth had had with being a child born into a marriage that was dissolved controversially, do you really think she'd set herself up to re-create the same situation for a child of her own? You know how different things were in our day, Dolly, when it came to divorce and the legitimacy of children, especially royal children. And even a simple country girl like me knew that the queen marrying my husband would have meant loss of prestige and political embarrassment for both her and our nation. With every day that came and went, I felt that I was doing a solemn duty as subject and patriot just by being Robert's loving wife and biggest obstacle."

"Let me get my ducks in a row here, Amy."

"Dolly! Are you a country girl too?"

"No, Amy; I mention the poultry strictly metaphorically. To recap, you were totally copasetic with your position as a betrayed wife."

"Totally, as you say, copasetic, in spite of the weight of responsibility that I bore, being the life that stood between my queen and the ruin of her reputation and her reign."

"Did you not fear for your life, Amy? You know the kind of thing—'will no one rid us of this cumbersome first wife?' People stepping up to the plate to do a bit of assassination to further their rulers' ends was certainly not unheard of in English royal history. And you know what they say: 'Murder's as near to lust as flame to smoke.'"

"My husband hadn't the goolies to order my assassination," Amy said simply.

At this, Lettice nodded knowingly, as she adjusted the ruffles at the end of her sleeves.

"Robert was all mouth and trousers, when you came right down to it," Douglas added.

"Surely mouth and stockings, in your day?" I said, doing what I could to repair my scholarly reputation.

"I had no fear of attack on my husband's part," Amy said. "And I trusted my queen, even if she was besotted with my husband, not to shed innocent blood by having me killed or by inciting others to do so. My fears began once I became ill. As the cancer spread through my body, I became weaker and weaker and suffered pain. The mental anguish was even worse. I knew that with my death imminent, my ability to be the bulwark between the queen and my husband was coming to an end. Then I knew fear. Fear for my queen and for her glorious future. Fear for my country and its future. So I did the only thing I could think of to do under the circumstances."

"What was that?" I asked.

"What any woman who was anybody did in the Tudor era when she was facing a crisis."

I recalled all I had heard in this place so far that night.

"Amy! You don't mean—"

Chapter Forty-Three
Keep Calm, Rest Still, and Call Cecil

I attempted to picture the meeting of the two minds that my surmise was painting for me. A long, Duck Dynasty beard figured prominently.

"It must surely be obvious to you, Dolly," Amy said, putting an end to my reverie. "I consulted Cecil."

"William Cecil, at that early point in the Elizabethan game," I said, stating the obvious, perhaps, but wanting to keep it as accurate as possible. His son, Robert Cecil, would not have been of an advice-giving age until much later on.

"Correct, Dolly."

"Wouldn't a physician have been more appropriate, Amy?"

"Not for the idea that I was brewing, Dolly—the idea that Cecil helped me bring to fruition."

"So you formulated an idea on you own before even consulting Cecil! That was enterprising of you. How did you manage such advanced planning, with things such as life and death on your mind?"

"The country life I loved so much came to my service, Dolly."

"You were imbued with inspiration as you sat soaking in the sweet air of the English countryside?"

"No. I happened to be out near the paddock when I saw one of our horses, sickly and old, being led off to the knacker's yard."

"Oh, my," I said, with trepidation. I sensed that things were about to get "of the earth, earthy."

"I guess I can assume what this sight suggested to you, Amy, considering your condition."

"Never assume, Dolly. When you assume," Douglas reminded me, "you make an 'ass' out of 'u' and 'me.'"

I thought this clever of Douglas, considering that the letter *U* was not in consistent use in the English language back in her day.

"'Never assume' is excellent general advice, Douglas," Amy said. "However, in this case, Dolly assumes correctly, or at least, I assume as much myself."

"Never assume, Amy," Douglas repeated. "Because when you assume—"

"Enough of it, Douglas!" said Lettice. "Get on with your story, Amy. Time is wasting, and we've still got me and Douglas with our tales to tell."

"Of course," said Amy indulgently. "I watched that decrepit horse being led off, and at first I thought, 'Poor creature.' Then I noticed the hang of its head, the lack of luster of its coat, its guarded movements. Soon the animal would be out of its misery, and the knacker would make sure that its carcass was put to good use. Surely it was the most comfortable and most utilitarian of all possible fates for that horse. What a blessing it would be, I thought, if I could orchestrate my own end to be that expeditious and constructive."

"You country folk are nothing if not practical minded!" I said.

"Well, Cecil was pretty practical minded too," said Amy, delivering a top-ten contender—excuse the oxymoron—for the most over-the-top understatement of Tudor history.

"So what did your horse sense, if you will pardon the pun, come up with, Amy? And what did Cecil's practicality bring to it?"

"I was able to discreetly summon Cecil to the country, and he readily appeared, incognito, of course. He arrived at Cumnor Place in the dead of night for a flying visit. His words were few, at first; in fact, he even shed a tear or two. I'm afraid I was looking pretty ill by then, and my looks saddened him."

"I don't think many saw Cecil's sensitive side, Amy. I suppose in a way, that was quite a privilege."

"'My dear Amy,' the man said to me, taking my hand gently, 'it is obvious you are not long for this world. You are suffering, aren't you?'"

I acknowledged I was. Cecil then got right to the point. He asked me if I wished to end my suffering. I admitted readily that I did. Cecil then said that he knew just the man to entrust the necessary pharmaceutics to. I squeezed Cecil's hand in gratitude for his perspicacity and efficiency. But Cecil proved himself to be even more efficient still."

"How, Amy?"

"By saying what he said next. 'That,' Cecil said, 'is not the only reason you contacted me, I am sure, Amy. Getting poisons and physics out here in the country is no great challenge with witches and wise women around every corner, brewing herbs. You didn't get the number one political mind in Europe down here in the dead of night just to get you a cyanide tablet.'"

"Not the humblest of men, was he?" I said.

"Perhaps not, Dolly," Amy replied. "But the man nailed my other reason for requesting his services pretty much instantly."

"Cecil got the scoop in one fell swoop! What did he say to you about that, Amy?" I asked.

"He said, 'Amy, you want to politicize your death, don't you? You want to make it matter. You want to make it count. I can help you to do that, to make your death significant, important, and effective for England—and for the queen—as well as brief and painless for yourself. Leave it to me, Amy. All will be as smooth as silk, if you just await my directions and follow them to the letter when you receive them.'"

"Which you did, Amy?" I inquired.

"Which I did," she affirmed.

"Did you ever see Cecil again?" I asked.

"Yes, I did see Cecil again a few days later, when he returned to Cumnor Place to deliver instructions and supplies personally. He was reluctant to entrust the supplies to a messenger or to commit the instructions to paper. He did not tarry long. He brought with him only a small pouch of powder and a calendar of days."

"Cecil was a man who knew how to travel light," I commented. "I can guess what that pouch of powder was. But what was Cecil doing with a calendar?"

"He knew," Amy said, "that the feast of Harvest Home was imminent and that in the country, it was celebrated with a festival or fair. He brought the calendar so that I could circle for him the day of the fair that year."

"Which was September 8, 1560?" I conjectured.

"Yes, Dolly, and a Sunday it was too. Cecil told me to empty the house on that day; to send all the residents, staff, and servants to the fair in Abingdon."

"There were, were there not, two ladies who would not play ball when the time came? Mrs. Owen and Mrs. Oddingsells, if I remember correctly."

"You are correct as to their names but not as to their not playing ball. Their presence, you see, was part of the plan."

Chapter Forty-Four
The Pair Who Missed the Fair,
or Of Potions and Emotions

"So Cecil had you empty the house except for Mrs. Owen and Mrs. Oddingsells. What was their role in the plan, Amy?"

"Trusted henchmen."

"Henchwomen, surely."

"'Trusted' is the operative word for their role, Dolly. They were needed to carry out the part of the plan that followed my demise. They were both old and faithful servants, countrywomen plain and true, who could accept and work with the realities of the plan. I knew I needn't worry about flights of fancy or any suggestibility or sentimentality leading them from the course of their duties as my death transpired. Like me, they were patriots. They understood the importance of the operation."

"Tell on, Amy."

"Cecil instructed me to take the powder he'd provided as soon after the house was vacated as I could on the day of the fair. It was, of course, the poison that would bring relief to my ailing body. All I had to do was stir it into a beverage and swallow it. He assured me its effects would be instantaneous and that within moments, all would be over."

"And did it turn out that way for you?" I asked, holding my breath as I waited to hear her response. I genuinely liked Amy and hated to think that she might have suffered at the hands of the "sure physician, death."

"It was, as Cecil promised, as smooth as silk. A little burp, a little rumbling in the tummy, and a slight weakness in the knees are all I remember prior to moving toward the light that took me out of one world and into the next."

I do think there is mettle in death, which commits some loving act upon her, she hath such a celerity in dying, I quoted silently to myself, relieved that death—and Cecil—had dealt so gently with Amy.

"As advised by Cecil, I was alone in my chamber and behind a closed door at the time of my death. Oddingsells and Owen were instructed to come into the chamber about twenty minutes after I had closed myself into it with the potion. Both were warned that they would find me dead upon entering. They had functioned as my maids over the past few months; they knew the extent of my cancerous illness and of the suffering that immediate death would spare me from."

"It must have been difficult for you, Amy," I said, "to find the courage, all alone, to take that poison when the time came."

"The emptiness of Cumnor House that day made for a fine environment for prayer, Dolly. I went down on my knees and prayed for courage, deliverance, and the desired outcome shortly before I retired to my chamber and took the potion."

"Mrs. Oddingsells listened to you pray, or perhaps, overheard you praying, didn't she, Amy?"

"No, Dolly. She prayed with me. It did me good to have a trusted friend by my side during that final prayer."

I'd gotten it wrong again but was glad to hear that Amy had had some gal power behind her in her final extremity.

"I am remembering, Amy, what Mrs. Oddingsells said when she was questioned about your death: 'I myself have heard her pray to God to deliver her from desperation.' That would have about summed up what happened, in all honesty, without giving anything away. She also said that if you were judged evilly because of her words, she was sorry she had ever said them."

"That sounds like Mrs. Oddingsells. Honest, efficient, and with the kind of country sense and integrity needed to pull the wool over the eyes of the more sophisticated minds of the court without telling an outright lie. Just the person to do what had to be done after I did my part and dispatched myself to my maker in the empty house."

I awaited with interest the lowdown on the Owen and Oddingsells show. I fancied it would be something like *Mission Impossible*. But really, it was just a case of two fine country gals proving "by wit, worth in simplicity."

Chapter Forty-Five
Of Empty Houses That Haunt Absent Spouses

"Mrs. Owen was discreet but not as old and trusted a friend as Mrs. Oddingsells," Amy said, continuing her tale. "Owen kept lookout for the enterprise. We emphasized to her how important it was for security to be airtight for the sake of myself, queen, and country. Mrs. Owen loved to feel important. She was more than happy to patrol the perimeter of the house and to take action if anyone returned to the house at an inopportune moment. As I learned after I crossed the bar, none had."

"So, having prayed your last, you retired to your chamber with your pouch of powder. Mrs. Oddingsells waited faithfully without, and Mrs. Owen did security rounds. Twenty minutes later, they opened your door. What happened then?"

"I had, of course, expired. Their first task was to make sure that was the case. Once they had, each had to execute her part in the next step of the plan."

"Owen and Oddingsells must have been ladies of great presence of mind to execute the political plan of a William Cecil, hot on the heels of finding a beloved mistress dead. What is it they were to do?" I asked.

"Owen, having supported Oddingsells through the first sad moments of finding me dead, returned to patrol duty. She was to let no returning servants into the house while Mrs. Oddingsells executed her part of the plan."

"Which was?"

"Which was to steal out of the house and to a spot behind the stables; there, she would find two men waiting."

"Two men sent by Cecil?" I asked.

"Correct, Dolly. Oddingsells brought them into the house and then went to join Owen on perimeter rounds while the men performed their task."

"Which was—I presume—to turn Cumnor into a crime scene. Am I right?"

"Yes, Dolly, you are! Cecil charged the men to make my death look suspicious but not too suspicious; just suspicious enough to make my husband too hot a commodity for the queen to marry but not a hot enough commodity to land him on the block for murder."

"And so they arranged for you to be found at the bottom of that staircase, neck broken, wounds to the head, and with your bonnet, amazingly, not one whit disturbed."

"That was Oddingsells's doing," Amy said. "Once the two men had completed their work, they got the two women and explained to them what they would find. With that, the men were off. When Owen and Oddingsells went into the house and saw me, I was apparently in quite a state. Oddingsells told me, when later we met in the hereafter, that the sight of my remains so *en dishabille* was quite upsetting to her. So while she and Owen awaited the return of the household servants, they fixed my dress and my bonnet to their satisfaction. Such was not their intention, but as Oddingsells tells it, it had the effect of making my end all the more mysterious."

"And we know what happened when the servants came home and found you dead. The alarm was sounded, and the rest is history."

"Yes," Amy said. "Oddingsells and Owen kept their secrets, and the case unfolded as well as we could have hoped. My husband was implicated and discredited enough not to be able to marry the queen. But he did not suffer any official punishment for my death, of which he was, of course, entirely innocent."

It was thus that I learned one of history's most pitiful victims was really one of its unsung masterminds, having outsmarted the great Elizabeth I herself. I was, to say the least, impressed, and I let Amy know it.

"Your doings certainly put paid to the idea that country folk are behind the eight ball, Amy. There was nothing plodding and unassuming about you. Talk about taking the bull by the horns!"

"I don't know that I'd call Robert Dudley a bull," Douglas said, pulling her ear thoughtfully. "He could be a randy old goat when he wanted to be. And of course, that is where I came in."

Chapter Forty-Six
Assumption and Gumption,
or A Dame in the Patriot Game

Douglas Sheffield assumed center stage masterfully, metaphorically speaking. She pulled her chair over near the fire and settled herself into it so that the glow of its flames did the kindest of things to her already lovely features. I rose from my chair, walked over to the large bed, patted out a spot for myself, and perched on it comfortably, able to look Douglas right in the eye. Amy and Lettice, allowing for Douglas's histrionic tendency, remained in the background sans any apparent resentment.

"Let me guess, Douglas," I said. "History is well aware of your affair with Robert Dudley and the son you bore him. The two of you may or may not have surreptitiously married. The truth about that has never been definitively established because of your inability to furnish evidence of the marriage during proceedings to establish your son's legitimacy. Surely you did what any desperate woman who was anyone did back then; you summoned Cecil."

"Wrong on both counts, Dolly. I was never desperate, and I never had occasion to summon Cecil."

"So Cecil plays no part in your story, Douglas."

"Wrong again, Dolly! I may never have summoned William Cecil, Lord Burghley, to my assistance, but recognizing my resourcefulness, he most certainly summoned *me* to *his*!"

The idea of a man of William Cecil's gravitas summoning someone such as Douglas to his aid did not exactly "follow, as the night the day." You'd think I'd have been used to such disclosures at that point, but I have to confess I was surprised by what I'd just been told. Douglas had always seemed to me, based on her history, to be a lightweight. Of easy virtue, she was used by Robert Dudley, the queen's at-arm's-length lover, to fill a base need. She was then handily rejected for the next thing to come along. It was one of the oldest stories in the book, even as far back as the sixteenth century. And yet a man of Cecil's standing had sought the woman's assistance. I was not at all sure what to make of it, and I guess my quandary showed on my face.

"You look perplexed, Dolly," Douglas said, a bit saucily, I thought.

I did not want to betray to her my initial estimation of her being nothing but, shall we say, unstinting generosity.

"You must be a woman of unsuspected depth, Douglas, to have had the great William Cecil as a supplicant for your time and talents." I assumed I knew what talents Cecil might have had reason to tap her for, but did not let her know this, knowing how she felt about what happens when people assume.

"I knew what men wanted, and I knew how to deliver it," Douglas said, looking more like her relative, the lubricous Catherine Howard, every minute.

"Surely there were plenty of other women at the court with that kind of aptitude, Douglas. What was it that made Cecil draft *you* for a mission?"

"I was a Howard before my marriage, Dolly, and the Howards were connected to the Boleyn family and therefore to the queen. A good patriot and loyal subject uses her talents without reserve in the service of the greater good of the nation and the queen. And when said patriot is a relative of the reigning monarch, the streak of loyalty goes even deeper. Cecil knew that when he first contacted me in the early 1570s."

"That is around the time that Gilbert Talbot went on record saying you and your sister Frances set your caps for Robert Dudley, isn't it?"

"Talbot made that statement in 1573, I think. I started my job before that, though. I don't believe in lollygagging around, you see; I went straight to work on the task Cecil had given me."

Chapter Forty-Seven
Of Climacterics and Tricks

"So Cecil set you loose on an unsuspecting Robert Dudley, Douglas?"

"Correct at last, Dolly!"

"Were you to seduce him?"

"I already had, Dolly."

"Were you to marry him, then?"

"Sort of."

"How do you 'sort of' marry someone, Douglas? Isn't that like being a little bit pregnant?"

"I suppose you could put it that way, Dolly. But whatever way you put it, I succeeded at my goal. You are not the only one around here who knows how to accomplish a mission, you know."

"But Douglas—your escapade with Robert Dudley was like a train wreck in slow motion. The affair; the letter, telling you in humiliating terms that he will not marry you because of the queen; the money offered to you to back off of your claim that actually, the two of you *were* married; your failure to prove the marriage; the birth of a son of unconfirmed legitimacy; the humiliation of Dudley sodding off and marrying someone else. None of that has the mark of the dignified, puritanical, and practical William Cecil about it."

"It had the mark of the *desperate* William Cecil about it, though."

"Desperate? Why was Cecil desperate?"

"He was desperate for the same reason everyone else at court was; the queen's time of life."

I considered the combination of Elizabeth I's well-known volatility and the trepidations of perimenopause. Surely having hot flashes in full Renaissance kit, complete with farthingale, ruff, and floor length garments, would make the edgy Elizabeth even edgier.

"No wonder Cecil was desperate; a climacteric Elizabeth I!" I said.

"The queen was around forty by that time. It was now or never for her, if she was to ever marry and pop out an heir to the throne. You know how hell-bent on unquestionable, direct-line heirs the Tudors could be."

"I do, indeed! Elizabeth of York dying in a last-ditch effort to produce the desirable 'spare heir' for Henry VII; Henry VIII's high jinks when it came to siring a male child; poor Bloody Mary Tudor, with her late-in-life false pregnancies. They put the 'hell' in hell-bent; that is for sure."

"Well, Elizabeth was not immune from the pressure that kind of precedent creates, and the strain of it was starting to tell on her. And when something told on the queen, it goes without saying that it told on everyone around her."

"Considering the stakes in the dynastic game of the time, the ticking of Elizabeth's biological clock must have been downright audible at court. Of course, her vanity would make it unmentionable—like the proverbial elephant in the room that no one talks about. That can't have been easy for the folks at court."

"I don't know anything about elephants in rooms," Douglas said, "but you've got the ticking part spot-on, Dolly. A clock ticking its way down to the inescapable end was exactly what the queen's biological clock, as you call it, was like."

"Issues around Elizabeth's fertility were Cecil's nightmare for pretty much all his career. What made him so especially desperate about it at this particular juncture?" I asked.

"No one knew the queen like Cecil did, not even Robert Dudley. Cecil had picked up on a statement or two the queen had let drop. He had reason to fear she might resurrect the idea of marrying Dudley in the hopes of popping out an heir at the eleventh hour of her youth, so to speak. And a Dudley marriage and heir were the last things Cecil wanted."

"Then surely Cecil would have wanted you to undisputedly marry Robert Dudley rather than just have a baby by him! That would remove him from the marriage market, plain and simple!"

"My marrying him would have been nothing a divorce wouldn't remedy. And Cecil had reason to believe that the queen, with that ticking clock of hers, had become less concerned than was her previous wont regarding the niceties, or otherwise, of marrying a divorced man."

"Well, the illegitimate child you gave him shouldn't have been a barrier to Dudley's marrying the queen! Almost any man who was anybody had illegitimate children about in the Tudor courts."

"True, Dolly. And that is why a shadow marriage was the only solution. Cecil and I orchestrated it very carefully, and, if I may say so, successfully."

I was beginning to feel even sorrier than I already did for Robert Dudley. He and Cecil went down in history as male frenemies of sorts, but I'd had no idea of the circles the crafty Cecil had apparently run around the man. I settled in and listened attentively as Douglas, like a very pretty spider, spun her tale.

"Cecil got part of his plan from his escapade with Amy, although, of course, I had no way of knowing so at the time. You see, this plan, too, hinged on a potion."

"Cecil's apothecary must have been one busy man."

"He didn't use just any apothecary, you know. He knew that the man for the job would have to be able, beyond a shadow of a doubt, to keep the whole affair hush-hush. A man merely bribable with filthy lucre would not do at all. It needed a man of patriotic principles, a man who would go to the wall for the queen. And there was really only one such man with the requisite qualifications."

"And he was?"

"Doctor Dee."

"Of course! Who would he be but Doctor Dee?" I said, wondering why it had not occurred to me immediately that it must have been him. My mind went back to my last visit here and to some information I had received from Ann Boleyn. Cecil's doings and his calling upon Doctor Dee to assist him with them made all the sense in the world.

Doctor Dee was one of the most fascinating men of the Elizabethan era, a diarist whose "almanac," as he called it, put Pepys's diary in the shade. At least it did if you have a taste for the strange and wonderful. Dee was Queen Elizabeth's astrological adviser, selecting for her the most propitious of coronation days—given the way the reign turned out, a job well done, for sure. He also advised the queen as physician, scientist, and magician. Mathematics, hermetics, alchemy, and navigation were among Dee's strong suits. And lest you think Dee was one of those boring, nerdy, scientists, think again—he was not above a little wife swapping, at least when he thought that the angels had ordained it.

"What sort of potion did Dee concoct for you, Douglas?"

"The potion was not for me, Dolly. It was for Dudley."

"An aphrodisiac, perhaps, to facilitate your plan?" I cringed a little as I recollected some of the things the Elizabethans considered to have aphrodisiac qualities: sparrow brains, prunes, chicken tongue, ruff starch. And of course, the ubiquitous lizard, which might have been known as skinks for skanks.

"The potion was part aphrodisiac, although I thought that was just overkill, myself. I had complete confidence in my abilities on that score. Cecil said he didn't want to take any chances, though."

I admired Douglas's aplomb and faith in her charms and in fact agreed with her regarding the unlikelihood of her needing chemical assistance in the seduction department.

"So if the potion was only part unnecessary aphrodisiac—what was in the rest of it?"

"A sedative and an amnesiac," Douglas answered, "and a little something to dim the wits."

I looked at Douglas; she was making some clothing adjustments. She shrugged her shoulders, making the neckline of her gown go even farther off the shoulder than it had started out. She tugged at the waistline of her dress, ostensibly to straighten the girdle at her waist but effectually tugging her plunging neckline a little lower while taking a deep breath in and holding it for a bit.

I felt even sorrier now for the horned up and stupefied Robert Dudley; he must have been putty in Douglas's able hands once he'd quaffed that potion.

Chapter Forty-Eight
A Team on the Same Beam

"Let me see if I have this straight, Douglas. Cecil was all for capitalizing on your relationship with Robert Dudley. When you had made sufficient inroads in that direction to facilitate Cecil's plan, he provided you with a no-fail potion. How, when, and why, exactly, did you make use of it?"

"In the winter of 1573, my liaison with Dudley was moving along nicely. I pressured him to marry me, as directed by Cecil. Dudley, of course, refused to do so."

"A very lengthy letter Dudley wrote to you to that effect has gone down in history, Douglas. It is as pusillanimous as it is long, in my humble opinion. The letter states—eventually—that you can expect no more from him than the on-the-side affection you had thus far enjoyed. 'And therefore ye first, I must this conclude, that ye same I was at ye beginning the same I am still toward you, and to no other or further end can it be looked for.' And then he suggests that you marry elsewhere. Not the most sensitive of men, was he; veritably 'a flesh-monger, a fool, and a coward'!"

"He wasn't the most concise of men, either. Has that marathon epistle of his really survived the ages?"

I assured Douglas that it had. "Don't feel bad about it, Douglas. It makes him look at least as much a wanker as it makes you look a pitiful reject."

"I told you that he was all mouth and trousers, Dolly! I was pressuring him to marry me, but he had no way of knowing that marriage with him was actually the last thing I wanted. I *wanted* him to think me a pitiful reject. I wanted him to think that I had taken the slap in the face of that letter meekly, accepting it for what it was. That lulled him into a false sense of security and set the scene for my implementation of the plan. In terms of the drama, Dolly, that letter provided me with motive, in Dudley's eyes, for what followed."

"What did follow, Douglas?"

"I arranged a tryst with Dudley—yet another in a long line of them. He had no reason to believe that this one would be any different than the others. Once I'd arranged the tryst, I got word to Cecil to send along the potion he had procured from Dr. Dee. He sent the potion to me, along with five able-bodied assistants."

"Five able-bodied assistants? Really?"

"Well, four were able-bodied, and one was rather elderly and frail, but who's counting, Dolly?"

"I'd have thought you'd want to keep the number of participants in a plan such as this as low as possible. You know—to reduce the possibility of word leaking out. I'd have thought the fewer involved in it, the better."

"Well, four of the assistants were already well tried in such doings and found to be sterling and entirely dependable about keeping their tongues."

"Were they high-level members of Cecil's coterie? Or perhaps members of Walsingham's world-class espionage machine?"

"I don't know how high-level the two strongmen were, but they were definitely henchmen of Cecil's. Cecil trusted them to assist me with my undertaking, and I trusted his judgment. I later learned that they were the same two he had entrusted to do the hatchet work on the Amy Dudley crime scene. They'd let nary a peep about that escape their lips."

"What about the elderly and frail assistant?"

"Another henchman of Cecil's. He had to have been well over ninety, and he shook all over with the palsy. Nature would take her course with the poor man soon enough, Cecil said, so he wasn't unduly worried about the old man shooting off his mouth once the plan had been executed."

"Well, those are three of your five henchmen—who were the other two?"

"Mrs. Owen and Mrs. Oddingsells, the two ladies who, I later learned, had performed so handily in the Amy Dudley case. Cecil pressed them into duty to move my little caper forward. They were pleased to do their patriotic duty and were quite cheerful and efficient women."

"We know how to select and train hired help out in the country," Amy said with pride. "None of your court-style 'it's not what you know; it's who you know' business practices in my establishment. I hired entirely based on merit."

"And you didn't go wrong with those two!" Douglas said.

"Well, Douglas, there you were with two strong men, two smart women, and an old guy with one foot in the grave and the other on a banana peel. I can't wait to hear exactly what the six of you did to the unsuspecting Robert Dudley during that wintertime tryst!"

Mind you, reader, there was nothing black and white in the answer I received; it would eventually turn out to be strictly shades of Grey.

Chapter Forty-Nine
Quaff, Drop, and Roll Is the Goal

I noticed, as Douglas was winding her way through her tale, that a pitcher and goblets were placed on a dresser across the room from where I was seated. I'd gotten thirsty what with all that had gone on and helped myself to a drink of what turned out to be sweet wine. I poured libations likewise for my companions and raised my glass to them.

"Come, ladies, I hope we shall 'drink down all unkindness,'" I ventured.

My companions and I bent our elbows and did justice to the wine. As it was very sweet indeed for modern tastes, I sipped at it slowly. Douglas picked up the threads of her tale.

"Robert reported for our tryst as expected. My assistants waited without in nearby rooms. After Robert and I had, um, tarried a bit, he felt he had worked up a powerful thirst and reached out for a goblet of wine. He did not know, of course, that I had spiked it with Cecil's potion. I was worried to death that Robert might be onto our plan when he said, 'Tastes rather skinky!' after the first sip."

The thought made me choke a bit on the wine I had been heretofore happily sipping. I coughed and sputtered and thought for a moment that I might be sick to my stomach.

"Are you all right, Dolly?" asked Douglas, all solicitude.

"I'm fine, really, ladies. That wine just went straight down the wrong way."

Douglas chuckled. "Well, when Robert Dudley quaffed that fateful beverage on the night in question, the wine went down exactly the right way. 'Zooks! That wine's gone straight to my codpiece!' is what he said, as I recall."

"Nice to know that the stimulant part of Dee's potion was on target," I commented.

"It got Dudley gunning for a bull's-eye, that's for sure!" Douglas said. "He lunged for me, but after only a moment or two more, he went down as though someone had cut his strings. Robert Dudley was where he never thought he would be—at my feet and totally under my control, at least for a little while; certainly for long enough to execute the remainder of Cecil's plan."

"What was your next move, Douglas?"

"It was the dead of night, of course, and no one was up and about. I grabbed a candle, stepped over Dudley, and made my way to the door of the next room to the left, where Owen and Oddingsells were stationed. Upon signal from me, they went to get the three men who were a little farther down the hall and set them to their tasks. I returned to Dudley to keep watch until they joined me. Once they did, everything was in the hands of those two strong men."

"And by everything, you mean..."

"By everything, I mean Dudley, Dolly."

"You transferred watch of the unconscious Dudley over to the muscle?"

"No, Dolly. Dudley was literally in their hands. They hoisted him up and toted him off to the sweet little chapel that we had fitted up in the manor house at that time. They handled Dudley as easily as they would have a doll. I led the way with my candle. Owen and Oddingsells followed behind me, Owen bearing my jewel box and Oddingsells a tray with wine and goblets. We were within the chapel in a trice and found the old man waiting for us there. He'd lit candles, opened a Bible, and donned clerical attire. The musclemen dropped Dudley none too gently into the first pew. Poor Dudley! He was always so fussy about his appearance, you know, and that little journey through the house, and its abrupt ending, had played havoc with his attire and his coiffure."

"And his wardrobe malfunction was just the beginning of the havoc that was about to be wreaked upon poor Dudley, wasn't it, Douglas?"

Amy pursed her lips and whistled. "You can say that again!" said Lettice, chuckling as she poured us each another goblet of wine.

Chapter Fifty
Caught Red-Handed and Wedding-Banded

I'd heard about shotgun brides before of course, but a groom looking like he'd been shot out of a cannon was a first.

"Well, Douglas, it sounds like you had all the fixings to make a bride of yourself: chapel, preacher, groom unable to raise objections, and trusted witnesses. Did you rouse Dudley to semi-consciousness and go through some sort of wedding ceremony with him?"

"Not at all, Dolly! We did nothing of the kind. All that had to be done was for Owen to slip two rings that Cecil had provided onto my and Robert's fingers, and for Oddingsells to pour each of us a goblet of wine. The henchmen made themselves scarce. The rest of us sipped our wine as we waited for Dudley to wake up."

"What happened when he finally did?"

"Dudley awoke to find myself, what appeared to be a clergyman, and two female witnesses enjoying a nuptial toast. He didn't know what had hit him. He was congratulated on a marriage and had no way of being sure that one had—or had not—taken place."

"So Dudley had reason to think you and he might be married, but he couldn't be entirely sure."

"Exactly, Dolly."

"I think I see how it all worked out, Douglas. The situation put paid to any possibility of the queen marrying Dudley to pop out an heir at her eleventh ovulating hour. Had you married

Robert legitimately, a simple divorce would have freed up Dudley to marry Elizabeth and sire children by her. Your 'maybe' marriage was an even more powerful tool against a Dudley-Elizabeth union than an indisputable one would be. There would always be the specter, the possibility, that some proof of the marriage would materialize *after* Dudley and the queen had married. And if it did, the legitimacy of the Dudley-Elizabeth union, and any of the children it might produce, would be destroyed. Elizabeth would be humiliated and the country subjected to yet another round of the kind of inheritance issues that so plagued the earlier Tudors."

"Yes, indeed, Dolly! And if anyone was alive to the desirability of clear-cut legitimacy when it came to royal heirs, it was the queen, bastardized off and on throughout her childhood."

"So that is why you did not provide the details of the date of your wedding to Dudley or the name of the cleric who performed it when pressed to do so. It always seemed so inexplicable to me that a woman could forget details like that. It wasn't inexplicable at all. You were just playing possum, Douglas. Nothing flighty and stupid about you; history has got it all wrong!"

"I did feel bad, Dolly, not being able to help my son more during his legitimacy hearing," Douglas confessed.

"This would be little Robert Dudley, Jr. He grew up to be quite the explorer, eventually suing, after his daddy died, for the benefits of being Robert Dudley Sr.'s heir. You were called upon to give information that would confirm your marriage to Dudley, but of course you could not; there was no marriage to confirm."

"Correct, Dolly. After it was all over, Owen and Oddingsells went back to the country a bit better off financially than when they had left it. The henchmen, I am sure, were compensated as well, but I never personally saw or heard from them again after that night. Our antiquated cleric died a month or two after that night, a perfectly natural death; Cecil let me know when it happened just to put my mind at rest."

"Dudley must have been pretty well conned into thinking there was a marriage of some kind; he offered you seven hundred pounds a year to disavow it, Douglas."

"And I refused, of course, with tears and wounded dignity. I eventually, as you probably know, Dolly, married Sir Edward Stafford."

"You explained that little move by saying you feared for your life because of Robert's wanting to do away with you. With the Amy Dudley scandal behind him, that allegation would be especially compelling."

"Exactly, Dolly. And my husband, Edward, had not the same aliveness to legitimacy that Queen Elizabeth had. He was perfectly content to marry me under the circumstances of the shadow marriage. He appreciated all that I had to offer a man," Douglas said, shaking her décolletage a bit, possibly to proffer evidence.

"''Tis but the shadow of a wife you see, the name and not the thing,'" I mused to myself, as I pondered poor Dudley's undoing.

"My new husband, Stafford, and I were off to France shortly after our own marriage was celebrated, starting a new life in a new place, with the past behind us."

"I've read, Douglas, that you became great friends with Catherine de' Medici during your tenure in France. That always surprised me."

"Why, Dolly?"

"Well, Douglas—Catherine was such a serious woman, so devious and single-minded when it came to her political doings.

Not your girly type at all. At least, that is how history has painted her. I wouldn't have thought she'd be the type to appreciate your—errrr—persona."

"You might be surprised by exactly what Catherine appreciated, Dolly," said Douglas.

"You might be surprised by what there was to appreciate about Catherine de' Medici as well, Dolly," added Lettice.

"Or," said Amy, mysteriously, "you might be surprised by Catherine herself, Dolly."

As it turned out, all three ladies were correct.

Chapter Fifty-One
The Chi-Chi English Lady and Catherine de' Medici

Catherine de' Medici was the Italian daughter of one of the wealthiest merchant families in Europe, but she was not royalty. The French royal family married the young, homely, and gauche Catherine to their spare heir to the throne strictly for her money and then promptly proceeded to look down their noses at her. Her husband's having a cougar mistress, and her own infertility during the early years of her marriage, compounded Catherine de' Medici's dilemma. But after her father-in-law, brother-in-law, husband, and then eldest son died, she came into her own as the mama bear to her remaining sons, two of whom took their turns as kings of France.

Catherine's surviving sons were a motley crew, but Catherine ruled France through them until 1588, having the last laugh at her early-in-life detractors. They were hard times for France, with the Saint Bartholomew's Day massacre taking place, sadly, on Catherine's watch.

I shared my French historical reminiscences with my companions.

"Your description of Catherine de' Medici is quite accurate as far as it goes, Dolly," Douglas said. "She was also wily and dedicated without question to the fortunes of her family. Why, with those characteristics, should she be a surprising friend for me to have?"

I was squirming a bit with having to answer this in a PC fashion. I did not want to insult Douglas, but I honestly could not see her going toe-to-toe with a powerhouse like Catherine de' Medici. I think she sensed my dilemma, and it amused her. She was kind enough to not let me stew in my own juice for too long, though.

"What does history tell of my relationship with Catherine de' Medici, Dolly?" Douglas asked.

"It tells of your advising Catherine on running her court more along the lines of Elizabeth I's, to the improvement of privacy and quality of life there in general. She was said to have been most appreciative of your advice."

"She was appreciative of more than that, Dolly. You see, she was privy to the whole Robert Dudley shadow-marriage plot."

"Douglas! Why ever did you confide in Catherine de' Medici about that? She was easily the most Machiavellian figure of Elizabethan times, and that was up against some pretty stiff competition. What were you thinking about, Douglas, putting yourself in that woman's hands that way?"

"I was thinking about queen and country, Dolly! Elizabeth was my blood relation. I wanted what was best for her and for our country. I agreed with my husband and Cecil—not to mention Catherine de' Medici—that a marriage between Elizabeth and a member of the French royal house would be that best of all possible worlds for her."

"So you told Catherine your story, the truth of it, because—"

"Because it reassured her that Dudley, Earl of Leicester, as my maybe, maybe-not husband, was effectively out of the running as a husband for Elizabeth. That information rekindled her interest in pursuing a marriage between Elizabeth and one of her sons."

"Is that really what you wanted for your cousin—one of Catherine de' Medici's unprepossessing boys?"

"My cousin Elizabeth was royalty, and it would be best for her to wed to royalty. She deserved nothing less than the best the royal houses of Europe had to offer."

"Even if that 'best' was more than a little bit unsavory? History has not exactly been complimentary in describing the physical and mental attributes of Catherine's surviving sons."

"I did not make the rules of royal destiny, Dolly. I just wanted to see them pay off for my country and my queen."

"So Catherine de' Medici, knowing your story, became your friend. I always perceived Catherine as a terribly straitlaced person. I'd have thought your, um, backstory, from before your French ambassadress days, might have put her off."

"Not when she knew my modus operandi, Dolly. I had not played the codpiece game only for fun, and I made that clear to her. She approved of codpieces yielding as little pleasure as possible."

"That sounds like her."

"I also made clear to her the complete trust that Cecil had in me. She approved of women who could get into the political arena with men and be appreciated for their skills."

"That sounds like her too."

"I told her about the effectiveness with which I completed my mission and my dab hand with a potion. That really won her respect."

"I can readily understand that, Douglas, rumor having lain more than one covert poisoning at Catherine's door."

"And then I told Catherine de' Medici about my undying devotion to Elizabeth and how I would do anything to ensure that she lived out her royal destiny. Family first! Catherine practically had tears in her eyes once I'd finished sharing."

"I'm not surprised, Douglas, given the devotion with which Catherine machinated for the benefit of those sons of hers, no matter how awful they were and no matter how dirty the deed. She could have invented the term 'family first'!"

Douglas drained her goblet of the last of its wine and drew and let out a deep breath. "Well, yes, some of those tears were about family matters. Some, though, were tears of—I don't know—relief, I suppose, at finding a kindred spirit in a world where she had so few of those. Machinations are hard on a girl, Dolly. There is so much to keep in, such a feeling of isolation as one protects one's secrets. My confession emboldened Catherine to confess one of her own machinating secrets to me."

"From what I've read about Catherine de' Medici, Douglas, she did not hold ambition of 'so airy and light a quality that it is but a shadow's shadow.' I'm not surprised that her considerable machinating weighed heavy on her. She must have just about wanted to bust out with it all, at least once in a while."

"Especially," Douglas said, "when she could bust out with someone whose machinations, at least in one small arena, were so identical to her own. You see, neither one of us realized that we were playing such identical games with Robert Dudley's fate."

"Catherine de' Medici was machinating about Robert Dudley? Long-distance machinating, surely, since she never made her way to England from the court of France. However did she manage it? Did she, like the ladies of England, call upon Cecil for aid and assistance?"

"No, she did not, Dolly," said Lettice; "she called upon me."

Chapter Fifty-Two
Circumspection and Escaping Detection

This time, I headed over to the old wine pitcher myself and filled my goblet to the brim. Lettice Knollys in cahoots with Catherine de' Medici? I hoped the wine would stop my scholarly head from exploding as I awaited details.

Lettice looked happy enough to finally have center stage. She arose and went over to the fireplace, where the fire was burning quite low. She leaned her back carefully against the outer edge of the fireplace mantel and draped an arm over the shelf above the fireplace. Amy brought a goblet of wine to her, placing it on the mantel shelf.

The light from the fire did wonders for Lettice's outfit and complexion, touching both from just the right angles, with light here and shadow there. A 1930s film star or modern-day fashion model could not have been more aware of lighting effects than Lettice was. Once positioned and illuminated to her satisfaction, she quaffed a bit of wine and set about telling her tale.

"No one was more surprised than I was when a messenger surreptitiously appeared at my door bearing a message from the queen mother of France herself," Lettice said. "It was early in 1578. Rumors of my having a liaison with Robert Dudley had been bruited about in England for some time and had made their way to France."

"What was going on with you and Dudley at that point, Lettice?" I asked. "History has indeed been rife with rumors about the two of you."

That was putting it mildly. There were those who said that the two were an item while her husband, Walter Devereux, Viscount Hereford, was still alive. Said husband's death after a disastrous military foray was, according to some, actually death by poisoning, orchestrated by his wife and her lover. Hereford's dying words, lamenting the frailness of women, added fuel to the speculative fire. A year or two after her husband's death, Lettice married Dudley "in a loose gown," Elizabethan-speak for pregnant. The marriage was reported to be a happy one despite Elizabeth's banishing the bride from court.

"Dudley and I had always been attracted to each other," Lettice confessed. "Of course, he was the property of my cousin, the queen, and that kept me on the sunny side of circumspection. His treatment of my other relation, Douglas," she said, nodding toward that lady, "made me stay on the sunny side of it. I had no idea that Douglas was involved in any kind of plot. I saw her as the rest of the world did."

"You saw her as used, abused, and losed," I said. "But only in the eyes of the larger world, of course," I added, raising my glass to Douglas, who saluted me back in kind.

"Exactly, Dolly," Lettice went on. "I was interested in Dudley, perhaps even tempted by him, but prudent. I was a countess and the queen's cousin. I respected my dignity and my family obligations. I was not about to make an ass of myself with Dudley, as I thought Douglas had done. And then came that surprise, to say the least, from France."

With that, Lettice turned to the door, and my gaze automatically followed hers. A stout, somberly dressed woman had entered the room, seated herself beside the door, and helped herself to a goblet of wine. At least I assumed she had helped herself, as I'd certainly not served her and had not seen Amy, Douglas, or Lettice, who were all within my sight, give her any such assistance. A black cat sat contentedly in the stout lady's lap, although I did not notice him at first as he blended so completely into the inky blackness of the lady's ensemble. I knew I was in a world where my companions were shadows, but this woman was more shadowy than most if she'd been able to set herself up so comfortably in the room, undetected. Her ability to do so despite the ampleness of her proportions, and with a cat no less, added to the mystery of the whole thing.

"I like to think of myself as a surprise from Italy via my adopted country of France," the stout lady said, rising and moving toward me, much to the consternation of that black cat. "Allow me to introduce myself, Dolly: Catherine de' Medici, queen mother of France, at your service!"

Chapter Fifty-Three
By Dint of Madame Serpent

The only ladies I had met here on my last visit who were imported from outside of England were Mary, Queen of Scots, and her four Maries—brought to you by Scotland via France via Scotland—Katharine of Aragon, and Anne of Cleves.

"I am here, Dolly, for a brief, ad hoc visit only. I am not in residence like the rest of these fine ladies are," she said, bowing to Amy, Douglas, and Lettice. "Word does get around in the afterlife, you know. I was granted permission by the powers that be to visit for a spell while you were here, Dolly. I've wanted to meet you ever since hearing about your apologia for Henry VIII's six wives."

"I made no apologies on behalf of the six wives, Catherine. No excuses, either, and very short shrift to tragedy, if I do say so myself. My contribution to their history was just the facts, ma'am, from a new perspective. But anyway—what has that to do with you?"

I was talking, as I so often do, off the top of my head, and the words were hardly out of my mouth when I realized that I had, yet again, said something very silly indeed. Of course, resizing the facts had everything to do with Catherine de' Medici. When you are known, in your own life and times, as Madame Serpent, your reputation likely needs all the help it can get. Catherine de' Medici was, by this time, staring at me pointedly.

"All right, Catherine," I began. "So it's out there, in the afterlife, anyway, that I do reputation rehab for Rennies like nobody else does. And you need reputation rehab for Rennies like no one else does. I take it you wanted to meet me to see if I could do something for you along those lines?"

"Well, as you get to know me a little better, Dolly, who knows…" Catherine de' Medici's words trailed off as she headed for the wine setup. With her back to me, she refilled her own goblet and then filled another. Then she turned to face me.

"Drink, Dolly?" she said, proffering me a goblet. The goblets were starting to pile up, I noticed; the cleanup crew was going to think that we'd had one heck of a party.

"No thank you, Catherine; two is my limit for any good given night," I said, telling—as anyone who has partied with me would know—one whopper of a lie. I just did not have it in me to accept a drink on short notice from the woman who was known in her time as Europe's poisoner-in-chief.

Catherine sighed as she put down the glass. "Well, it's not as if I'm not used to this sort of thing," she said resignedly. Actually, she said it more than resignedly; she said it with misty eyes and a hint of a sniffle. I felt badly, especially when Amy Robsart grabbed the goblet and quaffed the wine with nary an ill effect. I reminded myself that Amy was already dead, and I was not, and felt a little less guilty.

"You will pardon me, Lettice, if I do not join you by the fireside," Catherine said, returning to her chair in the shadow of the door. "Firelight does not do the same things for my looks that it does for yours."

Even in the shadows in which she was hiding, a life of wear and tear was manifest in the face of Catherine de' Medici.

The woman had the Italianate complexion, thought sallow by the French court, which history has attributed to her. It actually looked quite dramatic against her hair, a warm brownish-black streaked with ribbons of white. Her eyes were large, piercing, and black. They suited the stout, dignified lady of a certain age that I saw before me. I could see, though, that in the face of a younger and slimmer Catherine, those same eyes might have indeed appeared the bulging, protuberant organs described by contemporaries. It took some nerve to look past her piercing gaze and into the eyes themselves. There was strength there, as well as pain; enough pain to have done an average person in, emotionally speaking.

There were no crow's-feet around Catherine's eyes, a gift, possibly, of her Mediterranean genes. There were no laugh lines about her lips either; not surprising, given that life had brought her precious little to laugh about. Around her neck and jaw, however, deep and numerous lines were visible in her skin. Here was indisputable evidence of a lifetime spent with jaw set firmly against the outside world. Words and the emotions that went with them, pent up in self-defense, had, like a junkie's needle, left tracks. I could see why letting it all go for a while with Douglas had been so comforting to Catherine.

"I must say, I approve of your dress sense," Catherine said to me, gesturing with her hands to include the totality of my outfit. "Those rich colors suit you. And the fluid lines of the ensemble—understated without being dull. They knew nothing about 'understated' at the French court, Dolly. There were times during my sojourn there when I felt, in my basic black, like the sole voice of fashion dignity at a circus of Harlequins! You, though, have taste that is in keeping with my own leanings.

Elegant indeed, my dear! With your looks and coloring, Dolly, you couldn't have made a better choice than to pay tribute to an Italian classic."

I like to return one compliment with another but was not sure what to say. Catherine's somber outfit was black mourning, which she is said to have worn in perpetuity after the death of her cheating husband. The potential comments struck me as a minefield, and I trod accordingly.

"Thank you, Catherine! Your approbation is a compliment indeed, coming from someone as cosmopolitan as you are, versed in the worlds of both Italian and French fashion."

Catherine smiled and bowed forward a bit in acknowledgment of my compliment. Her movement made the candlelight in the room play onto her bosom, and I noticed that she was wearing a remarkable brooch. It was a single diamond; even bigger, I thought, than the Mirror of Naples that I had seen adorning Mary Tudor on my last visit here. It was cut in an impressive fashion, with what seemed like literally dozens of individual reflective surfaces; I had never seen anything quite like it.

"Your brooch is breathtaking! The way it reflects the candlelight against the background of your gown! It looks like the aurora borealis shining in the night sky."

"Thank you, Dolly!" Catherine said. "Come and take a closer look at the brooch. It was known in my time as the Briolette of India."

I didn't have to be invited twice. As an antiquarian, I leaped at my only chance, probably, to see the oldest diamond known to man. The fact that it had also once been in the possession of the legendary Eleanor of Aquitaine only added to its fascination.

"I've read about this jewel and so appreciate the opportunity to inspect it close up!" I said. "I never realized a jewel could be cut with such precision as this one is. I guess you could say it is multifaceted—just like I believe you must be."

"Thank you, Dolly, for that compliment," Catherine said. "My detractors at the French court used to say that I had many faces—too many. It is nice to meet someone who knows the difference between two-facedness and multisidedness."

"Survival in the French politics of your day pretty much demanded multiple facets and diamond hardness, Catherine. Take Henry IV, for example—the man who assumed the leadership of France after your death. A Catholic turned Calvinist who turned coat and went Catholic again when the need arose—you know, the famous 'Paris is worth a mass.'"

"The man had a talent for insouciance. The French appreciate insouciance. Which is why, I suppose, they did not appreciate me," Catherine said. "Certainly, the man's demeanor allowed him to get away with a volte-face in a way that I could not."

"Henry IV is doing volte-faces to this day. During the French revolution, his remains were disinterred and his body separated from his head, which was lost to history until the twentieth century, when a mummified Renaissance head turned up. It was eventually but tentatively identified by forensic science as belonging to Henry IV. DNA evidence, however, has been interpreted both as supporting and disputing that the head is Henry's."

"What is DNA?" Catherine asked.

"Matter in human tissue by which, among other things, biological lineage can be indisputably traced."

"It's a good thing we didn't know about DNA in our day!" said Douglas with feeling. "There'd be more than one girl in an awful lot of trouble if we had."

Catherine took a more global view of the matter. "Royal houses might very well have toppled had we known about this DNA back in the day," she said, hugging her black cat. "The ramifications of such a thing are frightening."

"The thought of Ann Boleyn hearing you all talk about people playing fast and loose with a disembodied head is frightening as well!" said Lettice, peeking around the doorway just to make sure *la Boleyn* was not within hearing distance. "Can we change the subject, please, and get back to business?"

"Yes, of course; the business at hand; the heretofore unknown story of Lettice Devereaux and Catherine de' Medici, partners in crime. Bring it on, girls!" I said.

Chapter Fifty-Four
Solution Convolution

"It's quite a simple story, really; simpler than most of what I had to deal with in my political life," said Catherine. "I wanted one of my sons to marry Elizabeth I. Negotiations thus far had failed. I suspected that Dudley, the Earl of Leicester, was the fly in the ointment. I'd never met Elizabeth, but I know human nature. As long as her beloved Dudley was in with a chance, she would never marry someone else. At least, that is what I suspected. So I decided to do something to remove Dudley from the equation."

At the word "remove," I put my wine goblet down rather abruptly. It was reflexive; I just couldn't help it.

"No, Dolly, I did not attempt to—in fact did not even consider—poisoning the man. The chemical solution is the way out for the desperate or the politically nonacrobatic. I was neither, at any point in my career."

"I'm glad you've cleared that up for me," I said, taking a contented sip of wine from my goblet, as Catherine smiled.

"As I said, Dolly, I know human nature. Dudley and Elizabeth I were the same age in 1576: forty-three. It was late for Elizabeth to be having children. In fact, it was doubtful that she'd still be fertile at that point. Dudley had no children—at least no legitimate ones. And he came of a tribe that was invested in having the family name leave its mark on the world down through the generations."

"I remember," I said, "some of the lines from that interminable Dudley-Douglas letter—

> my brother you see long married and not like to have children, it resteth so now in myself…yet is there nothing in the world next that favour that I would not give to be in hope of leaving some children behind me, being now ye last of our house.

"Dudley seemed pretty clear," I continued, "about how important it was to him and his family for him to leave behind a legitimate heir."

"It was also pretty clear the type of woman Robert Dudley liked, if he liked his queen; elegant, intelligent, slender, and ginger," Catherine continued. "The queen's cousin, Lettice, was known to be just that type, and Dudley had already shown an interest in her. And in 1576, Lettice's husband very conveniently died."

"Not as a result of any chemistry on your part?" I asked, still unable to completely let go of the image of Catherine de' Medici as a "mother hourly coining plots."

"No, indeed, Dolly," Catherine said.

"And he did not die because of exertions on your part, Lettice, or on Dudley's?" I inquired of Lettice. "Rumors abounded at the time regarding the two of you doing your husband in. You know the sort of thing: 'foul whisperings abroad, murder most foul, unnatural deeds breeding unnatural troubles.'"

"I am innocent of the charge, Dolly, and so was Dudley. My husband died a natural death," Lettice said.

"So, with poor old Walter Deveraux out of the way—what happened next?" I asked.

"As I've said, it seemed to me that Dudley would want to leave his mark on the world, DNA-wise," said Catherine. "His family history certainly seemed to suggest such a penchant for posterity, as you point out, Dolly. Dudley would need a wife to do that, of course, since illegitimate children could not so easily inherit in our day," Catherine went on, bowing to Douglas.

"And Lettice—all elegance, intelligence, ginger, and slimness—was still young enough to be reliably fertile and was conveniently available for wifely duty. The ideal combination for the furtherance of your plan to get Dudley out of the way of your son's marriage to Elizabeth," I surmised.

"I opened up communications with Lettice as to my intentions," Catherine confirmed. "We corresponded for several months via messenger about her possible marriage to Dudley. I explained to her the reasons I thought that her queen's marriage to my son, the Duke of Anjou, would be politic for England and for Elizabeth herself. I explained to Lettice that by removing Dudley from Elizabeth's marital equation, she could do her cousin and her country a great service. I was also able to reassure her about the Douglas shadow marriage, based on what Douglas had told me about it. Unlike Elizabeth, Lettice knew she had nothing to worry about on that score, in terms of the legitimacy of any children she might have with Dudley."

"And how did you respond to that, Lettice?"

"Well, Catherine's politics struck me as spot-on, and my personal inclination toward Dudley made the proposition even more attractive. The problem was to get Dudley on board. I was unable to get him to take the marital plunge on my own. Ambition and affection for my cousin Elizabeth had too strong a hold on him; he knew the price he would pay in regard to both if we ever married. I informed Catherine of my quandary and awaited word from her. What I got was more than word; I got, in fact, the solution for the problem."

"Which was?" I asked.

"Well, I'm not sure what was in it, exactly, Dolly," Lettice said.

"Beg pardon?" I asked Lettice, a bit confused. "What answer had Catherine for your problem?"

"I told you, Dolly. A solution."

"Which was?" I asked again, getting a bit tired of going around in circles. "Catherine, if Lettice won't tell me what the solution was, will you?"

"I most certainly will not," Catherine said. "What happens at the apothecary's stays at the apothecary's."

"I thought you said chemical solutions were only for the desperate, Catherine," I said, putting my goblet down again.

"That is in regard to poison, Dolly. I would not reduce myself to that. But when it came to a potion that would make a man broody? Well, certainly, no harm in that."

"Can you make a man broody? I always thought that was more of a woman thing."

"With the right ingredients, almost anything is possible, Dolly."

I wondered what kind of ingredient would go into a broodiness potion for men. Fearing it had something to do with avian backsides and amphibian orifices, I decided not to inquire too closely about it. An unrelated question about potions did occur to me, though.

"Catherine, if you were proficient in chemistry of that kind, why didn't you brew up a potion for yourself—one that would have secured your husband's affections to you and away from his mistress?"

Catherine's hatred for her husband's longtime cougar mistress was the stuff of legend. I awaited her answer with interest.

"I wanted the man to love me, Dolly, of his own accord and for who I was. I wanted it to happen naturally. If it could not, so be it. His love would not have been worth the having if it was the result of necromancy. It was that simple."

I got a little teary thinking of the complex career of Catherine de' Medici, a woman who knew how to make things happen. The one simple thing she wanted was the love of her husband. She could have made that a reality but did not, in accordance with her personal guiding lights. My respect for the woman was growing, as was my affection.

"So, Catherine," I said, picking up the threads of the Dudley plot, "you forwarded a male broodiness potion across the sea and over to Lettice. I guess she will have to take the story from here."

Lettice happily took up the challenge. "Everything fell right into place once that potion arrived. It was in 1578. Once I'd gotten that stuff into Robert, I was amazed at the effect. He went from wanting to be Elizabeth's consort to wanting to be a paterfamilias in no time flat! He lost all fear of any repercussions from the Douglas Sheffield situation when it came to the legitimacy of any heirs of his—he went from cursing the situation to pooh-poohing it overnight!"

"A pooh-pooh from out of the blue," I said.

"Now that you mention it, the potion did have an azure cast," Catherine recollected.

"At any rate, once I'd administered it to him," Lettice continued, "we started sleeping together regularly, and a short time later, I was able to inform him of my pregnancy. There was no holding him back once he knew about it! He said he wanted to do the right thing by his child—he was convinced it would be a son—and by the family name, for posterity's sake. Since I knew he felt no such compunction when he was involved with Douglas, I had no doubt that it was the potion that had done the job. We were married that September, and as I am sure you know, Dolly, we eventually had a son. Sadly, the child did not survive to adulthood."

"'Out, out, brief candle,'" I said, thinking of the short lifespan of both Dudley's son, the touchingly nicknamed "Noble Imp," and poor Dudley's aspirations for posterity.

"And so ended Dudley's chances of seeing his DNA legitimately descend down through the ages," Catherine said, as if she could read my thoughts.

"The poor man!" I said. "I knew he was thwarted when it came to his relationship with his queen. Little did I know he was thwarted, not to mention made use of, in so many other ways as well."

"He played right into my hands; that much is for certain," Catherine said, taking the tale back again. "I sent my ambassador, Simier, to England in 1579 to open negotiations for marriage between Elizabeth and my son, the Duke of Anjou. The queen, not surprisingly, was still smarting from Dudley's defection. I've always thought that's why she made something of a fool of herself with Simier."

"History tells us," I said, "that there was quite the flirtation going on there. I guess I can see where that kind of action might have assuaged Elizabeth's wounded pride somewhat, in her own eyes, at least, if not in anyone else's."

"And of course, things only got hotter and heavier when my son arrived in England to personally press his suit with Elizabeth," Catherine said, looking quite the proud mama.

"The middle-aged Elizabeth is said to have gone quite overboard showing your much-younger son lots of love and affection," I recalled. "I guess maybe she thought she was rubbing things in Dudley's face a bit."

"Perhaps," said Lettice. "That is certainly what people at court were saying. At least, those who were brave enough to come visit me out in the country, whence my cousin Elizabeth had banished me after I married her darling Dudley."

"And unfortunately, Lettice, yours and Catherine's well-laid plot did not achieve its final end. For all her flirtations with Simier and the Duke of Anjou, no Franco-English marriage took place, even though negotiations went on for literally years and years."

"Yes, my cousin Elizabeth had, without knowing it, the last laugh. She was good at that sort of thing. As you will soon find out, I am sure, Dolly," said Lettice, as Blanche Parry crested the door.

"Elizabeth has sent me for you, Dolly; outfit reparations for her and her sister have been completed," she said.

Blanche gave Catherine a friendly pat on the arm and her cat a playful rub behind the ear, causing the animal to purr loudly. She then addressed Lettice, Douglas, and Amy. "The three of you, I am sure, have regaled and illumined Dolly with your very best," she said. "Well, you've entertained her very well anyway," she continued, "if the condition of the wine decanter and multiplicity of goblets about the place is any indication."

Lettice, Douglas, Amy, and I looked sheepish for a nanosecond or so until we saw the glimmer in Blanche's eye.

After a moment, we all relaxed into a companionable—and, for some of us, wine-enhanced—giggle.

"Well, now that Dolly has been so admirably turned out and fortified by our efforts," Blanche said, bowing to the ladies in the room, "it is time for her to move on to the more challenging part of her time here. Are you ready, Dolly? Is there anything you need to take with you to make you, or keep you, comfortable?"

"I can see why you were made chief gentlewoman of Queen Elizabeth's most honorable Privy Chamber, Blanche. I admire the way you look to the comfort of those around you and the way you rally and enliven the troops. What you have just said, though, has me worried a bit."

"Whatever are you worried about, Dolly?"

"The 'take with me' part. Am I going somewhere? On my last visit here, I never left this room, you know."

"In fact, I did know that, and so did my mistress. She has a highly developed—what shall I call it?—sense of theater, you know."

"That would be the term for it," Catherine confirmed.

"Well, that being the case, Dolly, my mistress thought you might enjoy meeting with her and her entourage in a new and different setting—a setting to do her justice. A setting that has benefited from my mistress's considerable decorating sense, the hard work of the staff here, and the carte blanche the Almighty gave us as to works of art when we were furnishing the place."

A million questions sprang to mind, but the best I could do was to compress them into a monosyllable with a heartfelt "huh?"

"*Per farla breve*," said Blanche, showing off her Italian as she smiled at Catherine de' Medici, "we have been instructed to take you to the portrait gallery, Dolly. And it does not do to keep Elizabeth waiting. *Andiamo!*"

Chapter Fifty-Five
A Gal in a Gallery

I followed Blanche along a barren corridor with stone walls relieved only by the odd candle sconce. That monochrome stroll only heightened the impact of what I saw when we reached our destination and entered the portrait gallery. I actually staggered back in awe at what I saw. Fortunately I entered the room ahead of my companion, who was able to right me and get me steady on my feet again.

I think the glare was the first thing that sent me reeling backward. Candelabra were everywhere, and very strategically placed, as were the mirrors that reflected the glow of the candles. The second thing that knocked me off my feet was the sheer amount of color in the room. This large, round room most certainly lived up to its reputation. The walls were studded, at eye level and slightly below and above it, with portraits, all of the Renaissance era. "Studded" is actually probably too weak a word; "packed" would be more accurate.

There was no one else in the room yet save Blanche and me. There were, however, seven chairs arranged in a semicircle, facing a single chair at a distance of a few feet. The proxemics of the room brought me back to my first visit here and my interview with the six wives of Henry VIII; the chairs had been similarly arranged on that occasion. The room was also amply furnished with cushions and contained several salvers set up with pitchers—of wine, I supposed—and goblets.

"You may be seated while you await Elizabeth, Dolly," Blanche said, motioning me to what I already knew was to be my seat.

"Thank you, Blanche, but if it is all right with you, I would rather browse the portraiture a bit." It seemed like most of the prominent folk of the Tudor era were represented, but the preponderance of the portraits were of Elizabeth I in various regalia. I pondered for a moment whether it was a blessing or a curse for the world at large that the woman had missed the selfie era by several centuries.

I was roused from my reverie by a familiar voice from behind me.

"My portraitists did me proud, didn't they, Dolly?"

"Elizabeth!" I said, turning to see that my old friend, the Virgin Queen herself, had entered the ring.

I had learned during my last visit here that the resident ladies could present themselves to me as they had looked at any age; the choice was theirs. I had interacted back then with both Elizabeth the young princess and Elizabeth in a somewhat blowsy middle age. The Elizabeth I that I saw today was the woman in her prime. She was grown out of teenage skinniness but was far from the slackening and thickening of late middle life. Tall, stately, slender, but with feminine curves in evidence, she looked lovely. Her eyes had not quite lost all the restlessness of adolescence.

We hugged as old friends do when they meet again.

"I do admire your outfit, Dolly!" Elizabeth began. "An unusual choice, to be sure, but it suits you right down to the ground."

"And I am in awe of your outfit, Elizabeth. To be perfectly honest, I wouldn't have thought a gal of your strawberry blondness could get away with wearing such a rich red, but I stand corrected. You've captured what makes an old-fashioned Christmas both warm and elegant with your ensemble. I recognize it from the *Hampden Portrait*, I think."

"Well, Dolly, I see you've not lost your penchant for putting your foot in your mouth; most would not point out to a queen regnant that she has been caught wearing the same outfit twice."

"Yes, but what an outfit! The red velvet puts me in mind of the outfit your grandmother, Elizabeth of York, was wearing when I met her. You've definitely taken red velvet a step further, though, with the gold-and-white embroidery. I like that it is simple and understated stitching; it lets the full impact of that red glow through. The golden hue of your ruff continues the theme beautifully and makes the perfect frame for that burnished red-gold hair of yours. And the touches of green on the flora on your hat and flower brooch; genius!"

My assessment of her couture seemed to assuage Elizabeth's pique. She went from offended fashionista to woman-in-charge in an instant, as she addressed herself to Blanche Parry.

"Blanche, you may leave us now, and tell the others to come in here and take their seats in the semicircle. The business of the evening is about to begin in earnest."

Chapter Fifty-Six
Genial Genealogy

As promised, the seven chairs opposite me were occupied in good order. Elizabeth herself, not surprisingly, took the center seat.

The two ladies who occupied the seats immediately to either side of her were women I had met on my last visit here: Jane Grey, the Nine Days Queen; and Mary Tudor, aka Mary I or Bloody Mary. Another old friend, the one and only Mary, Queen of Scots, graciously deferred sitting until the remaining three ladies who had joined us had seated themselves. I'd not met any of those three on my last visit here. They all had a Tudor look to them; I wondered which members of the family they were. My curiosity was soon satisfied.

"Dolly," said Jane Grey, rising and gesturing to two of the ladies, "allow me to introduce my sisters, Mary and Catherine."

I did not need to ask Jane which was which; history has handed down descriptions that our meeting proved quite accurate. The tiny little gal with marked scoliosis was no doubt Mary. The woman next to her, who might have been called the flower of her family back in the day when such sibling rating was permissible, I took to be Catherine.

"And allow me, Dolly," said Mary, Queen of Scots, following suit and gesturing to the remaining unidentified lady, "to introduce my aunt and mother-in-law, Margaret Douglas, Countess of Lennox."

"Allow me to recap the relationships of my old and new acquaintances now present from the starting point of their relationship to Henry VIII and his progeny."

"As you wish," Elizabeth said graciously.

"I have Henry's two daughters, Elizabeth and Mary."

"Your hostesses, if you will," Elizabeth said.

"Likewise," I continued, "I have their cousin, Margaret Douglas, the daughter of Henry's eldest sister, Margaret Tudor. And, from this same elder-sister line of descent, Mary, Queen of Scots."

"Correct."

"And via Henry's younger sister, Mary, we have the Grey girls: Jane, Mary, and Catherine."

"Our cousins, as we like to think of them," said Elizabeth, as her sister Mary Tudor nodded agreement.

"Of course," I pointed out to Elizabeth, "Mary, Queen of Scots, Jane Grey, and Jane's sisters are not your direct cousins; they are cousins once removed."

"Dolly, really!" said Mary, Queen of Scots. "Execution awareness, if you please!"

"Hear, hear!" said Jane Grey.

Leave it to me, I thought, to start off on the wrong foot in such a big way with two women who had been executed at the orders of Elizabeth and Mary Tudor, respectively. A diversionary tactic was well in order.

"Well, the Tudor gang's all here, at least in latter-generation distaff terms, isn't it?" I asked Jane.

"Among those missing tonight are my mother, Frances Brandon; my aunt, Eleanor Brandon; and Eleanor's daughter, Margaret Clifford."

"Eleanor and Frances were the daughters of Henry VIII's younger sister, Mary Tudor Brandon," I confirmed.

"Exactly, Dolly. None of these women enter directly into the history you are about to be told," Jane said authoritatively.

"Yes, Auntie Eleanor and her daughter were a couple of bores compared to the rest of us," Catherine Grey offered.

"And as for our mother," Mary Grey piped in with spirit, "the less we see of her, the better we like it."

"Amen to that!" seconded Jane Grey.

While Eleanor Brandon and her line pretty much faded from the pages of history, Frances Brandon made a place for herself among its footnotes as the mother of the Grey sisters. Having this historical light shone upon her, however, illuminated some rather unpleasant aspects of her character (e.g., high-handedness, a bent for scheming, and not being above using physical abuse with her children). Frances, like all the Tudors, has had her apologists down through the years. The last two comments from her daughters, however, seemed to confirm that the traditional view of the woman was spot-on.

"Rumors about your mother's heavy hand with you have made their way down through posterity, Jane. All those 'pinches, nips and bobs'! I can't say that your comment about your mother today surprises me."

"It was Mother's nature, I suppose, to be bad-tempered," Jane said, "although I don't know where she got it from. I never met my grandmother, Mary Tudor, but I have been told she had a rather docile temperament."

"I don't know where that temperament came from in the line of our Tudor forebears, but Frances was not the only one in the family to inherit it," Margaret added. "My mother, Margaret Tudor, certainly had her share of difficult temperament."

"So I recall," I said, harking my mind back to my meeting with that lady on my last visit here.

"Yes, and thereby hangs a tale, quite literally," commented Elizabeth. "Margaret, you shall start things off by elaborating on the statement that you just made."

Margaret Douglas appeared to be in late middle age. She was known as the beauty of the Tudor court in her heyday, and one could still see the vestiges of pretty, red-gold hair among silvery strands and of a winning smile within the laugh lines. Like her great-grandmother, Margaret Beaufort, she favored rather severe dress, and black at that. She took full honors for having the smallest ruff in the room.

"It will be my pleasure to commence," she said. "How exciting to be the one to begin our story!"

I wondered silently about the pronoun "our," as Margaret settled in to speak her piece.

Chapter Fifty-Seven
One Tear More or Less and the Devonshire MS

"You are familiar, of course, with my mother's story, Dolly," Margaret began.

"Yes, indeedy!" I affirmed. "Margaret Tudor started off well enough as an English Rose making a successful marriage into Scottish royalty. It all went downhill with the death of her first husband, King James IV of Scotland. She made two politically and personally disastrous marriages after that. She managed to gain the upper hand politically at times and then would be ousted from power as a result of her own bad choices. She was downright pathetic when pleading with her brother, Henry VIII, for resources after her own had been plundered by her husbands."

"My mother was a loving parent, Dolly; let us not judge her harshly on that account, at least," Margaret said.

"I'm not surprised to hear it," I said, remembering the glimpses I'd had into the emotional nature of Margaret Tudor. "She seemed to me, when I met her, one of those ladies who could love well even if not too wisely."

"Yes, but Mother's lack of judgment made my life as her daughter something of a trial," Margaret confessed. "There were her skids into and out of power as the guardian of the young King James V of Scotland, who was her son by her first marriage. There was Mother trying desperately to keep custody of the boy and not let him fall into the hands of her second husband, my own father, Archibald Douglas, Earl of Angus. My mother actually fired cannons at my father in her efforts!"

"That's domestic violence and then some. You poor thing!" I said to Margaret, who continued her tale of family dysfunction.

"I think the worst was my half brother, James, king of Scotland, elevating my mother's motley third husband, Henry Stewart, to the earldom of Methven and then allying himself with that misguided couple. Insanity!"

"It's wonderful how you managed to crystallize the Scottish politics of your day into one word," I said.

"English politics was no maypole dance either," Margaret said. "Neither was my mother's status as a welfare case when she eventually made her way to the court of my uncle—Henry VIII—in England. It wasn't easy living with my mother and the fallout that surrounded her, I can tell you."

I hated to see Mama thrown under the bus that way.

"What you say is true of course, Margaret, and I can only imagine what that was like for you, when you were young. I can't help but recollect, though, what I know of Scottish Renaissance history. All the chaos and infighting of the clan system; bloodshed and murder; religious division; the quixotic battles fought, and for the most part lost, with England. More savvy politicians than your mother were done in by the Scottish politics of the day."

"As an older woman, I learned to understand that," Margaret said, walking over to a portrait of Henry, Lord Darnley, and looking at it admiringly. "Marrying my oldest son, Lord Darnley, to Mary, Queen of Scots, made me understand all too clearly the quagmire one could get in when love, familial loyalties, and Scottish politics mixed. Such," she said, looking like my friend Marge did when she talked about either of her sons, "a promising boy!"

"And such a sad end," I added. Said Lord Darnley met his death at a very young age in the contemporary equivalent of his boxers, in the courtyard of a building that had been blown up to kill him. When he managed to survive the blast, his enemies resorted to strangling him. Darnley had not been much of a man, as his wife, Mary, Queen of Scots, could attest. Nevertheless, it saddened me to think that his mother, the lady before me, had to come to an understanding of her own mother's troubles in such a traumatic way.

"You know our history, Dolly, so you know that as a young woman living at the English court, I reacted to the chaos in my family life by acting out myself. First it was with Lord Thomas Howard, to whom, against all the rules set out for royalty, I became secretly engaged."

"Just your luck that he was Ann Boleyn's uncle and that the news of your relationship with him broke *after* Henry VIII had gone sour on Ann."

"Yes, Thomas and I were both imprisoned; I, unlike Thomas, eventually emerged."

Margaret wiped away a single tear, as she remembered her lost love. As I recollected the story, though, there was one more lost love to go. After a moment, Margaret continued her story.

"In 1540, Dolly, I fell in love unwisely once again; it was as if I were modeling my mother. The object of my affection this time was Sir Charles Howard."

"He was the brother of Catherine Howard, Henry VIII's fifth wife, wasn't he?" I asked, pondering, as I had on my last visit here, the Tudor predilection for members of the Boleyn-Howard clan.

"Yes, and of course, the relationship did not endure," Margaret said, again wiping a single tear.

"Your eventual marriage, though, is said to have been a success," I reminded Margaret, hoping to give the conversation some positive tone. "The Earl of Lennox, of course."

"He was the best of husbands, if not the love of my life," said Margaret. "And he, too, knew about a chaotic youth; his father was killed in one of those interminable Scottish power struggles, and he had lived in exile in England. Being close to the Scottish throne by birth himself, he understood the tempestuousness of royal life. What he did not personally experience, though, was the kind of chaos a rampant mother can cause. Nor had he been tragically crossed in love as I had been. Much as he commiserated with me, he could not empathize with me effectively on either score. And he *so* wanted to ease my distress, to help me in some way. He loved me very much, you know," Margaret said, smiling, while wiping away yet another single tear.

Those single tears of Margaret's, evidence of both strong emotion and Herculean self-control, were more affecting than any more copious or obvious waterworks would have been. Here was a woman we might in modern times describe as intense, or perhaps complicated. In a Tudor world where men did not always appreciate these characteristics, I was glad to know that Margaret had bagged a winner for a husband after all her trials.

"Your Earl of Lennox must have been a fine man," I said, a rather more conventional comment than I like to make, but Margaret did not seem to mind.

"My husband *was* a fine man, and a wise one as well, Dolly. He eventually came up with an excellent suggestion for helping me to cope with all my life's tragedy and trauma."

"Well, since they didn't have therapy in your day, I'm not sure what he could have come up with—prayer, maybe?"

"No, Dolly. He suggested that I consult a friend—a particular woman friend. And I did so. That woman friend suggested that I vent my feelings in writing."

"What an excellent suggestion! The woman was certainly ahead of her time. In our day, journaling is offered as a way to cope with pretty much any of life's difficulties; a book with a pretty cover and plenty of blank pages, a decorative pen, a glass of wine, and your troubles are over. I am not much of one for it myself, but perhaps you found it therapeutic, Margaret."

"I am not much of one for keeping a diary either, Dolly. Even if I were, it would have been far too risky an undertaking for someone in my position at court."

"Well, Margaret, I know you were a creative writer, if not a diarist; you were a contributor the *Devonshire* manuscript, were you not?"

"I am flattered, Dolly, that you recall that part of my story," Margaret said, beaming not a little bit. A look of pleasure, such as the one my artistic reference brought to her features, definitely did something for the woman's face. A little softness, a little glow, and a bit of extra confidence made all the difference. I could see why those lusty Howard boys had fallen in love with the young Margaret.

"The *Devonshire* manuscript," I reminded myself aloud, "was a catchall of random but important early Renaissance writing and included most famously some of the works of the poet Thomas Wyatt. The story goes that it was passed from hand to hand at the Tudor court, giving the unsung talents who lived there an opportunity to try their poetic hands as well."

"That is correct, Dolly."

"Madge Shelton, one of Henry VIII's mistresses, was said to have been on Team Devonshire. Was she?" I asked Margaret.

"She was," Margaret confirmed.

"They say Ann Boleyn may have contributed to the manuscript as well. I have to know—did she?"

"You've met her," said Mary Tudor, from across the room. "Do you really think Ann Boleyn would have passed up an opportunity to put her oar in, when one came along?"

Knowing Ann Boleyn as I did, I took this to be a yes on the *Devonshire* question. Elizabeth gave her older sibling a sisterly noogie on the shoulder but made no comment. I directed the conversation back to Margaret Douglas.

"Your own addition to the *Devonshire* manuscript was some love poetry, as I recall, Margaret."

"It isn't entirely accurate for me to use the words 'my own' in reference to the work; I had a co-contributor, you know."

"You did indeed have a literary partner for your contributions, Margaret. It was your lover—your first love—Thomas Howard."

"Thomas and I wrote our parts of the manuscript as our romance unfolded, from its dreamy beginnings to its tragic end."

"It was in the form of a sort of exchange between the two of you—love poetry and a riff on some Chaucer, wasn't it?"

"Yes, Dolly. And my memories of that joint literary endeavor informed the first of the therapeutic writings I undertook at the behest of that sagacious female friend my husband advised me to consult."

"Who was this wise, advising chum of yours?" I asked.

"Catherine Willoughby," Margaret replied. "She and I were such great friends, and when it came to my writing, her advice proved spot-on! I knew it from the relief I began to experience almost as soon as I put pen to paper on my first clandestine work. How right she was when she said, 'Let it all go!'"

My gratification at this revelation was considerable; I had quite an interest in Catherine Willoughby, even though the two of us had never met in this place.

Chapter Fifty-Eight
On Sorrowing and Borrowing

"Why was your work clandestine, Margaret?" I asked. "You weren't afraid to come out of the closet with your love poetry."

"Poetry, in our time, was considered a genteel undertaking and not unsuitable for royalty. The writing of common plays most definitely would not have been considered *comme il faut* for a lady of royal blood."

"Theatrical waters at that juncture were muddy indeed. Biblical and historical pageants and allegorical morality plays were giving way to spins on classical dramas with provocative themes, farce, and elements of the budding *commedia dell'arte*. Not exactly the pool a delicately reared lady should be seen dipping her literary toe into, I suppose."

"I think it was just that crossroads quality, the idea of so much change and possibility in the theater, that made the idea of being part of it, even secretly, so irresistible."

Margaret's companions nodded silently in acknowledgment of the importance of keeping up appearances and the lure of Tudor-era dramaturgy.

"So, Margaret, you wrote a play, based on the Chaucer that you and Thomas Howard bandied about when you were lovers under the gun. Tell me more about it."

"My play dealt on one level with the truncated nature of my and Thomas's relationship; a brief period of idyllic ecstasy and a night of love, followed by inevitable separation, driven by political and familial conflict."

"And on what other levels did your play operate, Margaret?"

"Thomas and I were both imprisoned because of our romance and engagement. I knew that I, as the king's niece and favorite, would eventually be released. There came a point when we both realized, though, that Thomas would die in prison. He managed to communicate with me while he was incarcerated. He said he was resigned to dying for the sake of our love, but that it galled him to think that, eventually, I might move on with my life and find another love when he was out of the picture."

"How did you feel about this selective selflessness of your beloved?"

"In a word, Dolly, *guilty*—I felt guilty. Much as I loved him, I knew he was right; eventually, I would marry someone else. I was young and of the highest rank at court; my marrying—and marrying well, eventually—was inevitable. Time and maturity helped me to see, in my golden years, that this was simply the natural course of things. But at the time of my and Thomas's tragedy, and for some time after, it felt like perfidy, plain and simple, that my love and my heart would go on."

"So, Margaret, you worked out your feelings of guilt in your play?"

"Yes, I did. And I threw some politics and martial exploits into the play too, for good measure. I had seen the chaos that both could create, and I wanted to try to capture the futility of it all."

"Sounds like you had a lot going on in this work of yours, Margaret: love, sex, politics, futility, and guilt, not to mention the Chaucer. Which of Chaucer's works inspired you?"

"*Troilus and Criseyde*," Margaret replied. "And this was not the only instance of my weaving a beloved author's material into a work of my own. I followed my first romantic play with a second, and this time, I worked in some references to Dante's *Inferno*."

"I guess you don't hold with the conventional wisdom of 'neither a borrower nor a lender be,' do you?"

"I'm sure both Chaucer and Dante would have been honored to have their talents tapped by a royal personage," said Margaret, bringing all her full regal mien to bear. Elizabeth and Mary Tudor nodded approvingly, and Mary, Queen of Scots, gave a robust and vaguely Scots-burred "Hear, hear."

"Well—um—yes," I said, duly chastened. "What was your second romantic play about, Margaret?"

"It was a tale of young, star-crossed lovers, passionately attracted to each other from their earliest encounters. Lovers kept apart by family loyalties and politics. Imagine it, Dolly; a man dies, thanks to his beloved's relatives and to his own lack of judgment; a woman, unable to bear it all, ends her own life. In conclusion, some corrective recapitulation, as the subject families learn how to better get along."

"That doesn't sound much like Dante's *Inferno* to me," I said, recalling the tenor of that primordial heaven-and-hell epic.

I borrowed the names of my protagonists from Dante," Margaret explained; "the Montagues and the Capulets."

"Just-like-Romeo-and-Juliet," I sang, doing the twist to my very respectable cover of the 1950s doo-wop hit by the Reflections. The twist was an immediate hit with all the ladies present; as we danced together, I felt that we had, in a way, become closer, like girls at a sleepover. A DVD viewing of *Dirty Dancing* would have cemented our newfound unity even further, but you can't have everything.

"Dolly," Margaret said, gamely dancing along with us all, "my second play *was Romeo and Juliet.*"

Chapter Fifty-Nine
Star-Crossed and Pillow Tossed

I felt as star-crossed as those famous lovers for a moment; the shock made me produce a most unladylike sputter.

"*You* wrote *Romeo and Juliet*, Margaret? *You?* Not Shakespeare? *You?*"

"Yes, Dolly, *me*, who better than me to write about star-crossed love?"

Mary, Queen of Scots, Catherine Grey, and Mary Grey all raised their hands and looked pointedly at Margaret.

"Point taken," Margaret admitted. "Still, there is no denying that I was crossed in love not once but twice. I saw internecine familial strife cause the rupture of my first romance and the death of my first love. Getting all the emotion of that out of me and onto paper was marvelously unburdening. And I flatter myself that I made more than one person who saw *Romeo and Juliet* think twice about what can happen when one interferes with young love."

"No doubt you did," I conceded. "Leonard Bernstein, Stephen Sondheim, and Jerome Robbins, to name three."

"Fathers who disapproved of their daughters' lovers?" Margaret asked.

"No, Margaret; men who set *Romeo and Juliet* quite memorably to song and dance. Think of them as Team *West Side Story*."

"How charming!" Margaret said, after I had I sung a few bars of, and did a little dance to, a medley of "I Feel Pretty", "Tonight", and "Maria".

"Thank you, Margaret. But I am still unable to quite take this all in, I must admit. Just to confirm; you *are* telling me that Shakespeare did not write *Romeo and Juliet*—and that *you* did?"

"Yes, Dolly, dear; I assure you that it is true. My cousin, Elizabeth, will vouch for me, I am sure," Margaret said, turning to the redheaded menace in question.

Elizabeth nodded slowly and with gravity. "What my cousin says is true, Dolly."

The ever-practical Jane Grey saw me swaying a bit from shock; in fact, I was even starting to slide down in my chair.

"Catherine! Mary!" Jane called to her sisters, "bring some cushions for Dolly and Margaret to sit on. I think it might be best if Dolly remains at floor level, at least for the immediate future."

Jane's no-nonsense and practical side tickled me, reminding me of my dear and unflappable cousin Jean. Catherine and Mary, scrambling around for the cushions, made for a much less methodical picture. They looked, in fact, like Merrie and Katie, blundering around our college department. I had seen them literally run into each other as they dashed about the office in their efforts to complete a project on time. Mary and Catherine Grey did the same thing, their vision obscured by the armloads of cushions they were carrying. I admired, as I watched their farthingales sway at the impact, how they were able to stay upright after the collision.

I recalled that the ladies of the Renaissance often sat on cushions on the floor as a way to accommodate their farthingales most easily when in repose. That thought made the cushions seem like a good idea, for comfort's sake.

I realized a little later that Jane was thinking more about my safety than my comfort when she requisitioned the cushions. After all, if one is going to lose one's equipoise, one won't have so far to fall if one is already on the floor.

Chapter Sixty
Termagants and a Song and Dance

"Let me get this straight," I said, settled onto my cushion in ladylike fashion after a brief tutorial in farthingale management from Jane. "Your second romance, Margaret, was *Romeo and Juliet*. I guess I'd best ask the name of your first play—the one with the Chaucer connection."

"My first play was named after its protagonists, *Troilus and Cressida*, Dolly."

"As in Shakespeare's *Troilus and Cressida?*" I asked.

"Well, yes and no, Dolly," Margaret said. "I know what you mean when you say Shakespeare's, but really, it was mine."

My mind was reeling with the knowledge that Margaret Douglas, who coulda been a contender for the English throne, had actually written two of Shakespeare's plays. If Team *West Side Story* had written a tune called *Well, I'll Be Dipped*, I'd have been singing it.

Jane handed me a much-needed glass of wine, and I chugged it down with much less ladylike finesse than I'd had when handling my farthingale.

Elizabeth rose and walked over to where Margaret and I were sitting on the floor. She looked down at my empty wine glass and made a *tsk-tsk* sound.

"Guess I am setting myself up for a heck of a hangover when I get back to the real world," I said.

"Not to worry, Dolly," Margaret said. "The effects of libations quaffed in this world do not carry through to your world."

"That's a relief," I said.

"I should think so," Elizabeth said, turning her attention to my pillow pal, Margaret.

"Margaret," Elizabeth said to her cousin, "tell Dolly about your other three plays now. The comedy first, if you will. You know it is a personal favorite of mine."

I had a million questions just from the announcement about the first two plays but swallowed them down and waited for Margaret to continue. Elizabeth's commanding demeanor was one that did not brook questions on the set agenda.

"I've told you, of course, Dolly, about my experiences with my, shall we say, turbulent mother," Margaret continued. "Well, my comedy is based on those experiences."

"However did you manage to make a comedy out of the trauma you suffered from your mother's political and marital vicissitudes?" I asked.

"What I did was apply some corrective fantasy recapitulation to the root of the situation."

"In other words?"

"In other words, I wrote a story about an unbridled, rampant woman being brought to order and control in spite of herself. In my childhood, I'd wished a million times for that to happen to my mother. Sadly, it did not. So I made it happen in my story, and in a comic way. It was a most satisfying experience!"

"Looks like it must have been," I said as Margaret started glowing even more. In the excitement of telling her tale, she had run her hand through her coiffure, inadvertently pulling strands of Tudor gold and silver hair around her face in a flattering way.

"My heroine, unlike my mother, was able to modify her behavior based on the ups and downs that she experienced. They were silly ones, of course, unlike what my mother had to go through.

Still, it did me good to correct on paper a situation somewhat akin to the one that I could not correct in real life."

A therapist, I am sure, would have known the right thing to say about this rather Freudian information dump. I satisfied myself with asking about the name and the particulars of the play.

"All the wine you've had this evening has made you lazy, Dolly. Now that you know I wrote *Romeo and Juliet* and *Troilus and Cressida*; surely you can figure out the name of the play of which we are speaking now."

"*Kiss Me, Kate!*" I exclaimed as the lightbulb went off. Or, perhaps I should say, given the surroundings, as the candle was lit.

"Well, that is a quote from my play, certainly," Margaret conceded.

"The play, of course, was *The Taming of the Shrew*; it's true, isn't it?" I asked.

"Yes, Dolly," said Margaret, quite bursting with pride.

I sang a few bars of "Wunderbar" from the Broadway musical *Kiss Me, Kate* and got to my feet and did a little dance with Margaret for good measure, just because there is no wrong time for a little Cole Porter. Mary Tudor even cut into our little waltz for a moment or two; she was surprisingly light on her feet.

"And a fine play *Shrew* was too," said Elizabeth, not one to brook the attention being on others for very long. "A rollicking comedy; I heartily enjoyed it!"

"I'm rather surprised to hear you say that, Elizabeth," I said, resuming my seat on the pillows. "Most modern feminists take exception to the play. They feel a man roughhousing a woman out of her spiritedness is offensive."

"Spiritedness and arrogant willfulness are two different things," Elizabeth commented. "I myself was an example of what you would call *spirited*."

All six of Elizabeth's companions examined their shoes as Elizabeth glanced at them for confirmation.

"My aunt Margaret," Elizabeth went on, "though a loving woman, could be both arrogant and willful at her worst, as our younger Margaret here has pointed out. Such behavior benefits from correction, in my opinion. We know that in modern times, marital behaviors and expectations are different from what they were in our era. Given how life and relationships were when we were alive, no one thought, in our time, that the nature of the taming was out of line with the provoking behavior."

"And I did set it in Italy," Margaret pointed out, "where people are, after all, of a more passionate nature."

I recollected the doings in Padua when the determined Pertruchio wedded the shrewish Katherine, and the depredations of dress, transport, and table that he exposed her to in order to take her down a peg. I recollected also the benefit the taming had on the fate of the shrew's sweet younger sister, Bianca; I suspected that right there was a good deal of the corrective recapitulation Margaret had mentioned.

"So, Margaret, you were adept at both comedy and romance. Quite versatile when it came to style, weren't you?"

"When one is a writer, Dolly, one learns that all kinds of different writing have their times."

"'A time to every purpose under heaven,' as Shakespeare had it," I said, trying to hold my own literary end up.

"That is from the Bible, Dolly—Ecclesiastes chapter three—and as true when written as it was when I was alive, and I am sure it is still applicable today. It certainly applies to the circumstances under which I wrote my last two plays."

Chapter Sixty-One
The Party Line on a Maligned Spine

"Yes, do get on with the story of those last two plays, Margaret; wasting time does not count as a purpose under heaven!" Elizabeth said with what she herself would no doubt have called spirit, though I would have called it pure bossiness. Clearly, Margaret was used to it, however, no doubt from all that practice she had with her mother. She took up her tale without turning a hair.

"The last two were of a more sensible nature than my other plays. Catherine Willoughby suggested I write them; she had been impressed with my other works but felt that they lacked a certain groundedness."

"That sounds like her," I said, recalling that she was, like me, a woman of academic bent.

"These two serious works of mine were meant to affirm, in the uncertain world of European politics, the absolute rightness of the Tudor family being on England's throne."

I could see that the Margaret before me had inherited more than one thing from her grandma, Margaret Beaufort, the family matriarch who had made it her life's work to toot the Tudor horn.

"My last two plays were straightforward historical dramas, Dolly, telling the tale of my family in recent generations. One was about Richard III, the other about Henry VIII. They were named after their heroes."

I recollected that both of these relatives of Margaret's had plays bearing their names in the Shakespeare canon. *Henry VIII* was generally considered a minor work; *Richard III*, however, was another story.

"'A horse! A horse! My kingdom for a horse!'" I cried lustily. I imagined myself as an onlooker at the Battle of Bosworth Field, where Richard III died ignominiously and Henry VII established the Tudor dynasty.

Mary Tudor piped up as I settled back onto my two little flat feet. "We recall from your last visit here, Dolly, how anxious you were to leave us and get back to the real world. You know horses will not get you out of here, any more than wishes will, before we have finished with you."

Mary looked over at Margaret, puckishly grinning, and they both laughed. I decided to forebear any further Shakespeare quotations for the moment and to offer Margaret the apology I felt she deserved on behalf of my fellow historians.

"Margaret, the Shakespearian depiction of *Richard III* gave history one of its ultimate bad guys, in all his evil glory. You made him so evil that anyone would thank Henry VII for doing him in. Why, in the play, you even have Richard III murdering those poor York boys, the legendary Princes in the Tower."

"I've been told, Dolly, that you were brought up to speed on the specifics of what *really* happened to those boys the last time that you visited this place," Margaret said. "That was something I myself had no way of knowing until I arrived here."

"I *was* brought up to speed on the story of the Princes in the Tower," I assured Margaret. "And now, it is *my* turn to bring *you* up to speed on something!" I said with what I trusted was spirit rather than the commonplace stealing of a march.

"You portrayed Richard III, Margaret, as having a marked spinal deformity—what we in modern times would call severe scoliosis.

Many of my fellow historians had decried that description over the years. They accused Shakespeare—I guess I should say, you—of trying to make Richard seem more evil than he was through giving him certain physical characteristics. The Shakespearian twisting of his body as an indicator of a twisted mind has been called unfair, inaccurate, and offensive. However, recent findings in the real world have vindicated you; we now know you were simply reporting the truth about the man's physique."

"What happened to change things, Dolly?" Margaret asked.

"Richard III's remains turned up in a parking lot in 2012," I explained. "His skeleton clarified that your description of his back curvature was spot-on. You were not being unduly unkind or taking literary liberties; you were just reporting the history accurately."

"What is a 'parking lot'?" Margaret asked. "Is it an ignominious place for one's remains to turn up?"

"Well, yes, I suppose you could say it was," I answered.

"Good!" chorused all three Grey sisters in impressive unison. "The man was a bully, and he deserved what he got," Jane said with feeling.

"Ladies," I said, "a little retrospective pity, please, for the man who ended up dead under a parking lot, uncrowned, and with a stab wound to the butt! As the Bard so movingly put it, 'The mystic chords of memory will swell when again touched, as surely they will be, by the better angels of our nature.'"

"I think you will find that Abraham Lincoln said that, Dolly," said Mary Tudor.

"How do you know about Abraham Lincoln?" I asked.

"His wife, Mary Todd Lincoln, was brought here to discuss first lady theater-going protocols," Mary, Queen of Scots, informed me. "She was warned off of it, in a general way. We've always doubted she took the advice she was given here; she seemed rather a stubborn character."

"And high-handed, as well," said Elizabeth, blissfully unaware, I was sure, of the adage about the pot calling the kettle black.

"I think I can safely say that Mr. Lincoln's first lady, unfortunately, failed to take your advice," I said. "But right now, ladies, if I may, I'd like to take the conversation from the subject of advice to the subject of questions."

Chapter Sixty-Two
The Royal Matron and the Literary Patron

"Am I even allowed to ask pointed questions here?" I inquired. "There was a moratorium on my asking any during my last visit here, but they seem all right now. Am I correct in this?"

"You are, Dolly. Ask away!" said Mary Tudor.

"Well, I'd like some of the background on how five plays written by Margaret Douglas made their way into the Shakespeare canon. My curiosity about this is understandable, surely."

"I should say so!" said Jane, looking as professorial as is possible for a sixteen-year-old to look. "Any scholar who calls herself a scholar would feel the same."

"Well," Margaret said, "it started with my turning for assistance with my literary career to a highly placed individual who was the obvious go-to man for the job."

"William Cecil?" I asked, feeling confident.

"No, Dolly. Robert Dudley."

Accompanied by the hissing sound of the air escaping my deflated ego, Elizabeth let a hint of a smile pass over her lips at the mention of her lover, Robert Dudley, Earl of Leicester, and Margaret began her story.

"The year was 1578," Margaret began. "I had a premonition that my time on earth would soon be over. As a royal personage, my thoughts of course turned to the legacy I would leave behind me. My sons had reproduced and put children tauntingly near the English throne. I had no control, in the last days of my life, over how the fates of those grandchildren would play out."

"Your grandchildren were the future King James I of England and Arabella Stuart," I recalled. "Guess you could put it at fifty-fifty."

"I knew I needed to leave my grandchildren to fate," Margaret said. "But I also had my literary works to leave to posterity. I wanted my plays to be put out into the world and credited to me *after* I was gone. I dreamed of the glory of literary immortality without the social burden of having to live down being a female member of the royal family who wrote common plays."

"And so you contacted Dudley," I said. "You certainly took that down to the wire, Margaret; as I recall, you dined with the man the night before you died. People at the time viewed it with suspicion."

"And people at the time were incorrect in suspecting Dudley of wrongdoing, Dolly. I dined with him on that last night to pass my five plays into his possession. As the patron of a dramatic troupe and a close friend of the family, he was the best bet I had for the safekeeping of my plays. His troupe had, as part of its warrant, the ability to perform plays with minimal censorship. Given the ribald nature of *Shrew* and the political football that *Richard III* could become, I couldn't think of a better way to ensure that my plays would see the light of day and meet an audience."

"His troupe was called the Earl of Leicester's Men, was it not?" I asked. "The legendary James Burbage, builder of the first known modern English theater, was among the members of the troupe. Its motto was 'more stars than there are in the heavens,' wasn't it?"

"No, Dolly," said Mary, Queen of Scots. "That was the motto of a movie studio, called Metro-Goldwyn-Mayer, I believe. Mistress Greta Garbo mentioned it when she was here for advisement about her motion picture career. We suggested that she be true to herself in her roles, and she responded by simply saying, 'I want to be alone.' We told her to go with that."

"It worked for her too," I said, remembering some of the first words spoken on film by the Swedish silent film star and how they had become her tagline.

"At any rate," Margaret went on, "I entrusted my plays to Dudley, directing him to put them into the hands of his players. He was not to reveal my authorship of them until after I had died. I learned in the afterlife that he had not carried out my wishes exactly as I had expected him to."

"Pretty rum of the man to bollocks up your last request that way."

"Well, Dudley wasn't exactly the only iron I had in the fire on this matter," Margaret said. "I also employed a contingency plan to at least hint to posterity that my plays were mine."

"A contingency plan?" I echoed.

"That's what I said, Dolly," Margaret affirmed as she fingered a brooch she was wearing. "I had a contingency plan."

Chapter Sixty-Three
The Accessory That Tells a Story

I couldn't help but notice the beautiful intricacy of the brooch that Margaret's touch was calling my attention to. Realizing that I was staring at it, she invited me to have a closer look at it.

"Margaret—is that the famous Lennox Jewel?"

"It is, Dolly," Margaret confirmed.

I'd read about the thousands of words of juvenilia that the Bronte children had scribbled into little booklets only inches high. They had produced a complex literary world that you could literally hold in the palm of your hand and close your fingers over. This brooch was surely the jeweler's equivalent; romance, drama, tragedy, history, philosophy, inspiration, jewels, flora, and fauna, all in a colorful heart-shaped cameo well under three inches square.

Margaret removed the brooch and let me hold it in the palm of my hand. The intricacy of the piece was astonishing. It was replete with the kinds of images that I knew would have been highly symbolic to people in the Tudor world. But I, a woman of the twenty-first century, needed an interpreter if I was going to fully appreciate it.

"I admire this brooch tremendously, Margaret, but I'd be lying if I said I understood it. There is just so much going on! It's like an HBO miniseries on a couple of inches of enamel."

"This brooch, Dolly, carries symbols of my life, my loves, my royal heritage, my religion, and my family's history," Margaret informed me. "But in the interest of time, I will direct your attention to the bits of imagery that relate directly to my plays."

"Go ahead and coach me on the brooch, Margaret!"

The jewel was even more multifaceted than I had realized at first glance. Margaret flipped open both a crown and a heart that appeared on the front of the brooch. This revealed, among other things, two hearts pierced by arrows, a green horn, two clasped hands, a skull and crossbones, and the words "death shall dissolve." I touched them gently with my fingertip.

"References to *Romeo and Juliet,* surely," I said. "And that green horn; what does that symbolize?"

"The horn is the time-honored symbol of the cuckold, Dolly; the man Troilus thought himself to be when his Cressida took up with another man."

"And that skull and crossbones; is that the wholesale death and destruction of the Trojan War, as seen in *Troilus and Cressida?*"

Margaret nodded and revealed that the jewel could open yet again; she flipped up the entire front of it to reveal quite a scene.

"You see these two warriors, Dolly," she said, pointing to one triumphant and one who was clearly in dire straits on the ground. "The fallen one is Richard III; the tall fellow, standing upright—obviously a fellow who would excel at the joust—is Henry VIII."

I couldn't help but notice the image adjacent to these two. "That lady being dragged by the hair by a man in a green shirt—is it a depiction of *The Taming of the Shrew?*" I inquired.

"Correct again, Dolly. And now I would direct your attention to two of the quotes on the jewel."

I saw the words "Time causes all to learn" near the images of an hourglass and an unclad woman. Margaret closed the jewel, and I was again looking at its front. The white enamel border surrounding the jewel contained words that, if translated into modern English, would read "Who hopes still constantly with patience shall obtain victory in their claim."

"You covered all the bases, Margaret; all five of your plays and the acknowledgment of the waiting you were willing to do for the right time for all to be revealed about them," I said. With that, I turned the jewel over to see what the back of it held in store. Among some pretty impressive dragons was a reclining fellow with what looked like a giant cockscomb flower—no pun intended—growing straight up out of his groin. The plant was at least as tall as the man was long, and the flower was golden.

"*That* doesn't look very Shakespearian to me," I said, pointing to the image.

"It is a highly personal and meaningful image to me, the details of which I have no need to share with you or anyone else. All you need to know, Dolly, is that it is indeed *not* Shakespearian. I suppose "Freudian" would be the better word for it."

"You know about Freudian psychology?" I said, surprised.

"Yes, a Fraulein Anna Freud was among the guests brought here by the queens for career advice. She was thinking of going into her father's line of business; who better to advise someone about that than the latter-generation Tudor women?"

"What advice was she given?" I asked.

"It was suggested that she capitalize on her father's legacy but find a way to branch out and do something uniquely on her own. We never did learn how that went."

"Pretty well, I think. Anna Freud made quite a name for herself specializing in the psychology of children."

"Well, I am glad that worked out," Margaret said, appearing relieved to have attention diverted from that giant groin flower.

"All right, Margaret," I said. "The Lennox Jewel was your contingency plan for demonstrating to the world your authorship of your plays in the spirit of the Renaissance world and its absorption with symbolism. And I guess it is a good thing that you had a contingency plan if, as you said, Dudley didn't carry out your last wishes the way he was supposed to. What exactly did the man do?"

Chapter Sixty-Four
Being Practical and Waxing Theatrical

"Dudley did with Margaret's plays what he thought was best to do at the time," Elizabeth said, taking the narrative over. "He took the trouble to read one of the five plays—*Henry VIII*. He did not find it impressive and assumed that the other four were of a similar quality. He passed them on to his theatrical troupe through James Burbage, feeling it was his duty to a dead friend to do so."

"Seems legit so far."

"Dudley did not tell Burbage who wrote the plays, feeling he was protecting the royal family from embarrassment. All Burbage was told was that the plays were written by a highborn lady and that Dudley was passing them on to him simply to satisfy a promise. Burbage, based on the opinion he got from Dudley, never bothered to do anything with the plays. Eventually, though, the plays found their way into the hands of Burbage's son, Richard."

"The same Richard Burbage who played with the Lord Chamberlain's Men, later known as the King's Men—the troupe associated with William Shakespeare. The same Richard Burbage who made a Shakespearian name for himself as an early Richard III and quite probably as an early Romeo as well," I posited.

"Yes, Dolly, the same," Elizabeth said. "Burbage had been told about the association of the plays with an unknown but very highborn lady. When he realized just how viable the plays were as contemporary theater, he was chomping at the bit to have them put into production. However, out of an abundance of caution, he decided to confer with someone in power regarding any possible political repercussions of going live with these mysteriously sourced plays. It was well into the 1590s by this time; Dudley was dead. So he turned to—"

"William Cecil?" I asked.

"Correct this time, Dolly. Cecil, likewise one for an abundance of caution, asked to see the plays in question. Recognizing the handwriting of the plays and realizing they had been written by my late cousin Margaret, he brought them to me. I was not surprised to see the plays; Dudley had told me about that last dinner of his with Margaret. I was surprised, though, by the quality of the plays; my dear Dudley had missed the boat entirely by not reading all five of them."

It occurred to me that Robert Dudley was a byword for missing the boat entirely, but I kept the thought to myself.

"As soon as I realized the excellence of Margaret's plays, I instructed Cecil to go ahead and permit Burbage to use them," Elizabeth said. "Margaret Douglas's name, however, was to be kept strictly out of it, at least for the time being. Plays were not a common undertaking in the social world we lived in, and I had the Tudor family standard to maintain. Margaret may have been dead and past all worry on that score, but I was not. I directed Cecil to have Burbage and the Lord Chamberlain's Men attribute the plays to one of their company. They suggested William Shakespeare, one of their actors, a poet, and a would-be playwright, for the time being. I myself would determine when the plays' true provenance was to be made known to the world and how that news would be leaked. Shakespeare, Burbage, and the company were more than happy to take credit for such high-class plays with no effort whatsoever, and only a modicum of discretion, required on their part."

"Old Will must have been absolutely thunderstruck at having that kind of luck come his way," I said. "Talk about an unbeatable, unrepeatable, once-in-a-lifetime opportunity!"

"Well, yes and no, Dolly," said Jane. Proving herself a mighty princess, the slender little thing toted several large cushions over to where I was seated and, along with her sisters Mary and Catherine, hunkered down on the floor with me as Margaret vacated the vicinity. And thus with three if not fifty shades of Grey, yet another Tudor tale was about to unfold.

Chapter Sixty-Five
The History of the Sisters Grey, or the Thwarted Departed

The Grey sisters were a lesson in the word "thwarted," even in a place as full of thwarted plans as the Tudor-era court was.

The eldest, Jane, has gone down in history as the Nine Days Queen. Her ambitious family put the adolescent on the throne for a brief spell after the death of Edward VI. She was arguably entitled to it, but Mary Tudor ousted young Jane and had her executed for the sake of the stability of the realm. History has painted Jane as scholarly and sweet, and my meeting with her the last time I was here had done nothing to disabuse me of that notion. On this occasion she was wearing what probably passed as a party dress, if you were the scholarly sort in the middle Renaissance. It was a very flattering fawn-colored number with jewel-tone embroidery.

Jane's younger sisters, like Jane, were a very real threat to Mary Tudor's throne, and later to Elizabeth I's, because of the unquestioned legitimacy of their births and claims. Unlike Jane, neither Catherine nor Mary Grey went down as a byword for intelligence; in fact, quite the opposite.

The elder Jane having gotten all the brains in the Grey family, all the looks fell quite naturally to the lot of the second Grey daughter, Catherine. She was, quite simply, lovely. Unlike the demurely dressed Jane, Catherine knew how to use color, texture, and line to make an outfit count. Her natural blond beauty was emphasized and accentuated by the elegant black, white, and gold ensemble she was wearing.

With brains and looks already spoken for, there wasn't much left for nature to bless the youngest Grey daughter with. Mary was tiny, well under five feet tall, and had an obvious scoliotic curve to her upper spine. Perhaps as a compensatory mechanism, the tiny Mary's black-and-white outfit with pale salmon-colored accents was conspicuously sumptuous, embroidered to a never-you-mind and all about the pouf. I say *sumptuous* because it is hard to qualify overdressed when it comes to Elizabethan fashion; the girl did, after all, share DNA with the sartorially over-the-top Elizabeth I.

Mary Grey had a face that was homely in the good sense of the word. It was nonthreatening, simple, and wholesome—a face that aimed to please. There was something of the ovine in her expression; here we had a follower, not a leader, I thought.

"You got to know *me* the last time you were here, Dolly. I will therefore allow my sisters to tell you a little bit about themselves before I tell you what I have to say," said Jane, bowing her head graciously toward her sister Catherine.

I wondered if I was about to hear, from the horse's mouth, the actual facts about one of the Tudor era's oddest marriages.

It turned out that I was. But that particular comedy of errors was just the tip of the iceberg.

Chapter Sixty-Six
On Disparaged Marriages

Catherine grasped the hand of her sister Mary before she addressed me.

"You are a Tudor scholar, Dolly. You know, therefore, that both Mary and I were, shall we say, unlucky in love."

"Not unlucky in *love*, Catherine," said Mary stoutly. "Unlucky in *marriage*, I would say, was more accurate. Neither of us have any complaint to make about the devotion of our husbands."

"Granted, Mary," said Catherine.

"Nor had we reason to complain about their personal attributes," said Mary, blushing a little.

"You are one of those girls who believe that size matters, aren't you, Mary?" I asked. "After all, you married Thomas Keyes, who was said to be almost seven feet tall." It occurred to me that the pair of them must have been like the Mutt and Jeff of the Tudor court, but I did not give voice to the mental picture.

"My husband was a giant of a man in spirit as well as body, Dolly, in spite of his humble birth. And yet everyone said he was beneath me."

"Surely, not with a straight face," I said, looking down into the eyes of the four foot-ish Mary.

"The joke was on everyone who did not realize what a fine man Thomas Keyes was!" she snapped, pinching my arm by way of comeuppance for my thoughtless words.

Though she be but little, she is fierce, I thought, surprised at the ire that the little dynamo before me could summon up.

"Thomas could look down into my eyes without looking down on me as a person. He was the only man I knew who could do that. Do you blame me, Dolly, for loving him, even though he was only a gatekeeper?"

I was as impressed with Mary's dignity and simple forthrightness as I was with her spirit. Because I was thus impressed with her, I felt it only right to be honest with her in return. "I do not blame you for *loving* the man," I replied. "I have to wonder about your wisdom in *marrying* him, though, given the climate of the Tudor court. You had to know that the queen—Elizabeth at the time—would be furious. You had to have also known how just about everyone else at the court would react, as well."

"You are forgetting my gynecology, Dolly," Mary said.

"Oh my—this conversation is about to get *way* too up close and personal, isn't it?" I asked, feeling, I conjectured, like a manly man being forced by his girlfriend to watch *Call the Midwife*.

"I think you will find that the girl means *genealogy*, Dolly," said Mary Tudor. "If *anyone's* gynecology is worth forgetting, surely it would be my own."

I winced as I recalled the phantom pregnancies that had marked Mary Tudor's short reign and blighted her final months on earth.

"After my father's death," Mary Grey resumed, "my mother married her master of the horse, Adrian Stokes. It was a marriage that was beneath her yet a very happy one in every way."

"So you thought, Mary, that you would be wise to follow your mother's example?"

"Not just my mother's example, Dolly. You are forgetting your history again, and I am, quite frankly, surprised at you. Surely you of all people realize who else's example I was following."

I thought a moment about those who might have been romantic exemplars for the little Mary.

Mary looked at me fixedly; in fact, everyone in the room did. It reminded me of the way the four Maries of Mary, Queen of Scots, had looked at me on the occasion of my last visit here.

I knew, now, what the diminutive Mary was alluding to.

Chapter Sixty-Seven
Mary Grey's Matrimonial Testimonial

"Your mother wasn't the first one in your family tree to eschew aristocratic suitors and make a surprising match; your step-grandmother, Catherine Willoughby, did so as well, didn't she?"

"She did, Dolly; she was a most outspoken component of marrying for love."

"I think you mean proponent, dear," Jane said sweetly.

"Well, anyway—her decidedness on the matter influenced my own mother. Witnessing the happiness that both my mother and my step-grandmother knew helped me to make my own decision."

Since my last visit here, I'd had reason to be particularly interested in Catherine Willoughby, the gal voted most likely to succeed Henry VIII's sixth wife, Catherine Parr. Her chance at fame as Henry's seventh consort ended with Henry's predeceasing his last wife. This happened between Catherine Willoughby's arranged marriage to Mary Grey's grandfather, Charles Brandon, and her later marriage for love to Richard Bertie, her gentlemen usher.

"You know, Mary, that as an academic, I am familiar with your history, but it never occurred to me that you had such compelling examples set for you when it came to your marriage. Now, suddenly, it looks less like foolhardiness and maybe more like a fusion of courage and family tradition."

"I appreciate that acknowledgment, Dolly."

My eyes got misty as I considered the history of this romantic little lady and how her story—the long and the short of it—ultimately played out.

"Unlike your mother and step-grandmother, you did not get away with your less-than-noble alliance. Both you and your husband were imprisoned almost immediately after the ceremony."

"And we never saw each other again," said Mary, sniffling.

"Your husband, while kept well away from you, eventually left prison and lived a free man thereafter until his death," I recollected. "You were kept under house arrest in a series of places, including the home of Catherine Willoughby. You eventually achieved a degree of social rehabilitation but died at a young age and with little to your name."

"What I had in jewels, I bequeathed to my step-grandmother—the jewels, that is, and a few other particulars."

"Other particulars?" I asked, my interest piqued.

"I refer, Dolly," said Mary, smiling, "to my literary works."

Chapter Sixty-Eight
A Little Ire and Irons in the Fire

"Not you too!" I said to Mary.

"Why *not* me, Dolly?" Mary asked, stamping her foot in pique at my statement. I supposed it was true what they say about how "the smallest worm will turn being trodden on," and changed my tack.

"The emphasis there was on the *too*, not on the *not you*, Mary. I've got no reason to doubt that you might have had literary leanings. Actually, given what I've just learned about Margaret Douglas, I suppose I might even think it runs in the family."

"You can say that again," said Mary, Queen of Scots.

"Don't encourage Dolly like that," Elizabeth said. "She talks enough as it is. Time is of the essence, and there is more than one tale left to be told. "Dolly," said Elizabeth, "will hold her tongue and let our little Mary get on with her tale."

"I guess that is your spiritedness showing, Elizabeth, and not arrogant willfulness," I said sweetly.

"I think maybe it is Elizabeth's unfeelingness showing," said Catherine, hugging her sister Mary about the shoulder and leaning her head against her sister's. "Calling Mary *little*, indeed! You know how sensitive she is about her height, Elizabeth."

"And you oughtn't to use words like 'unfeeling' to me," Elizabeth said, with, well, feeling.

"In all fairness, Elizabeth has tried very hard to live down her reputation for imperiousness ever since Mistress Hillary Clinton was here to visit us," Jane said.

"For marital advisement from the six wives?" I inquired.

"No, for career advisement on running for high office," Mary Tudor said. "We talked a lot about showing one's softer, human side."

"Only not too much," said Mary, Queen of Scots, the voice of too much of a good thing.

"Our advice to Mistress Hillary led me to some healthy introspection and a reassessment of my own *modus operandi*," Elizabeth said. "Mistress Hillary and I struck up a bargain; I was to work on what she called the warm and fuzzy on this side of the great divide, and she was to work on it on the other side. I refer to it on my end as my 'farthingale pledge.'"

"And you call it your 'farthingale pledge' because?"

"Because Mistress Hillary accused me of having an iron arse under an iron one," Elizabeth said.

"My sister got her own back though," Mary Tudor said, with sibling pride. "She referred to Mistress Clinton's preferred garb as 'brass-tacks slacks.'"

My mind imploded a bit at the thought of this grand bargain across the ages, between farthingale and pantsuit, so to speak, and at the sheer amount of collective work that would have to be done.

"Elizabeth does *try* to let her softer side show nowadays. Let's not hold it against her if she fails miserably at it at least as often as she succeeds," said Mary, Queen of Scots.

I thought the sentiment very big—if a bit passive-aggressive—from someone who had actually been executed at the command of the woman she was defending.

Elizabeth's sister was not about to jump on the *poor Elizabeth* bandwagon with Mary, Queen of Scots. Bloody Mary Tudor was, in fact, going to show a little iron farthingale of her own.

"Let us not forget, ladies, that we are all Tudors; we are all above getting our feelings hurt over trivialities."

"Yes," I chimed in, "let's not get our knickers in a twist."

"Dolly," Margaret Douglas pointed out, "none of us is wearing knickers. They didn't come into fashion until after Elizabethan times."

We all had a hearty laugh as Jane assumed the unlikely role of bartender, passing fully charged wine goblets all around. Now that we were drinking buddies, it felt as though we had grown closer as a unit. We settled in with our libations to hear what Mary Grey had to say about her heretofore unsung literary endeavors.

Chapter Sixty-Nine
Mary Grey Tells It to Liz Like It Is

"My works were cries from my heart as I languished in my various custodial situations," Mary began.

"I supposed they would have had to be," I said. "You married at a young age—around twenty, as I recall—and spent the rest of your dozen or so years in custody of one kind or another for doing so."

"Being in custody gave me a lot of time to think," Mary said, "about my many grievances. The thing that wrangled the most was what I considered the two-facedness of the queen, Elizabeth, when it came to romantic matters."

Elizabeth's face, or faces as Mary would have it, went a bit purple at this statement. I was not entirely clear if this was because of Mary's grammatical error or the personal insult. Either way, little Mary Grey knew an oncoming smack when she saw one and fielded it masterfully.

"You told me to get on with my tale, Elizabeth, and getting on with it is what I am doing. I speak of feelings I harbored in life in the real world. We may be above all that now, but we weren't back then. You were so hell-bent in life, Elizabeth, on keeping all the ladies in your coterie out of romantic involvements. How any of us who acted on normal romantic impulses were made to pay the price for it! And all the time you were making a fool of yourself over Robert Dudley. The duplicity of it was so unfair!"

"Well, rank does have its privileges," Elizabeth offered in her own defense.

"She's right," I said, remembering the stories of military life that my dad had told me when I was a child.

"Be that as it may, the irony of the situation festooned in my soul," Mary admitted.

"I'll bet it festered, too," I said, correcting her as gently as I could. She seemed grateful for the consideration.

"As you've mentioned, Dolly, one of my wardresses during my time in custody was my own step-grandmother, Catherine Willoughby. She noticed my languishing spirits during my time in her care."

"Yes, she is on record as saying that you wouldn't eat as much as a chicken leg over the course of two days."

"You know how grandmothers are. She eventually wheedled out of me the thing that was undermining my spirits the most. Once she had, she took great pity on me and did her best to help raise my spirits. She eventually made an excellent suggestion as to how I could relieve myself of my feelings."

"A suggestion," said Margaret Douglas, beaming with pride, "that she got from me, during one of our many friendly visits together."

"What happened on that visit?" I asked Margaret.

"Catherine Willoughby shared with me her concern about Mary Grey's bitterness with the virgin queen duplicity situation, as we shall call it; she said it was eating the poor child alive. She wondered how Mary could get it out of her system. I reminded Catherine of how she had started *me* on my literary endeavors and of how very cathartic I had found the writing of my plays. I had no qualms about recommending that she advise Mary Grey to do the same thing: to get her feelings out on paper."

I don't know who first noticed that history repeats itself. Whoever he was, he'd have felt totally vindicated if he could only have been a fly on the damp stone walls that surrounded me.

Chapter Seventy
Iniquities and Ditties

"All right now, Mary. The spotlight is on you! Tell Dolly all about those plays of yours," said Catherine Grey, rubbing her sister's shoulders as she spoke. The pair of them looked for all the world like a prizefighter getting ready to go the next round and his manager giving him the old pep talk; the only things missing were the towel, the sweat, and *Rocky's Theme.*

The subflyweight Mary came out swinging. "I'll get straight to cases, Dolly. I took my grandmother's suggestion about getting my feelings out by writing. Before I knew it, the habit consumed me. I spent most of my captivity writing, drafting and redrafting my plays, obsessed with making them as perfect as I could."

"They say that when you were under Sir Thomas Gresham's charge in Bishopsgate Street, you spent all your time locked in a room with your books. I guess what you were doing in there is not so much of a mystery now."

"I wrote two plays themed on the feelings that were crushing my soul. The first dealt with the unnatural idea of eschewing normal sexual relations, put forth as Elizabeth's command."

"Mary Grey versus the celibacy agenda, round one," I said, the wine having hit me a bit, I'm afraid.

"My plot concerned a ruler who has sworn off sexual relations for the sake of study and has his companions do the same. The presence of lovely and highborn ladies, desirable and suitable in every way, puts a chink into the—as you would call it, Dolly—celibacy agenda. The ladies demand a reasonable period of proof of love—one year—at the play's end, leaving the field open for eventual consummation of the various unions sought by the characters."

"Sounds like a "Love TKO" to me," I said. "It also sounds a lot like Shakespeare's *Love's Labour's Lost.*"

"That's because it *is Love's Labour's Lost,* Dolly," said Mary, rising from her cushion. Elizabeth came and stood beside her, all five-feet-eight or so of Elizabeth next to the Lilliputian Mary. "And," Elizabeth continued, "I must have my say—"

"Elizabeth takes after her mother when it comes to having her say," quipped Mary Tudor. "And, she takes after her in another way as well—a propensity to stealing other people's thunder." It occurred to me that as the daughter of Katharine of Aragon, Mary ought to know about the stolen thunder. "Really, Elizabeth! Let Mary Grey tell her own tale, in her own way," Mary Tudor continued.

"I was just going to take exception to her comment about me," Elizabeth said. "The insinuation that the standards I set for my ladies were unrealistic is quite uncalled for. I mean, really—a little sexual tension never hurt anyone."

"Elizabeth takes after her mother when it comes to her philosophy on human relations as well," said Mary, Queen of Scots.

"I've never had much patience when it comes to sexual tension," I confessed.

"Neither have I," admitted Mary, Queen of Scots, perhaps unnecessarily. I wondered briefly what the Renaissance equivalent of *hot pants* was; *farthingales afire* came to mind.

"I also have no patience when it comes to having secrets revealed," I continued. "I want to hear the rest of Mary's tale!"

"Thank you, Dolly," Jane interjected. "Now, Elizabeth, please let my sister have her say." This time it was Jane who was rubbing

Mary's shoulders, getting her ready for the next round. Mary went in gamely.

"My second play," she continued, "involved the hypocrisy of someone who held others to a strict standard of sexual conduct while being far from beyond reproach oneself."

Elizabeth bridled, but remembering, perhaps, her farthingale of iron, said nothing. I could tell it pained her though; her face got redder and redder.

"'Hail, virgin, if you be, as those cheek-roses proclaim you are no less,'" I said, bringing a little bit of the Bard into the conversation, a bit cheekily, I must confess.

Elizabeth lunged as if to box me on the ear, but in reaching down to the floor to do so, lost her balance, and landed on her bottom beside me. Mary Grey, standing now, was just tall enough to look down on both of us. She got between us and held us apart from each other at arm's length, going from protagonist to referee in an instant. The feeling of power, one she'd had so little experience with, seemed to do her a world of good.

"Elizabeth, control yourself! Remember your farthingale pledge. This is no time to go backward in your efforts at being kinder and more salacious."

"You mean solicitous, surely, Mary. And while I may have pledged to try to be more solicitous, I certainly never pledged to be downright servile. I think Dolly owes me an apology."

"I do not agree, Elizabeth," said Mary, bringing Elizabeth to a state of complexion that made it pretty much impossible to tell her skin from her trademark red hair. "Dolly was not making a comment about you, Elizabeth. She was simply quoting from that second play of mine, *Measure for Measure*. Weren't you, Dolly?" said Mary sweetly, turning to me.

"*So Love's Labour's Lost* is yours, and *Measure for Measure* is, Mary, as well?"

"Correct," Mary confirmed. "And both must have turned out to be quite well-loved and familiar plays, for you to have identified and quoted them so easily. Is it so, Dolly?"

"Two of my favorites," I said, stretching the truth more than a little bit in what I trusted was a good cause.

"And the favorites of others as well? Of others," Mary asked hopefully, "who were inspired by them to write beautiful songs, like those that were inspired by Margaret's plays? Please, Dolly, tell me it is so!"

Jane and Catherine, in serious big-sister mode, gave me the "you'd better not let her down, or you'll have us to deal with" look. Fortunately, I am able to think fast in a crisis.

"Absolutely!" I said, finding the truth amenable to a little further stretching. "One of the favorite songs of my childhood, in fact, comes from *Love's Labour's Lost*. It is called *Jacquenetta*, after the sweet country girl in the play."

"Sing it please, Dolly," Mary requested.

I am also, fortunately, able to riff on a tune at short notice. And so I sang: *Ja-que-net-ta, Ja-que-net-ta—dormez vous? Dormez vous? Sonne le matina, sonne le matina, ding dong ding, ding dong ding.* My vocal range allowed me to do full justice to the old "Frere Jacque" tune, even if my French was not quite up to the lyrics.

"Your French, Dolly!" said Elizabeth. "We'd heard it was bad, and I can see why."

"Farthingale pledge!" Mary Tudor called out.

"You carry a lovely tune though, Dolly," Elizabeth said, gamely getting back on track.

"I am not so bothered by bad French," said Mary, Queen of Scots, former resident of France. "One had to get used to it, living at the Scottish court."

"I think it is a lovely song, and I am so glad that Jacquenetta has been immortalized in song. Dolly," Mary said, hugging her sister Catherine. "Has Julietta from *Measure for Measure* been likewise immortalized?"

I wondered why Mary should be worried about one of the down-the-list supporting characters in the play. However, mine was not to question why, and I broke into song once more.

"Julie, Julietta, do you love me? Julie, Julietta do you care?" I sang, as Mary and Catherine clapped and smiled at my slightly adulterated cover of Bobby Sherman's bubblegum classic.

"I am so glad about that!" Mary said. "The character of Julietta, you see, was my tribute to my sweet sister Catherine, her giving nature, and her trials and tribulations. There was a lot more of her presence in my original draft of the play than survives in the final version; the play was heavily edited, I'm afraid."

"The same thing happened with the character I used to pay tribute to my sister Mary in one of *my* plays," Catherine said. Her moue of disappointment was nothing compared to the drop of my jaw, as I awaited the explosion of yet another Tudor literary bombshell.

Chapter Seventy-One
Time for Catherine to Chime In

"Let's cut right to the chase," I suggested to Catherine, earning a beam of approval from the time-conscious Elizabeth. "Are your works part of the Shakespeare canon as well?"

"They are: one a drama and the other a comedy," Catherine said.

Remembering the "though she be but little, she is fierce" line from *A Midsummer Night's Dream*, I asked Catherine Grey a question.

"Is *A Midsummer Night's Dream* the comedy currently in question? And is the character of Hermia based on your little—I mean younger—sister?"

"You've got the right idea but the wrong play," Elizabeth commented, rising. "Surely even on short acquaintance you can tell that Catherine is hardly up to the subtlety of *Midsummer*, and Mary an unlikely Hermia. Where is your head, Dolly?"

"Elizabeth, really! I wish you'd be more decapitation-sensitive with your language when I am around," said Mary, Queen of Scots.

"Ditto, Ditto!" said Jane Grey, grasping the hand of the Scottish queen approvingly.

"And should you really hold it against Dolly if her literary judgment is somewhat deficient in this case?" Margaret asked. "After all, the character of Hermia, being so notably, shall we say, petite, is an understandable red herring."

"I don't appreciate being called unsubtle, either, Elizabeth," Catherine complained.

"And I can't help but wonder if that *short acquaintance* crack was aimed at me," Mary Grey said. Such was her ire and her simple dignity that she was actually able to stare down Elizabeth while only coming up as high as her chest.

Elizabeth seated herself again on her cushion. She looked so dejected by the group disapprobation that I felt sort of sorry for her. Putting my pride in my pocket over her doubts as to my intelligence, I tried to pour some oil on the rough waters.

"Ladies," I began. "I made a wrong guess about which play was Catherine's comedy, and I was called on it. It happens. Let's not make much ado about nothing."

My companions broke into laughter, and it was wonderful. A room full of royal women, mutually touched by violence, tragedy, imprisonment, and profound disappointment, were giggling like schoolgirls and, for another one of those magical moments, just being cousins together.

I cracked up as well, when I realized what they were laughing about.

Chapter Seventy-Two
Character Building and Gilding the Lily

Having established that *Much Ado about Nothing* was the work of Catherine Grey, my task was now to figure out which of the characters in the play was based on her sister Mary. Neither the confident, spiky, and clever Beatrice nor the circumspect Hero seemed to me to have much in common with Mary Grey. I put up my hands in a gesture of defeat.

"Which of the lovely ladies in *Much Ado* is your sister Mary in disguise, Catherine?"

"Neither, Dolly. I told you that the play was heavily edited. Well, the Mary character and her presence in the play were greatly abridged."

"Not just abridged," Mary Tudor pointed out.

"No, indeed," said little Mary Grey. "My character was emasculated as well."

"I think you mean quite the opposite, Mary dear," Elizabeth said. "Emasculated means a man hasn't got the use of his own balls."

I thought about poor old Dudley for a moment and his relationship to his inamorata, the termagant Elizabeth. Mary Grey seemed to read my mind.

"You ought to know, Elizabeth," she said. "About the grammar, I mean of course." Mary was looking all innocence as she said it, but her arm reaching down to mine, her pinky linking victoriously with mine in an old-fashioned pinky promise hidden in the folds of our gowns, belied the guilelessness. "Do I perhaps mean masculated?"

"If that's the word for having balls put on," Catherine said, "then perhaps you do."

"Mary's tribute character in *Much Ado* is a male?" I said.

"Yes. But even so, one aspect of Mary's personality survived the editorial depredations: the duality of the wily if misdirected mind at work behind the deceptively bumbling exterior."

"That and one other thing," said Elizabeth, looking like she was getting ready to ride herd over the unsuspecting Mary Grey. Fortunately Jane Grey, big sister extraordinaire, headed her off at the pass.

"That," she said, "and Mary's occasional *lapsus linguae.*"

My Latin was a little rusty, and I was embarrassed to admit it. Fortunately, Mary Grey was likewise challenged but much more humble.

"Translation, please, Jane; you know how musty my Latin is."

"It is a reference, dear," said the gentle and quick-thinking Jane, "to the robustness and creativity of your vocabulary."

"Horse hockey," Elizabeth said under her breath. The passive-aggression may have been deplorable on Elizabeth's part, but it made a lightbulb go off in my head.

"Dogsberry!" I said aloud, naming one of the most engaging of the Shakespearian supporting characters.

The main action in *Much Ado*, of course, is about two sets of lovers. The supporting set, Beatrice and Benedick, get together after some Tracy-and-Hepburnesque verbal sparring and initial friction. The primary protagonists, the lovely Hero and the stalwart Claudio, likewise get together once Hero has been cleared of false accusations of easy virtue. Dogsberry, local law enforcer and man of many malapropisms, catalyzes some of the important action of the play.

"Even with their mutual, er, robust and creative vocabularies, it seems quite a leap from Mary Grey, English flower, to Dogsberry, Italian cop on the beat. Although, as the man himself says, 'Comparisons are odorous.'"

"As I explained to you, Dolly," Catherine said, "my comedy was heavily edited. My drama was as well."

Chapter Seventy-Three
Confinement, Wine, and On Down the Line

"Your life and times certainly gave you plenty of material for drama, Catherine. You were, as a Tudor cousin, very arguably next in line to the throne of Elizabeth I; you were rumored at one point, in fact, to be named as heir. Then you clandestinely and without royal permission married Edward Seymour, first Earl of Hertford—an act that was treasonous. Within months of the wedding, the only witness to the ceremony was dead, your husband was abroad on a grand tour, the clergyman who performed your ceremony had very sensibly gone to ground, and you were heavily pregnant."

"Yes, and I was desperate with it. I did not know where to turn for guidance on how to break the news to Elizabeth. I turned first for advice to Bess of Hardwick. The woman seemed to have the answer to every question."

"Whether you asked her or not," added Mary, Queen of Scots, no doubt basing her comment on her long acquaintance with the lady during her days as royal prisoner on the woman's premises.

"Well, I did ask Bess, but she refused to help based on the fact that to do so would be foolish at best and treasonous at worst. She said that *she* wasn't going to have the queen cross with *her,* just because *I* didn't know when to keep *my* legs crossed."

"That sounds like Bess. Perhaps she believed, as the Bard did, that 'discretion is the better part of valor.'"

"Well, whatever she believed, she feared the queen's wrath most frightfully," Catherine said.

"Well, in Bess's defense, as the Bard also reminds us, 'Hell hath no fury like a woman scorned.'"

"I think you will find that that was William Congreve, Dolly," said Mary Tudor.

"Well, he was right about the fury part, anyway," Catherine said. "And fearing that fury myself as well, I eventually turned to the person I felt would be best at appeasing the fury of my cousin Elizabeth."

"Her beloved Robert Dudley, Earl of Leicester," I recalled.

"Yes, and he wasn't best pleased to have a heavily pregnant and hysterical female enter his chamber in the dead of night, especially when she was a political as well as gestational time bomb. But at least, unlike Bess of Hardwick, he had the sense to immediately apprise me of what was going on," Elizabeth said.

"And there you were, Catherine," I said, "with your word being the only proof of your marriage; there was no one to attest to it, and you had no paperwork to indisputably confirm that the ceremony had taken place and was legal. Talk about being a day late and a dollar short!"

"Exactly, Dolly. And so Elizabeth sent me to the Tower. I was not angry about it at first. My son was born while I was in prison, and I was allowed to keep my precious animal companions as pets. My husband eventually returned to England and was imprisoned along with me. The conjugal visits allowed us by a kindhearted guard and the eventual birth of a second son helped to pass the time and keep my spirits up."

I'd read about the conditions in the Tower of London, to which were added, in Catherine's case, major depredations on her own premises there by her menagerie of dogs and monkeys. It all seemed pretty unsavory, and I commented that she must have been relieved when Elizabeth eventually had her removed from prison and remanded to court exile and house arrest in various country estates.

"I suppose Elizabeth thought that exile in the country was more comfortable and suitable detention for me. She had separated me from my husband, though, and of course eventually annulled my marriage. I was terribly lonely without my husband, and time hung heavy. I did, however, correspond with my sister Mary, who understood what I was going through because of her own similar experience. She wrote to me of how her literary endeavors improved her mood. Desperate to raise my own spirits, I thought I would give it a try. I wrote my comedy first, in an effort to divert my mind. It worked to a point, but I still was not relieved of the burden of the central tragedies of my life. The most galling of them became, eventually, the themes of my drama."

"You saw a lot of hardships in your short life; I can see that all of them might have been a little too much to work into one play. Which of your tragic circumstances did you consider the central ones?"

"Imprisonment and exile; loss of rank and privilege; the cruelty that power can lead to. And star-crossed love, of course. Unfortunately, the latter theme was edited out of the play."

The wine favored by Renaissance folk tended to be very much on the sweet side, and the several glasses I had consumed were telling a bit on the old tum. I think it was my gastric churnings as much as the thematic musings of Catherine Grey that suggested to me the name of her play.

"I am assuming by now that your play was one I'd associate with Shakespeare; I am thinking, therefore, that it is *The Tempest*."

"Got it in one, Dolly!" Catherine said, taking my arm up over my head and holding it there in true championship style.

"Dolly does seem to be getting into the swing of things," commented Mary Tudor.

"The exile bit was the giveaway," I said.

I could see where Catherine could have put a lot of herself, or at least her themes, as she called them, into *The Tempest*. The tale begins, of course, with power gone bad, and the wizardly Prospero and his daughter, Miranda, are exiled as a result of it. Their island home is also residence to spirits with experience of entrapment and, thanks to Prospero's magic, to some shipwrecked folks from home. Eventually, love and magic conquer all. Prospero resumes his rightful place as Duke of Milan. Miranda resumes her place as Milanese heiress and gets on the fast track to being the princess of Naples as well by marrying one of the castaways, Prince Ferdinand.

"If only my own story had had as happy an ending as Miranda's," Catherine said, and I was suitably silent as I considered her eventual death at the age of twenty-seven while still in custody.

"Your story has a happier ending than you think, Catherine," I pointed out to her a few moments later.

"How so, Dolly?" she asked.

I was pleased to be the one to deliver surprising news for a change. "Well, through the line of your oldest son, Edward, you are a progenitress of the current royal family."

"Am I? How so?" Catherine asked.

"Yes, we know that *I* have the privilege of being a progenitress through the line of my son James," Mary, Queen of Scots, said, looking slyly at her cousin Elizabeth as she did. "But the news we receive here comes about piecemeal, at best. How is it that Catherine is linked to the current regnant?"

"Elizabeth II's mother, Elizabeth Bowes Lyon, is a descendant of your son, Catherine."

Catherine was crying with joy at her long-delayed happy ending. Her sisters, Mary and Jane, cried right along with her, as did I.

"Dolly is much more emotional than she was the last time she was here," Mary Tudor remarked.

"Hard not to be, under the circumstances," I said in my own defense. "I remember similar tears of joy cried by your mother, Katharine of Aragon, the last time I was here," I told Mary.

Mary Tudor broke into a huge grin at the mention of the word "joy" in relation to her mother, whose life had not exactly gone down in history as a byword for it.

"*Touché*, Dolly! Mother told me all about that, and I will thank you, belatedly, for making her so happy on that occasion," Mary Tudor said, kneeling down on the floor next to me and giving me a big hug while she squeezed out a tear or two herself.

Once the minitempest of tears had cleared up, I got back to the literary subject at hand.

"*The Tempest* has come down through history as one of Shakespeare's final plays," I informed Catherine, "released decades after your passing. Perhaps that considerable lapse in time and the changing times, tastes, and mores accounted for the heavy editing that Shakespeare applied to your play."

"Shakespeare was *not* the one to edit my play," Catherine said. "Well, there may have been minor edits at production time, no doubt, but it was not Shakespeare who was responsible for shaping the final version of *The Tempest* as the world knows it."

"Who edited your plays, then?"

"The same person who edited mine," Mary Grey said.

"And my play as well," said Jane Grey, as the nine-day queen prepared to demonstrate that she was more than just an eight-day wonder.

Chapter Seventy-Four
Holy Folio!

Jane Grey lived an even shorter life than either of her sisters, dying at the age of sixteen. Her end was not the drawn-out demise of the prisoner but the swift, sudden death by execution that was so much a feature of Tudor court life. Her death in fact kicked off the bloodshed of the reign of "Bloody" Mary.

Because Jane and I were old acquaintances from my last visit here, we did not dance around the literary subject at hand very much but rather got right down to business.

"So you managed, Jane, to write a play during your sixteen short years on the planet?"

"My sixteen years on the planet were indeed short, Dolly. The six months I spent in prison awaiting my execution, however, were very long."

"And the perfect time to engage in some literary endeavors," I surmised.

"Indeed," said Jane.

"It couldn't have been at the behest or suggestion of your sisters, as your death preceded their literary efforts."

"I wrote at no one's behest, Dolly. Those last six months of my life were the time of my greatest introspection."

"Given your reputation for bookishness and studiousness, that is saying something," I said with respect.

"As my thoughts turned inward, I realized that what I wanted most was to leave my very own mark upon the world before I died. My political life was not of my own making; I was a mere pawn when it came to that. But something good did come out of it; that nine days' reign that I was shoved into by others informed the literary endeavor that would be my own, personal, crowning achievement."

"How so, Jane?" I asked.

"Because of all that happened to me, there were timeless themes that I could speak to in a new and unique way, thanks to my experiences. Themes that concerned *me* just then but that I was certain would concern many others down through the ages."

"I'd guess your leitmotifs were really more like heavy motifs, given the circumstance," I said.

"Justice, mercy, and a world in which a woman could advocate for herself and others in law. Those were my chosen themes, Dolly."

"I understand your needing to make a statement about those things, Jane, but I am rather surprised that you went about doing so by writing a play. History paints you as so serious and scholarly. That doesn't really comport with your being a playwright; at least it didn't on the literary scene of your day. I'd have expected some sort of scholarly treatise on the subject from you."

"Serious and scholarly though I was, Dolly, I was also a girl. Locked away as I was, without having to prove my scholarly prowess to anyone, I was able to let my hair down a bit and indulge in some drama. It was quite enjoyable, really, after a lifetime of heavy academic work, to explore something more fanciful. There was no holding back once I got started. I wrote, in fact, right up to my final hour, leaving the very last scene of my play not quite completed; I had to stop and make arrangements for its dispatch just before I was executed."

"'Because I could not stop for death, He kindly stopped for me; The carriage held but just ourselves and immortality.'" The Bard could have been saying those words about you, Jane."

"He could have been, Dolly, but he was not," Jane pointed out. "Emily Dickinson said them."

"Did Emily visit here at some point?"

"So we're told, but it is all pretty mysterious. Apparently they couldn't get the poor thing out from under the bedclothes once she'd arrived."

"Perhaps she'd heard about my cousin Elizabeth and her iron farthingale," said Mary Grey.

"I think we can let Elizabeth and any of her ferrous tendencies off the hook this time," I replied. "Emily Dickinson was a byword for reclusiveness."

"Well, Dolly," Jane resumed, "your quote attribution may have been off base, but you were spot-on about the immortality bit; my play survived me, even if in a somewhat abridged form."

I wondered how Jane knew what had happened to her works after her death. I had learned the last time I was here that the residents, other than Henry VIII's six wives, were all voluntarily exiled and cut off from sources of information other than what they could glean from each other or the various guests they had entertained down through the ages.

"All three of you Grey sisters know that your works were edited; you seem to know who did the editing; and you seem to know what the final product looked like. How so?"

"As you've been told, Dolly, we have been allowed, on a limited basis, to bring various of our possessions here to make us comfortable. One of Elizabeth's courtiers, Emilia Lanier, when she was due to arrive here, was worried about being caught short with nothing to read."

"Any bibliophile would sympathize," I said, thinking of my own stash of lightweight, portable Tudor paperbacks in car, travel bag, and bathroom. Mary Tudor, Mary, Queen of Scots, and Elizabeth nodded in agreement.

"Emilia likes to travel light, so she brought with her a single volume: Shakespeare's *First Folio*," Jane said.

"I'd hardly call nine hundred pages worth of Shakespeare 'traveling light,'" I commented.

"Well, when you consider the entertainment value contained in those nine hundred pages, I think you will agree it is a pretty compact option for the enlightened reader; as Emilia herself described it, 'Tears and laughter for all time.'"

"That was the poetess Elizabeth Barrett Browning commenting on the Bard, surely," I said, pleased, for once, to be the one correcting the quote.

"Well, I'm sure Emilia said it as well. They say great minds think alike. Was Mistress Browning a poetess like Emilia was?"

"Yes, indeed; possibly the best known British poetess. And Emilia, of course, while less well known to the general public, was the very first woman in England to professionally claim to be a poetess."

"Well, Emilia may not be very well known to the general public, but she is well known here, especially in regard to her being a most giving person," Jane said. Since the lady in question was mistress to at least one elderly theater patron and, as rumor would have it, to Shakespeare himself, I had no reason to question Jane's assessment of her generosity.

"Emilia's *Folio* is the only copy of Shakespeare that we have here. You'd think, with its being so valuable and with so many readers in the house, that she'd tend to be protective of it and keep it close. Not Emilia! She's encouraged us all to share and enjoy it. That, of course, is how my sisters and I were able to follow up on the final condition of our works."

I think Jane may have had a little more to say, but I did not catch it. I was too busy salivating and trying not to let it show.

"Dolly," Jane said, my efforts at concealment having failed completely, "would you like to flip through the pages of the *Folio*?"

I dabbed my lips with my sleeve as discreetly as I could and addressed Jane's offer. "How would I like to hold a priceless first edition of Shakespeare's *Folio* in my hot little hands? Jane—*let me count the ways!*"

As a Tudor scholar, I had seen, and in some cases handled, more than one important centuries-old publication. The thing about that is that the books were, well, centuries old. They looked old, they smelled old, and they felt old beneath the fingers. They had to be handled gingerly, like newborn babies, if one was permitted to handle them at all.

Because of the cosmic nature of the place I found myself in, the *First Folio* I held had not aged at all since its 1623 publication. Without the patina of age, the elegantly but simply bound work looked and felt like a volume in one of those upscale *Classics of Literature* collections that the well-read once ordered by mail and received at the rate of one volume a month, never to read. Leafing through it one was one of the strangest experiences that I have ever had in my life; and you must remember that as

I handled it, I was on my second visit to an alternate-universe astral Tudor plane.

As I perused the pages, familiar passages came and went: Polonius's advice to Hamlet; Lear's rant on the heath; Lady Mac's OCD breakdown. Eventually I reached one passage that was such a favorite that I read it aloud.

> I am a Jew. Hath not a Jew eyes? Hath not a Jew hands, organs, dimensions, senses, affections, passions? Fed with the same food, hurt with the same weapons, subject to the same diseases, healed by the same means, warmed and cooled by the same winter and summer as a Christian is? If you prick us, do we not bleed? If you tickle us, do we not laugh? If you poison us, do we not die? And if you wrong us, shall we not revenge? If we are like you in the rest, we will resemble you in that.

"Dolly," Jane said, "you read that with such feeling! Are you a Jewess, dear?"

"No," I informed Jane; "Polish-American, and a proud Catholic school survivor. One doesn't have to be Jewish to appreciate this passage. Anyone who has ever felt marginalized might identify. And anyone who values justice and equality cannot help but be stirred by such a simply but movingly phrased speech on the subject. It is probably my favorite speech in the entire Shakespeare canon."

"I am flattered at your estimation of my work, Dolly," Jane said. "That speech is one part of my play that has survived verbatim. You've read the words exactly as I wrote them. The rest of the play, of course, is something of another story."

Chapter Seventy-Five
Doggy Style for a Little While

Upon my complimenting her work, Jane had gone from demure English flower to incandescence in a moment, and the change enhanced her resemblance to her redheaded cousin, Elizabeth. Such happiness on a usually serious countenance emboldened me to vent my fulminating curiosity in a joke.

"''Splain please, Lucy!'" I begged, feeling a little like Ricky Ricardo, flummoxed at redheaded vagaries.

"We've heard that before," Elizabeth said, chuckling inordinately.

"Well, Elizabeth, that may be so, but I don't think it's very kind of you to laugh at my being out of the loop," I said. Since everyone else was laughing as well, I had to confess that my feelings were getting ready to be a little bit hurt.

"We are not laughing at your puzzlement, Dolly," Catherine said, being the first of the group to regain her composure. "We are laughing because you've reminded us of our old friend, Mistress Lucy."

"Lucy? You mean—Lucille Ball?"

"That's right, Dolly," Mary Tudor said.

"Lucy was here with you ladies? Whatever did she visit you for, Mary?"

"She was a career advice case, Dolly. She was a very young woman when she came to see us, an all-around performing artist. She was wondering if she should specialize in comedy."

"I remember some of Lucy's roles when she was a beautiful young movie actress in the 1930s; drama, melodrama, comedy, musicals. She did specialize in comedy once she went over to radio and television, though. And what a good decision that was!" I said.

"I am glad she took our advice as to her career," Mary, Queen of Scots, said, looking pleased. "Such a talented comedienne; I did want to see her get on."

"Permit me to ask, Dolly, if Mistress Lucy took another piece of advice that was offered to her while she was here," Elizabeth requested.

"Ask away, Elizabeth! I'll answer any question I know the answer to. Are you wanting to know what happened with Lucy and her husband, Ricky? I mean, Desi?"

"No, Dolly, that's not what Elizabeth was curious about. Romantic decisions were our mothers' department, not ours," Mary Tudor reminded me.

"That's right, of course," I answered.

"What I want to know," Elizabeth said, preening a bit before a mirror that had come to her hand, "is if Mistress Lucy took my advice as to the coloring of her hair. I suggested she adjust her shade of red so that it would be precisely the same shade as my own. I was wondering if she had done so. All she would say about it while she was here," Elizabeth said, looking chagrined, "was that she would think about it."

I answered that Lucy had indeed taken Elizabeth's suggestion and then burst into laughter myself.

"What is so funny, Dolly?" Elizabeth asked.

"'If you tickle me, do I not laugh?'" I said. "It tickled me, Elizabeth, to think that Lucy turned the tables on you like that. You have gone down in history as the monarch least likely to commit to anything; you drove the statesmen of your era mad with your shilly-shallying. Leave it to Lucy, the *Vitametavegamin Girl*, to give you a taste of your own medicine!"

I got myself a heaping helping of Elizabeth's medicine in short order. "When I smack you," Elizabeth said, suiting the action to the word, "do you not sting?"

"Well," I said, rubbing the ear that Elizabeth had boxed, "I can see now why Lucy once said that she was not funny so much as she was brave."

Mary Grey had quietly gone and gotten a glass of wine; she reached up and handed it to Elizabeth, who quaffed it with salutary effect.

"My apologies, Dolly," said Elizabeth, extending me a friendly hand. "My efforts at improvement do fall short on occasion."

"Apology accepted, Elizabeth," I said, extending my own hand to her. "No worries, I assure you. I understand completely. Old habits die hard."

"Yes, you know what they say about teaching an old dog new tricks," said Mary, Queen of Scots, provocatively.

"And I shall refrain from smacking my Scottish cousin as well, in spite of her making a bitch of herself with that dog comment."

"No pun intended, surely, sister?" asked Mary Tudor.

"Since, as Dolly pointed out, being a conundrum is my trademark, I will leave you to wonder about that, sister dear."

"I wish I could be mysterious and cunning," said the sweet and uncomplicated Catherine. "It's a shame that Elizabeth should have all the fun that way."

"Not being a dog in the manger, are you, Catherine?" Elizabeth asked.

"Not calling my little sister a dog, are you, Elizabeth?" asked Jane, her flashing eyes indicating active big-sister mode.

"Don't get your hackles up, Jane. We all know Elizabeth's bark is worse than her bite," said Mary Tudor with what would pass, on this occasion at least, as sisterly affection.

"'Cry havoc, and let loose the dogs of war!'" I said, wanting to be in on the fun.

"I think this conversation is going to the dogs, ladies," said Mary, Queen of Scots.

"A real dog's dinner," Margaret Douglas offered.

Yet again, I got to watch these legendary relatives, embattled in life, dissolve together into giggles at shared silliness. However, all good things must come to an end, just as every dog must have his day.

The incandescence that my earlier compliment to Jane had brought about had not lasted long; the girl was looking downright hangdog.

"Why so sad, Jane? I mean, really—*Merchant of Venice*—what a play it was!"

"Well, I feel like such a slacker; each of my sisters wrote more than one play," Jane confessed.

My heart broke for the poor, sweet overachiever who felt that writing *Merchant of Venice* at the age of sixteen made her an also-ran. The other women present clearly felt the same. There were even tears in the eyes of Margaret Douglas, Mary Tudor, Mary, Queen of Scots, and Elizabeth, all of whom, I knew, had lived in the pressure cooker of having to grow up as Tudor-era prodigies. Jane had clearly struck a chord.

Catherine and Mary Grey each grasped one of Jane's hands consolingly as we all set out to show *Merchant of Venice*, and Jane, more than a little love.

Chapter Seventy-Six
Hypocritically, Literally?

"Since Dolly shared that the Tickle Speech was her favorite from among the Shakespearian canon, I suppose I shall share that my own favorite comes from *Merchant* as well," said Mary Tudor.

"Really?" said Jane. "You never told me that before."

"Well, the subject never came up," Mary Tudor said.

"Let's hear it, then," said Margaret Douglas, passing the Shakespeare *Folio* over to her royal cousin.

"I don't need that," Mary Tudor said, her own inner overachiever shining through. "I can recite the passage by heart."

> The quality of mercy is not strained;
> It droppeth as the gentle rain from heaven
> Upon the place beneath. It is twice blest;
> It blesseth him that gives and him that takes:
> 'T is mightiest in the mightiest; it becomes
> The thronèd monarch better than his crown:
> His sceptre shows the force of temporal power,
> The attribute to awe and majesty,
> Wherein doth sit the dread and fear of kings;
> But mercy is above this sceptred sway;
> It is enthronèd in the hearts of kings,
> It is an attribute to God himself;
> And earthly power doth then show likest God's
> When mercy seasons justice.

The assembled Tudors applauded Mary's feeling rendition of the speech.

As for me, I got up and got myself another goblet of wine; I felt like some fortification was definitely in order. After all, I had just heard the woman known to time as Bloody Mary, maker of nearly three hundred martyrs by fire, and executioner of the speech's author, discourse with eloquence and a straight face on the subject of mercy.

I searched for the right words to say, and it wasn't easy to find them. My hope that one of Mary's relatives would start off the commentary died pretty quickly; they all looked at me expectantly.

"Some speech!" was what I eventually settled on, although, after all the wine I had taken on thus far, it came out more like *thum thpeech*. It did at least thtart, I mean start, the conversational ball rolling.

"I know what you are thinking, Dolly," Mary Tudor began. "Bloody Mary, discoursing on mercy; she has one hell of a nerve!"

"Downright pharisaical, one might even say," Jane ventured, coming out swinging with some of the best vocabulary of the evening. I wasn't quite sure if pharisaical was actually a word but figured that as one of Mary's first victims, she ought to know what she was talking about.

"Tartruffery would not be too far off the mark," Elizabeth said, adding some Moliere and one-upmanship to the mix.

"Brass balls, if you ask me," Mary, Queen of Scots, added. I wondered briefly if her experience with kilts informed this comment at all.

"A veritable whited sepulcher, to quote the Shakespeare canon," said Mary Grey.

"That was the Bible, dear. Matthew, chapter twenty-three," said Margaret.

"A wolf in sheep's clothing, then," offered Catherine, her inner animal lover shining through.

I expected Mary Tudor, aka Bloody Mary, to look crushed at all this, but she didn't. My next guess would have been that she would look defiant, in defense of her actions, but that was not the case either. She looked like the chief mourner at the funeral looks, when the deceased has passed on after a long illness; pale, yet composed; sad, but resigned.

"I am afraid," the woman said with feeling, "that you have all got the wrong end of the stick."

Chapter Seventy-Seven
Remorse, of Course

"I think I know what my cousin means," said Mary, Queen of Scots, walking over to her and standing behind her with her hands firmly on her shoulders. The Scottish queen's perspective on this whole issue would certainly have been unique. She herself was an executed martyr—but also, like Mary Tudor, a devout Catholic.

"It's all about nature versus nurture, isn't it?" asked the queen of Scots. "I let my loving emotional nature lead me away from my strict Catholic nurture, to my own detriment. My cousin here let her Catholic nurture lead her away from her loving emotional nature, to *her* detriment. It's easy for others to judge us on this, after the fact, without having to make the decisions themselves."

"So true!" said Mary Tudor. "I never knew," she said to her Scottish cousin, "that anyone understood my dilemma so well." Mary, Queen of Scots, bowed her head forward to nestle it against that of her cousin for just a moment. "Bloody" Mary Tudor relaxed her face into blissful serenity with the gesture.

Mary Tudor's face, in repose from the torments of conscience, was well worth a look. Contemporary portraits of her show the rigid funereal face of a frustrated, spinsterish extremist. None of them capture the beauty the woman had when she could share with a kindred spirit the blessed relief of acceptance.

"I was the child of Katharine of Aragon, who upended a kingdom in defense of her Catholic religious tradition," Mary Tudor began. "I was a grandchild of Ferdinand, Isabella, and the Spanish Inquisition. My Catholic position had the support of the papacy, which I had been brought up to respect as the highest authority on the planet. Those forces were constant in my world."

"As opposed to the other force in your world—specifically, your father, Henry VIII," I said.

"The next highest authority in my life—my father—cast nurture and Catholic tradition to the winds and followed his emotional nature," Mary continued. "We all know how that worked out; the hell of abandonment for my beloved mother and myself, and shame and total loss of credibility for him."

"Six wives and a historic weight problem to boot," I added.

"Such were my examples when it came to making the choice between the option of following my heart and my nature, or that of falling in with the stability of the religious tradition of those who nurtured me. I chose the latter. In the tempestuous times for religion that I lived in, that meant hard, life-and-death decisions, and many of them. Each and every one of them that went in favor of execution and death for religious dissenters went against my nature, none more so than that which sent my cousin, Jane, to meet her maker, in order to stabilize the kingdom in my native faith."

Jane walked over to Mary Tudor and pressed her head against her cousin's, as Mary, Queen of Scots, had done before. The two looked into each other's eyes and smiled. It seemed, unusual for here, that no words were needed for this cousinly détente and coming to terms. The professor in me almost swooned at the historical significance of it, and the woman in me simply melted. After a brief silence, Mary Tudor spoke once again.

"History thinks it was some kind of female disorder that led to my death—a uterine cancer, they say."

As a historian, I was able to confirm that Mary's end at age forty-two, after months of abdominal distention she mistakenly thought a pregnancy, had indeed come down through the ages that way.

"I was eaten alive all right, but not by any physical cancer," Mary said. "I was eaten alive by each and every religious execution I authorized. I did not and do not harbor guilt for them in the traditional sense because of my Catholic upbringing. I harbored, and harbor, the pain that comes from violating the feelings of my own heart. I was not and am not a mean, vindictive, or cruel woman by nature. My upbringing and what I considered my duty called for me to act like one. And so I have had to answer for my actions, down through the ages, not to the lights that guided me, but to my own heart. It has not been easy."

"That's got to be one of the worst scenarios of nature versus nurture imaginable," I said, with heartfelt sympathy. "How, then, Mary, do you come to be so fond of the quality of mercy speech?" I asked. "I would think that if anything, it would torture you with remorse even more than you torture yourself."

"Don't you see, Dolly?" asked Mary, Queen of Scots, proffering the tearful Mary Tudor a hankie. "My cousin isn't *claiming* personal mercifulness when she recites those lines from *Merchant*. She is *asking* for mercy—for herself."

"I no longer have to ask mercy from my Maker; he showed enough to allow me to come here, where I've been able to spend time with the beloved mother I was so cruelly separated from in life," Mary Tudor said. "And thanks to your auspices, Dolly, he has now permitted me to come to terms with my cousin Jane, a woman who has proven by her gesture just now that she is well and truly the last word when it comes to mercy. What a relief! Now all I wish for is mercy from the world at large and from history; I hope, Dolly, that somehow, when you tell our story, you can arrange for at least a little of that for me."

It was a tall order for a postmodern world, but I felt comfortable with a promise to do what I could.

Chapter Seventy-Eight
Hindsight Is All Right

After the naked emotion of Mary Tudor's revelation, the remaining shared praises of *Merchant of Venice* were tame indeed. Still, they served their purpose of bolstering Jane's ego quite nicely.

"The use of literary devices in *Merchant* is simply brilliant," said Margaret Douglas. "The three caskets is one of my favorite bits of business in the whole Shakespeare canon."

I recalled the three caskets as one of my favorite parts of the play as well. "The lovely Portia's suitors are asked to choose one of three caskets—gold, silver, or lead—in a sort of lottery for her hand. The gold one says, 'Who chooseth me shall gain what many men desire.' The silver one says, 'Who chooseth me shall get as much as he deserves.' Both of these weed out suitors who are looking strictly to gain wealth by marrying Portia. The third leaden chest, which says, 'Who chooseth me must give and hazard all he hath,' would be the choice of a man who is more interested in giving to Portia, than in what he can get from her."

"Wish I'd thought of a lottery like that when it came to marrying Darnley!" Mary, Queen of Scots, said, recalling her marriage to one of history's great opportunists. "He'd have given himself away as a silver casket man for sure. He had a big head and an entitlement attitude to go with it."

"Even if he had given himself away that way, you'd probably have made the same decision. Cooler heads seldom prevail when there's a strong sexual attraction," said Jane, based presumably on her academic base of knowledge. The poor thing had only a brief arranged marriage prior to her execution and was reportedly dragged kicking and screaming to the altar.

"Nothing like a tempting codpiece to cloud one's judgment," Catherine said knowingly.

"True," Mary, Queen of Scots, admitted, "and Darnley had that going for him even if he had precious little else."

"I should think, daughter-in-law," Margaret said to the queen of Scots, "that you'd have been wiser to have forsworn silver caskets altogether."

I was taken aback by Margaret's reference to the infamous Casket Letters of Mary, Queen of Scots. Eight epistles housed in a silver box, they were damning evidence against Mary in the murder of her husband, Darnley, and in regard to her sexual relationship with the macho Earl of Bothwell. The historical jury remains out on the letters' authenticity, but they were certainly political dynamite in their day, blowing up in the face of the Scottish queen.

"My mother-in-law is correct about that!" was all Mary, Queen of Scots, would admit to.

There were so many questions that my professorial heart longed to see answered here. Were the letters really written by Mary, Queen of Scots? Had they been altered or forged? Was she complicit in Darnley's murder? Was she romantically involved with Bothwell before her husband's murder? Was her relationship with Bothwell after the murder consensual, or was she an intimidated hostage?

None of these questions were to be answered, at least for the time being. "Unraveling your convoluted story, cousin Mary," Elizabeth pointed out, "would require that Dolly have a two-night stay here at least. We simply haven't the *time* for that."

My emotions were mixed; I lamented a missed opportunity but applauded the idea of moving on.

"I can tell you what literary device *I* think is most impressive in *Merchant*," I offered. "The pound of flesh, hands down."

I was speaking, of course, of the bargain made between two of the protagonists in the play: a pound of flesh removed from the debtor for nonpayment of a debt, at the creditor's discretion, and the anticipated death of the debtor as a result.

"The pound of flesh is unique in its reference to something between revenge and repayment," I said. "People in the modern world know immediately what is meant when they hear the words. But ask someone to describe it using other words, and they have difficulty. Some might say it parallels 'an eye for an eye,' as the Bard says, but the pound of flesh goes much deeper than that."

"'An eye for an eye' is from the Bible, Dolly. Book of Matthew, chapter five," Elizabeth reminded me. "And that pun about the pound of flesh—intended?"

I shrugged my shoulders as Elizabeth took over the conversation.

"As to the literary devices in *Merchant*," she said, "I myself am most impressed with that of Portia's ring, given in earnest by her to a man she loved and given away by him so very readily."

"As my daughter-in-law would have been wise to stay away from silver caskets, I would hazard that you, Elizabeth, would have been wise to steer clear of promise rings," Margaret said, eyeing the cameo "Essex promise" ring on my finger. I could see Margaret's point. I could also see that although she never made queen of England, Margaret could easily be the queen of After-the-Fact. I buried my hands in the fold of my gown just in case Elizabeth's glance should follow Margaret's. Thankfully, it didn't.

"Well," Jane said, looking quite confident again, "I would like to thank all you ladies for your kind appreciation of my play and for your support. I am feeling—if my cousin Mary Tudor will pardon the expression—quite sanguine about it again."

Bloody Mary Tudor raised an eyebrow at Jane and rose to pour glasses of wine for everyone. The flask of wine we had present must have been a magical one; it never seemed to run dry. My own glass seemed fuller than the glasses of the others. I asked why.

"You are going to need it," Jane said.

"You see," Mary Tudor said, "the identity of the editor of the Grey sisters' plays is about to be revealed."

I took a good sip of wine and did a pretend drumroll on the cushion next to me. "And the editor is…"

The assembled Tudors looked at me pointedly. I was again reminded of the four Maries of Mary, Queen of Scots, and their reaction to my earlier debut here in a French hood.

I rose to my feet and prepared myself for the editorial revelation. I was pretty sure, though, that I already knew who it was: my unmet soulie, Catherine Willoughby.

The already-mentioned Catherine Willoughby, Duchess of Suffolk, Twelfth Baroness Willoughby de Eresby, was about as connected to the Tudors as it was possible to be without actually being one of them. She was born the daughter of Maria Salinas, the BFF of Katharine of Aragon, Henry VIII's first wife.

When the child Catherine was eventually orphaned, she wound up as a ward in the home of Mary Tudor, Henry VIII's baby sister, and her husband, Charles Brandon. When Mary died, Charles married Catherine, who was then thirteen and the heiress of a considerable fortune. Charles Brandon also died in the fullness of time, leaving Catherine a young, wealthy, and desirable widow.

Catherine Willoughby was a witty, learned, and seriously Protestant woman and was great friends with the like-minded Katherine Parr, Henry VIII's sixth wife. When Henry was on the outs with his last wife, it is rumored that he was lining up her friend Catherine Willoughby as wife number seven. The woman was saved by the bell—and Henry's death. She went on to marry Richard Bertie and had two children, Peregrine and Susan.

Catherine also had, as a result of her marriage to Charles Brandon, three step-granddaughters: the three Grey sisters now present—Jane, Catherine, and Mary.

Chapter Seventy-Nine
Execution, Exile, and Exculpation

"Let's take it in chronological order," said Jane with authority. "That is probably our best chance to get the story of the editorship across clearly in the time frame we've got to work with."

"It also means you get to go first," said Catherine, showing a little middle-sister petulance.

"Well," Jane said, taking a deep breath and no notice of her sister, "the reality is that in July 1553 I was headed for the block, leaving behind a play that I wanted desperately to see the light of day: my final words on justice and mercy. I knew that if I could get that play into the right hands, the tame, final words that I'd speak in the shadow of the block need not be my last."

"'Cleanse me with hyssop, and I will be clean; wash me, and I will be whiter than snow,'" Mary Grey quoted.

"A final request of yours, Jane?" I asked. "For grooming aids, perhaps?"

"No, Dolly. My sister quotes the Book of Psalms, a selection I recited at my execution. Psalm fifty-one. It begins–"

"'Have mercy on me, O God, according to your loving kindness; according to the multitude of your tender mercies blot out my transgressions,'" quoted Mary Tudor. "You see, Jane, at the time of your execution, we were both praying from the same psalm."

Jane brushed a tear from her cheek and continued her tale. "Well, immediately before my execution, I penned my last epistle on earth, and it was to my step-grandmother, Catherine

Willoughby. I enclosed my manuscript for *Merchant* in the correspondence."

"So, Jane, am I correct in assuming that Catherine Willoughby was the editor of the Grey-Shakespeare plays?"

"Yes, Dolly. Could there possibly have been a better choice?"

"I can hardly give an unbiased opinion on that, Jane, being as big a fan of Catherine Willoughby as I am."

"Well, I knew that the time for my work to be made public, and attributed to me, would be a while in coming. It certainly would not occur during the reign of the woman who had executed me, and probably not for a long, long time after that."

I had to agree that four hundred years and counting did indeed qualify as a long, long time.

"So," Jane resumed, "I realized that I had to get my work into the hands of someone with an eye to the long view. I knew also that the work would need some polishing; my expedited end meant that while I had finished a good first draft of the play, I didn't have the opportunity to put the finishing touches on it. So the person to whom I entrusted my play would have to function as editor as well as keeper of the flame."

"Given her precarious position under Mary Tudor's rule, I suppose it was courageous of Catherine Willoughby to be in communication with you during your imprisonment. Not to mention her accepting from you, via a trusted messenger I presume, a lengthy and mysterious document that was all about justice and injustice."

"My step-grandmother knew little fear," Jane said, "but was likewise one who would let nothing get in the way of self-preservation. I knew my play would survive the Marian counterreformation in her capable hands."

"You were right there," I commented. "Catherine was nothing if not a survivor."

"That sounds like Grandmother," Mary Grey confirmed.

"I was fortunate enough to die knowing that my manuscript had reached my step-grandmother," Jane said, "and to be able to tell, even from her brief and cryptic message back to me, that all would be well."

"What word did she send you?'

"Simply the words 'Ruth three:eleven.'"

"Since Catherine Willoughby was so famously devout, I am not at all surprised she employed Bible code as a way to communicate with you. I recall that Ruth was one virtuous woman, according to all sources, but I'm not savvy enough to identify the words in that verse. Can you help me, Jane?"

"'And now, my daughter, fear not. I will do for thee all that thou requirest, for all the city of my people doth know that thou art a virtuous woman.'"

"Short, pithy, and to the point," I commented. "I expect being circumspect and expeditious with her communications around that time was especially important. She surely must have been planning, if not executing, her flight from England as one of the Marian exiles," I said.

Catherine Willoughby was a staunch reformer and Protestant, and by all accounts rather shirty about it. She had made enemies in the Catholic camp in England and would have been, under Mary Tudor's rule, a marked woman. Like many of the Catholics in England at the time, she went into voluntary exile to avoid the fate of those martyred by Mary Tudor. Catherine and her husband wound up in Lithuania, of all places, where they supported themselves doing administrative work for the king of Poland.

"So Catherine Willoughby accepted, guarded, edited, and polished your *Merchant of Venice,* Jane. I've got a question I'd like to ask about that; there is something that troubles me about the play. I hope you don't think it too nervy of me."

"There is little you could say in the way of nerve that would surprise us, Dolly," Catherine said.

"It is about the—well, frankly—anti-Semitic tone of the play. Perhaps it is not for me to judge on the complex cross-religious mores of the Renaissance, but I cannot help but confess I find it painful."

"That aspect of the play did not come from me or from my step-grandmother," Jane said. "My Shylock was a more simpatico character than the one who has come down through the ages, and I know my own language, in the play as in life, had little disparaging to say about anyone. Grandmother has told me that she assumes the altered Shylock was the work of Mr. Shakespeare or one of his company when the work got to them. All she lays claim to is grammatical and stylistic corrections where needed, the Nerisa subplot, and some considerable reworking of the character of Portia to make her personality more in keeping with my own, as my grandmother saw it."

I liked the idea that Jane's editorial "we" included Catherine Willoughby and that Catherine's talent had come down through the ages in such a hitherto unknown way. "How far a little candle can throw its beams!"

Chapter Eighty
How They Were Hand-to-Handed, and Whence They Landed

"I was told earlier that Jane's work was edited by the same person who edited her sisters' works. So, just to recap, Catherine Willoughby was responsible for the final product of all three of you Greys. Have I got this right?" I asked.

"You have, Dolly."

"Well, I know how Jane's work made it into Catherine Willoughby's hands. How did your works get there?" I asked Mary and Catherine.

"Unlike my sister, Jane, I was not confident enough in my work to be passionate about it seeing the light of day. I did not, quite frankly, know what to do about it when I realized my end was imminent. In the event, all I did was direct that all my personal papers go to my sister, Mary, upon my death. Mary," said Catherine, saluting her little sister, "over to you!"

"Discovering, from her effects, the excellence of my sister Catherine's plays spurred me on to greater effort with my own works," Mary said. "Like her, though, I was unsure about what I wanted the fate of my works to be when I was gone. When I found myself ill and with my days numbered, I made a will leaving my jewels and my personal papers—which included, now, my sister Catherine's, as well—to my step-grandmother, Catherine Willoughby. I didn't know what I wanted her to do with them. I just trusted that with her wisdom and connections, she'd be the right one to figure it all out."

"I'd love to hear from her, directly, about what she did with your plays!" I said. "Will I get to meet Catherine Willoughby while I am here? I was not able to on my last visit, after learning of the very special bond the two of us share. And now, knowing that we are both involved—on opposite chronological ends—in the sourcing of these plays of yours, I feel even more connected to her and would like even more to meet her!"

"Sorry, Dolly, but that is against the rules," Elizabeth informed me.

Mary, Queen of Scots, took pity on me, no doubt moved by my crestfallen face, and proffered me yet another glass of wine. I rose to my feet and accepted it. Fortified after a couple of sips, I took umbrage with Elizabeth.

"You told me, Elizabeth, during my last visit here, that there was only one rule about my visit: *favete linguis,* a religious silence. That I was not to reveal to the world, ever, that I had been on a visit to this Tudor astral plane. So what is this other rule that keeps me from meeting Catherine Willoughby?"

"I don't make the rules here, Dolly," Elizabeth said, rising, as she and all the others looked skyward. "I just enforce them. We have been informed that you and Catherine Willoughby are not to meet. We didn't know that was a rule until we were arranging your current visit here; the Almighty, realizing that the question might come up because of the nature of our discourse, made this rule known to us."

I must admit that I was pretty unhappy about this rule, not to mention a little the worse for all the wine. I flung my goblet at the fireplace; in its trajectory, it narrowly missed bathing Elizabeth in wine.

"Dolly!" she said, "don't shoot the messenger. I am only doing what I've been directed to do by a higher authority."

I thought for a moment about how very many of Elizabeth's staff must have felt the same way as they carried out the orders of their mercurial queen.

"There is something ironic about the fact that, in enforcing the inexplicable, you are essentially living the nightmare that you put the Cecils and so many of your other staff through, Elizabeth," I said. I probably had a smirk on my face but did not have a mirror on hand to confirm.

A wine goblet flung by Elizabeth crashed on the wall behind me and splashed a few drops of wine on my gown. Fortunately, they did not show very much on the wine-colored velvet.

"Farthingale pledge!" Mary, Queen of Scots, reminded her.

"I think Elizabeth can be excused for being so upset about having the tables turned on her like that," I said, rising up with my hand extended to Elizabeth for a conciliatory handshake. "It was probably unfair of me to throw her behavior in her face like that, not to mention the wine goblet. It's just that I have always pitied poor Cecil and all the others so vulnerable to the royal whim."

"'Excused' is not a word one uses to a queen of England, Dolly! "*I* do not require pardon from *you*! I will deign, however, in light of my pledge, to excuse *you* for your impertinence. Shake?"

We shook hands happily enough.

"So," I asked, "if I can't hear the story of the Grey-Shakespeare plays from the Catherine Willoughby firsthand, can I at least hear it as secondhand news?"

"Easily done, Dolly," said Jane. "Our step-grandmother informed my sisters and me, when we all met here, that she had edited and polished all our plays as she saw necessary. She wanted our work, and at that point, hers, to be performed in public to a contemporary audience. She also wanted to be sure that the works descended down into posterity and did not just become flashes in the pan. As she felt her end drawing near, in 1580, she did not feel that English theater was ready yet for the plays; the industry was not sufficiently developed to do justice to our works. She felt confident that it *would* be in the not-so-distant future but knew that her own time on earth would not take her to that point."

"What did she do about the plays, then?" I asked.

"She left our works in the hands of her daughter, Susan Bertie. Susan was to ensure that the plays were performed pseudonymously in her time so that a contemporary audience could enjoy them without compromising the Grey sisters' reputation. Their authorship was to be a temporary secret, not a permanent one—to be revealed when theater and playwriting gained credibility as respectable literary outlets."

"Well, the latter part of that directive obviously has yet to happen."

"Which is where you come in, Dolly," said Mary Tudor.

"Yes, I know; you want me to reveal the true authorship of these plays to the modern-day world. I'm going to need more information if I'm to perform my task, though. Why, or how, did Susan Bertie fall down on the job? What happened?"

"Susan Bertie did *not* fall down on the job, Dolly," Jane said. "She safeguarded the plays with her eye on the Lord Chamberlain's Men and some of its players and playwrights to help her execute her task. By the time her own end was imminent, she felt that the troupe was on the brink of being ready to be part of the fate of those plays but still not *quite* ready yet. So she turned the Grey plays over to a trusted accomplice to await the full development of the troupe into the means that would bring the plays to life and immortality."

"Those plays got passed around more than a pre-Truman buck," I commented. "Who got them next?"

"Susan Bertie left them in some very capable literary hands—in fact, probably the most capable hands there were for the job."

"Cecil's?" I conjectured.

"No, Dolly. Susan passed the plays off to her protégé, Emilia Lanier."

And so Shakespeare's Dark Lady made her way into the tales of the evening.

Emilia Lanier, early English poetess, was also the mistress of Lord Hunsdon, Shakespeare's patron; possibly the mistress of Shakespeare himself and the inspiration for his *Dark Lady* sonnets; and a well-placed individual in the ambit of Elizabeth I. Capable hands seemed to about cover her credentials.

"And through Emilia, the plays found their way to old Will and to fame and glory—at least fame and glory for Will," I said.

"Those plays found their way to old Will through Emilia but with my gracious permission," Elizabeth pointed out. "Emilia knew dynamite when she saw it and wisely sought my permission to forward the tales to the Lord Chamberlain's Men through William Shakespeare. She felt that, because of his romantic interest in her, he would do right by them as a favor to her. That made sense to me. Emilia was a discreet girl and great favorite of mine; I felt comfortable trusting her with the task and with the Grey plays."

"Did you read them before they were passed along, Elizabeth?"

"Yes, I did, and mightily entertaining they were too."

The Grey sisters beamed at Elizabeth's approbation, and she generously let them bask in the center stage for a nanosecond or so before drawing the attention back to herself.

"And now, Dolly," said Elizabeth, joining hands with Mary Tudor and Mary, Queen of Scots, "it is time for the three of us to tell you about our contributions to the Shakespeare canon."

Chapter Eighty-One
Paeans to Three Queens

Knowing my history as I do, I probably should not have been surprised that the Renaissance era's three most famous queens were not about to be outdone on any level by their also-ran relatives. Still, I was not entirely sure how to respond to this latest and biggest bit of heretofore unknown literary history. I assumed the best posture I could manage in a farthingale, as I felt fitting to the occasion, and addressed myself to the three queens.

"I have to admit that at this point, I'm beginning to rethink using the word 'Shakespearian' around here altogether. My goodness," I said in exasperation, "did the man write *anything* that I thought he had?"

"The man's sonnets, so far as we know, are his own, Dolly," said Elizabeth. "And possibly that dubious *The Two Noble Kinsmen* that came along after the main Shakespearian fact."

I felt on somewhat more solid ground with the sonnet information than I had in some time and addressed myself to Mary, Queen of Scots, Elizabeth, and Mary Tudor once more. "So, your cousins have enumerated the plays from the Shakespearian canon that *they* actually created. Which of the remaining plays does history now have to credit you three ladies with?" I asked.

"All of them," said Mary, Queen of Scots. "The assembled works of the ladies now present before you, Dolly, comprise the entire canon of the theatrical works heretofore attributed to William Shakespeare; the *bona fide* works of his *First Folio*."

Back onto my cushion I flumped; there is no other word for it. I was floored, literally, by the ramifications of this information.

"You realize that history of all kinds—political, social, literary, royal, and feminist—will be rocked to the core and have its socks knocked off by this revelation! It almost seems that it couldn't possibly be so."

"'Couldn't' is not a word to use to royalty, Dolly," Elizabeth reminded me. "And as I informed you on your last visit here, 'denial is more than just a river in Egypt.' We are telling you the truth and entrusting you with the task of revealing it to the world."

"Before I can reveal anything, you've got to float me across that denial river on a raft of information. Who wrote what? How did it wind up credited to Shakespeare? I need answers!"

"I think my cousin Jane had the right idea when she talked about taking things in chronological order. Being the firstborn among us, I would therefore like to begin the proceedings, if everyone else doesn't mind," said Mary Tudor.

"It seems only fair to me that, on this occasion, we give Mary Tudor her head as first in line," I said.

Mary, Queen of Scots, took over from Elizabeth in the keeping-me-in-line department by hitching up her skirt a couple of inches and applying her slippered foot to my behind.

"Execution awareness never goes out of fashion, Dolly," she reminded me.

"Point taken," I said as I rubbed my sore backside.

"And graciousness never goes out of fashion either," said the Scottish queen, addressing Mary Tudor now. "You may go first, as you request, Cousin."

Elizabeth chimed in with some younger sis sass.

"I have no problem deferring to you, Mary; after all, it is what I did when our brother Edward died and the English throne was up for grabs. You get to go first now, as you did then. And you know what they say—age before beauty."

I couldn't help but notice Mary Tudor wince. I had always thought, from what I knew about her life, that her self-esteem when it came to her attractiveness had probably been beaten pretty much to death by the behavior of her less-than-gallant husband, Phillip II of Spain. This made Elizabeth's potshot seem mean and unnecessary, and I sprang into corrective action.

"'Beauty is only skin deep,'" I reminded Mary. "'But ugly,'" I said, staring directly into the eyes of her sister, "'goes clean to the bone!'"

"Isn't that what our friend Mistress Dorothy said when she was here?" asked Margaret.

"Mistress Dorothy? Do you mean Dorothy Parker?" I asked.

"Yes, that was her name. She was here for career advisement. I found her most amusing!" said Elizabeth, her pleasure at the memory of her old acquaintance clearly visible.

"I'm not surprised," I said, remembering the caustic wit and acerbic tongue of that famous New Yorker.

"What was it that Mistress Dorothy called her witticisms?" Elizabeth asked, trolling the collective memory in the room.

"Wisecracks!" Mary Grey said. "She called them wisecracks."

"And pithy they were too. What was the one she made about my father's fifth wife, Catherine Howard?" asked Elizabeth.

"'You can lead a hor-ti-culture, but you can't make her think,'" said Mary Grey, long on memory if short on inches.

"I rather liked her 'what fresh hell is this?'" said Mary, Queen of Scots. "It was the story of my life, really, if you think about it."

"What career advice did you ladies have for Dorothy?" I asked.

"She was looking for—what did she call it?—a gimmick. We were flummoxed for a while, I can tell you. Eventually she spoke to our grandmother, Elizabeth of York," said Mary Tudor. "You recollect my grandmother's obsession with the Camelot legends, Dolly. Something she said about the Arthurian Round Table really resonated with Mistress Dorothy. She said it was just what she was looking for!"

I remembered the history of Dorothy Parker and the Algonquin Round Table, that epicenter of 1920s urban culture and literary criticism. Around it, the New York City literary world's best and brightest met daily at the landmark Algonquin Hotel for lunch. The resultant wit and acerbity were shared with the waiting world in publications such as *The New Yorker*. Elizabeth of York's suggestion had clearly been just what the doctor ordered.

"Do you think Dorothy remembered the advice our grandmother gave her and put it to use when she returned from here to the real world?" Elizabeth asked hopefully.

"Well, I think I can tell you what Dorothy would have said about that," I replied. "'Women and elephants—they never forget!'"

Chapter Eighty-Two
Family Dysfunction Junction

"So!'" I asked, returning to the subject at hand, "When, so to speak, did your literary party start, Mary?" It turned out that the outset of Bloody Mary Tudor's literary career, like the rest of her life, wasn't much of a party at all.

"My literary output began while I was resident with the last of my stepmothers: Katherine Parr."

"It's said that she united Henry VIII's children in a haven of love and security, at least for a time. It must have been a welcome respite for you after all you went through during your father's various marriages. Your fidelity to your mother's principles put you on thin ice with him on more than one occasion, to say the least. It must have been nerve-racking for you, living that way."

"It was, Dolly! I was feeling as if I had just about reached the end of my tether by the time my father made his sixth marriage. Fortunately for me, my fifth stepmother was committed to doing the right thing by *all* my father's children, and I could appreciate her for that. She and I had our religious differences, of course, me being Catholic and her being a confirmed reformer. Nevertheless, the combination of her kind heart and the point of emotional exhaustion that I had reached by then allowed us to come to an understanding."

"That is impressive indeed, considering the reputation for unbending dispositions that you both had," I commented.

"Never underestimate girl power, Dolly," Mary said.

"After my experience with Henry VIII's six wives," I responded, "not bloody likely!"

"Really, Dolly! Language, please!"

I apologized sincerely for my thoughtless words, and Mary continued her story.

"I felt sufficiently comfortable with Katherine Parr to confide in her how my feelings about my father's second marriage, and all that ensued from it both emotionally and politically, were eating me alive."

The story of Henry VIII's fascinating second wife needs little retelling. Leaving the middle-aged Katharine of Aragon—Mary's mother and Henry's first wife—in the dust, Ann Boleyn led the until-then sane and stable Henry VIII a merry dance. The world's most famous divorce, the upheaval of English Catholicism, and the eventual decapitation of Ann Boleyn left behind a now despicable Henry VIII, eating his emotions for all eternity.

"I was consumed with hatred for Ann Boleyn for obvious reasons in terms of my mother, Dolly," Mary recounted. "She rendered mother's dower years a time of humiliation, misery, ignominy, and privation. And of course, Ann Boleyn made my own life sheer hell as well. Perhaps worst of all, though, was the ongoing wreck that Ann Boleyn made of my father. Henry VIII was my hero and everyone else's before Ann Boleyn's advent. After Ann, he became an object of fear, hatred, and ridicule. My resentment about it all did not end with my mother's death or with Ann's and seemed unlikely to end even with my father's. My anger raged on inside me, day and night. There was no respite from my feelings; I ruminated on the matter constantly."

"I guess you took after your mother in that respect, Mary."

"What, when it came to ruminating? You're not insinuating that my mother was a cow, are you, Dolly?"

Mary was obviously, and understandably, hypersensitive when it came to her mother. I tried to talk her down as best I could.

"No, of course I was not! I was thinking more of the propensity the two of you had to hanging on to things, no matter what. The two of you were like a couple of Renaissance-era pit bulls; you just couldn't let go."

"That sounds like the Mary I know," said Elizabeth, giving her sibling a sisterly chuck under the chin.

Mary smiled and resumed speaking. "We shall return to that particular topic, I am sure, Dolly. To resume my chronology, Katherine Parr sympathized with me in my dilemma as best she could, and I cried many a tear on her strong and comfortable shoulders. When she was at a loss to tell me what I might do to relieve myself, she asked if she might consult a trusted friend on how to advise someone in my situation. She said she would do it discreetly, in general terms, and without revealing my identity. I agreed to let her do this."

"And in whom did Katherine Parr confide on your behalf, Mary? Let me guess—Catherine Willoughby!"

"She was the ideal person to ask, Dolly; she was my stepmother's best friend, after all. And of course, my own mother and Catherine Willoughby's mother were best friends back in the day, as well."

"I presume that my home girl, Catherine Willoughby, advised Katherine Parr to counsel you to expose, examine, and process your painful feelings on paper. Correct?"

"It didn't take much to figure that out, did it, Dolly?" asked Mary. "The novel, of course, did not really exist yet in any meaningful way in my life and times, but playwriting was, as my cousin Margaret pointed out, at an intriguing turning point. I decided to take my stepmother's advice, and try my hand at the drama."

"So there you were, pen in hand, ready to work out the volcanic emotions you had about your father's downfall, as you perceived it, at the hands of the original complicated woman, Ann Boleyn."

"I wouldn't exactly call her the *original* complicated woman, Dolly."

"Well, in any event, it can't have been easy for you, capturing so mercurial a woman in prose. The Bard might have said of her 'that time could not wither, nor custom stale, her infinite variety.'"

"Spot-on, Dolly. That is exactly what the Bard—I mean what I—wrote about Ann Boleyn!"

Chapter Eighty-Three
The Spin on Ann Boleyn

"Mary, who'd have thought it? You—responsible for *Antony and Cleopatra!*"

Mary beamed. "I did think rather well of it once I'd finished it," she admitted, with an author's pardonable pride.

"Pardon my asking about this, Mary; I hope I am not being persnickety here," I began.

"What is your question, Dolly?"

"*Antony and Cleopatra* was said to have been based on Thomas North's translation of Plutarch. And that came after your time."

"Dolly," Mary said, "do you not recall the discussion that you, Elizabeth, Jane, and I had on your last visit here—about scholarship and my own, my sister's, and my cousin's credentials?"

"Yes, I remember," I said.

"I do too," said Elizabeth. "The only one of us who got to favor Dolly with her Greek on that occasion was *me*. She has had no proof, Mary, of *your* proficiency in the language."

"If writing a play in English based on Plutarch's *Parallel Lives* from the first century in the original Greek is not proof enough of proficiency, I shall eat my snood!"

As she spoke, Mary primped the crocheted hairnet that corralled her locks behind her simple white French hood with red embroidered filigree. The rest of Mary's ensemble was likewise a simple red and white, but it was sumptuous, in velvet and brocade. It reminded me of the elegant outfit that her grandmother, Elizabeth of York, had been wearing when I met her.

"Plutarch's work would have given you ample material to work with when it came to analyzing the character of Marc Antony," I said.

"The parallels between Plutarch's Marc Antony and my father were considerable. And when you look at Cleopatra and the parallels to Ann Boleyn, well—"

"Hold on a minute, Mary!" I said, remembering the pyrotechnics that tended to follow Ann Boleyn around. "Are we about to judge the character of Ann Boleyn, out loud, right here, on her own turf? It was mentioned earlier that Ann is visiting here; is she likely to appear at any moment?" I asked, peering suspiciously around the corner and mentally preparing myself for an explosion.

Elizabeth reassured me. "My mother is present but will not be appearing while we here in this room make our revelations to you, Dolly. My mother—"

"And mine as well," Mary Tudor added—

"Have promised not to steal our thunder on this momentous night," Elizabeth concluded.

My panic meter moved down from ten by about four degrees but still had a ways to go.

"I also cannot help but mention that we will be judging Ann Boleyn's character in the presence of her daughter," I said, motioning to Elizabeth. "It will not be easy for Elizabeth to hear home truths about her mother from someone who has as big an ax to grind with the woman as you do, Mary."

Elizabeth pulled the elastic that was holding my sweet little pillbox hat on my head and then let it go. It snapped back and smacked me under the chin.

"Execution awareness, Dolly!" she reminded me.

"Like mother, like daughter, Elizabeth," I said, rubbing my chin. "I do apologize for my thoughtlessness. Still, given the history and current circumstances, I have my reservations about a frank and honest discussion of your mother's character in your presence."

"Man up, Dolly!" Elizabeth commanded me. I expected further directives about having the heart and stomach of a king, or perhaps a queen, but they were not forthcoming. "If I can take it," she continued, "you can too!"

With that, Elizabeth rose from the floor, and she and her sister Mary squared off. I watched as little Mary Grey casually grabbed a pillow and held it up against herself like a shield, preparing herself for any possible fallout.

Did I follow her cautious example? You bet your asp I did.

Chapter Eighty-Four
A Quote or Two to Float Your Boat for You

"'We cannot call her winds and waters sighs and tears. They are greater storms and tempests than almanacs can report—'" Mary quoted. "I think I summed up Ann Boleyn's propensity to create turmoil quite nicely there."

"The drama queen revealed, in twenty-five words or less," I agreed. "And of course, you went on to capture the way she was able to turn this potentially unattractive characteristic into an asset. To wit:

Fie, wrangling queen!
Whom every thing becomes, to chide, to laugh,
To weep; whose every passion fully strives
To make itself, in thee, fair and admired!

Mary, taken aback that she may have inadvertently complimented Ann Boleyn, bristled discernibly. Her recovery, though, was almost instantaneous.

"'Would I had never seen her!'"

Mary quoted, "'As Marc Antony said of Cleopatra. I heard my father say that more than once about Ann, as well, after the tingle became a chill.'"

"To which the character of Enobarbus," Elizabeth pointed out jubilantly, "said: 'O sir, you had then left unseen a wonderful piece of work which not to have been blessed withal would have discredited your travel—'"

"A bootlicker that bails out at the very end! You are welcome to Enobarbus, Elizabeth, if you would have him," Mary said.

"Probably not the most fortuitous choice of quotes, Elizabeth," I said. "You see—"

"Are you taking sides, Dolly?"

"Certainly not. I just wanted to point out that the phrase 'piece of work' has a different connotation in modern parlance than it did, perhaps, in your day."

"Well, what is the modern meaning, then?" Elizabeth asked.

"Hard to put into words, really—you could say that calling someone a piece of work is like calling them a hot mess, I guess."

"That wasn't very helpful, Dolly. Try again," said Mary, Queen of Scots.

"Well—how about a strong and unusual personality with serious character flaws?"

"You certainly could have called our father a piece of work, then," Mary Tudor said, "at least, when it came to his trajectory during and after Ann Boleyn. Although I thought, 'The triple pillar of the world transform'd, Into a strumpet's fool: behold and see' covered Father pretty well," she went on. "And I managed to get it in only about a minute into the first act, as well."

Elizabeth picked up a plumy quill that was lying on a desk in the room. "Well, since Father laid claim to England, Ireland, and France in his day, I can live with the 'triple pillar.' What I cannot live with," she said, gently bitch-slapping Mary with the feather, "is my mother being called a strumpet in front of company."

"You will be more copasetic, I am sure, Sister, with my lines from Marc Antony on men and the impact their behavior can have on women. I would think we can agree in feeling on that.

Take, for instance, these words, Elizabeth—germane to the fate of my own mother and in a way to yours—

> Why, then, we kill all our women:
> we see how mortal an unkindness is to them;
> if they suffer our departure, death's the word.

We were all silent for a moment out of respect for two if not more of Henry VIII's wives.

Mary quoted:

> Under a compelling occasion, let women die;
> it were pity to cast them away for nothing;
> though, between them and a great cause, they should be esteemed nothing.

"It is germane to my mother's fate in the king's Great Matter, as he liked to call his divorce and the English Reformation. It also sounds like your mother, though, Elizabeth, doesn't it? I mean, later on, when she was cast aside as a nonstarter in father's sire-a-son project."

"Agree," Elizabeth conceded.

"I should think Katharine of Aragon's wily adversary, Cardinal Wolsey, might have been in on the action of that last quote as well," I commented. "Wolsey was tossed aside as readily as Catherine was, when he ceased to be sire-a-son proactive."

Mary's expression changed suddenly; it was hard to describe what it showed. Not quite pain, not quite anger, not quite guilt. Disquiet probably best summed it up.

"Perhaps I shouldn't have reminded you about Wolsey," I said to Mary. "A man with big enough balls to tussle with your immovable mother! I can see why a mention of the Cardinal would make you see red."

"The Cardinal being as fat as he was, it was hard *not* to see red when he was around," Mary said. "And your mentioning him and his relationship with my mother dredges up painful feelings that I have harbored about her."

"Her tragic fate as a castaway first wife; her end-of-life exile in a drafty and remote castle; her final illness and death, endured alone except for a faithful few. It was a sad fate indeed for a princess of Spain, daughter of the legendary Ferdinand and Isabella."

"Actually, Dolly, that wasn't what I was referring to at all," Mary said sheepishly.

Chapter Eighty-Five
Of Druthers and Mothers

It pained me to see Mary looking so discomfited, so I attempted to buck up her feelings.

"You are said to have adored your mother, Mary, and understandably so; what an example she was of noble steadfastness! And you certainly did your level best to hove to her party line on Catholicism and the validity of her marriage. She'd surely have been proud of you."

"It was almost immediately after Mother's death that I started having feelings of anger about her expectations of me, Dolly. I wondered time and again what my life—and hers—would have been like had Mother taken the path of least resistance. What if she had bowed to the inevitable and exited her marriage by taking the veil as an abbess, for instance, instead of digging her heels in for a protracted divorce? She could have preserved her position and mine that way and saved us both so much misery."

"I've wondered that about the convent option myself," I admitted.

"Then, of course, after having such thoughts, I would emotionally flagellate myself for being so weak and pusillanimous a daughter to such a powerfully staunch and devoted mother. My emotions were in a constant state of agitation about it, Dolly. And once I'd felt the relieving outlet of getting my emotions about my father and Ann Boleyn out on paper with *Antony and Cleopatra*, I decided to apply the same form of therapy to my feelings about my mother."

I trolled my mind for Shakespearian works in which mothers prominently featured.

"*Hamlet?*" I ventured.

"No."

"That should have been obvious, shouldn't it? When it came to attitude, the voluptuous Gertrude wouldn't have had much in common with Katharine of Aragon. How about *The Winter's Tale*, with poor Hermione undeservedly cast aside by her royal husband?"

"A better guess, Dolly, but still not correct."

"One of the 'absent mother' plays, then—reflections on the mother you lost?"

"No, Dolly," Mary answered. "Try again."

"And if I may," Margaret Douglas suggested, "I'd advise you to think big this time, Dolly. Really big."

"I don't remember any Shakespearian mothers making particularly big names for themselves," I said. And as I said the words *big* and *name*, it came to me.

"Voluminous!" I said. "Or rather, Volumnia, the mother of the poor, harried Coriolanus."

"I'd read about Coriolanus in Plutarch," Mary explained. "His inability to deviate from his devotion to his mother's wishes, and what it cost him, resonated with me."

"Yes, I can see where Coriolanus's pivotal 'Pray, be content: Mother, I am going to the market-place' would pretty much be Renaissance-speak for 'Yessss, Mother,' and all it implies," I said.

"'Thy valiantness was mine, thou suck'dst it from me,'" Mary said, quoting Volumnia's words to her grown child, the martial Coriolanus. "My own mother said very similar words to me before we were parted. There is no forgetting something like that, Dolly."

"I suppose that your mother, who is said to have sent Henry VIII a jacket soaked in his dead enemy's blood at one point in their marriage, had more than the usual stomach for discussing bodily functions and fluids," I said. "There is more to that quote, though, isn't there? 'But owe thy pride thyself,'" I mused aloud.

"Which brings me to another way I could identify with Coriolanus, Dolly," Mary said. "We shared the burden, he and I, of pride—or at least the appearance of it—and a woeful lack of what has been called the common touch."

"We can't all be *Miss Congeniality*, Mary," I said, trying to soft-pedal the fact that the woman has come down through history as one of the least charming queens ever.

"Of course, I rode into my reign on a tide of popular approval and love," Mary said. "Just like the hero of one of my other plays: *Julius Caesar*."

"You are responsible for *Julius Caesar* as well as *Coriolanus*?"

"Yes, Dolly. I wrote *Julius Caesar* toward the end of my reign, when I could see the vultures circling around me, metaphorically speaking. Everyone who was anyone at court wanted nothing more than for me to be dead and out of the way during the final months of my reign," Mary said. "What a comedown from the triumph of my taking the throne!"

I thought of the middle-aged Mary of that time. She'd convinced herself that she was pregnant, but it was clear to all around her that she was really terminally ill.

"That had to have been hard for you, Mary," I said. I got unduly emotional as I thought about Mary's sad end and spoke through tears. "You were so alone! Your husband had bolloxed off to Spain, and your only immediate relative, your sister Elizabeth, was the flashpoint of all the courtiers who were against you."

"Yes, indeed, Dolly. 'There are more that look,' as it is said, 'to the rising than to the setting sun,'" Mary quoted.

It sounded very familiar, but in my emotional state, I could not quite place it. "*Julius Caesar*?" I ventured.

"No, Dolly; me!" said Elizabeth. "*I* said it! It was no easier for me to be the rising sun, than it was for Mary to be the setting sun. My sister and I had our differences, but I in no way wanted to be involved in action against her. Of course, with the politics of the time being what they were, Mary and I were very much at odds, but I had no way of convincing her that I meant no harm to her."

"I admit to being quite paranoid about my sister, at the end," Mary said, "and that was painful. I was so convinced that she, like everyone else, was against me."

Someone had to say it; I figured it might as well be me. "'*Et tu, Brute?*'"

"Exactly," Mary said. "That final paranoia was the denouement to an adult lifetime of bad feelings about my relationship with my sister. Being as alone as I was in the crowd of the court, I wanted nothing more than a sister I could confide in. Of course, the political and family situations we were in made that impossible. And I resented the person who was responsible for that."

"You know, Mary, as the Bard said, 'Resentment is letting someone you despise live rent free in your head.'"

"I think you will find that was Mistress Ann Landers, Dolly," Margaret said. "Another one of our guests, you know. She was brought here for career advice but wound up giving more advice than she received."

"I'm not surprised," I remarked.

"Anyway, Dolly, your point, or rather hers, on resentment, is well taken," Mary said. "The longest lasting resentment I ever bore was toward my father for separating me from my sister. Elizabeth and I were the last two survivors of our family debacle but separated so cruelly by circumstances that persisted long after the deaths of our parents. I had few friends in life, Dolly, and a close sisterly relationship with Elizabeth would have meant so much to me! "

"This is an interesting revelation, Mary, especially as history has largely come down on the side of you wishing Elizabeth had never been born at all."

"Elizabeth started out in the whole sorry affair of our family dysfunction by being born into it; unlike my mother or anyone else involved, she had no choice in the matter. My sister's heart cried out for a relationship with Elizabeth, while as a queen, I feared and resented her as a threat to my throne, if not my life. As a Catholic, I bemoaned her religious leanings. I resented my father for creating this situation between me and my only sister! There was a time when I decided to get all those feelings out on paper as well, because they were cutting at my heart like a knife."

"Or perhaps more '*like a serpent's tooth*'?" I asked. I was pretty confident that I was about to hear that Mary Tudor was responsible for the last, or perhaps the first, word on daddy issues and sister acts from the dark side.

Chapter Eighty-Six
The Concussed and the Nonplussed

The story, of course, is well known. In his dotage, King Lear makes the fatal mistake of misreading his three daughters and inadvertently setting them against each other, creating chaos in general. He eventually winds up on his uppers and pretty much naked on a stormy heath. In the fallout that follows, the old man loses his mind and learns too late the value of a true and faithful daughter. By the time it's all over, the entire family and their retainers, both faithful and otherwise, have bitten the dust.

"Am I correct in assuming that *King Lear* was the result of the cathartic exercise you just mentioned?" I asked Mary, just to be sure.

"You are, Dolly," said Mary.

"You couldn't have gotten that one from Plutarch though; King Lear was an ancient British king."

"I was inspired by the work of Geoffrey of Monmouth," Mary said. "My grandmother, Elizabeth of York, owned a copy of his work. I never knew her, of course, but I had access to the book. I'm told she treasured it because of its telling of the Arthurian legends."

"Yes, she gave me quite an earful about that the last time I was here," I said, recollecting Elizabeth of York's startling revelations about her life, the Arthurian legends, and her brothers, the mysterious Princes in the Tower.

"The story of Lear and how his unsound ideas ruined the relationship of the three sisters, Regan, Goneril, and Cordelia, was just begging to be retold, it seemed to me," Mary said. "So I retold it."

"You were prescient, Mary, in telling a tale of a king of unsound mind," I said. "Or at least that is what some modern historians would say."

"How so, Dolly?"

"It has been suggested that Henry VIII's jousting injury of 1536 was at the bottom of a lot of his, shall we say, otherwise inexplicably vicious behavior," I said.

"That fall was a bad one," Mary said. "I remember it well. Father was unconscious for hours, it seemed, before he came to. We feared he would die."

"The shock of it caused my mother to have a miscarriage," Elizabeth recalled. "And the lost child was, ironically, the much-wanted royal boy."

"Well, in the modern era, we've learned that the seat of emotions as well as thoughts is in the brain. An injury such as that which your father suffered is called closed-head trauma. Such injuries can bruise the brain or cause bleeding within the skull that puts pressure on the brain. The sufferer of such an injury may be subject to changes in behavior, thought, and emotion. Issues with controlling impulses, anger, and suspicion can occur, and judgment and cognition can suffer."

"Well, Father's judgment was questionable *before* that injury, at least as far as the whole Ann Boleyn affair goes," said Mary.

"Can we leave my mother out of this, please?" asked Elizabeth, coming at Mary again with that feather.

"Well, moving on from there, Father seemed to degenerate in kingship after that fall, even in matters *not* related to Ann Boleyn," Mary admitted. "And certainly, his temper got worse."

"And what you say about suspiciousness and impulse control rings a bell, Dolly. Kat Ashley told me that my parents had always had an up-and-down kind of quality to their relationship but that things changed after Mother had that miscarriage—all downs from then on out. Everyone at the time, including Kat, blamed Father's general churlishness from that point forward on disappointment about losing that boy. But perhaps there *was* more to it than disappointment. A paranoid quality, would you say, Mary? I, of course, was too young to remember the immediate postfall period," Elizabeth pointed out.

"Well, I was all for Father's casting off Ann Boleyn, of course, and given her actions in relationship to my mother, I did not think much of her personal integrity and chastity. I have to admit, though, that the things father suspected her of and executed her for were a bit over the top. Even *I* don't believe she was guilty of relations with all of the men father eventually had arrested and questioned as her lovers. What you said about pathological suspiciousness fits the picture, Dolly. Father was downright paranoid a lot of the time after that jousting fall."

"Thomas Cromwell would have seconded that, I am sure," Elizabeth said, recalling the friend and right-hand man that Henry VIII also had executed because of his incipient suspiciousness.

"Yes, and the part about poor impulse control fits Father to a T, as well," said Mary. "Remember him going off to meet Anne of Cleves before their wedding? He acted like a schoolboy, against all royal protocol!"

"Well, we might chalk that up to romantic notions," Elizabeth said. "But the exception he took to the woman immediately afterward was inexplicable. She wasn't at all unpleasant, unreasonable, or unattractive," Elizabeth said. "And yet he divorced her on a whim."

"Speaking of whims, there was the changeability of Father's feelings about you and me, Elizabeth, as he made his way through his four marriages after our mothers' deaths. One or the other of us, in favor, out of favor, in favor, out of favor—like some kind of insane emotional morris dance."

"And Katherine Parr, bless her, could attest to the man's temper," Margaret pointed out. "The things he threw around the sick room when the woman was trying to play nurse for him. Unspeakable! Poor Katherine had to dodge more than one loaded chamber pot, I can tell you!"

"So you are telling us, Dolly," Mary said, voice strained and hands shaking, "that these behaviors on Father's part were because of his injury and were not simply because of his personal choices?"

"You're telling us," said Elizabeth, likewise trembling, "that the man wasn't gratuitously cruel and unfeelingly changeable? That he was, well—sick?"

"Quite possibly sick, if you buy into the traumatic brain injury theory we've been discussing. And on top of that, given the abysmal state of medicine in the early Renaissance era, he was probably being medically managed, or rather mismanaged, by men who had no idea what they were dealing with. Your father could quite possibly have been 'more sinn'd against than sinning,' one might say," I told them, venturing to quote from *Lear*. "The theory opens up an intriguing line of thought, if nothing else."

Mary and Elizabeth clearly found it all more than just intriguing. The two hugged, shedding tears of joy. I was reminded of their mutual tomb back on earth and its inscription: "Consorts in realm and tomb, here we sleep, Elizabeth and Mary, sisters in hope of resurrection."

"Dolly," Elizabeth said, turning to me after embracing her sister, "Do you realize that, in a way, you have given me my father back? Had he not had that accident, he may never have executed my mother!"

Mary turned to me next.

"Well, Mary, we can't use the traumatic brain injury theory to exculpate Henry VIII from his treatment of *your* mother," I said. "That was a done deal well before the accident."

"Yes, Dolly, that is true. Father is not off the hook in any way for all that happened before that accident. But you see, when I was living the nightmare of Father's Great Matter, I always felt that if only Ann Boleyn were out of the picture, things might get better between my father and me. Once he had her executed and she *was* out of the picture, however, things did not improve very much at all."

"In favor, out of favor, in favor, out of favor," I repeated.

"And now I find out that it was all because of this medical condition of Father's," Mary said.

"I don't know about the word 'all,'" I said. "The traumatic brain injury theory is, of course, only a theory. And even if the theory is correct, there was still a lot of other context around Henry VIII's actions," I pointed out.

"Still, Dolly," Mary said, looking at Elizabeth, who nodded her head in agreement, "it is as though, in a way, you have given us a gift. There are now many grievances, small and large, against our father that we can let go of, based on the fact that he may not have been in his right mind when the events occurred."

"It must feel good to let go of that," Catherine Grey said.

"And since so much of Henry VIII's behavior set the two of you at odds, it must feel good to be able to let go, at least to a degree, of some of your sisterly rivalry," said little Mary Grey, hugging her sisters Catherine and Jane in an extension of sibling joy.

"This letting go *does* feel good," Mary confessed.

I was glad to have relieved both Mary and Elizabeth, at least to some degree, of some of their bad feelings about their father and maybe even each other.

"Well, Mary," I said, "we've discussed your finding ways to come to grips with your painful feelings about four of the pivotal people in your life: your father, your mother, your sister, and Ann Boleyn. It occurs to me, though, that there might be one more unsatisfactory relationship in your life that we have left uncovered."

"Actually, two more," Mary answered.

Chapter Eighty-Seven
Literary Notions and Going through the Motions

"Well, I think I can guess who one of those remaining unsatisfactory relationships of yours was with, Mary."

I hesitated about going too deeply into the details of Mary's marriage; in fact, I hated to even mention it. I worried that to do so would be painful for her. She married, as her mother would have wished, Phillip II, then Prince Phillip of Spain. This Catholic marriage was, to say the least, not popular in the increasingly Reformist England and even led to the Wyatt Rebellion. As a husband, Phillip was reportedly dutiful if not devoted, at least when he was actually present in England, which was a far cry from all the time. His final words about Mary—'I felt a reasonable regret for her death'—seemed to pretty much sum up the marriage, at least from Phillip's side.

Mary, on the other hand, was described as being almost besotted with the man who so failed to appreciate her. Presumably, at least in earthly life, she was spared the knowledge that very shortly after her death, her widower would be considering his options with her sister, Elizabeth. Word on the street was that Phillip was attracted to the girl even before Mary's death; hopefully, in life she'd been spared that knowledge as well.

Mary, it seems, read my mind as the thoughts were formulating themselves. "You know, I am sure, the story of my marriage, Dolly. My husband was away from me so very much of the time!"

Phillip's being one of the inbred and unprepossessing Renaissance-era Hapsburgs, and by all reports something of a prig, may have made this a plus rather than a minus for some women. Clearly, though, this was not the case for Mary.

Mary walked over to a portrait of herself and Phillip, and I followed her to it. I was familiar with the work by Hans Eworth and made note of its details once again as Mary spoke.

"I put a good face on it, but I knew that my husband was just going through the motions when it came to our marriage and to our, shall I say, intimate relations."

I looked at the Phillip in the portrait, all freakishly large head, short little arms, impossibly skinny legs, and big feet. The thought of him going through the marital motions with Mary or anyone else did not make for the prettiest of pictures.

I chose my words carefully, going for the ever-popular open-ended questions. "Tell me about the emotions your relationship with Phillip inspired and which of them you committed to paper," I suggested.

"To be entirely correct, it was not so much emotions as the situation we both found ourselves in," Mary said. "For me, it was being the chooser in our relationship and unhesitatingly selecting him, all starry-eyed and anticipating reciprocal affection. For him, it was having no personal voice whatsoever in a political marriage and having to pretend an affection that he did not feel. I put a good face on it, of course; I was my mother's daughter, after all. But I knew in my heart that with every bit of emotion I showed to Phillip, I simply made him more and more uncomfortable."

"That can't have been easy for either of you."

"And of course, the pressure on both of us to produce a pregnancy only made it all worse, especially as my health became so unpredictable."

Mary's false pregnancy symptoms are of course part of the stuff of Tudor legend. Amenorrhea, abdominal girth, and nausea convinced everyone at first that the perimenopausal Mary had defied all the odds and had indeed become pregnant by Phillip. The only thing missing was the baby—none appeared after months if not years of pregnancy symptoms.

"It was early on in what I thought to be my pregnancy that I wrote my play about the problem of Phillip and me," Mary said. "As I wrote, I harbored a slim hope that the baby I thought I was carrying would solve the whole relationship problem in one fell swoop."

"You wouldn't be the first to put all your hopes on the baby solution to a problematic marriage," I said.

"She certainly would not have!" said Elizabeth. "There was my mother, for one; she certainly had reason to believe that a baby, or at least a male one, would solve her marital problem."

At all these mentions of the word "problem," I thought about Shakespeare and the plays that, being neither comedies nor dramas, fell under the rubric of problem plays.

"You certainly did have a problem there, Mary. And if I am correct in my guess about which play you wrote about it, I can safely say that literary history agrees. 'If ever truth were pregnant by circumstance'—" I said, feeling confident that Mary's marital play and Shakespeare's most cynical problem play were one and the same.

"Your choosing your husband, and your husband being, shall we say, less enthusiastic than you'd have liked about being chosen—the template for the dilemma of Helena and Bertram, was it not?" I asked.

"Yes, Dolly, it was. I got the idea for the play from one of the tales in Bocaccio's *Decameron*."

"Helena earns the right to marry Bertram; Bertram is not happy about this. He says he will not marry the girl until she can get both a ring and a baby from him, things he is certain will never take place. Helena contrives to make both of these things happen, though, making use of the rather unfeminist principle that one woman is pretty much like another in the dark. And so, Helena and Bertram are united in a—what should I call it? 'Happy ending' doesn't quite seem to fit the bill," I said.

"That's why I called it *All's Well That Ends Well*," Mary said.

I was sobered by just how little Mary seemed willing to satisfy herself with in terms of a romantically satisfying conclusion. I was about to be even more sobered when I learned which was the last of Mary's plays.

Chapter Eighty-Eight
The Riled and the Exiled

"Enough about my husband and me though," Mary said. I have to admit I was glad to move on from an awkward subject. Unfortunately, the next subject at hand was even more awkward still.

"We are now left with the last of the relationships that I felt the need to process in a fictional work," Mary said.

"Well, we've covered mother, father, sister, and husband; who is left?" I asked, flummoxed.

"My kingdom remains, Dolly; my subjects, courtiers and commoners both. My relationship with them is the subject of my remaining play."

Given that Mary Tudor had come down through the ages as Bloody Mary, the least popular of English monarchs, I figured another problem play was in with a chance, a tragedy was an even better bet, and a comedy was pretty much out of the question.

"I started my reign with such high hopes, Dolly! I wanted to bring the people of England back to the old religion, Catholicism. I considered it a gift I could give to them. And they did not want what I had to offer."

"Not unlike your relationship with Phillip, was it?" I said.

"Rejection by those I valued was certainly a theme in my adult life," Mary admitted. "It seemed to me that the influential and reasonably well-off were the first to abandon me after I began my reign; so many of them chose exile from the country over converting to my faith. Catherine Willoughby," Mary added meaningfully, "was one of them."

"She had a lot of company," I said. "There were said to have been over eight hundred Marian exiles, as they came to be called."

"And I considered each departure a slap in the face, and a failure on my part. So I stepped up my game."

"To the tune of two hundred and eighty-three," I remarked. There was a moment of silence as we all recalled those lost in the Marian executions for political or religious intransigence.

"A bit of me died with each and every one of them," Mary admitted.

"And yet, you went on," I said, merely ruminating on the fact. Jane of all people stepped up, not to Mary's defense exactly, but to remind me of some of the context of the Marian executions.

"Please do remember, Dolly; in Mary's father's reign there were wholesale religious executions as well."

"Yes, of course; easily two hundred during the Pilgrimage of Grace alone, with some estimates going into the thousands."

"And there was the Prayer Book Rebellion during the reign of her brother, Edward VI," Jane pointed out.

"Well over five thousand down over that one, they say," I recalled.

"And my cousin Elizabeth's reign; so many executions during the Northern Rebellion alone."

"Up to eight hundred, according to Elton."

"Make that eight hundred and one, if you think about it," said Mary, Queen of Scots.

"All right, ladies. Point taken about the context of the executions of Bloody Mary; 'everything is relative,' as the Bard says."

"I think you will find that was Leon Trotsky, Dolly," Jane said.

"How in the world did you get the skinny on Leon Trotsky?" I asked. Surely the early twentieth-century Russian communist had not sojourned here.

"We had one of the members of the Romanov dynasty—Alexandra—here for a consult. As empress of Russia, she was going down a very bad road with a cleric named Rasputin. Unfortunately, there was no talking her out of it. We heard that that ended badly."

"It's surprising the things you have and haven't heard here, over the years," I commented.

"We've learned a lot, of course, from our guests over the centuries; sometimes, it is blanks filled in about things that happened relevant to our legacy after we died. But mostly, it is about how very much things have changed over the centuries. Hence, we understand why someone from the twenty-first century may not fully understand the dynamics of executions in our day," Elizabeth said.

"But surely, Dolly," Mary added, "some feelings are timeless. Can you imagine how I felt well into my reign knowing that my people hated me in spite of all my good intentions? Knowing that all my generous and motherly impulses, my desire to guide my people back to the true religious path, were denigrated and thwarted? Do you know what that's like?"

"Trying to talk a girlfriend down off a loser boyfriend and being flipped off for my pains is probably about as close as I've come to it, but I think I can imagine, at least, what your feelings might have been."

"Then surely you can see, Dolly, why I was so intrigued with the story of *Timon of Athens*, as told in Lucien."

"Poor old Timon!" I said. "The most generous man in Athens, and everyone was his friend as long as the money held out. Then, when he was down on his luck, everyone deserted him. He left town and lived in the wild, hating and cursing mankind rather fruitily all the while, wishing for nothing more than to destroy the people who'd abandoned him."

"You know the work!" Mary said, pleased.

"Well, to be honest, it is considered one of the minor works of the Shakespeare canon, but it does have its fans, of which I am one," I admitted. "Timon's last banquet before leaving Athens, with the stone and water cuisine served on gold and silver plates, is one fine set piece," I said.

"If you are familiar with the play, then you know what happened to Timon after that very same banquet while he was out in the wild."

"Yes! He stumbles upon some hidden treasure and gives it to Alcibiades to fund an invasion of Athens. The Athenians beg Timon to save their city, but he is so disillusioned by then that he wants no part of it. Timon dies, angry and alone, after acknowledging only one true and deserving friend in the whole world."

"Flavius," Mary said. "That character was a tribute to my dear friend, Jane Dormer. She was the one true and steady person in my world, which was otherwise so full of people I had reason to fear, hate, or distrust."

"I can see why the story of the misanthropic Timon would have had so much appeal for you," I said.

"'Here lies a wretched corse, of wretched soul bereft: seek not my name,'" Mary quoted. "I certainly worked out a lot of negative emotion while writing about Timon's sad but defiant end."

"He is surely one of the most melancholy characters in the Shakespearian lot, and that is up against some pretty stiff competition," I said.

"Well," Mary said, smiling a little, "at least I didn't end up quite as badly as poor old Timon in the end—naked, hairy, eating raw meat, and throwing rocks at people from a cave."

All of us, including Mary herself, laughed at that mental picture and at hearing the dour Bloody Mary make light of herself in that way.

"Tell me, Mary, about the immediate fate of your plays; how they went from your little world to Shakespeare's Globe," I said, when the hilarity had subsided.

"I think it is fair to say," she replied, laughing again, "that they got to the Globe in a most roundabout way."

"Mary, have you just punned on the rotund intentionally?"

"You bet!"

Chapter Eighty-Nine
Tiswas at Amboise

"When I knew my end was near," Mary began, "I thought, as an author would, of the fate of my works. We've spoken already about my position during my reign and of the dearth of people I could trust. There was one, though, who I knew would come up trumps."

"It was Jane Dormer, of course; trusted lady-in-waiting, and probably your only friend by the time you were on your deathbed."

"Correct, Dolly. I handed off my works to Jane in my final days, and died knowing she would do the right thing by them. I little suspected how roundabout a path she would set my works on, but life can be funny, can't it?"

I looked at my reflection—all Renaissance splendor—in a mirror on a distant wall. I had to admit that life could indeed be funny.

"When I arrived here, Jane was able to fill me in on the *first* leg of the journey of my plays."

"The *first* leg?" I said.

"That's what I said! You will recall of course, Dolly, Jane's career after my death."

"Yes. An ardent Catholic, she married the Spanish ambassador, and returned home with him to Spain. She lived out her life as the Countess de Feria, most religiously, and died in a convent. Did your works wind up in that Spanish convent, Mary?"

"No. My works never saw the sunny skies of Spain."

"Well then, what skies *did* your plays see?" I inquired. "Just rainy old England's? Did Jane leave them in your homeland with someone she trusted?"

"No. Jane took my works with her when she left England. She did make a stop on the way over to Spain, though."

"Of course she did—at Amboise, in France. It's said that Jane Dormer and Mary, Queen of Scots, became great friends during that layover."

"We did," said the Scottish queen. "And that is why Jane left her mistress's plays in my hands."

"Whatever did you think, holding the plays of Mary Tudor in your hands, a gift from the other side from your cousin and fellow Catholic and queen?"

"I am a bit embarrassed to admit that I did not give the plays the attention they deserved. The advent of Jane and the plays occurred during that brief, gaudy hour when I was queen of both France and Scotland."

"It was not much more than a year that you were queen of France," I recalled.

"And of course, I was so young, not yet out of my teens. The French court was such a glittering place, and I was newly raised to the highest prominence in it. Lording it over my mother-in-law, Catherine de' Medici, and picking out gowns for the day's and evening's wear were the highest priority for me in those halcyon days."

"'Your salad days, when you were young and green of experience,'" I offered.

"Green was never my color, Dolly," Mary said, laughing.

"As I recall, you dressed in white to receive Jane Dormer when she arrived at Amboise in 1560. I suppose that was the fashion equivalent of being young and carefree, back in the day."

"Jane was a pretty serious young woman, and she spoke to a side of me, hidden pretty deep in those days, that could be intelligent and serious too, when it wanted to. Since that side of me was so little brought out by my frivolous life at the French court, I came to value Jane's friendship even after a very short acquaintance."

Mary Tudor smiled benevolently at her cousin's commendation of her friend.

"I was flattered, during our visit, when Jane entrusted me with Mary Tudor's plays. I knew how much her mistress meant to her and how seriously she took her duty to those works. She felt that putting them in family hands, and Catholic hands, was important. So she was thrilled when the opportunity presented itself to hand the plays off to me. Once Jane left France, though, I have to admit that I was flummoxed about what to do with them."

"I guess that would be a bit of a conundrum for a young French queen; what to do with one's dead elderly cousin's secret potboilers."

"That is exactly what I thought they were, Dolly. English was not my first or even second language, so when I read the plays at the time, I understood but did not fully appreciate them. And not long after Jane left, of course, my own troubles, you might say, began."

"You refer of course to your first widowhood and the untimely death of Francois II," I said.

"Correct, Dolly. Overnight I went from being the premier woman at the French court to being a dowager while still in my prime. I wasn't having *that*, young and proud as I was."

"And so you were Scotland bound, to take up in earnest your career as queen there," I said.

"That's right, Dolly. As I prepared to leave France, those plays *did* weigh on my mind. I decided against taking them with me to Scotland. What with the puritanical bent of my homeland's culture, I knew that the plays I'd read would have little hope for a future there. French theater, on the other hand, was more developed, thanks in part to the popularity of the *Commedia dell' arte*. And of course, my husband's ancestress, Marguerite de Navarre, while most famous as a religious poetess, had also reportedly popped out the odd play. Overall, I thought that Mary Tudor's plays would be best served by being left in France. I put personal feelings aside and placed them in the hands of the most capable person I knew at the French court; my mother-in-law."

"So you left Catherine de' Medici holding the bag—I mean, the manuscripts."

"I did. And she held them for quite a long time. I left them with her in 1561, and they stayed with her, I later learned, until 1579."

"What happened in 1579?" I asked.

"Some of the most fun I ever had in my life!" Elizabeth said, actually slapping her thighs—or as close as she could get to them in a farthingale—with merriment. It made me wonder what it might have been like to party like it was 1579.

Chapter Ninety
The Gift That Fixed a Rift

Once her mirth subsided, Elizabeth took me by the hand and led me to a portrait of a man who, at first blush, looked all nose, jaw, and ruff. The lettering on the painting told me that the man who'd set Elizabeth's farthingale a-twitching that way was none other than the Duke of Anjou, son of Catherine de' Medici and brother-in-law to Mary, Queen of Scots.

"In 1579, the French Duke of Anjou came to pay court to me," Elizabeth began. "He was the only one of my royal suitors to actually appear in person. He was so sophisticated and bohemian. What a change his advent made from the usual dour royal courtship rituals, all dusty ambassadors and even dustier portraits."

"You nicknamed him your 'frog,' Elizabeth. History indicates that your frog was something of a dog as far as princely suitors go. He was by all accounts pretty unprepossessing at best—his own brother called him a little monkey."

"Well, looks aren't everything, Dolly."

"The man wore one of those padded, push-up codpieces, as well. At least, that was the rumor at the French court," Mary, Queen of Scots, added.

"Well, size isn't everything either. And what a pleasure that he had such tremendous wit," Elizabeth said. "I also learned, from my dalliance with him, just how well founded the French amatory reputation was."

"I guess old Anjou was G-spot on when it came to knocking your stockings off," I said to Elizabeth.

"Of course, the man was also about twenty years younger than I was, and being courted by such a youthful and engaging swain was like a breath of fresh air," Elizabeth said. "At least, it was at the time of life I had reached by then."

"A May and December romance; or perhaps I should say a December and May romance, given that you were the elder of the two of you," I said.

Elizabeth started glowering after my unthinking reference to her age. I diverted her attention quite nicely with a fair rendition of the "September Song." She wasn't best pleased about the long, long while from May to December but had warmed up quite a bit by the time the days dwindled down to a precious few in September and November.

"And of course," Elizabeth said, mollified, "the fact that Anjou came bearing the plays that had been written by my dead sister, Mary, made his arrival at court that much more of an event for me."

"I see! Catherine de' Medici punted the plays to her baby boy, the Duke of Anjou, and he hand-delivered them to you, Elizabeth. What a courting gift! What was it like, receiving, as it were, a message from beyond from your departed sister? We've already discussed the difficulties of your sisterly relationship in life. How did you feel about hearing from her again, so to speak, after so much time had gone by and with a good few years of being queen now under your own belt?"

"Well, Dolly, I'd been writing plays myself, secretly. To know that my sister had done the same made for a bond between us, even though she was gone. For a long time—for years, in fact—I held on to those plays and treasured them as though they were private correspondence between the two of us. Those plays healed a lot of sisterly sore spots and helped me to let go of a lot of negative emotions, particularly those about how suspicious Mary was of me during her reign."

Mary Tudor got teary at this, and so did I, I must admit. The Grey sisters satisfied themselves with joining hands.

"I read and reread those plays," Elizabeth went on. "I was inspired by them, and in some ways they informed my own work. I realized, as I became more and more familiar with them, just how good they were. It seemed unfair, eventually, to keep them to myself. But of course, the English mores of the day meant that I couldn't reveal them as having been written by my sister, an anointed queen. I wanted to do justice to them, though, and happily, I found a way to do so and keep it in the family—my own family, if not my sister's—at the same time."

Chapter Ninety-One
See 'Em Later, Alligator

"How did you manage to keep those plays in the family?" I inquired.

"Through the auspices of one of my Boleyn cousins—Henry Carey, First Baron Hunsdon."

"Of course!" I said. "The man was the patron of the Lord Chamberlain's Men, the theatrical company that Shakespeare was associated with."

"Well, he wasn't patron yet when I passed the plays off to him, but he was interested in the theater at the time and in making it more accessible and acceptable to all the public, both the plebian and the well-to-do. I wanted to support the effort, and I wanted to find a way to get Mary's plays out. So I turned the manuscripts over to him for future use, for when he had operationalized his plan for subsidizing and patronizing a theatrical troupe."

"Did Hunsdon know about your own playwriting efforts?"

"No. He was not privy to that or to the identity of my sister as author of the plays at hand. I had copied Mary's plays out in a disguised hand as a precaution. I authorized him to attribute the plays as necessary to get them before the public, telling him that I would take the revealing of the true authorship into my own hands, to occur in the fullness of time, after my death. I think he suspected that the plays were mine. I did not disabuse him of that notion because it meant he would be all the more assiduous about assuring the success of the plays."

"And did everything work out to your satisfaction?" I asked.

"Well, yes and no," said Elizabeth. "I passed the plays off to Hunsdon in the late 1580s, and he died in 1596. By the time of my death, in 1603, I'd seen only two of Mary's plays, *Julius Caesar* and *All's Well That Ends Well*, performed. I'd liked to have seen them all, but that was not to be. I left it to faith that my sister's other works would see the light of day after my death, just as I hoped that my own works would."

"'Behold, the farmer waits for the precious fruit of the earth, and has long patience for it, until he receives the early and latter rain,' as the Bard has said," I pointed out.

"That is the Bible, Dolly. James chapter five, verse seven," Margaret said.

"Darn! Goofed again! I hate to mess up like this, especially in front of such erudite ladies as yourselves."

"Well, Dolly, 'into each life some early and latter rain must fall,'" said Mary, Queen of Scots. "Although in my own life, I suppose it was all latter rain, really."

And so Mary, Queen of Scots, the *décapitée* who put the "gal" in gallows humor and knew a segue when she saw it, set the stage for her own revelations.

Mary was Queen of Scots from earliest infancy because of her father's death in one of the worst military drubbings in the history of Scotland, a country with plenty of such drubbings to its name. The child queen was eventually shipped off to France to be held in some very gilded cold storage until she was old enough to marry the French prince. She was quite a prize, you see, being not only the Scottish queen but an heir to the English throne as well, at least by strictly Catholic lights.

The child grew up a beauty, and the French marriage went off as planned, but the groom died in his teens from an ear infection.

Widowed and at a loose end, the elegant Mary returned to rough-and-ready Scotland to assume the reins of government. It was the world's worst case of cultural dissonance and an unmitigated disaster. After some of the poorest decision making on record, Mary wound up making a run for her life to Elizabeth I's England. The back-door advent into her country of the woman that Catholic Europe thought should be ruling it in her place paralyzed Elizabeth's faculties of resolution; the result was close to twenty years of house arrest and imprisonment for the Scottish queen. Mary, Queen of Scots, was finally executed under Elizabeth's orders in 1587.

Mary was dressed in the same black and white that she had favored for several of her extant portraits. It suited her perfectly. Her headpiece was a lacy, white French hood with billows of even more lace falling behind into a veil. She wore a large, lacy ruff, and the bodice of her gown featured soft white linen with curlicue embroidery. The effect was enchanting, as if her face was nestled in a cloud somehow.

"I don't like to brag, Dolly," the woman began.

"But she won't let that stop her," Elizabeth finished.

"The pot calling the kettle black, surely," Mary Tudor offered.

"I think that when it comes to bragging, my Scottish cousin 'does it with better grace,' but Elizabeth 'does it more natural,'" Jane said puckishly.

"Well, I bested Elizabeth on one thing, and I am not ashamed to crow over it," said Mary, Queen of Scots. "In fact, on this one thing, I bested everybody else in this room."

"Your particular accomplishment?" I asked.

"Being prolific," she said.

"With one child to your name? Surely not," I said, thinking of Catherine Grey and Margaret Douglas.

"I wasn't speaking about fertility, Dolly. I was talking about literary output. I wrote more of the plays in what is known as the Shakespeare canon than anyone else here."

Chapter Ninety-Two
Propinquity with Antiquity

"Well, I guess your literary fecundity is hardly surprising. Close to twenty years of incarceration must have given you plenty of time to write," I conjectured.

"Yes, and to ponder long and hard the role that sex and violence played in my life and my downfall," Mary said. "Four of my dozen were dramas that amplified those recurring themes in my experiences."

"And the other eight?" I inquired.

"The castles in which I served my time were places that were, shall we say, off the beaten path. Those who resided in them were isolated from others, and from opportunities for entertainment such as the masques and plays that I had enjoyed when I lived at court, and that I missed so much. Those various castles all had, as a result, generously furnished libraries. During my confinement, I had access to all sorts of tomes that I could use for my research."

"Your research into—what?"

"History. The remaining eight of my plays all dealt with history, Dolly. *King Henry IV, Part 1*; *King Henry IV, Part 2*; *King Henry V*; *King Henry VI, Part 1*; *King Henry VI, Part 2*; *King Henry VI, Part 3*; *King John*; *King Richard II*," Mary recited, proud as a peacock.

"I can't help but notice that you stopped at *Richard II*," I said. "Did you know that Margaret Douglas was covering the subsequent stories of Richard III and Henry VIII?" I asked.

"No, Dolly; I took the modern history of England in numerical order of its kings, and the project wiled away many a dreary hour during my captivity. Unfortunately, I ran out of time, or perhaps I should say, luck, before I could get past Richard II," Mary said.

"You wrote in English, rather than Scots or French; that was certainly in keeping with your subject matter."

Mary nodded. "And of course, everyone around me in my captivity spoke English, and my reference works were in English, so writing in the language seemed the natural thing to do," Mary said.

"I'm surprised you chose English history over Scottish, though," I said. "You were, after all, the queen of Scots."

"Well, Dolly, the preponderance of my plays involved English history because that is what I had access to in my confinement," Mary said.

"Edward Hall's *Chronicle*, I suppose?" I asked.

"Yes, among other things."

"It always tickles me to remember that he came from the Parish of St. Mildred's in the Poultry," I admitted.

"Holinshed's *Chronicles* were available in the latter half of my imprisonment, as well," Mary told me. "And there was some history in there that allowed me to pay tribute to my native Scotland with one play, at least."

Not being one to tempt fate, I chose my next words carefully.

"That would be *The Scottish Play*, of course."

"I know why you refer to my play euphemistically, Dolly. Mistress Sarah Bernhardt, when she was here for career advisement, told me about the suspicion that now surrounds my work of Scottish history. As its author, though, I feel I am exempt from the curse and will call it by its name: *Macbeth*."

Chapter Ninety-Three
The Lots of Some Scots

The Scottish Curse, as it has come to be known, holds that in theatrical circles, it is bad luck to refer to *The Scottish Play,* or even to the surname of its husband-and-wife protagonists, by name. Elaborate cleansing rituals, such as turning three times or reciting a particular Shakespearian line, are said to be antidotes to inadvertent mentions of the forbidden word.

"I guess Sarah Bernhardt would have known what she was talking about when it came to *The Scottish Play*," I said. "When her theatrical career was at an impasse in the 1880s, she pulled her chestnuts out of the fire with a very successful portrayal of Lady Macbeth. Based on what I've been hearing since my arrival here this evening, I have a feeling that idea of hers may have come from a visit here for career counseling."

"You are correct, Dolly, but before we go any further, you must perform a cleansing ritual for saying the *M* word out loud just now. Three times around, please!"

"Does it matter if she goes clockwise or counterclockwise?" asked Mary Grey.

"Good question. 'The devil is in the details,'" said Catherine, who, if anyone, ought to know.

"I think the direction of Dolly's choice will be quite satisfactory," Mary Tudor said.

"I don't know," said Elizabeth. "My mother says that widdershins is bad luck."

"Widdershins?" I asked, as I rose from my seat on the floor.

"Yes, Dolly. It is an old-time mystical word for counterclockwise."

Remembering my last encounter with Ann Boleyn, I realized that she ought to know as well.

Three times around clockwise I spun myself, and let me tell you, it wasn't easy. The mini-Bernoulli effect that the endeavor created around my farthingale nearly knocked me off my feet.

As I spun, I considered the plot of the *Scottish Play*, aka *Macbeth*.

Macbeth, incited by the prognostications of three witches, embarks on a mission to attain the Scottish throne. Sharing in his ambition is his wife, Lady Macbeth, the one who wears the hose and doublet in the Macbeth family. Macbeth wavers in the blood spilling required to operationalize his plan, but his wife, who is so tough that she doesn't need a first name, eggs him on. Eventually, guilt and mental illness set in. Macbeth starts seeing things, and Lady Mac goes all OCD about washing the blood of their victims from her hands and eventually kills herself. Macbeth himself is killed at the hands of MacDuff, whose family Macbeth has killed to further his ambitions.

"The *Scottish Play* must have crystallized for you much of what you experienced in your life in Scotland," I said to Mary. "The clans and their fierce bloodline loyalties; the ruthlessness and the violence; the magic and mystery of the old ways; and of course, the abysmally bad Scottish weather—you got it all in there!"

"*Macbeth* was satisfying to write in a number of ways. As with all my plays, writing it helped to pass the time, a crucial function when one is a captive."

"Too true," said Catherine with feeling.

"The play also served as a crystallizing of my own political experiences, as you say, Dolly; ambition, murder, and mayhem.

Of course, it also allowed me to show some Scottish pride by memorializing a piece of my country's ancient history. It served one other function that may be a little less obvious to you, Dolly."

"It's hard to believe you could have fit any more meaning than that into the play," I said.

Mary, Queen of Scots, raised her hand to her mouth, as if to hide a guilty giggle.

"Well, whatever else it was that you worked in, I'm glad it gives you something to giggle about," I said.

"I can't help it," she told me. "I feel so wicked when I think about what I did!"

Chapter Ninety-Four
Stitch and Bitch

"Out with it, Mary! What did you do?" asked Elizabeth. "I'm as curious to know as Dolly is."

"Me too!" said Mary Tudor. "It must have been really something to make someone with a track record like yours feel wicked."

"'Naughty' is probably a better term," the Scottish queen confessed, enjoying the mystery she had created. "I will give you a hint. It involves someone you all know."

"Not poor old Dudley getting raked over the coals again," I said. He'd met the Scottish queen when he'd been proposed as a potential husband for her; of course the relationship had gone nowhere.

"No."

"Well, since everyone here knows the person involved, I'm going to go out on a limb and assume he or she is English," I said.

"Correct, Dolly."

"Then it is likely someone you met while you were imprisoned here," said little Mary Grey.

"Well, then, the pool of candidates can't be all that large," said Catherine. "One doesn't get around much under house arrest."

"When one is on house arrest, one takes one's friends and amusements as one finds them," the Scottish queen said.

"Well, now I know that you had your writing to help pass the time during your captivity, Mary. Other than that, all I know about your pastimes during your incarceration is that you did a lot of needlework to entertain yourself and while away the hours. You and Bess of Hardwick, your primary wardress, embroidered many a panel together, and a number of them are still extant."

"Are they, Dolly?" asked the Scottish queen.

"Yes," I answered, "and I've seen some of them. I like to do a bit of cross-stitch myself, so viewing historic textiles is something I indulge in whenever the opportunity presents itself."

"Which of Bess's and my embroideries have survived?" she asked, with a craftswoman's concern.

"Panels of animals, both real and fanciful, that the two of you embroidered," I said. "Some of them were emblematic, some personal, and some just plain charming and fanciful. I recall fishes, birds, an elephant, a monkey, a cat and a mouse, and a strikingly beautiful peacock attributed to Bess. And, of course, my favorite of them all, attributed to you," I said admiringly.

"And that was?" the Scottish queen asked.

"An embroidered rendering of a pet dog of yours," I said. "In addition to its being a lovely piece of embroidery, it is a glimpse into your day-to-day life as well. The dog is called Jupiter. He was a white dog with black markings."

"That dog adored me," Mary, Queen of Scots, said. "I called him Jupiter as a kind of joke. He was about as unlike his namesake, the god of thunder and lightning, as he could possibly be. He was a sensitive animal, fearful of sudden noises and of storms. And he could read people as though he were human himself. Strong personalities and tension between individuals upset him terribly."

"Can't have been easy for the poor old pup, living around Bess of Hardwick," Elizabeth said.

"I'll bet," I said.

"Bess thought it ridiculous that I called the dog Jupiter," Mary, Queen of Scots, said. "She thought that dogs, like people, should hold up their end. She really didn't see the point of Jupiter at all. She insisted on referring to him not as Jupiter but as Spot. She felt the name suited him better."

"How did poor old Jupiter feel about Bess of Hardwick?" asked Catherine, her inner animal lover showing through.

"He sensed her disapprobation of him, and it distressed him. He made his distress known the way dogs usually do."

"Shoe chewing?" asked Catherine.

"No," said Mary, Queen of Scots.

"Nipping?" Catherine inquired.

"No."

"Spite peeing or spite pooping, then?" I asked, figuring somebody had to.

"Exactly, Dolly, and usually on or near Bess's shoes. Bess would get so upset if the animal came into the room when she was present! I can hear her now, addressing that poor little dog."

"What would she say?" asked Catherine, getting ready go all PETA if the need arose.

"She'd shake her fist at that dog," Mary, Queen of Scots, recollected, "and say, 'Out, damned Spot!'"

Chapter Ninety-Five
In the Stir with the Green-Eyed Monster

"Out, damned Spot!" I echoed. "That is Lady Macbeth's tagline! 'Will all great Neptune's ocean wash this blood clean from my hand?'" I continued, quoting Lady Mac at her guilt-ridden, hand-washing best, or maybe worst.

"Three times around, Dolly," said Mary Grey. "You've said the *M* word again."

"I'll have to send for Kat Ashley to wash your mouth out with soap if you can't control yourself better than that, Dolly," Elizabeth said.

I declined to quote Lady Mac further, not wanting to put any more ideas about ways to discipline me into Elizabeth's head.

"Are you telling us, Mary, that Lady Mac, as I will call her, is connected somehow to Bess of Hardwick?"

"It wouldn't be inaccurate at all, Dolly, to say that Lady Mac *is* Bess of Hardwick!"

"You never told me that!" said Elizabeth. "I think that the attribution is, if I may say so, *spot*-on," said Elizabeth.

"Nice pun!" I commented.

"And if Lady Mac was Bess, Mac himself, of course, must have been poor old George Talbot," said Elizabeth, naming the erstwhile sixth Earl of Shrewsbury.

The Scottish queen nodded in affirmation. "I lived with Bess of Hardwick and her husband, George Talbot, for fifteen years," said Mary, Queen of Scots. "Thrown together as we were, a royal prisoner and her keepers, we got to know each other quite well.

I watched day after day, year after year, as Bess henpecked poor old Talbot pretty much into the ground. Her husband was a good man and a strong man—but not strong enough to outman Bess."

"What man possibly could be?" Catherine asked.

The assembled ladies gave a synchronized shoulder shrug, having trolled the collective database and come up with no contenders.

"So you based the Macs, both the ambitious but wavering husband and the ambitious and unwavering wife, on the Talbots, George and Bess," I recapped.

"Well, Dolly, the characters' actions and fates are out of the pages of history. However, the nuances of their individual emotional tenors, and that of their relationship, were pure Bess and George."

"It *was* awfully naughty of you to send them up that way," Elizabeth said, herself now the one giggling behind a hand held over the mouth.

"I don't usually like to be meanspirited, but Bess really started getting on my wick after the first ten years or so," Mary admitted.

"The fact that you held out that long is a testament to your endurance," said Margaret Douglas.

"'Like patience on a monument, smiling at grief,'" I suggested.

"Indeed, Dolly! 'Grief' was the word for what both I and poor old George Talbot got, at least in the end. Bess and I managed to be companionable enough over the early years. You know how it is when women do needlework together. It's easier to let go of certain things when you are working on a common project and randomly sharing your thoughts."

"Hen therapy is cheaper than any other kind, and with stitchin' and bitchin', you get textiles when all is said and done," I said.

"Yes, and I can imagine who most of the bitching was about," said Elizabeth, bringing her plume out of retirement and giving her cousin a playful slap across the face with it.

"Actually, Dolly has a point. Our shared craftsmanship made Bess's…shall we say, personality tolerable for quite a long time. Toward the end of our tenure together, though, things changed," the Scottish queen admitted.

"The 'green-eyed monster,' wasn't it?" I asked.

"Yes. After all our peaceable years together, Bess inexplicably took it into her head that her husband was interested in me romantically. If he was, he certainly didn't make it known to *me*. But you know how Bess is; once she has an idea in her head, there is no talking her out of it."

Everyone in the room nodded in synch. It was an impressive testament to the fact that Bess of Hardwick's head was as hard as her ass.

"And so, with Bess being jealous and her henpecked husband not having enough starch in his ruff to handle his wife, relations between the three of us became quite strained. I am afraid I took out my frustration about it all in my delineations of Lord and Lady Mac."

"Well, Bess is such a priceless character, I think it is marvelous that she's been captured in cameo to survive the ages," I said, quite taken with the whole Bess-Lady Mac connection. "I presume Bess does not know about the little, shall we say, literary liberty that you have taken with her and her husband?"

"No, she does not; at least I have no reason to think she does," said Mary, Queen of Scots.

"I do think it best that we keep it that way," Mary Tudor suggested, eliciting another one of those impressive synchronized group nods.

"You know how Bess can be, and as a needlewoman, she always has access to sharp objects and scissors. I think keeping her cameo appearance in the Scottish play a secret would prevent a lot of storm and strife, if not actual bloodshed," said Mary, Queen of Scots, shuddering.

"You'd certainly have more reason than most to abhor gore," I said, thinking as I did so of the Rizzio murder to which Mary was a witness.

"What you say is true, Dolly," the Scottish queen acknowledged. "The irony of the fact that I penned three of the goriest works of the Shakespearian lot is not lost on me."

Chapter Ninety-Six
Gore in Store and Walking the Floor

"Well, when the words *goriest* and *Shakespeare* come up in the same sentence, the words *Titus* and *Andronicus* cannot be far behind," I reasoned aloud.

"It was my final work, Dolly, penned in haste during the last few weeks of my life while I pondered my imminent execution at Fotheringay. I'm afraid it wasn't the most polished of works, given the compressed time frame. I am certain the rush showed in the final product."

"Literary history agrees on that point," I said. "One Shakespearian critic used the words 'heap of Rubbish,' with a capital "R," no less, and went on to say, ''tis the most incorrect and indigested piece in all his works.' From my own viewpoint," I added, not wanting to end on so critical a note, "I think I can say that the execution overlay is definitely robust."

"Thank you," Mary said proudly.

"Nine revenge-driven onstage murders, several others off stage, and one man buried alive. Not too shabby for an evening's worth of drama. And then of course, the tragic rape and dismemberment that is central to the action of the play."

Titus Andronicus's story is driven by revenge on numerous levels. His daughter, Lavinia, is raped in an act of vengeance and has her tongue and hands cut off in an unsuccessful effort to prevent her from identifying her assailants. She does, however, get her own back, at least somewhat, by using her stumps to hold the bowl that her father uses to drain the blood of her assailants when he slits their throats, preparatory to grinding them up and serving them to their evil mother in a pie. Sadly, Lavinia is eventually killed by her father, who is himself killed as well; in fact, by the end of the play, only about three from a full cast of characters are left standing.

"I would guess that your experience with Bothwell informed this play as well," I conjectured, recalling the rape-kidnapping that became one of the most controversial crimes in history.

"You could say that," was all Mary said.

"Bothwell's ending was like something out of *Titus Andronicus*, when you think about it," I continued.

While Mary, Queen of Scots, languished in her relatively comfortable English captivity, Bothwell did time in the much less well-appointed Draghsolme dungeon in Denmark. He was reportedly short-chained to a pillar in appalling conditions and died insane after ten years. They say that the groove he wore in the floor, pacing the arc of his tether, can still be seen in the dungeon.

"True," Mary said. "But the Bothwell saga is a tale for another night; compressed time frame, Dolly."

It occurred to me that the motif of Lavinia's being so signally restricted in telling her story must have been especially compelling to the Scottish queen. Surely she herself had a hands-tied feeling during her trial at Fotheringay, where her guilt was a foregone conclusion and her ability to advocate for herself was limited. We did not get to discuss the details, though, as Mary was so all about moving things along.

"You may be disappointed of learning more about the Bothwell story, Dolly, but you can, at least, have a little bit of the Lord Darnley experience. That particular Mr. Wrong's antics formed the basis for my two remaining plays."

Margaret looked a bit pained at Mary's mention of her son but said nothing. Jane poured Margaret a nice, big glass of wine, and the Scottish queen embarked on a little well-deserved former-husband bashing.

Chapter Ninety-Seven
About a Lout

Lord Darnley, Margaret Douglas's eldest son, was a lightweight pretty boy thrust suddenly into a position of rank and privilege when he became the second husband of Mary, Queen of Scots.

"Being the husband of the queen of Scotland went to Darnley's head a bit," his widowed wife admitted.

"Did you say *a bit?*" I asked, finding her restraint surprising, given the history. The jumped-up lord and would-be king ticked off pretty much everyone at the Scottish court, including his wife, with an arrogance fostered by his unearned power and prestige. Proclivities for both the high life and the low life also emerged, further deteriorating the man's judgment and standing.

"I wasn't at all surprised when things went to Darnley's head," Elizabeth said, doing a bit of Monday-morning quarterbacking. "After all, there was plenty of free space available in there."

"Are you referring to my son having a big head or an empty head?" asked Margaret, her inner mama bear having *its* head. I cringed for her mother's heart as I anticipated the obvious answer.

"Both," Elizabeth said.

"Don't take it too hard, Margaret," said Mary, Queen of Scots. "There is no denying that Darnley wasn't emotionally or mentally up to the position he found himself in as my husband. But that doesn't mean that he mightn't have emerged as a better person, a more successful person, had circumstances been different."

"I didn't realize you recognized that, Mary," said Margaret, wiping another of those single tears from her eye.

"I had a lot of time to think during my imprisonment," Mary said. "An inventory of what one did right and what one did wrong in one's life is inevitable. From the perspective of years, I occasionally wondered if I had not wronged Darnley by inadvertently putting him into an untenable position when I married him. Maybe I should have realized that life in the hotbed of the Scottish court would have been too much for him to handle."

"I've often wondered if I should have realized the same thing as well before I talked him into pursuing marriage to you," Margaret said.

Margaret's wine glass was empty, but Jane did not attempt to refill it. Clearly, she knew that there was not enough wine in the entire world to wash away mother-guilt.

Mary and her erstwhile mother-in-law hugged over their mutually admitted little secrets. "I feel like I can let go of some of the anger I've harbored against you, dear, now that I know how you've felt about the matter of my son," Margaret said to the Scottish queen.

"And I was able to let go of a lot, if not all, of my feelings about the man through the catharsis of the two plays I wrote about my experiences with him," Mary said.

I considered what Mary, Queen of Scots, might want to be letting go of, metaphorically speaking, when it came to that second husband of hers. He'd screwed up in so many ways that she was pretty much spoiled for choice, but I thought I could identify the one thing that must have rankled the most.

"Darnley, drunk with power, or the illusion of it, after he married you, indulged in some pretty nefarious behavior," I recollected. "Drinking, whoring, antagonizing and alienating the rich and mighty, being abusive, and in general embarrassing him and you, Mary. But surely the worst of it all was what he did to Rizzio."

David Rizzio was the right-hand man of Mary, Queen of Scots. An Italian musician for starters, he eventually assumed the role of Mary's secretary, and she put a great deal of faith and trust in him. Driven by jealousy of the man, Darnley was instrumental in his murder; Rizzio was stabbed a grand total of fifty-six times by Darnley and a crew of henchmen. The murder took place as the diminutive Rizzio clung pitifully to the skirts of a heavily pregnant Mary.

"I don't want to dwell on what happened to David," Mary said, very understandably. "But we will talk about the emotions that were at the bottom of what happened there and what drove so much of the rest of Darnley's behavior as well: jealousy and insecurity. I bemoaned the price of them in both my Darnley plays."

"Jealousy and insecurity?" I said. "Well-o, well-o, I think I know the fellow!"

Chapter Ninety-Eight
Moor and More

"*Othello!*"

"Yes, Dolly, I did retell the story of Othello, with Darnley in mind. I had a copy of Cynthio's work available to me at Wingfield, and the idea suggested itself."

"I follow you on the jealousy and insecurity part," I said. "But other than that, Othello seems pretty different from Darnley. Othello is effective and respected, outside of the fatal sexual jealousy he has regarding his wife, Desdemona."

"Think about it, Dolly. For one thing, Othello was a Moor, and as such, an outsider in Venetian society in spite of his rank. My second husband was likewise an outsider at the Scottish court. As an effete Englishman among a court of rough-and-ready Scotsmen, he stuck out like a sore thumb, and his being married to me was not enough to mitigate that."

"Point taken," I said.

"And don't forget, Dolly, that through his mother," Mary said, taking Margaret by the hand, "Darnley was pretty much as royal as I was, at least, when it came to the English throne. Arguably, absent of me he was next in line to it."

"He was a contender to the Scottish throne as well, through his father," Margaret pointed out.

"Yes, one does tend to forget Darnley's rightful place as Tudor and Scottish heir and the relative strength of that against the other, largely female or questionably legitimate candidates.

Perhaps he was so very much eclipsed because of the glare of your own incendiary persona," I said, raising my hat to Mary.

"And then, of course, there was Darnley's suggestibility," Mary pointed out. "He was as easily manipulated by the canny Scots of my court into killing Rizzio as Othello was manipulated by Iago into smothering the innocent Desdemona in her bed."

"I'd not considered the suggestibility angle," I admitted.

"Suggestibility came into play in my other Darnley work as well," Mary pointed out.

"I can't quite make a guess as to which one it is," I said. "I'm afraid I'm developing a bit of Shakespeare fatigue."

Elizabeth picked up two silver trays that were at hand and clapped them together, lustily crying out, "Hint!"

Chapter Ninety-Nine
Imogen and Imagining

"Cymbals," I said aloud. "Of course—*Cymbeline*! Suggestibility added to the jealousy and insecurity mentioned earlier—that about sums it up."

In *Othello*, the title character's sexual jealousy, whipped up by the evil Iago on evidence as slender as a stolen hankie, causes him to murder his wife, Desdemona. When Othello learns that Desdemona is innocent of any such behavior, he kills himself in remorse.

The hero of *Cymbeline* comes off much more lightly for his sexual jealousy. Convinced this time by a pilfered bracelet, the jealous husband puts a hit out on his wife, Imogen. Fortunately for all, the hit man correctly deems Imogen innocent and fails to carry out the hit. Eventually all comes right, and everyone, even the evil Iachimo, lives happily ever after in the kingdom of Cymbeline, Imogen's father.

"So, in *Cymbeline*, you explore what might have happened had circumstances treated Darnley a little differently," I said to Mary.

"Yes," Mary admitted. "I had the story of *Cymbeline* from Hollinshead, and I compared it to the story from Cynthio that inspired my *Othello*. Darnley didn't have the bottle to have committed the Rizzio murder himself; he may have gone to his grave an innocent man had he not found himself at the Scottish court, surrounded by the kind of men who knew how to exploit a weaker character."

At the words "gone to his grave," I was reminded that the jury was still very much out on whether Mary was complicit in the eventual murder of her husband, Darnley. However, Elizabeth was chomping at the bit to take over, now that Mary had covered all her plays. The story of Darnley's murder—one of the great unsolved crimes of all time—like the Bothwell kidnapping would be one more story for another night.

"Well, Mary, now that we've covered the round dozen of your literary output, perhaps you will answer me a question. However did your plays make it from your castle prisons into the hands of William Shakespeare?"

Elizabeth stepped next to Mary, Queen of Scots, and the two joined hands.

"I guess you could say it was a cousinly secret," Mary said; Elizabeth just smiled.

Mary, Queen of Scots, kept plenty of secrets from her cousin Elizabeth in life—to wit, two attempts, the Ridolfi and Babington Plots, to seize her cousin's throne and possibly end her life.

Elizabeth, who liked to keep everybody guessing, likewise was not forthcoming with her Scottish cousin; Mary's imprisonment had to have entailed twenty years or so of just wondering what Elizabeth was thinking.

It was a treat, really, to see these two legendary protagonists with a secret actually *shared* between them. At least I assumed there was a shared secret; they certainly had the look of coconspirators if ever I saw it.

"Am I correct in guessing, Mary, that your works found their way into Elizabeth's hands after your death?"

"No, Dolly. They found their way to Elizabeth's hands *before* my death."

"How odd that you thought to trust your plays to the woman who was about to have you executed," I said. "Who delivered them to Elizabeth for you? Was their route as roundabout as that of the plays of Mary Tudor or of the Grey sisters?"

"No, Dolly, their route was not circuitous at all. In fact, it was quite direct; quite literally, hand to hand."

And with that, I learned that famous meeting places such as Yalta, Appomattox, Worms, and Runnymede didn't have much at all on the once-upon-a-time castle of Fotheringay.

Chapter One Hundred
A Gem of a Stratagem

"You handed your plays to Elizabeth yourself?" I asked the Scottish queen.

"Yes," Mary affirmed.

"But history tells us that you and Elizabeth never met; that nonmeeting is looked upon as one of the great ironies of the Tudor age, considering the drama that took place between the two of you."

"Well, Dolly, that is one more thing you can set history straight on," Elizabeth said. "I may be the kind of girl who can have my own cousin executed—"

"Runs in the family, after all," Jane pointed out.

"As I was saying," Elizabeth said, "I may be the kind of girl who can have her own cousin executed, but I am *not* the kind or girl who would do so without meeting with said cousin face-to-face for an airing of our mutual grievances."

"So did you bring Mary to see you, Elizabeth, or did you go to see Mary?"

"After the Babington Plot blew open, I was pressed into a corner about doing something about Mary, who had plotted twice at that point to take my throne and my life. She was too hot a commodity to be moved, even covertly. So I arranged to go to Fotheringay in the latter part of 1586 to meet with her in secret and discuss affairs."

"How did you manage it secretly?" I asked Elizabeth. "It can't have been easy for you to have left court without its being noticed."

"My Scottish cousin was brought to Fotheringay for the trial that established her guilt in the Babington Plot late in 1586," Elizabeth began. "I myself was at Windsor until Parliament met that year to discuss the whole Queen of Scots situation. I retreated to Richmond once Parliament was in session."

"Well, avoidance was your forte, after all."

"Not for avoidant purposes on this occasion, Dolly. Cecil and I felt it would be easier to make arrangements from Richmond."

"Arrangements?" I asked.

"Yes. Cecil was, at that point, increasingly insistent on Mary's being executed, and I knew the Parliament that was then meeting would likewise soon be hot on my heels with the same agenda. I told Cecil that I could not consider such a thing as an execution without seeing Mary personally first. He then shocked me by suggesting that he arrange for a private and secret meeting between just the two of us, Mary and me."

"Why as private as that?" I asked.

"Cecil believed, as did I, that there are some things best left to women to sort out between themselves," Elizabeth said.

"Smart man," I said. "Tell me, how did Cecil sneak you out of Richmond and over to Fotheringay?"

"On the day in question, I let on that I had a sick headache, a sore throat, and a touch of laryngitis. I took to my bed, demanding a day or two of being left strictly alone, with meals being delivered to my chamber. Given my, as you call them, Dolly, avoidant tendencies and the Parliamentary goings on of the moment, no one questioned it. Once I was behind closed doors, Cecil had a trusted female agent smuggled in from the country to take my place in the bedchamber."

"One of the members of Team Owen and Oddingsells?" I inquired.

"Spot on, Dolly. Mrs. Oddingsells was well up for the proceedings to follow. Fortunately, she was about my age and size, and Cecil had her dye her hair to a similar color to mine."

"How did Cecil manage to introduce her into your bedchamber?"

"Cecil arranged for *his* staff, rather than mine, to be in charge of providing my food for the duration of my indisposition. He said it was heightened security, necessary to head off any chance of my being poisoned at such a critical political juncture. Oddingsells brought the first meal, and we traded places and outfits without anyone being the wiser. My capable replacement from the country managed to be in the privy, or under the covers, whenever servants appeared with my later meals or any of my ladies popped in to check on me. No one was the wiser that I was gone for a little while. Or, if they were, they were smart enough not to mention it."

"And how were you introduced into Fotheringay?" I asked.

"Cecil contacted Sir Amyas Paulet, who had charge of Mary at that time. Amyas was very security conscious, and Cecil knew it. Cecil told the man that he, too, was concerned about the airtightness of arrangements for the Scottish queen at Fotheringay. Amyas had no reason to question Cecil's demand to make a personal and confidential survey of Fotheringay and of Amyas's procedures to ensure that all was in order. Cecil told Amyas that he was bringing with him one person only for the inspection; an expert, he said, in prison security."

"Walsingham?" I conjectured.

"No, Dolly; it was me. I was dressed as a man, of course; hat pulled down over my brow and ruff pretty much up to my eyeballs. I said nothing to Amyas during the proceedings—only nodded at him—and he didn't recognize me. Or if he did, he had the sense not to let on."

"How did you get access to your cousin, once you were there?"

"Cecil dispatched me to make an investigation of the physical plant while he discussed policy and procedure with Amyas. Cecil told Amyas that I was to have run of the house and that the servants were to do my bidding, no questions asked. He made clear that he wanted me to have private and unrestricted access to Mary's chamber while she was in it. All her servants were to vacate the room, though, lest any of them were in cahoots with Mary somehow, Cecil said. They were to wait just outside her room, where she could easily call out to them if needed. No one thought to question Cecil, or through my association with him, me. I was alone with Mary in her chamber before I knew it."

Chapter One Hundred-One
Amnesty, Your Majesty

"What was your first thought, Mary, when Elizabeth revealed her identity to you?"

"Quite frankly," Mary said, "my first emotion was one of annoyance at being caught unawares. It was late in the day, and I had retired for the evening. I hadn't my wig or any properly supportive foundation garments on, or any accessories in place. For someone with my lifelong reputation for elegance, even in difficult circumstances, this was upsetting to the equilibrium. I felt as though Elizabeth had wanted to deliberately put me at a disadvantage, and I told her so."

"She calmed down," Elizabeth said, "when I pointed out to her that I, dressed as a yeoman of the guard, was not at my elegant best either."

"At that point, inexplicably, we both started laughing uncontrollably," the Scottish queen said, smiling at the memory.

"Nothing inexplicable about that," I said. "Put girl cousins alone together and add an inside joke, and there can be only one outcome, at least initially," I said. "Tell me what happened when the laughing jag subsided."

"We talked awhile about family resemblances," recalled Mary, Queen of Scots. "I'd never met any of my Tudor relations, so it was interesting to know who I looked like. Elizabeth told me that I took after her aunt, Mary Rose, Henry VIII's younger sister."

"You do, at that! I'd not noticed it before," I said, remembering my meeting with that lady the last time I was here.

"And Mary was surprised at how ample my curves were," Elizabeth said proudly, thrusting out what I would estimate was a 34C bustline. "She'd been led to believe that I was skinny, like an old maid."

"Then we talked about the difficulties inherent in being a queen," Mary said. "I could talk about it only from past experience at that point, but still, I could validate a lot of what Elizabeth had to deal with. She and I were the only two queen regnants in our part of the world, so the opportunity to vent to each other was quite therapeutic."

"And I could validate a lot of what my Scottish cousin was experiencing at Fotheringay, based on my own quasi-imprisonment during my sister's reign," Elizabeth added.

"We talked about my brother-in-law, the Duke of Anjou, whom I had not seen since I left France. Hearing Elizabeth talk about his courtship escapades was like being back with my adopted French family for a while," Mary added.

"We discussed John Knox's *Monstrous Regiments* and agreed that his stance against women queens was quite out of order," Elizabeth said, swatting at an imaginary Knox with her plume.

"Nothing like a common enemy to bring people together," I said.

"That reminds me, we did chew the fat about Bess of Hardwick and that poor henpecked husband of hers. We had quite an enjoyable little gossip," Elizabeth said.

"The fact that each of you was plotting to kill the other didn't come up at all?" I asked.

"It did," Elizabeth said, "but what was there to say? Self-preservation motivated us both. When we were able to accept that basic premise and ignore the religious and political dust storms that surrounded it, we were in a position to let go of a lot of our resentments and come to an understanding."

"For me, the Ridolfi and Babington plots were the only ways I had to try to bust myself out of English custody and away from the possibility that at any time, I might be put to death. I did not feel unjustified in participating in them," Mary said, "and I was able to make Elizabeth accept that."

"And I helped Mary to come to terms with the fact that my setting her up with the Babington Plot was the best way *I* had to obtain the proof I needed to make a case for executing her. She understood perfectly well that her existence was a direct threat to my own life."

The Ridolfi and Babington plots were espionage capers carried out by the Catholic world for the cause of Mary, Queen of Scots, and her replacing Elizabeth on the English throne and restoring England to Catholicism. Walsingham, Elizabeth's spymaster, had double agents planted for the Babington Plot and so was able to set Mary, Queen of Scots, up for trial and execution for plotting against Elizabeth's life.

"For my part," Mary said, "I was growing weary of life; almost twenty years in prison had taken a toll on my health and day-to-day comfort. I was coming to realize that my best fate might be in Catholic martyrdom rather than any restored glory in the earthly world. Once I met Elizabeth, and got to know her, I saw her as the person who could be brave and resolute enough to dispatch me to that fate. I felt, strange as it may seem, grateful that she'd be able to steel herself to do it."

"For *my* part," Elizabeth said, "it was not as passive a fate as that. Not for me to rely on someone else's courage; I was going to have to find enough of it in myself to have the only other anointed queen I knew, my own cousin, executed. Even though Mary pretty instantly came to grips with that reality and embraced her fate and my role in it, I couldn't rid myself of a nagging feeling of self-reproach. I wanted to do something for Mary, something to ameliorate that burden on me."

"And I had just the thing for it," the Scottish queen said. "There was a way Elizabeth could make it up to me for any self-recrimination she felt about my end. Well, two ways, actually. One was that she would name my son as her heir, to take England's throne after she died."

"Which she did, albeit at the eleventh hour," I said.

"The other way she could make things up to me was to take charge of my plays and see that they, like my bloodline, survived for posterity. Imagine my delight, Dolly, when Elizabeth accepted the charge and shared with me that she, too, was a playwright. It was yet another bond between us. We parted that night not as mortal enemies but as two women who had become, if not the best of friends, at least perfectly *sympatico*."

"I eventually made the same arrangements for my cousin's plays that I made for my own, to go into effect after I died," Elizabeth said. "Between the time I received the plays and that point, I read my Scottish cousin's plays many times. They were entertaining, and they reminded me of our bargain, helping to relieve, at least a little, the painful feelings I carried about being the cause of her death."

"I learned after we met here just how much Elizabeth enjoyed and was inspired by my plays," Mary said. "In fact," she added, bringing a little much-needed passive-aggression to this cousinly love fest, "I do not mind at all that she hijacked the favorite of all my characters in my plays and used him for one of her own."

Chapter One Hundred-Two
Ruff and Bluff

Now that we were down to the last nine of Shakespeare's plays, guessing games such as the present one were getting easier. In fact, I was able to take charge of the conversation, at least a little, while I figured things out.

"Well, we've *Hamlet* to go, but there are no repeaters there that I can think of. Ditto the pastorals, *Midsummer* and *As You Like It*. The lost mother plays, *Pericles* and *Winter's Tale*, do not qualify, nor do the mistaken identity plays: *Comedy of Errors, Twelfth Night*, and *Two Gentlemen of Verona*. That leaves *The Merry Wives of Windsor* and of course, John Falstaff."

Falstaff is one of Shakespeare's best-loved characters, the original bad influence with good intentions. He is Prince Hal's boon companion in the Henry IV plays and appears as a fat and dirty old man in *Merry Wives,* trying unsuccessfully to take advantage of two ladies who are far savvier than he is.

"Well, Elizabeth, legend has it that you asked Shakespeare to write a play featuring Falstaff in love, and that he came up with one of his minor works, *Merry Wives,* in response. Is that why you wrote a play about Falstaff—to see him in love?"

"First off, 'minor' is not a word for royalty, Dolly," Elizabeth reminded me, executing a jump kick to my backside with a *finesse* that I wouldn't have thought possible in a farthingale. "I wrote a play around Falstaff because I wanted to see William Kempe play him. I was a big fan of his, you see. The *Henry IV* Falstaff was terribly amusing and with some ripening could suit Kempe right down to the ground. Maturing Falstaff from boon companion to bumbling and lecherous old man was a natural progression and one that made the role ideal for Kempe."

I'd always pictured Kempe as sort of like John Belushi in *Blues Brothers*, or maybe like Chris Farley or Lou Costello in a ruff. Known for physical clowning and for actually dancing across England, Kempe is said to have gone from shareholder in the Lord Chamberlain's Men to penury and death around the turn of the seventeenth century. I was a little surprised that the elegant and erudite Elizabeth would be such a big fan of the *commedia del arte* style of a John Kempe. I was not surprised, though, at the knowledge of human nature that her Falstaff progression showed, having watched many an old high school bad boy age into a pitiful, old, bar-crawling horndog.

Elizabeth preened while I rubbed my backside. For the sake of my aching behind and the integrity of my farthingale, a change of subject seemed in order.

Chapter One Hundred-Three
Bucolic Frolics

"I guess it's time we moved this conversation on to greener pastures," I said.

"As you like it," Elizabeth replied.

"Thank you," I said.

"That was not permission, Dolly. That was my introducing the first of my two pastorals to your attention."

"Of course—*As You Like It* and *A Midsummer Night's Dream*! Which of the two came first?" I asked.

"*As You Like It* followed closely on the heels of *Midsummer*, Dolly, during my progresses of 1591 and 1592."

Elizabeth, being a wise ruler, made annual summer progresses, or journeys, to country homes during much of her reign. Her peregrinations served multiple purposes.

"Those progresses gave the common folk outside of London a chance to be exposed to you as you traveled through and were entertained in the hinterlands. They cemented your reputation as the people's choice," I noted.

"Absolutely," Elizabeth said. "I tried to be at my grandest as I traveled in the country. It gave my subjects such a thrill to see that I wasn't known as Gloriana for nothing."

"A visit was also your way to show favor to a particular noble family or to keep tabs on folks who lived away from the hurly-burly of the court and might be worrisome because of their religious or political leanings."

"Yes, we turned up more than one Papist relic at Catholic country houses but generally chose to look the other way," Elizabeth said.

"You didn't want to 'make windows into men's souls,'" I said, remembering Elizabeth's famous comment on religious tolerance.

"Nor to have drama introduced into my stays in the country. That is precisely *not* what I went there for."

"Of course; your progresses also served as much-needed vacations, allowing you to hunt, party, soak up local culture, and generally chill in the lovely English countryside."

"There was not much opportunity to chill in August, Dolly, which was when I often made my progresses. My hosts were usually very good about creating shady corners for me and my courtiers, though, if that is what you mean."

"They were also very good about providing you with expensive gifts. Those gifts, like everything else involved in entertaining you, were usually replete with symbolism. It was quite a mental exercise for your hosts, wasn't it, to come up with something symbolic and clever?"

"Some were more up to the job than others, Dolly. I probably have one of the largest golden key collections on record."

"Where did you head for your 1591 and 1592 progresses? Theobalds? Kenilworth?" I asked, naming two of the most famous of Elizabethan progress destinations and the country homes of William Cecil and Robert Dudley, respectively. "The entertainments they put on for you were the stuff of legend, fueled as they were by a little friendly, or not-so-friendly, competition."

Cecil and Dudley, being two of the top men at court, really put on the dog when it came to entertaining Elizabeth in the country. They were more fortunate than some of her hosts in terms of being able to afford it. More than one man went broke setting up his country home to impress the queen and curry favor with her. Off-season agriculture, rearranging landscape features, and producing exterior statuary and waterworks were all part of the drill. So was organizing elaborate plays and masques for the queen's pleasure.

"In the summer of 1591, I sojourned at Cowdray with Viscount Montague. I was particularly looking forward to relaxing as much as I could during my stay in the country that year. To that end, I brought along some lighter literature than was my wont to read when at court: Thomas Lodge's *Rosalynde*. The tale was enchanting. And the entertainment that Viscount Montague arranged for me was most rustic. So many characters met among the oaks; anglers, ruffians, gentle ladies, buffoons, and country dancers. It was well done and in a simpler and more natural vein than I was used to seeing at Theobalds and Kenilworth. That and *Rosalynde* gave me the idea of turning my playwright's pen to a pastoral."

"And so *As You Like It* got its start," I said.

"Yes. It was easier to write in the country than at court, so it came along quite quickly."

"How did you manage to write your plays, in the country or otherwise? You must have had precious little privacy, not to mention time."

"One can make privacy and time when it matters," Elizabeth said. "I was known among my ladies as a night owl, and I did most of my writing in the wee hours. My ladies were asleep, or wished they were, and never looked too closely into what I was writing, assuming it was some of my voluminous correspondence."

"I see," I said. "And so there you were in the wee hours, writing your country story."

"It was more than just a country story, Dolly. It starts off, as I may remind you, with the younger of two brothers, Orlando, being unfairly treated by his older sibling."

"You were working through your feelings about your troubled relations with your own older sibling even then, when you were entering your golden years."

Elizabeth flicked my shoulder in rebuke. "I was ageless, Dolly, and all my years were equally golden. You are correct, however, in that I worked through some of my feelings about my sister and our relationship in that play and, to some extent, allowed them to drift away."

"You were able to arrange the happy ending in art that Mary and you did not have in life through the characters of Oliver and Orlando. In *As You Like it*, Oliver reforms his ways, and he and his younger brother live happily ever after."

The sisters, Elizabeth and Mary Tudor, joined hands and smiled.

"I worked through and was able to let go of some of the resentments I had about the banishments in my early life as well," Elizabeth said.

"I'll say! Duke Senior and his lords, Rosalind, Orlando, Celia, and Adam all know exile, one way or another. Of course, during your father's and your sister's reigns, you also knew what it was like to be cast to the margins of the world you lived in."

"I knew what it was like to go about dressed as a man as well, thanks to my visit to my Scottish cousin. It was one of my most interesting experiences, and I wove that into the play as well."

"Of course; through Rosalind, who dresses as a man to escape detection, using the deception to advantage with her lover."

In *As You Like It*, star-crossed lovers Rosalind, Orlando, Celia, Oliver, Phoebe, Silvius, Touchstone, and Audrey all manage to sort things out in the forest of Ardenne. The backdrop of wrestling matches, courtly love, wandering royalty, roaming lions, shepherds, shepherdesses, and cross-dressing only adds to the fun.

"I think the fact that you worked on that play in the country shows through; even with the heavy personal themes involved, in the end, one gets the sense that you had fun with it."

"I did!"

"And the homoerotic tones in the play; very ahead of your time," I commented.

"You know how it is when you set people loose in country houses," Elizabeth said. "There is always plenty going on for the observant writer to use as literary capital. People *will* let their hair down."

"Not to mention their pants," I said.

"You've spent time in country houses too, Dolly!"

"No, but I enjoyed *Brideshead Revisited* as much as anyone."

"I finished up *As You Like It* early in my 1592 progress to Bisham," Elizabeth went on. "It was while I was there that I also started on my second pastoral."

"*A Midsummer Night's Dream*, of course."

"Those *will* happen when one overindulges in all the exotic new-world fruits and vegetables that are presented to one during the typical summer progress," Elizabeth said.

"You mean the play started with your actually having a dream while you were staying in the country?"

"Yes. Some indigestible fruit was lying on my stomach, and a few things were lying on my mind. I was just finishing *As You Like*

It and was in a rare writing mode. I wanted to line something up to be started the moment I was done with it to take advantage of the muse when she was at her best."

"That's understandable."

"Of course, the lady of the house at Bisham being so very literary a person also served to get my writer's plume a-twitching."

"Who was she?"

"Elizabeth Russell, aunt of Francis and Anthony Bacon. She was a poetess, a translator, and a deviser of entertainments; at least she was when I was on progress to her country home. She wrote a pastoral for me herself and had it performed for me during my stay; she called it *The Lady of the Farm*. It was Arcadian revels of the usual sort, but she was quite proud of it; nymphs, Pan, wild men, verdure, mythological figures, the lot. Elizabeth Russell was not unlike Bess of Hardwick when it came to personality. Her bragging about her works made me want to brag about mine, and of course, I couldn't. Writing masques for at-home use was genteel and acceptable, unlike writing plays like mine, for eventual public consumption. The woman brought out the competitor in me; I wanted to do Arcadia in a way that would set the standard for all future works of that nature."

"You certainly succeeded," I said.

"Well, the reading material for that particular progress was also on my mind, or at least in my subconscious."

I wondered aloud what Elizabeth's equivalent of a beach read would be.

"Edmund Spenser's *Faerie Queene*," Elizabeth said. "It had come out a year or two earlier. Since it was a tribute to me and my reign, I knew I should reread it sooner or later, and this progress seemed the ideal opportunity."

"How did you enjoy it?"

"Well enough. It was the timing of my reading it that mattered. The country masques and entertainments tended to be a little heavy on fairies, sprites, and mythological creatures to begin with, and with Spenser's work added on, it all became somewhat overwhelming."

"So, between exotic fruit overload, hostess envy, and faerie burnout, you—"

"I had the most vivid dream I'd ever had!" Elizabeth said. "*Midsummer* was the easiest of my plays to write because all I had to do was transcribe that dream."

"You literally dreamed up all those woodland characters—Bottom, for instance?"

"I think I know how Bottom made his way into the dream. At dinner the night before the dream, Lady Russell was complaining about her husband, and how he left all the attention to detail about my visit up to her. She said the man just went around with his head up his arse."

"That about covers Bottom," I said.

"I think I know how Peaseblossom, Cobweb, Mote, and Mustardseed got into the dream as well," Elizabeth said.

"They *do* seem a bit Beatrix Potter for someone of your, shall I say, less than fanciful character. How did they find their way into your dream?"

"I remember discussing with my ladies, as we retired after dinner, that the housekeeping at Bisham left something to be desired. There were all sorts of detritus under the furniture and in the corners. I was only calling things I found as I actually saw them on the Bisham floors."

"Oberon, Titania, and the foundling prince Titania refuses to relinquish to her husband; what made you dream them up?"

"Gilbert Talbot, Bess of Hardwick's son-in-law, was among those present at Bisham. He was in hot pursuit of a handsome young dogsbody his wife had just hired. Gilbert had recently inherited the Shrewsbury title, and had just been created a Knight of the Garter; his wife didn't want anything beneath his dignity to happen during the progress. Ergo, she kept Gilbert on a very short leash and wouldn't let him near the young man."

"I guess Gilbert hadn't changed much from when he'd been milling around hallways, trying to chase the likes of poor, old Marlowe around," I conjectured.

"Lady Russell's two daughters made it into the dream too. Their mother was bound and determined to get them positions with me as maids of honor. To that end, those two girls were in my face, so to speak, wherever I turned at Bisham. Their mother even made them part of the entertainment; they played two sisters, Sybilla and Isabella, 'two virgins keeping sheepe, and sewing their samplers.'"

"It wasn't much of a leap from there to your dreaming up Hermia and Helena, was it?" I asked.

Mary, Queen of Scots, quoted:

We, Hermia, like two artificial gods,
Have with our needles created both one flower,
Both on one sampler, sitting on one cushion,
Both warbling of one song, both in one key,
As if our hands, our sides, voices, and minds,
Had been incorporate. So we grew together…

Elizabeth was touched by the tribute to her play. "Fancy you remembering my play so well!"

"It's the needlework reference; it hits me where I live, or at least lived, all those years I was captive and embroidering away for dear life. It isn't often that one finds a literary reference to the hobby that saved one's sanity."

"You are not the only one to appreciate the play," I said. "It is probably the most popular of the Shakespearian comedies."

"More popular than my *Much Ado about Nothing?*" Catherine Grey asked plaintively.

"And my *Love's Labour's Lost?*" little Mary Grey added, making a most becoming moue of disappointment.

"I'm afraid so," I said as Elizabeth gave Catherine and Mary each a caress of condolence, brushing their faces with her plume.

Jane Grey was having none of it; her sisterly pride came to the forefront. "All I can say about that," Jane said, "Is '*what fools these mortals be!*'"

Chapter One Hundred-Four
Winter's Chill Fits the Bill,
or Nothing Finer than Paulina

A guttering candle caught my eye, and reminded me of both how far we had come and how far we had yet to go. Mary Tudor noticed my gaze.

"Let's keep things moving," she suggested. "I think you should tell Dolly about your absent mother plays next, Elizabeth. They are," she said, turning to me, "among my favorites in the entire canon."

"I can see why," I said, remembering how tragically Mary had been separated from her own mother, Katharine of Aragon.

"They strike a chord with me, too," said the Scottish queen. She sighed and walked over to a picture of her own mother, Mary of Guise. The woman was beautiful; she looked, in fact, like Deborah Kerr in a French hood.

"Of course, you were separated from your mother when you were only five or six years old," I recalled. "And you saw her only once again in your lifetime, when she made a visit to France."

"Probably my fondest memories are of that visit," the Scottish queen said.

"We just *wished* that our mother could have been absent," Jane Grey said, speaking for all three Grey sisters.

"That is something I cannot imagine," Elizabeth said, in a rare moment of unvarnished vulnerability. She was the only woman in the room who, in life, probably had no recollection of her mother at all, with the woman having been executed when

Elizabeth was just a tot. As she held her breath, her fair skin took on almost a bluish hue for a moment or two. Finally, she exhaled slowly, and the color returned to her cheeks.

"'A sad tale's best for winter,'" I said, quoting from *Winter's Tale*.

"Well, we have no seasons here, but I will take your cue, Dolly, and start with the story of my *Winter's Tale*," said Elizabeth. "It was suggested to me as I was reading Robert Greene's *Pandosto*. The parallels between the first part of the story and that of my own family were too marked for me to ignore."

"Let me see—a king who erringly and publicly accuses his wife of adultery, leading to her shameful death. Baby daughter of said wife abandoned by her father and brought up by surrogates in a manner she ought not to have faced. Sounds like your family, all right. That is the first part of *Pandosto* covered, and the first part of *Winter's Tale* as well."

"In the second part of *Pandosto*, the king happens upon his daughter once she has grown up but does not know her identity. He falls in love with her. When he learns that the girl he has fallen in love with is his own daughter, he kills himself."

"Pretty deep waters there but nothing applicable to your own family story, surely."

"Exactly, Dolly. That is why I decided to adapt the story into a play and change the second half of it. I wanted to give my family something that it had never had: a happy ending. Even if I could do it only in fiction, it seemed worth doing."

"And you succeed so well with that in *Winter's Tale*. Corrective recapitulation done right! The lost daughter grows up to be a real catch and marries happily ever after. She is also reunited with a now-repentant father after the space of sixteen years. And best of all, the wrongly accused wife is vindicated and turns out not to be dead at all but in hiding. She is reunited with her husband and her daughter, and all live happily ever after."

Elizabeth nodded in affirmation. I wondered how much longer my ability to recap Shakespearian plays without mixing up the plot of one with another would hold out.

"You accomplish in the space of a short play something that would take modern family therapy years to achieve," I said.

"I'd wondered at times, as I was writing the play and afterward, if the happy ending was perhaps a little too easy on my father, given the extent of his crimes against my mother. However, after what you've told us about the head injury theory, I can let go of that concern."

"Glad to be able to give you that gift," I said.

"I tried to give my mother an allegorical gift in *Winter's Tale* by gifting her counterpart in the story, Hermione. Hermione had something that Ann Boleyn never had in life—something that might have made all the difference in my mother's story, or at least might have comforted her in her trials."

I had a feeling I could see where Elizabeth was going with this and offered a quote accordingly.

"'I would rather walk with a friend in the dark than alone in the light,' as the Bard said."

"Actually, Dolly, I believe Helen Keller said it. And truer words about friendship were never spoken."

In *Winter's Tale*, the wronged queen, Hermione, has an ace bestie named Paulina. Paulina goes to bat for the queen even when it is dangerous for her to do so. She keeps the wronged queen safely under wraps for years and years and eventually engineers the woman's dramatic reentry into the life of her husband and daughter.

"Paulina is one of literature's all-time great friends," I said; "faithful, wise, brave, patient, and with a flair for the dramatic. Ann Boleyn had no such support in her short life. She had ladies-in-waiting and cousins, but history has not suggested to us that Ann Boleyn had any really close and trustworthy female friends. I wonder what her story would have been like if she'd had someone close by who would stand up for her when the whole world was rallied against her."

"Her story may or may not have ended any differently," Elizabeth said. "But the quality of her life would surely have been improved had she had at least one really good woman friend. And so when I wrote my story, I gave her one, providing Paulina to Hermione."

"It takes a good friend to be one," Mary Tudor said.

"Helen Keller again?" I inquired.

"No, Dolly; just me, talking common sense. In life, Ann Boleyn was a lone wolf, or more accurately still, a lone hunter, like a cat. No pack instinct at all. It's hard for someone like that to make friends or to inspire Paulina-style friendship in others. Elizabeth would have had no way of knowing this, her mother having died when Elizabeth was too young to remember her. I of course was old enough to assess Ann Boleyn's character from close up, in life."

"Well, fortunately, my mother has mellowed since your last visit here, Dolly. She and Katharine of Aragon have formed a bond of friendship that, while not perfect, gives satisfaction to them both," Elizabeth said.

"Frenemies, perhaps, is how I see them," I said.

"That would pretty much fit the bill," Mary Tudor said.

"It would fit the bill for more than one relationship here!" Margaret pointed out.

"And of course, since your last visit here, Dolly, and what it accomplished, Henry VIII's wives have had much wider scope to rub elbows with other queens who came after them," Jane explained. "Ann Boleyn made great friends with Queen Marie Antoinette of France, for example."

"Yes, she has," Elizabeth said. "French fashion, the decapitation motif, and Marie Antoinette's unpopularity with the common people and generally bad press gave her much common ground with Mother."

"My own mother made a French friend too," Mary Tudor added. "Empress Josephine. You should hear the two of them go on about infertility and midlife marital abandonment—a couple of soul sisters, those two!"

"Our father actually got quite chummy with Josephine's husband, Napoleon. The difficulties that both went through to finally procure a male heir created a bond between them. That and the fact that, after all the effort they put into getting those sons, the immortality of line that they expected from it did not materialize, "Elizabeth said.

"Their first meeting would have been something to see! Imagine little Napoleon trying to do the French cheek-kiss salute with all six feet plus of Henry VIII! He'd have had both an altitude and an attitude problem to contend with there."

"The logistics would be challenging, but not impossible," said little Mary Grey, the voice of experience.

"'Tis time to fear when tyrants seem to kiss,'" I said, bringing us quite neatly, I thought, to Elizabeth's next play: *Pericles, Prince of Tyre.*

Chapter One Hundred-Five
No Greater Collaborator

Pericles tells the story of yet another orphaned and abandoned little girl. This child, Marina, is born during a maritime storm. Her mother, presumed dead from childbirth, is buried at sea. Unbeknown to her husband, Pericles, she washes up on a foreign shore alive and becomes an acolyte of the Goddess Diana. Pericles, meanwhile, leaves his little Marina in the safekeeping of a nurse, Lychorida, and a friendly neighboring king. Unfortunately that setup does not go well, and Marina is eventually sold as a slave. However, her noble blood tells, and all comes out well at the end, with Marina, Pericles, and mother happily reunited.

"*Pericles* is the one Shakespearian play omitted from the *First Folio,* Elizabeth. What a shame you didn't get to see the final product of it once Emilia and her copy of that work arrived here. You must have been disappointed about that."

"I wasn't the only one!" Elizabeth said.

Having discussed the themes of the absent mother, abandonment, and corrective recapitulation already, I was not inclined to rehash them in relation to *Pericles*. There was, however, an academic question for which I wanted an answer.

"Shakespearian scholars are pretty united on the fact that *Pericles* was the work of more than one author," I said to Elizabeth. "Did you work with a cowriter while you were writing it?"

"Well," said Elizabeth, "yes and no."

"Your hem and haw sticks in my craw," I informed Elizabeth. "Come clean, girlfriend. Did you have a collaborator with you when you were writing the story or didn't you?"

"The person who wrote the first half of *Pericles* died without finishing it. I simply brought the story to its conclusion for her. And while doing so, I took the opportunity to memorialize her in one of the minor characters of the story—Lychorida."

"Lychorida is little Marina's faithful nurse and protectress," I recalled.

"It should be obvious to you then, Dolly, who she was based on."

"Kat Ashley, of course; your own nurse, teacher, surrogate mother, and guard dog all rolled into one."

"She certainly has the proportions for such a creature," Mary Tudor said, looking gratified at the group giggle she evoked.

"It wasn't much of a tribute, if you don't mind my saying so, Elizabeth. Poor old Lychorida dies before the family is reunited and doesn't get to be part of the happy ending."

"Dolly, all my life I viewed Kat as a mother figure. It was a perfectly satisfactory way for me to look at things as a very young child. When I grew into adolescence, though, and started developing faculties of analysis, things changed."

"Faculties of analysis don't go easy on a girl," Jane said.

"No, they do not," Elizabeth agreed. "Once I could start analyzing the story of my mother's life for myself, I could not buy into the stock story of the court, the story of an adulteress and all-around evil witch."

"Surely Kat Ashley didn't speak that way about your mother to you!" I said.

"Kat herself always spoke respectfully of my mother, on the rare occasions that we spoke of her at all. Kat was so attached to me—as though I were her own daughter. She did everything she could to keep that illusion of our being mother and daughter alive, for herself probably as much as for me. Those efforts included minimizing discussion of my real mother."

"How sad for you," I said. "I guess blended families weren't as well done as they might have been back in Tudor times."

"You aren't dissing Kat, are you?" said Elizabeth, going into instant tigress mode. I'd have sworn that the pile of the velour on the back of her dress rose up a half inch or so along her spine.

"No, I'm not," I was able to say with honesty. "I'm basing it on a lot of what I've heard during my visits here."

"Dolly *has* spent considerable time with Bess of Hardwick," Mary, Queen of Scots, reminded Elizabeth.

"Whatever Kat may have done out of an excess of motherly feeling, I do not hold against her," Elizabeth said. "She was in a difficult position, and so was I. Once I started to feel that my real mother, Ann Boleyn, had been a victim rather than a villainess, I started to feel guilty about my daughterly feelings toward Kat. I felt as though indulging those feelings was somehow making me disloyal to Ann Boleyn. And of course, when I started feeling daughterly toward my dead mother, I'd feel guilty about not giving Kat her due. She was, after all, the woman on the spot."

"As was Lychorida," I said, "if I might bring us back to *Pericles*."

"What we need to bring it back to, Dolly, is John Gower. Kat was a big fan of Gower's; I knew that much about it all while Kat was alive. What I didn't learn until after she was dead, though, was just how touched she was by the story of Pericles, the child orphan of the storm, and her faithful nurse as told in Gower's *Apollonius*. "

"How did you find that out?" I asked.

"I was going through some correspondence of hers after she had passed on. I found that Kat had started but never finished a play based on Gower's work."

"Like surrogate mother, like daughter; both of you surreptitiously writing plays."

"Kat knew about my writings in the wee hours. I suppose she wanted to emulate me and eventually surprise me with a completed play about an orphaned child and faithful nurse. It would have been yet another bond between us, and one my natural mother could not have shared. Kat died with the play only half-finished."

"And you completed it," I said. "Shakespearian scholars have always supposed that *Pericles* was penned by two authors, based on the difference in the first and second halves of the play. Over the years, one George Wilkins has won out as likely coauthor. Who'd have ever guessed it was our girl Kat?"

"Finishing her play helped me to grieve Kat's death and come to terms with the relationship between Kat, my natural mother, and myself. I was able to let go of a lot of the guilt and mixed emotions by the time I was finished with it."

As if on cue, Kat Ashley herself actually entered the room. She stood right in a narrow beam of light that had made its way in through one of the arrow slit windows. The sun was coming up; our night together was coming to a close.

"I've come to hurry you girls along!" Kat said. "You ought to have finished by now."

"We're almost done," Elizabeth assured her.

"How done is almost?" she asked pointedly.

"Four plays to go."

"Four to go! Really, now, you must move things along. Condense, my dear, condense!"

"If only you could take your own advice," Elizabeth said saucily, tapping Kat on her ample behind.

"*I* don't need to take my own advice. *You* need to take my own advice," Kat replied. After rapping Elizabeth on the knuckles, Kat turned to me.

"Gloriana she may be, in all her splendor, but she still needs me to keep her on track," Kat said, now holding Elizabeth by the hand and glowing with substitute maternal pride—and likely a healthy dose of codependence.

"I don't know what Elizabeth would do without you, Kat!" Jane said kindly.

"You are my saving grace, dear, and always will be," Elizabeth said to Kat as she walked her to the door. "We'll be done here very shortly. You can start priming the others to take over from us in a few minutes."

Kat made her way out the door and down the hall, and I prepared for some of the condensing Kat had so enthusiastically suggested; we had four plays left to cover in those few minutes I'd just been promised.

Chapter One Hundred-Six
The Rom-Com Bomb, or a Winning Way with Twinning

"All right, Elizabeth, we are on the fast track now. Let's tackle the three remaining comedies first. A capsule version of how each came to be, if you please!"

"Easily done, Dolly. We will start with *Two Gentlemen of Verona*, since that was my very first play. I wrote it when I was in my teens, after the Thomas Seymour debacle. Sexual attraction and what it will drive people to; loyalty and its demands; the impact trusted servants have on our lives; deceit; banishment. You can see why all those things would have been on my mind."

"Of course I can. Tom Seymour's sexual escapade with you when you were a vulnerable teenager certainly would have involved all those things. It happened while you were living with Katherine Parr, who was his wife and your stepmother. It also happened on Kat's watch, and some say with her misguided encouragement. And of course, at the end of it, you were banished from the home of a respected stepmother."

"That about sums it up," Elizabeth recalled aloud.

"How did you manage to make a comedy out of a smarmy story like that?"

"'Smarmy' is not a word to use to the princely, Dolly!" Elizabeth snapped, tickling me under the nose with her feather till I sneezed. "A lot of soul-searching followed that escapade, and it helped me to grow into a wiser girl than I was. A lot of advice from others, and discipline, also followed, and you know how those can feel to an adolescent. I rebelled against it internally all the while that I was kowtowing to it on the outside."

"Holy kowtow! I mean, holy cow!" I said, wondering what it would have been like to see Elizabeth kowtowing to anything.

"Because my brother Edward found my behavior during that escapade, as you call it, to be questionable, he sent me some reading material to guide me into the channels of more circumspect comportment. Thomas Elyot's *Book Named the Governor* was popular for such training purposes at the time; his treatment of the story of Titus and Gisippus intrigued me. I shared this thought with a family friend, who suggested that as a scholastic exercise, I attempt to rewrite the story myself. Little could she know that with the fractiousness of adolescence, I would take her advice, but with a grain of salt: I would write out the story as a brash comedy instead of as an academic polemic."

"Let me guess; it was Catherine Willoughby who started you on the playwriting path?"

"Who else?" Elizabeth asked.

"Well, Elizabeth, many consider *Two Gentlemen* Shakespeare's weakest work; I guess it was just your youth and inexperience showing through, wasn't it?"

"I may have been young and inexperienced at points in my life, Dolly, but weak I never was! I was, however, on rare occasions, a little the worse for the wine. It happened once during Twelfth Night revels."

"It happens," I said. "For most of us, the end result is a crying jag. Fancy you turning the experience into a classic play. At least, I am assuming that is what you did—turned the experience into *Twelfth Night.*"

Twelfth Night has a lot of the hallmarks of Shakespearian theater rolled into one neat package: mistaken identity, cross-dressing, star-crossed love, and some goofball comic relief, to name a few.

"So you conceived the idea for *Twelfth Night* when you were four parts pissed," I said.

"Beg pardon?"

"You were drunk. Tanked up. Crocked. Soused. Smashed, as it were."

"'Smashed' is not a word to use with crowned heads, Dolly."

"'Smashed' and 'crowned heads' certainly don't go together if one is being execution aware," I pointed out.

"I suppose 'stewed' would about cover it," Elizabeth said gamely. "It was a few years shy of the turn of the seventeenth century that year. I was feeling my age, I suppose. Revels do take more of a toll on one as the years go by."

"You must have felt like a stewed prune," I said.

Elizabeth reached over and pulled the plume out of my hat in retribution, and then continued her tale.

"As I lay in bed, half-asleep, half-awake, and feeling a hangover coming on, I'm afraid I perseverated a bit on the poor quality of the entertainments that were provided for the revels that year. I considered that I could do better in the way of comedy than that, and set about to start a play to prove it. I actually started the work that very night. Some of the practical joking that was going on during the revels that year gave me a lot of very suitable material for my Malvolio subplot."

"And the cross-dressing Viola; yet another heroine inspired by your escapade with your cousin Mary, Queen of Scots?"

"Yes, indeed."

"And I suppose the overriding themes of marrying outside of one's station, or not, would have been informed by your experience with Robert Dudley."

"Not intentionally, but now that you mention it, it's probably not unlikely that there was some subconscious element to that particular subtext of the play. You're neglecting to mention my very favorite thing about *Twelfth Night,* though, Dolly."

"That being?"

"That being Sir Toby Belch."

Sir Toby, of course, is one of literature's great buffoons. It occurred to me that Elizabeth, in her comedic writings, had quite a sideline going in uncouth party animals.

"Sir Toby was inspired by Edward de Vere, the seventeenth Earl of Oxford. He was being a bigger ass than usual during the revels that year," Elizabeth said.

de Vere was a very high-ranking English peer, a poet of note, a theatrical patron, and a contender for the role of Shakespeare ghostwriter, according to some conspiracy theorists. He could also be, as Elizabeth pointed out, an ass, going about knocking up women, brawling, stiffing literally hundreds of tradesmen, and frittering away a large family fortune.

"Why did you call the de Vere character 'Sir Toby Belch'?"

"Well, I started out calling him 'Sir Toby Breakwind,' in memory of that epic fart of de Vere's, but I worried about that being a little over the top. So I muted it to 'Sir Toby Belch.'"

"Is it true what they say about de Vere having the misfortune to inadvertently fart when bowing obeisance to you?"

"Perfectly true. And a loud one it was! It reverberated throughout the court. I thought poor old Cecil would have an apoplectic fit, trying to keep a straight face."

"And is it equally true that the man was so ashamed of his flatulence that he avoided the court for seven years?"

"Not quite as long as that, but he did lay low abroad for some little time."

"And is the less-than-charitable greeting that history has attributed to you upon his return likewise accurate?"

"Me? Less than charitable? Never! What words does history credit me with on that occasion?"

"'My lord, I had forgot the fart!'"

"What could possibly be more charitable than blessed forgiveness for letting one rip in the royal presence?" Elizabeth asked, her laughter belying any claim to anything like sweet charity.

"Seeing that you are the only queen I know of who is on record as making a fart joke, I must say that I am surprised at your delicacy in defaulting to a belch when you named Sir Toby. Even thusly toned down, though, the man is still a comic masterpiece. Allow me to offer you a salute for Sir Toby!"

"If you follow that up with a fart, I shall smack you!" Elizabeth said, and she looked like she meant it. I gauged the way the wind ought to be breaking, or not, and decided that a change of subject was in order.

"I love that you named the heroines of *Twelfth Night* Olivia and Viola. They are two of my favorite names for baby girls."

"Fancy!" Catherine said. "I always rather liked Luciana but never had girls."

"Luciana is a lovely name," Elizabeth agreed.

"You worked that name into your *Comedy of Errors*," I recollected, "along with the equally lovely name Adriana. I don't know what you were thinking with the names Antipholus and Dromio, though, for the twin male characters in the play."

"My fancy took me where it would," Elizabeth said. "*Comedy of Errors* was suggested to me back in the early 1590s, when one of my courtiers, a father of twins, mentioned how much he'd enjoyed the twin-driven plot of Plautus's *Menaechmi*. It seemed excellent fodder for reworking into a comedy for the contemporary stage. I was studying some Aristotle around the same time, and the classical unities were on my mind. Put it all together, and you've got *Comedy of Errors*."

"The classical unities, of course, were unity of action, time, and place, all three factors being visible, as it were, to the audience viewing the proceedings upon the stage. You used that structure to give the theatergoer a very full evening's worth of theater, not to mention two sets of twins."

I pondered for a moment on all the fictional lookalikes who'd followed after the twins in *Comedy of Errors*. *The Man in the Iron Mask* and Louis XIV; Dickens's *Prince and Pauper*; the Bobbsey twins; Patty Duke and Kathy; witches Samantha and Serena; the *Star Trek* and *Gilligan's Island* doppelgangers; and Phoebe and Ursula, just to name a few.

"You've no idea how robust a legacy your twinning work has been to the entertainment industry at large down through the ages," I said to Elizabeth.

"Thank you, Dolly," Elizabeth said modestly, or as close to it as she could get. "And of course, I think I can flatter myself that my remaining play was also a boon to the theatrical world."

"And what a play it is! You show a gift for understatement when you describe it in generic terms as a boon. It is, in fact, the greatest play in the Shakespeare canon, if not in all the world."

Margaret Douglas, Mary Tudor, the Grey sisters, and Mary, Queen of Scots, all looked a bit nonplussed at being summarily taken out of the running.

"Sorry, ladies, but I am nothing if not honest to a fault. Talented as you all are, the plume has to go to Elizabeth for the greatest of all the Shakespearian plays: *Hamlet.*"

Chapter One Hundred-Seven
Validating Vacillating

My mother was always an advocate of saving the best for last, but I was a little disappointed that we would have to address *Hamlet*, of all the plays, in as constricted a time frame as we were left with. In keeping with the Shakespearian mode, the word "alas" escaped my lips.

"You're going to quote the Yorick speech, aren't you?" Jane asked.

I wasn't, but just to prove that I could, I did. I had no skull to hold in my hand, so I made do with a candlestick.

> Alas, poor Yorick! I knew him, Horatio; a fellow of infinite jest, of most excellent fancy; he hath borne me on his back a thousand times; and now, how abhorred in my imagination it is! My gorge rises at it. Here hung those lips that I have kissed I know not how oft. Where be your gibes now? Your gambols? Your songs? Your flashes of merriment, that were wont to set the table on a roar?

I bowed gratefully to the applause I received. "You are all too kind," I said. "Who could go wrong with those powerful words on the transience of life?"

"No one," said Elizabeth proudly. "But those powerful words were not meant to be a statement on the transience of life. They were my coming to terms, in maturity, with the whole Tom Seymour situation of my youth. From a vista of years, I was able to salute him, to forgive him, and to move on from the embarrassing and terrifying memories of the whole affair. I might have lost everything, you know, just because Tom Seymour was up for a little slap and tickle and I was young enough to be foolish about it. Anyway, I had the last laugh, and knowing that, I was able to write my little summary of the whole saga in that passage and move on from it."

"Literary history has it that the character of Polonius, with his trite but true platitudes and his plodding wisdom, was modeled on William Cecil, Lord Burghley. Was he?"

"He was, Dolly; Polonius was a tribute to the wisest if least scintillating man I ever knew. *William* Cecil was thus immortalized in *Hamlet*; his son *Robert* was the catalyst for my writing the play in the first place."

Robert Cecil, first Earl of Salisbury, secretary of state and lord high treasurer, was obviously as ace a politico as his father. He has gone down in history as small in body but big on brain.

"Robert Cecil led you to write *Hamlet*? How?"

"By haranguing me on the same subject that his father harangued me about during *his* entire career."

"I've got it!" I said. "'This is the tragedy of a man who could not make up his mind,'" I quoted in my best Shakespearian manner.

"I don't recall having written that into the play," Elizabeth said.

"You didn't. Laurence Olivier added it in when he filmed it in the 1940s."

"He was the husband of that lovely young woman who was here with us for career advice," Elizabeth recalled. "Mistress Vivian Leigh. She was an English actress, troubled about taking on an important role that would require she speak with an American Southern accent. She was so talented that we encouraged her to pursue the role. We've always wondered how it worked out."

"Well, fiddle-dee-dee," I said, "it worked out brilliant-lee! There's been no other real Scarlett O'Hara since Vivian Leigh; she made the role her own and had the Oscar to prove it. Everyone recognizes her as Scarlett O'Hara on sight. It was quite a coup for her."

"We're glad that worked out. And what a coincidence it is that her husband did a production of my *Hamlet*."

"Getting back to the Cecils—it was your famous, or perhaps I should say infamous, inability to make up your mind that Robert Cecil was twitting you on, wasn't it—just as his father before him had?"

"Yes, Dolly. It was toward the end of my reign, when the Essex disaster was playing itself out. I had a decision to make—whether or not to execute the man. Robert Cecil knew, as I did, that Essex's execution was necessary. But I could not bring myself to give that final, fatal order. Cecil lost his patience at one point and had at me quite roundly for not being able to decide unequivocally on a course of action. He blamed it on my being a woman. 'Imagine what would happen to the kingdom,' he demanded, 'if a *man* in your position prevaricated the way you do!'"

The little man with the big brain also, apparently, had very big balls. "What did you say to Robert Cecil after that?" I asked.

"Very little," Elizabeth said.

"You were awestruck at the man's courage?"

"No, Dolly. I was doing what the man requested: imagining a situation at court in which a man could not nail his colors to the mast and stick with a decision. The theme haunted me for days, like a tune you can't stop humming. I could not get it out of my head, until I started to write it out of me by beginning another play."

"So you wrote a play about what many consider, if you will pardon me saying so, the primary flaw in your character?"

"*Flaw* is not a term for monarchs, Dolly!" Elizabeth said, defiantly flinging her plume down to the floor. She tried to be defiant, at least; the plume, not playing ball, floated about in the air for what seemed like a long time before it finally landed at my feet.

"Don't you see?" Elizabeth continued. "As a woman, I made *an art* of not coming to conclusions and a science of second-guessing. What you call a character flaw was really using a woman's way to make my reign the greatest epoch in British history!"

It occurred to me that Queen Victoria might take exception to the "greatest epoch" bit, but otherwise I could see that Elizabeth was spot-on.

"A *man*," she continued, "would have made nothing but a mess by endlessly rethinking and hedging his bets. It is a feminine—not a masculine—art, in my opinion. And so I decided to give the world a tragedy about an indecisive man, based on the dark side of what made my own persona tick."

"And the Hamlet legends, of course, were well established by your day and age, ready for you to borrow to achieve your purpose."

"Exactly."

"I guess the writing of the play helped you to work through the Essex situation too, in the end," I said.

"It did, Dolly. I was eventually able to let go of some of my doubts and move forward with the Essex execution."

"Good for you!" I said.

"But not so much for Essex, of course," as Mary, Queen of Scots, pointed out.

Chapter One Hundred-Eight
Fare-Thee-Wells and Dare-Thee-Tells

"'What light through yonder window breaks,'" I said, looking at the ever-widening beam shining in through the window. "Ladies, it would seem that we've covered all the bases—the entire canon of Shakespeare's plays, brought to the world not by the Bard but by all of you. Referring to your collective body of works as the Shakespeare canon seems kind of ridiculous now, doesn't it?"

"Well, the man does still have his sonnets," Catherine Grey reminded me.

"I like the term *royal plays*," Elizabeth said. "It captures the essence of the thing perfectly, in my opinion."

"Well, it will be an honor and a privilege to share the story of the royal plays with the world."

"It will be after you've figured out how to make the world believe it," Mary Tudor said with concern.

"'The devil can cite scripture for his purpose,'" I reminded her.

"Well, I'm sure you'll figure out something!"

"'There are no tricks in plain and simple faith,' Mary. I am absolutely certain that this will all come right, eventually."

"I hope so, dear. Good-bye, and do take care," Mary said, giving me a kiss on the cheek.

Jane Grey came up and kissed me next. "If anyone can achieve the mission, Dolly can," she said sweetly.

"Thanks for the vote of confidence, Jane. 'So shines a good deed in a naughty world'!"

"Good-bye, Dolly," Margaret Douglas said. "And, Dolly, about the Lennox Jewel—"

"What about it?" I asked.

"That enormous groin flower depicted on it," she said. "You remember."

"How could I forget? Talk about flower power!"

"Dolly, should your research for our mission lead you to the story behind that flower—you will keep it a secret, won't you?"

"'What springs forth from forth the fatal loins,' stays in the fatal loins," I reassured her.

"Good luck, Dolly! You're going to need it, rewriting history like you will have to do. You won't know where to begin!" said Catherine, stroking my cheek in farewell.

"Oh, I think I will—'What's past is prologue,' you know."

"Won't you be daunted, Dolly, by such a Herculean task?" asked little Mary Grey, getting the big word right for a change on this auspicious occasion.

I replied:

Our doubts are but traitors
And make us lose the good we oft might win
By fearing to attempt.

"I feel confident that I can brave it out, Mary," I said, bending down to meet her as she got up on her tiptoes to hug me good-bye.

"I hope you aren't underestimating the inherent difficulties in this task, Dolly. Your fellow academics are not likely to take it lying down when you turn history on its head," the Scottish queen pointed out, so moved by the occasion that she actually forgot her execution awareness.

"'I shall screw my courage to the sticking place,' and not fail, Mary; no matter what it takes!"

Elizabeth hugged me with tears in her eyes—happy tears. "It's hard to believe that at last, our literary achievements will be made known to the world. The excitement is almost too much! I'm confident we've put our faith in the right place, Dolly, by entrusting you with the mission. I hope you are cognizant of the very high honor that is yours. You've made a name for yourself in historical circles with the story of my father's wives. With *our* story, you will rise to greatness in the literary world as well."

"I'm not afraid of greatness, Elizabeth. You know what they say! 'Some are born great; some achieve greatness, and others—'"

"'Have greatness thrust upon them,'" said two familiar voices in unison from the doorway.

Chapter One Hundred-Nine
A Toast That Is the Most

Katharine of Aragon and Ann Boleyn entered the room arm in arm, believe it or not, and laughing. Their daughters, Mary Tudor and Elizabeth, moved happily to their mothers' sides. Seeing a look of joy on all four of those faces at the same time was like witnessing a little miracle. Clearly, even after centuries in a ghostly otherworld, the enchantment of mother-daughter reunion had not worn off for any of them. The emotion was particularly evident in the face of Elizabeth, who likely had no memories whatsoever of her mother in life on earth.

"You've gained weight, Dolly," Ann Boleyn pointed out.

"Married life must agree with her," said Katharine of Aragon.

"You both look wonderful," I said. "Not a day older than when I saw you last."

"The afterlife goes much easier on a girl than the one that comes before does," Katharine of Aragon reminded me.

"I'm *so* glad your visit here coincided with mine. It is wonderful to see you again! And why didn't you bring the other four wives with you?" I asked, inquiring after the full contingent of Henry VIII's wives.

"This is *my* daughter's moment, and I didn't want anyone stealing her thunder!" Ann said; apparently sharing the thunder was OK, even if stealing it was not.

Katharine glowered at Ann. "All right," Ann conceded, "*our* daughters' moment!"

It was now the hour, or at least the moment, for the Grey sisters, Margaret Douglas, and Mary, Queen of Scots, to glower.

"All right," Ann said, correcting herself yet again and gesturing to include all the seven authoresses present. "It is *everyone's* moment!"

"We didn't come here to make a scene, Dolly," Katharine of Aragon said, elbowing Ann. "We just wanted to see you again and to wish you well."

"And to impress upon you the importance of fulfilling this new mission of yours, bringing our daughters even greater fame than they already enjoy," Ann added.

"If Dolly does as well with this task as she did with the last one, all will be well," Katharine said.

"Fancy seeing you two arm in arm; it's good to know that what I accomplished here last time was more than just a flash in the pan. What an amazing development!"

"Thank you," Ann said.

"Any amazing new developments back in your world, Dolly?" Katharine asked politely.

"Just one, but I think you should know about it!" I said. "What a thrill to be the one to tell you about the Succession to the Crown Act of 2013!"

"Tell us about it!" Ann Boleyn demanded.

"Well, around the time that the current second-in-line to the English throne, Prince William, was expecting his first child, the rules of inheritance were changed by Act of Parliament. Absolute primogeniture has eclipsed male-preference primogeniture. Girls, you will be happy to know, are now on an equal footing with boy children when it comes to being in the lineup for the English throne!" I said.

Ann Boleyn and Katharine of Aragon wept tears of joy, hugged each other, hugged their daughters, hugged me, hugged everyone else in the room, and then wept some more. The depth of their feeling could be gauged by the fact that Ann Boleyn was absolutely speechless for some time.

Wine all around, served by Jane Grey, cleared up the tears and gave us all the means to toast the good news.

"*Who rule the world?*" I asked, raising my glass.

The assemblage raised their glasses in response. Katharine of Aragon and Ann Boleyn, just for good measure, linked elbows to be able to drink out of each other's glasses when the toast was completed.

"*Girls!*" they all replied.

Chapter One Hundred-Ten
What's Supposed to Be Sub-Rosa

Once everyone had consumed their wine, we got back to the business of wrapping things up.

"Time for me to remind you of rule number one for our departing guests," Elizabeth said. "You must maintain a religious silence about your experience here, Dolly."

"No one knows of my last visit here or of the personal details that the six wives so willingly shared with me. Based on what they told me, I was able to troll the primary sources available to the modern historian and interpret them correctly to develop the women's true stories. I maintain that it was all totally aboveboard in regard to rule number one."

"Well, your actions in that situation are what made us realize you were the girl to handle our stories," said Elizabeth, speaking for all the latter-generation Tudors if their nodding heads were any indication.

"It occurs to me that you could have gotten your story out a century and a half or so earlier if you'd entrusted it to Delia Bacon," I said. "Did you ever consider it? She was the original Shakespeare conspiracy theorist and spot-on about the Shakespeare plays having been a group effort. Of course, she had the candidates all wrong though; Raleigh, Spenser, Francis Bacon, and the Earl of Oxford."

"We heard of her doings," Elizabeth confirmed, "and did consider her for the assignment. We came to the same conclusion that her contemporary, Ralph Waldo Emerson, did, unfortunately."

"With genius, but mad," I recalled, remembering that after publishing her *The Philosophy of Shakespeare's Plays Unfolded,* Delia Bacon went all OCD about digging up Shakespeare's grave and had a nervous breakdown. She died in an asylum shortly thereafter. "I guess you made the right call there."

"Girls, it is time to be leaving Dolly to her task. You've all had enough gallivanting for one night!" said Katharine of Aragon in tried-and-true motherly fashion.

The Grey sisters led the charge out of the room, with Mary, Queen of Scots, and Margaret Douglas right behind. I waved a final good-bye to them all. Mary and Elizabeth tarried.

"When shall we three meet again?" I asked, rather rhetorically.

"'In thunder, lightning, or in rain,'" Elizabeth said.

"Yes, Dolly. Look for us to communicate with you in that way if ever you need our help on the other side in completing your mission," Mary affirmed.

Katharine of Aragon, Mary Tudor, Ann Boleyn, and Elizabeth lingered at the door for one more moment, hands joined. I addressed, for the last time that night, Elizabeth, the legendary Gloriana.

"I may be thinking ahead a bit, Elizabeth, but there's something I'm going to need to know a little bit more about. How did your works and those of Mary, Queen of Scots, get from you, or your designees, to Shakespeare? You've not enlightened me on that particular nugget of information."

"That," Elizabeth said, motioning to two as yet unmet ladies who were about to enter the room, "is their job. The art of leadership is in delegation, you know. I leave you in their capable hands." With that, Elizabeth gently touched my cheek in a final farewell salute as she left the room.

"Isn't my daughter *brilliant?*" said Ann Boleyn, squeezing one of my hands with her free one for a moment as she exited the room.

"Yes, your daughter is brilliant," Katharine of Aragon acknowledged as she waved me good-bye and exited the room with her daughter, Mary. "*She takes after her older sister that way!*"

Chapter One Hundred-Eleven
Enigmas, Anyone?

One of my new companions was a tall, elegant, pale redhead; the other, a petite Mediterranean type, was very mysterious and sexy.

"Good evening, Dolly," said the redhead, with a marked Scandinavian lilt. She was dressed with elegant and tailored understatement in a black velvet dress and poufy white hat.

I consulted my academic memory for legendary Nordics of the Renaissance era. This beautiful and very feminine young woman couldn't possibly be Queen Christina, the eccentric, awkward, and inelegant Swede who hightailed it off to Papal Rome from Lutheran Sweden. I was at a loss, though, to figure out exactly who she was.

"A pleasure to meet you, Dolly," said the dark young woman. She didn't have an accent, exactly, but her tone and inflection spoke of roots not strictly British and likely from points south. I was as much at a loss for placing her as I was for the redhead. Like her companion, she was dressed in black. Her outfit, however, was flowing and sensuous, with bell sleeves and a low-cut neckline.

"Ladies," I said. "This night has been forever, and my memory has been reduced at this point to about an inch."

"Well, that is the long and short of it, if ever I've heard it," the redhead said, laughing. "Talk about the bloody obvious!"

"What is not bloody obvious," I confessed to them both, "is your identities. I take it," I said, turning to the redhead, "that you are from points north of the Tudor clan's England?"

"I am," she confirmed. "I hail from Sweden but lived most of my life at Elizabeth's court, privileged to serve, as maid of honor, the greatest woman of the age I lived in."

"Helena von Snakenborg!" I said, coming out of the fog I'd been in and—if the woman's smiling and clapping was any indication—nailing it first time out.

"At your service!" she said.

Helena von Snakenborg came into Elizabeth's ambit as part of the entourage that came to England in 1565 to tempt Elizabeth to marry Sweden's king. Helena's intelligence, looks, and charm won everyone over, including Elizabeth and the elderly Marquess of Northampton, whom she eventually married. Given that he was the brother of Henry VIII's sixth wife and Elizabeth's beloved stepmother, Katherine Parr, Helena had more or less married into the extended Tudor family. When the elderly marquess died a few months after the wedding, Helena rose to the dizzying heights of the rank of marchioness in her own right overnight.

As was the wont of more than one of Elizabeth's courtiers, Helena married down when she chose her second husband, one Thomas Gorges, a relative of Ann Boleyn's and therefore of Queen Elizabeth's. As was the wont of Elizabeth in these matters, she roundly punished the pair for marrying. However, Helena was eventually rehabilitated socially and regained her place in Elizabeth's favor. As Elizabeth entered old age, Helena was her chief deputy in many affairs. In the fullness of time, she was the chief mourner at Elizabeth's funeral.

Having placed Helena, I turned my attentions to the dark lady next to her. "You remind me an awful lot of Ann Boleyn," I said. "Are you a relation, perhaps?"

"I am no relation to Ann Boleyn, or to anyone at the Tudor court, except for my father. I lived there rather as 'a stranger in a strange land,'" she said.

"Not so very much a stranger," Helena pointed out. "The man who kept you was, after all, a cousin of Queen Elizabeth's."

"One of the Carey clan?" I conjectured.

"Yes," the dark lady answered. "Henry Carey, First Baron Hunsdon."

"He was the patron of Shakespeare's theatrical troupe!" I recalled. I could vaguely see pieces of a puzzle coming together and grew quite excited.

"He was," the dark lady confirmed.

I realized then that in thinking of this mysterious woman as the dark lady, I had actually hit upon her very identity. She had to be, of course, Emilia Lanier, England's first self-proclaimed poetess and the reputed subject of Shakespeare's *Dark Lady* sonnets.

"It is a privilege to meet each of you, and your personal histories would be something I'd love to dish with you about," I said. "But time being of the essence, we need to get down to business. I was told that you two would tell me how the royal plays of Mary, Queen of Scots, and Elizabeth I were transferred over to William Shakespeare. I know already that the works of Margaret Douglas got there through the auspices of Robert Dudley, and that Mary Tudor's made it through thanks to Lord Hunsdon. The works of the Grey sisters were, last I heard, in your hands, Emilia, ready to get passed to the Lord Chamberlain's Men and, I assume, to your friend, William Shakespeare."

"Susan Bertie realized by the late 1590s that the Lord Chamberlain's Men were just about ready to bring the Grey plays to life," Emilia began. "She also conjectured that the troupe's success and popularity would eventually make playwriting a more acceptable literary specialty. So it was that at that time, with her life coming to its end, she turned the Grey plays over to my possession, to be turned over to the troupe as I saw fit. I feared doing *anything* with plays by royal relatives without the queen's blessing, so I went to her with the Grey plays, as you've already been told, and sought her permission to pass them on to, as you call him, my friend Will."

"Were you and Shakespeare lovers?" I asked.

"No, we were not, even though he wanted us to be," Emilia said. "The possibility of my giving in was something I dangled in front of him to keep the development and production of those plays going along the way I wanted it to. It worked, of course."

"The old Ann Boleyn strategy done right, not to mention the sonnets that were written about it," I said. I recalled sonnets 127 154, the beautiful *Dark Lady* series in which Shakespeare immortalizes the passion and desperation he suffers at the hands of a taunting brunette.

> She walks in beauty, like the night
> Of cloudless climes and starry skies;
> And all that's best of dark and bright
> Meet in her aspect and her eyes...

Emilia listened with raised eyebrows as I quoted a few lines. "Very lovely, Dolly, but that was George Gordon, Lord Byron—spot-on about brunettes, but well after my time."

"Hell's bells; so much for my poetry credentials! But I guess that's what I get for straying from the topic at hand. Getting back to it—tell me about how you handled the Grey plays that made their way into your hands."

Chapter One Hundred-Twelve
Routing and Outing

"As I began to tell you," Emilia said, "I sought permission from the queen to forward the Grey plays to Will. She felt that the time was right for the plays to be incrementally forwarded to the Lord Chamberlain's Men but not right for the royal identities of the authors to be revealed. She and I collaborated on feeding those plays, one by one, to Will over a period of years, as we saw fit; each play had its own right time. I'd been privy to the way my lover, Lord Hundson, handled the plays that I later learned were authored by Mary Tudor, so I had a good idea of how to go about the logistics of it."

"'Sooth!'" I said.

"My story to Will was that the plays had been written by well-born women who preferred to remain anonymous. He suspected that *I* wrote them and had them copied out by other hands. I didn't do a lot to disabuse him of that notion, because it made him all the more compliant with my directions for bringing the plays to the public."

"And what about the plays of the two queens—Elizabeth and Mary, Queen of Scots? How did *they* make their way to Shakespeare?"

Helena Von Snakenborg picked up the tale. "Queen Elizabeth had possession of her Scottish cousin's plays, as has already been described to you. Elizabeth started to ponder her own mortality as early as 1590. I was her right-hand woman, her wing woman extraordinaire, her most trusted servant. Elizabeth was already involved with Emilia and the slow feeding of the Grey plays to Shakespeare, one by one. She wanted her Scottish cousin's plays, and her own, to be fed to him in the same way. She was fond of Emilia, fond enough to trust her with the plays of the Grey sisters, who were royal relatives but not—discounting Jane Grey's nine-day disaster—queens. She wanted someone of a little higher standing to come into the picture for the output of actual reigning monarchs."

"She couldn't have done better than you, Helena; you can't get much higher up than a marchioness!"

Emilia Lanier, a product of her age, did not seem one whit disturbed by the whole class issue. She, while a poetess in her own right and the mistress of one of England's leading men, was not of the noblesse or even the gentry. Her Italian father was a musician at Elizabeth's court.

Helena continued her tale. "The queen trusted me implicitly with her plays, as she had with so many other things over the years. I had proven myself worthy of such trust again and again; I was, to use her words, 'tried and true.'"

Take it from me; you have not heard the words "tried and true" until you've heard them spoken with a Swedish lilt. Helena continued her tale.

"The queen was very concerned that the royal plays, as she called them, not be attributed to their rightful authors until after her death. So she passed the physical manuscripts of all the plays in her possession, including her own later ones as they rolled off the press, into my care. She thought, for secrecy's sake, that they were safer in my charge than in anyone else's, including her own. Spies were everywhere about the court, and Elizabeth's papers were vulnerable."

"And the queen chose well when she chose Helena," Emilia said. "Helena kept mum about the whole thing quite admirably; in the hotbed of a Tudor court, she and I were truly the only two who knew about all those plays."

"I guess Elizabeth brought the two of you together when it came to working with her plays?" I asked Emilia.

"Yes. She met with the two of us and put all the cards on the table—or at least all the cards that had to do with her plays and those of Mary, Queen of Scots, Mary Tudor, Margaret Douglas, and the Greys. The queen then had me introduce Helena to Will Shakespeare, and Helena used the acquaintance to start funneling the royal plays of Elizabeth and Mary, Queen of Scots, along to Will, separately from my own project with the Grey plays. We funneled slowly, over a course of years."

"Wow!" was all I had left within me to comment at this juncture.

"For a time, we had Will convinced that the plays Helena was feeding to him were actually her own work and that of some of the queen's other ladies, who preferred to remain anonymous. His experience with the Grey and Douglas plays made that believable to him, at first. But eventually, he guessed that something more was going on. And then something happened that made him realize the royal plays were, indeed, royal."

"How did he figure it out?" I asked.

"The queen did her share of attending theatrical productions and saw any number of the Lord Chamberlain's Men's productions when they were given for the court. Of course, when she was in attendance, all eyes, including Will's, sought a glimpse of her. Once, Will was actually able to cadge a look at her while a play was being performed. He said that when she watched a production of

A Midsummer Night's Dream, her face was a dead giveaway; it was the face of a proud author, if ever he'd seen one. From there he started looking at the handwriting of the royal manuscripts, asking discreet questions, and checking details. He eventually came to me and confronted me with the true authorship of the various royal plays. The man was terrified, quite frankly. He did not know what to do or to think. He loved the fame and acclaim that the plays brought him. On that level, he was more than happy to keep the secret of the authorship of all those plays that seemed to just keep coming to him. On the other hand, he feared, as did everyone, inadvertently doing something to earn the queen's disapprobation."

"Gadzooks!" I said, rallying a bit from the information overload.

"Helena and I didn't dare let Elizabeth know that her secret was out if we hoped to keep our positions at court and our quality of life in general. It didn't take much to convince Will to keep the secret once we'd talked him down and assured him that *we'd* take any fall that had to be taken, should it come to that. That mollified him somewhat."

"Old Will was a trusting soul."

"Old Will was a horny soul and wanting to get under my farthingale. He'd have believed anything I told him," said Emilia.

"And so the plays kept moving along the Shakespearian pipeline," Helena continued. "We managed to maintain a very livable status quo until the queen's final weeks on this earth."

"What happened then?"

"She shared with me her final wishes. Among them was that the plays that we'd been dealing with, as well as the Margaret Douglas and Mary Tudor plays, be attributed to their rightful authors as soon after her own death as possible."

"So what did you do?" I asked.

"We went, Emilia and I, to meet with Will to address the situation. We had decided that a pact, or a covenant, was in order. Will agreed, as he had a request to make about the author identity situation as well."

"What was it?" I asked.

"His wish dovetailed fairly well with the queen's; he asked that the true authorship of the plays not be made public until after *his* death. He wanted to enjoy the fame and fortune they brought him to the last, or at least to *his* last, here on earth. Emilia and I felt it reasonable to agree. Since she was by the far the youngest among us, it seemed likely that Emilia would be the person in charge of revealing the authorship of the royal plays when the time came. She would need the original manuscripts to do this. Will had them well secured, he said, and would make arrangements for Emilia to receive them immediately upon his death. Given that Will lived away from the court and all its spies and intrigues, we felt that the manuscripts were safest with him and agreed to this plan. We furnished him with the originals of the Mary Tudor plays, which Elizabeth had passed into my hands, for the sake of completeness. And of course, we memorialized all this in a letter, a covenant, jointly signed by Will, Emilia, and myself and witnessed by a fourth, peripherally involved party."

"I thought that the three of you—you, Emilia, and Will—were the only ones in on this," I said.

"There was me as well, Dolly," said a plainly dressed, middle-aged woman, who had just entered the room.

"'Great Caesar's ghost'!" I said. "Not another one! Who are you?"

Chapter One Hundred-Thirteen
Spouse in the House

"I'm sorry I said 'not another one' when you entered the room," I said to the woman. "It was nothing personal. Just a little overwhelmed, you know."

"I understand, Dolly. Take heart. I am the last of the ladies you will meet tonight."

"And I take it that you are Mrs. Shakespeare, my dear?"

"You presume correctly," the woman answered.

Mrs. Shakespeare, nee Anne Hathaway, has been given the shortest shrift of just about any historical wife I know of. Shotgun wedding; significantly older than husband; left the second-best bed in deceased husband's last will and testament. That was about all that I, or posterity, had known about her until now. She was handsome enough for a woman of her age and wore a basic black-and-white ensemble. Her ruff was refreshingly diminutive, and on her head she wore a simple, white linen cap.

"So, Mrs. Shakespeare—Anne—you were the secretary and/or witness to the letter of the covenant between your husband, Emilia, and Helena?"

"I was," Anne Shakespeare said.

"Had to have been a bit awkward. I mean, you and Emilia working so closely together on something after your husband had written those steamy sonnets for her."

"Our marriage had deteriorated to pretty much nothing more than a business arrangement by that point, Dolly. I knew Emilia was the Dark Lady, and frankly, I didn't really care. What

I was most interested in was keeping the secret of the authorship of the plays sacrosanct. I was, of course, more than a little bit older than Will was, and I assumed he would outlive me. Had this turned out to be the case, keeping the Shakespeare plays under Will's provenance until his death would have meant that I could enjoy, *my* whole life long, the cache of being Mrs. Shakespeare, wife of the famous playwright. It was my claim to fame, so to speak, and I did not want to live to see it end."

"I guess Will's dying before you did must have upset that little applecart, didn't it?"

"It could have, but it didn't."

"It was another story for us though," said Helena Snakenborg. Emilia Lanier nodded in agreement.

"When Will knew he was dying, he turned the covenant letter over to my possession, the information therein to be disclosed to the world, eventually, by Emilia," Anne said. "He also disclosed to me the place where he had secured the manuscripts of the royal plays, which would be the documentary evidence of the claims made in the letter."

"That evidence did not make it down through the sands of time though; why not, Anne?"

"The queen had wanted the disclosure of the authorship of the royal plays to wait until after *her* death, and Will wanted it to wait until after *his*. Nobody thought to ask me *my* opinion on the subject. I did not want the information disclosed *at all!* The royalty had their claim to fame and posterity by heritage and right. My husband, Will, would have his claim to fame, even absent of those plays, thanks to his sonnets. Those sonnets meant a lot to him—even more than his plays did."

"They were the classier form of expression for the Renaissance writer," I said. Anne Shakespeare was not impressed by the argument.

"A bunch of ditties, and the best of them about a loose woman, no less! They weren't nearly as impressive, to my mind, as those plays were. Comedy! Drama! History! Romance! Family dysfunction! All seven of the deadly sins! There was something in those plays for everyone to enjoy. I had my eye on the future and on posterity. I felt sure that those plays, in the fullness of time, would supersede Will's poetry in the public eye."

"Not to mention the public ear," Emilia pointed out.

"Either way, I devised a means to protect those plays from being attributed to anyone other than Will and to secure, for as long as possible, my place in literary history as the wife of the man who wrote them."

"You destroyed the letter and the original manuscripts!" I said, feeling a downright visceral scholar's pain at the thought of the most significant primary source documents in the world of English literature going up in smoke.

"Actually, I didn't," Anne said. "Mind you, I thought about it, though. And I told Emilia and Helena that I had. My conscience, however, wouldn't allow for the actual destruction of the documents, putting the lie to the authorship of the plays for all eternity. I was too true a subject to my late queen to do that. My conscience was elastic enough, though, to put the lie to the authorship for at least my own lifetime and for an indeterminate while longer."

"What did you do with, or about, the documents?" I asked.

"I left the royal manuscripts where Will had put them. It was a safe place, a place no one would look for them, I was sure, while

I was alive. Once I was dead—well, it seemed to me that if the Almighty wanted the authorship of the plays to be revealed, then the plays would find their way out of their hiding place and into world. I trusted them, after my lifetime, to fate and to a higher power that would make arrangements for them according to his desire. Those plays have stayed in their place until now—until you, Dolly, came along."

"So where were—or maybe I should even say where *are*—the manuscripts of the royal plays hiding?" I asked.

"Take your best guest, Dolly," said Emilia meaningfully.

"Were they somewhere in the Globe Theater; a safe haven in Stratford-on-Avon?" I asked. It was the best I could do on short notice.

"Dolly," said Helena, speaking as meaningfully as Emilia had, "take your second-best guess."

Chapter One Hundred-Fourteen
Secreted and Defeated

"Of course! Those manuscripts are hidden somewhere in the second-best bed! The one that Will so cryptically endowed to his wife, leaving a baffled posterity to conjecture why."

"Will was a fair woodworker, in his spare time," Anne Shakespeare said. "He hollowed out the posts of that bed, which were enormous, and hid some of the manuscript pages inside of them. The rest of the manuscript pages were deposited into the headboard and footboard, and in the woodwork of the canopy."

"Where did the bed find its way to after your death, Anne?" I asked.

"My death came upon me suddenly, Dolly, but I did not die intestate. My daughter Susannah was the immediate beneficiary of my household furnishings. Neither I nor Will had given her any reason to suspect the contents of the woodwork of that bed."

"And what about the covenant letter? Is that in the second-best bed too?"

"No, Dolly. The covenant letter is not in the second-best bed."

"Well then, where is it?"

"In life, that letter never left Will's possession. He kept it on his person at all times, even when sleeping. It seemed to me quite fitting that that practice should not change with Will's death."

"So that letter; it—it—"

"It reposes in a grave at Holy Trinity Church," Helena said, kindly finishing my thought for me as I found my way out of my stutter.

"Of course—the covenant letter was buried with Shakespeare!"

"'Good friend, for Jesus's sake forbear,'" I said, quoting one of the most famous epitaphs in the English language:

To dig the dust enclosed here.
Blessed be the man that spares these stones,
And cursed be he that moves my bones.

"Very nicely recited, Dolly," Anne Shakespeare said. "I thought I did as good a job with that epitaph, if I do say so myself, as my husband would have done. Those little couplets of mine certainly served their purpose, at least until now. That little warning has put off the curious from disturbing that grave for nigh on four hundred years now and holding."

"And Emilia and Helena, having been led by you to think the manuscripts and letter were destroyed, never thought to look for either of them. At least, that is what I am assuming," I said, despite Douglas Sheffields's repeated warnings against assumptions.

"Correct, Dolly," Emilia confirmed. "Helena and I went to Anne Shakespeare as soon as we'd heard of her husband's death, and she told us that she'd destroyed the covenant letter and the royal manuscripts to protect her claim to fame as the wife of the age's greatest playwright. She was a convincing liar. It occurred to neither one of us that she might have spared, or hidden, the documents."

"Of course, I was devastated, Dolly, at this turn of events," Helena admitted. "I was devoted to my mistress and queen in her lifetime and to her memory posthumously. I had sworn to her that I would bring the authorship of those plays to the light of day. Yet with the manuscripts and the covenant letter destroyed, or so I thought, there was no way I could do so."

"You couldn't have just come forward with your story?" I asked. "You'd have had Emilia to back you up."

"Yes, and England's new monarch to wear us down," Helena said.

Chapter One Hundred-Fifteen
A Man of Parts, a Change of Heart, and a Departure

James I of England, and VI of Scotland, was the son of Mary, Queen of Scots. He'd been raised in her absence in the melee that was the Scottish court, living through the deaths of several of his regents while he was of tender years. His keepers and educators played some major mind games with him, particularly as pertained to his mother, the monarchy, and religion. It wasn't the typical life of a prince and a king, and he grew up to be not the typical monarch.

"King James was an unusual man, to be sure," I began. "He was conformist enough to bring the world the standard King James Bible, and maverick enough to make waves in the political arena by engaging in questionable relationships with rather unsavory male favorites. A man of mixed parts, I suppose one would have said in his day."

"Yes, Dolly, and he—like his mother and his predecessor Elizabeth—was an author," Emilia reminded me. "His *Basilikon Doron* was a bestseller in our day."

"A work directing his son in the proper comportment of royalty, was it not?" I asked.

"Yes, Dolly, and let me remind you of the tenor of its first book," said Helena.

> Remember, that as in dignity he hath erected you above others…A moat in another's eye, is a beam into yours: a blemish in another, is a leprous boil into you…Think not

therefore, that the highness of your dignity diminisheth your fault but by the contrary your fault shall be aggravated according to the height of your dignity…

"I get it," I said. "King James was all about the pomp and circumstance of the monarchy. His own mother and his predecessor engaging in common playwriting, which was not a distinguished pastime for the regal male, let alone the female, would not have sat well with him, or with the Puritan element that was becoming so prominent in England then. It would have been well beneath the royal dignity."

"King James was a great patron of the theater, of course. But in our day, there was a world of difference between being a behind-the-scenes patron and being involved in the dirty business of the nuts and bolts of making theater happen. And of course, there was a world of difference between what a man and a woman could get away with socially."

"I understand," I said.

"Then of course, there is what James had to say to his son about the literary arts in the third book of the *Basilicon*," Helena continued.

"'Use a plain, short, but stately style…and if your engine spur you to write any works, either in verse or in prose, I cannot but allow you to practice it: but take no longsome works in hand, for distracting you from your calling…'" Emilia quoted aloud.

"'Longsome' is as good a word as any to use when describing the Shakespearian, or royal, plays. Short and pithy is not what comes to mind when one thinks of Shakespeare. Except for some of the insults, of course," I said. "So you had plenty of reason to think that old James would not approve of the role that his mother and the rest of the royal playwrights played in producing the Shakespeare canon."

"'And because your writes will remain as true pictures of your mind, to all posterities; let them be free of all uncomeliness,'" Helena said, quoting again from the *Basilikon*. "Think about the content of those royal plays, Dolly!"

"Agree," I admitted. "The lowlife proclivities and horn-doggery of Falstaff alone would have been enough for James I to blackball Mary, Queen of Scots, and Elizabeth I as authors under the *Basilicon* criteria."

"Exactly," said Emilia.

"And of course," I considered, "there are the mommy issues James I had with Mary, Queen of Scots. He was raised to despise her. However, her DNA and his relationship to her were what qualified him to achieve his life's ambition: the crown of England. He had to have been conflicted about that, as he was about so many other things. Muddying the waters even further by bringing up the question of his mother's playwriting activities was probably the last thing he'd have wanted."

"We thought so too," Helena said, and Emilia nodded. "And so, when my time came, I went to my grave, carrying the burden of having failed my mistress and queen in the task she had given me regarding those plays."

"Imagine Helena's joy when she arrived here on the other side, to which I had preceded her!" Anne Shakespeare said, beaming.

"You came clean with Helena once she arrived in the afterlife? And told her that the covenant letter and manuscripts, though hidden, were not destroyed?" I asked Anne.

"I did. You see, my husband, Will, and I had preceded Helena—as had all the royal authoresses, of course—to the

Great Beyond. Not to mention Catherine Willoughby, Baron Hunsdon, Susan Bertie, Jane Dormer, and Robert Dudley. Word does get around in the afterlife, you know! Everything about the channeling of the royal plays was aboveboard once we all got to this side of the great divide."

"Well, everything was once *I* finally got here!" Emilia reminded Anne.

"So, there you all were, or I suppose I should say, here you all were, with the truth out in the open. That didn't amount to very much, did it?" I asked.

"Well, we waited a few generations to see if something would give with that second-best bed," Anne said. "Will's and my direct line gave out with our grandchildren, and from there the bed went into the Hall family through Will's sister, Joan. Eventually, though, we lost track of the bed."

"And of course, thanks to that epitaph of yours, no one has ever thought to exhume old Will and the covenant letter," I said.

"Correct, Dolly. We eventually concluded that only some one-in-a-million quirk of fate would ever bring the true authorship of the royal plays to light. The authoresses were disappointed, of course. I was not. At least, I was not until you came along and did what you did for Henry VIII's six wives."

"What did that change for you?" I asked.

"You setting the record straight about Henry VIII's wives made the royal authoresses realize that they finally had a real chance of receiving credit for their plays. At last, someone—you—had appeared on the horizon with the skill set needed to get the job done. You would play the final part in the drama of the revelation of the authorship of the royal plays!"

"I guess I will take my place with Catherine Willoughby and all the others who had a part in the saga of the royal plays. It is an exciting prospect, Anne!"

"The job you did with the wives' stories also helped me to understand that, after the passage of four hundred years, things have changed on my side of the issue as well. I've come to realize, over time, how much more desirable it would be for me to see the plays properly attributed than to see them continue to be credited to my husband, Will."

"How is that so?" I asked. "You wanted so much to remain known as the wife of the man who wrote the greatest plays of all time!"

"What you did for the six wives, Dolly, was to take them from being women memorable for their wifely status to being women memorable for their own lives, fates, personalities, and accomplishments. It made me realize that I could be more than just a reflection of Will, in posterity's eyes, if the truth comes out."

"Because?" I asked.

"Because," Anne said proudly, "if the truth comes out, I will be known as the woman who pulled the wool over the eyes of the historical and literary worlds for centuries and centuries! How clever people will think me when they realize how my beautifully simple plot stymied the world from learning the truth about those plays. I can go down in history a second time, not just as someone's wife but as a real and active player, in my own right, in the drama of the Shakespeare—now to be known as royal—plays."

"Well, I'll be," I said, "a monkey's uncle, or perhaps a bunch-backed toad. The historical reputations of so many people are riding on my outing the Shakespeare plays. Without a doubt, I certainly do have my work cut out for me!"

The sun was fully up save for a sliver of a shadow. My time in this place, I knew, was over. I took a last look around the room, kissed Helena, Emilia, and Anne good-bye, and took a deep breath.

"'We are such stuff as dreams are made on; and our little life is rounded with a sleep,'" I said. "Good-bye to you all. Wish me luck back in the real world!"

"You know what to do now, Dolly, to get back home," Helena said. "At least, that's what Elizabeth told us. The same thing you did last time you were here. She told us to remind you in case you forgot."

"How could I?" I said as I raised my skirts an inch or two and peeped down at my cordovan slippers. While they were not the ruby footwear of my last visit here, they were, if one was limited to selecting strictly from the primary colors, for all intents and purposes red. I clicked my heels together slowly, three times, and spoke my last words in that place: "There's no place like home!"

And behold, it was all a dream.

Act Three

Chapter One Hundred-Sixteen
Arise and Surprise

They say that "journeys end in lovers' meetings," and this one was no exception; I opened my eyes to find myself peering directly into Wally's.

"What happened?" I asked groggily.

"You fainted as you were ascending the steps to the stage to give your commencement address."

"Gadzooks!" I said. "What about my underwear—or should I say, the lack thereof? Tell me I didn't throw a shot at the academic universe as I went down for the count!"

"You didn't, dear; I had the situation under control. Didn't you hear me calling out to you as I crested the audience and came to your aid?"

"I'm afraid I didn't. What did you say?"

"I said something to the effect of 'don't worry, I've got you covered.' I meant it literally and figuratively!"

"Well, thank goodness!" I said, looking around. I appeared to be in an emergency room, behind a curtain, and I was now wearing a hospital Johnny coat.

"They must have caught me going commando, though, when they changed me from my doctoral robe into this hospital gown," I said, cringing with embarrassment.

"No, they didn't," Wally told me. "I suspected the whole commando situation, and just in case, as we were leaving the house, I slipped some of your undergarments into my inside jacket pockets and a little sleeveless dress of yours into a satchel. I learned in the Peace Corps that it pays to be prepared for every contingency. I declined the ambulance for your trip here and transported you in my own vehicle. I got the outfit onto you in the car, before I carried you in here."

"Thanks," I said.

"I was thanking my lucky stars that we made it here without having an accident or getting pulled over," Wally said. "I'd have had quite a time explaining to the police about the semiclad unconscious woman in my car, and the bra and panties in my pocket!"

Wally chuckled as he said this, and then his face relaxed into a broad grin. He had, in fact, been grinning ever since I awoke. I had expected something a bit more like concern from him, quite frankly. This kind of insensitivity was not at all like my Wally, and I called him on it.

"You seem awfully happy for a man whose wife is in the emergency room."

Wally was saved from having to explain himself by the entrance of the hospital doctor. He, too, was grinning from ear to ear.

"Wally Rolly!" the medic said excitedly, pumping my husband's hand in greeting and ignoring me completely. Wally, being a physician as well as a veterinarian and an engineer, among other things, occasionally did locum duty at the local ER, so he was fairly well known to the area's medical community.

"Well," I said, glancing over at the paperwork in the doctor's hand, "how am I?"

"You are," he asked, "Catherine Rolly, aka Dolly?"

"I am."

"Well, Dolly, all your tests came back negative, except for one."

"Which one?" I asked, figuring that all the stress eating I'd been doing lately had shown up on my lipid panel.

"The pregnancy test, Dolly! You're going to have a baby!"

With Wally's grin now so wide that I feared his ears would pop off, we got down to the nitty-gritty.

"You've known all along, haven't you, Wally?" I asked.

"Well, dear, I *am* a physician. I've suspected it for some weeks. That's why I've been hounding you to go see your doctor."

"Why didn't you just tell me about it?" I asked.

"I wasn't sure how your feminine ego would take *my* being aware of the possibility before *you* were. And pregnant women must be humored, you know."

"I like the way it's turned out," I said, snugging up against Wally's chest, "both of us hearing the news together, at the same time. Perfect! It's awfully unexpected, though. Not exactly what we had planned."

"Unexpected?" said the medic, digging his elbow into Wally's side companionably. "And you a physician, Wally!"

"Stranger things have happened," Wally offered in his own defense.

"And very recently too," I added, looking skyward and remembering the changes Blanche Parry had prognosticated when she read my palm.

Driving home from the hospital, Wally and I started to plan for the impact our blessed event would have on our lives.

"We can remodel the second floor of our Rainbow Chateaux to create a nursery," Wally began. "I knew my degree in architecture would come in handy one of these days!"

"Can you squeak an office out of that space as well?" I asked.

"Certainly I can, if you like, but why?"

"You know how Burr has been at me to move away from the world of Tudor academia and on to greener pastures. It occurs to me that freelancing and baby raising might go very well together."

"Abandoning your beloved Tudors?" Wally asked. "Frankly, I'm shocked."

"Not abandoning them, dear. Just taking a new approach to them is all; letting go of the old way and trying something new. There's only so much one can do about revealing the history when one is limited, by academic rigor, to the extant primary source documents that we have available to us. All those sources have been worked to death over the years. Maybe it is time for a fresher, less academic approach."

Wally looked a bit skeptical.

"For the next seven or eight months, dear, it's anything my little heart desires," I reminded him.

"Wrong, darling," Wally said. "For the rest of our lives, it's anything your little heart desires, Dolly."

Chapter One Hundred-Seventeen
The Shindig and the Big News

There was yet another surprise in store for me when I arrived home. Wally had arranged for a postcommencement address reception at our house, complete with all my friends, family, and coworkers. Wally had instructed them to go on with the proceedings in spite of my fainting spell, saying he would explain all when we arrived. He didn't have to, as it turned out.

"Dolly!" Miss Bess called out as I entered the front door. She was holding a drink in her hand, and unless I was very much mistaken, it wasn't her first or even her second. "You're glowing, Dolly! Have you had a drink already? Let me get you another."

"I'm afraid I'll have to say no to that, Bess."

"Why, Dolly? One more drink Morley or lessly won't matter," she said.

"Miss Bess, did you just say 'Morley'?" I asked, taken aback.

"She's drunk, Dolly," cousin Bella explained. "I've been mixing her drinks, and I've made them all doubles. It's fun to watch her when she gets like this."

"Passive-aggressive, but true," I agreed.

"Not drinking at a party, Dolly? That's not like you," said Kath, feeling my pulse at my wrist and putting a hand to my forehead to check for a temperature. "They let you out of that hospital too soon."

"Let me see what her palm says," said Blanche.

"I don't need to read her palm," Auntie Reine Marie said with a knowing smile, "to know that I'd best be getting my needles and pastel-colored wools out of storage."

"You can see it in Dolly's face, surely," said the ever-perceptive Jean; there was no getting anything past my wise little cousin.

"I see happy motherhood in Dolly's palm," Blanche said, peering into one of my hands. "But," she added, perplexed, "I do not see a little boy or a little girl."

"Time will solve that little mystery," Wally said.

The practical-minded Amy brought the conversation around to more mundane matters. "In my little home village, Dolly, we have a sovereign remedy for morning sickness. We call it the 'in-a-fix elixir.' Works every time! I'll bring some in to the office next week in case you should need it."

"We have a potion like that in my family too. We call it the 'gestation distillation.' It's nothing short of a miracle drug, I can tell you. I'll make some up for you, Dolly," Lettice offered.

Gladous was not to be outdone when it came to pharmaceuticals. "Out our way, it's 'in-the-club syllabub.' Absolutely the best thing for when a girl's gotta hurl," she said seriously.

"In my hometown in Italy, we have a surefire powder for morning sickness. A pinch of it mixed into a shot glass of milk does the trick. Loosely translated into English, it's called 'gravid granules,'" Demi said.

"You can all bring some of that stuff around for Katie too. She's still got a few weeks to go on her first semester, you know," Merrie said.

"I think you mean trimester, dear," said Katie, giving her office partner in crime a big hug.

"And I've got a linen, lanolin, and lavender belly binder that will do wonders for your stretch marks, once you get them," said Janie, Wally's research assistant and part-time herbal girl. "I got the idea for it during my recent trip to France. It's the one foundation garment every expectant mother should have!"

Marge brought a much-appreciated change of subject to the conversation, when she called my attention to the rather dramatic bouquet of flowers that graced the dining room table.

"Cockscombs, aren't they?" I asked, as I admired their jewel tones and ran a finger along the velvety surface of the flowers.

"They're what is blooming in my garden at the moment," Marge said. "'Yet my goodwill is great, Dolly, though the gift small.'"

"What kind of name is 'cockscomb' for a flower?" asked Miss Bess. "Sounds more like something you'd call—"

We were spared Miss Bess's conjecture by a bustle at the front door. Wally opened it to what turned out to be a trio of women: Helen, Emily, and Annie. I was concerned for a moment that he might refer to them as "those publishing women" to their faces, but I needn't have worried. He came out with their names like a trooper and even managed to apply the correct name to the correct woman, as we greeted them at the door.

"Dolly," he whispered to me in an aside, "I didn't invite them. How did they know to come?"

As if on cue, two more women popped out from behind the trio.

"Surprise!"

"Lizzie and Mary!" I exclaimed, welcoming in the daughters of my former fiancé, Harry.

"I hope you don't mind that we brought our mutual publishing friends around for the party," Lizzie began. "They and my sister and I have been doing some business together on the I Make a Whisper a Sell campaign. Well, when your name came up, Dolly, they told us about how they've been trying to get you to go mainstream with that Henry VIII treatise of yours."

"We couldn't agree with them more," Mary said. "And our campaign can help you make a success of that project, not to mention any others you might have in the hopper in that vivid imagination of yours, Dolly!"

"All very interesting, ladies, but that will all have to go on to the back burner, at least for today," Wally said, gathering me protectively into his arms. "You see, we've just learned—well, you tell them, darling."

"Wait just a moment, Dolly, before you tell us your news. I think," Lizzie said, looking at the car that had just pulled into the drive, "that is my mother and Mary's mother come to join us."

It did indeed turn out to be Anna Belinda and Kay. We welcomed them into the house, and Mary and Lizzie explained to their respective mothers that I was about to break some exciting news to them.

"Well, judging by the way Dolly's glowing—" said Anna Belinda with the look of an old-time wise woman who knows all.

"And," the ever-practical Kay added, "considering the subtle changes in her face and figure—"

"You've cracked it, ladies. There's a jolly little Rolly on the way, by golly!" Wally said.

"What's that I hear?" said a masculine voice from the direction of the library. Wally looked relieved as the speaker brought some much-appreciated additional testosterone to the proceedings.

"I was hiding out in the library from—if you will pardon the expression—all these complicated women," said Burr, my dear old mentor and favorite geek—aside from Wally, of course.

"Can't say I blame you," said Wally, "speaking as one man to another, of course. Not to be misogynistic or anything. It's just that I can see how so much high-powered feminine talent and brains in one room could be a bit overwhelming for a man on his own."

"So did I hear the news properly, Dolly? A baby on the way?" asked Burr, actually blushing at the word "baby."

"Yes, sir, you did!" said Wally, shaking Burr by the hand and mercifully leading him away and back into the library.

As Burr and Wally beat their retreat, I overheard Burr talking excitedly to Wally. "I've been reading Dolly's Henry VIII work again, Wally. I'd forgotten how intriguing it is. Really, it's a shame for the rest of the world to miss out on it, while it circles around aimlessly in academia. And you know—it's time for Dolly to follow up that project with another one. She must seek the next dream to pursue. Time is a-wasting!"

"I think, Burr, that a lot will change around here in the next year or so," Wally said, looking back at me and throwing me one of those smiles of his that makes me go weak in the knees. "In fact, Burr, I think Dolly may just find that she needn't look any further than her own backyard for her heart's desire, because if it isn't there—"

"Whatever are you talking about, Wally?" asked the ever-literal Burr.

"I think the rainbow's end that we all want for Dolly isn't far off at all, and that she will, in fact, give up her death grip on old ways and somehow find her future right under her very nose. Just a feeling I have. I think, Burr, that your wish for Dolly may come true sooner than you think."

"It would be 'a consummation,'" Burr said solemnly, "'devoutly to be wished.'"

Chapter One Hundred-Eighteen
Bliss and Synthesis

Blanche's prediction of neither a boy nor a girl proved true when I delivered twin girls, Olivia and Viola—or, as their father likes to call them, Ollie and Vollie. Good old Burr just couldn't be prouder of his two goddaughters, not to mention their Shakespearian monikers. Harry's girls are the children's godmothers. Lizzie, Mary, and I have grown dearer than ever to each other over the past few months. We're working closely together, along with the publishing women, to make their I Make a Whisper a Sell campaign the vehicle for bringing my Henry VIII treatise, as well as my in-development Tudor/Shakespeare research, to the world at large.

Based on my second otherworldly Tudor experience, I finally found myself able to let go of my university job shortly before the end of my pregnancy. Gravid as I was, I still felt light as a feather with the relinquishment. Once I'd delivered the children, I started in on revising the pedantic *Henry VIII, Man of Constant Sorrow* for consumption by the general public and began work in earnest on my Tudor/Shakespeare project. Nothing makes one better at multitasking than motherhood does. Between research, writing, nursing, diapers, and Wally, my days are pretty full.

Wally's home office and nursery project made him realize just how much he missed flexing his architectural muscles during all the years he'd been practicing as a veterinarian and physician. That, combined with his hobby interest in local archeology, has started him on a very satisfying new career of restoring historically relevant structures. Now that we are both working in the field of history, it seems that Wally and I are united on every front possible. Much of our most recent shoptalk has been about a Tudor-era lodge that Wally is rescuing from rack and ruin.

"I'm off to that antique auction now, Dolly."

"Good luck, Wally!" I said as I settled the girls into their little playpen. "Are there any promising beds up for grabs?" I asked, knowing that he was in the market for an antique one for this latest project of his.

"No bed out there is as promising to me as ours tonight is, dear," he said happily. "Still, there is one bed at this auction that might do for the current restoration. It's a very sturdy middle-Renaissance piece with a rather mysterious provenance. It has seen better days, though, according to the description."

"I should think so, if it is several hundred years old."

"No, not that, Dolly. It apparently has evidence of tampering."

"Tampering?"

"Yes, it's been taken apart and put back together again—and clumsily at that, it seems. I don't like to settle for second best in a bed when it comes to furnishing one of my houses, but I suppose it is worth a look."

"Did I just hear the words *second…best…bed?*" I asked.

"Yes, you did," Wally said. "Perhaps I'd better skip looking at that bed altogether."

Before the words were out of Wally's mouth, a clap of thunder shook our cottage, a bolt of lightning struck, and torrents of rain began to fall.

"How odd for that storm to have blown up so suddenly!" Wally said. "Up until a second or two ago, it was a perfect day."

"It's more than that, darling; it's a red-letter day! The girls and I are going with you to take a look at that bed. I can't wait for you and me to get inside it!"

"Dolly, I'm flattered. But I'm not eyeing that second-best bed for our personal use, you know."

"You grab a brolly, Wally, and I'll bundle up Ollie and Vollie. Take my word for it; once we crack open that bed, 'the world's our oyster'!"

Who's Who in *Seven Will Out*

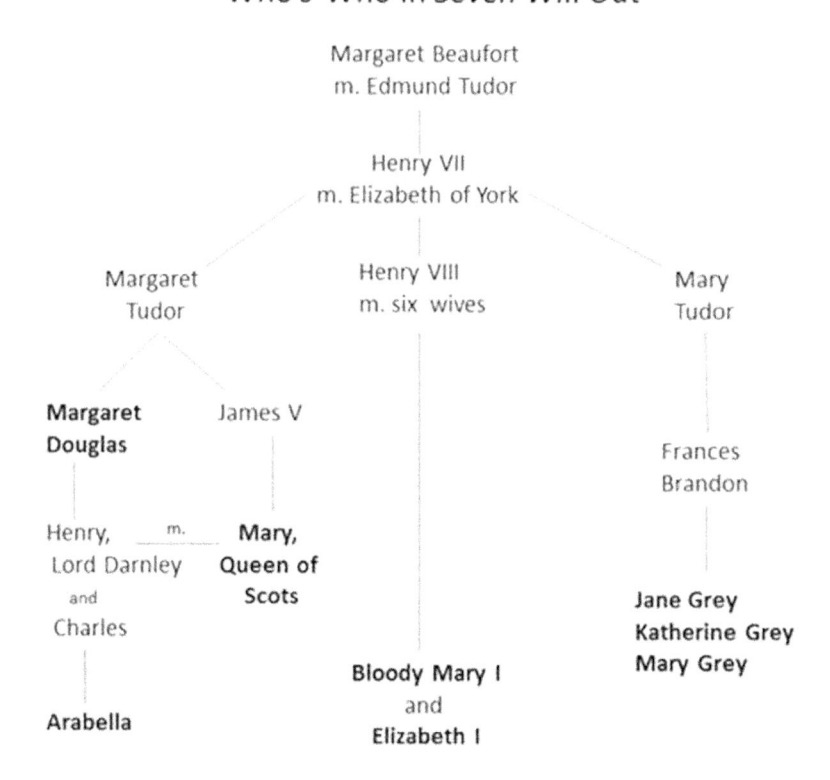

```
                    Margaret Beaufort
                    m. Edmund Tudor
                            |
                       Henry VII
                    m. Elizabeth of York
                            |
        ┌───────────────────┼───────────────────┐
    Margaret           Henry VIII              Mary
     Tudor            m. six wives            Tudor
        |                   |                    |
   ┌────┴────┐              |                Frances
Margaret   James V          |                Brandon
Douglas      |              |                    |
   |       Mary,            |              Jane Grey
Henry, m.  Queen of         |              Katherine Grey
Lord Darnley Scots          |              Mary Grey
and                    Bloody Mary I
Charles                     and
   |                   Elizabeth I
Arabella
```

Bess of Hardwick: Arabella Stuart's other grandmother and wardress of Mary Queen of Scots

Amy Robsart, Douglas Sheffield, Lettice Knollys: Robert Dudley, First Earl of Leicester's women

Catherine De'Medici: queen of France and mother-in-law of Mary Queen of Scots

Kat Ashley, Blanche Parry, Anne Bacon, Mary Dudley, Helena Von Snakenborg, Emilia Lanier, Philadelphia and Catherine Carey: ladies of Elizabeth I's court

Jane Dormer: Mary I's lady-in-waiting

Ann Boleyn and Katharine of Aragon: Henry VIII's first and second wives

Katherine Willoughby: would-be seventh wife of Henry VIII; step-grandmother of the Grey sisters

Sources:
Elizabeth Barrett Browning:
A Vision of Poets

William Congreve:
The Mourning Bride

William Cowper:
The Task

Emily Dickinson:
Because I could not stop for Death

Gilbert and Sullivan:
The Sorcerer

George Gordon, Lord Byron:
She Walks in Beauty

Christopher Marlowe:
The Passionate Shepherd to His Love
Hero and Leander

The Shakespeare Plays:
All's Well That Ends Well
Antony and Cleopatra
As You Like It
Comedy of Errors
Coriolanus
Cymbeline
Hamlet

Henry IV, Part I
Henry IV, Part II
Henry V
Henry VI, Part I
Henry VI, Part II
Henry VI, Part III
Henry VIII
Julius Caesar
King John
King Lear
Love's Labour's Lost
Macbeth
Measure for Measure
Merchant of Venice
Merry Wives of Windsor
Midsummer Night's Dream
Much Ado about Nothing
Othello
Pericles
Richard II
Richard III
Romeo and Juliet
Taming of the Shrew
Tempest
Timon of Athens
Titus Andronicus
Troilus and Cressida
Twelfth Night
Two Gentlemen of Verona
Winter's Tale